the

SHAPE

of

FAMILY

Also by Shilpi Somaya Gowda

Secret Daughter
The Golden Son

SHILPI SOMAYA GOWDA

the
SHAPE
of
FAMILY

A Novel

HarperCollins*Publishers*Ltd

Published by HarperCollins Publishers Ltd

First edition

HarperCollins books may be purchased for educational, business or sales promotional use through our Special Markets Department.

HarperCollins Publishers Ltd
Bay Adelaide Centre, East Tower
22 Adelaide Street West, 41st Floor
Toronto, Ontario, Canada
M5H 4E3

www.harpercollins.ca

Library and Archives Canada Cataloguing in
Publication information is available upon request.

ISBN 978-1-4434-5897-9 (hardcover)
ISBN 978-1-4434-5898-6 (trade paperback)

Printed and bound in the United States

LSC/H 9 8 7 6 5 4 3 2 1

For Mira & Bela,
may you seek widely, and always find home

We wanderers, ever seeking the lonelier way, begin no day where we have ended another day; and no sunrise finds us where sunset left us.

Even while the earth sleeps we travel.

We are the seeds of the tenacious plant, and it is in our ripeness and our fullness of heart that we are given to the wind and are scattered.

Brief were my days among you, and briefer still the words I have spoken.

But should my voice fade in your ears, and my love vanish in your memory, then I will come again,

And with a richer heart and lips more yielding to the spirit will I speak.

Yea, I shall return with the tide,

And though death may hide me, and the greater silence enfold me, yet again will I seek your understanding.

—from "The Farewell," Khalil Gibran

A young woman, hovering on the edge between adolescence and adulthood, is walking. She climbs over a bed of rocks that marks the border between city sidewalk and seashore. She wears clothing the color of snow, of clouds, of nothing. She wears nothing on her feet. She carries nothing.

She walks slowly but deliberately toward the Pacific Ocean, yet she possesses none of the regular trappings of those who do so at this hour—no fishing pole, no surfboard, no wet suit.

It is early morning, not long since dawn broke. The sun is beginning to spread its orange hue on the horizon, but the air is still brisk.

In one of the houses that line the cliff overlooking the beach, an elderly man rises and switches on the light in his kitchen. He is pondering whether it is a gift or a curse to wake at this ungodly hour every morning. It is peaceful, to be sure, but nothing else makes him feel more alone in the world.

As he fills the kettle at the sink, he looks out the back window, as he does every morning. There are few people out at this hour, usually only an intrepid jogger or dog walker. This morning, he peers closer. He squints his eyes and opens them again to verify what he's seeing.

She is almost a mirage, the young woman dressed in white. For a moment, from the pull of her hair into a loose knot at her nape, he imagines it is his late wife, come back to see him. This thought, however improbable, makes him smile.

As the water overflows the kettle, he returns to himself. From this angle, he now notices her olive skin, her youthful face. She walks with intention toward the roaring waves. Something is not right: a young woman, alone in street clothes on the beach at this hour. He places the kettle in its cradle, picks up the kitchen telephone and dials the police.

HOME

1 | karina

2007

Karina sat outside the principal's office, kicking her feet against the wooden bench. She knew the noise was annoying the receptionist, who glanced up periodically with a stern look from behind the tall barrier. Karina didn't care. What else could happen to her? She was already waiting in the principal's office; her mother had been called. The only redeeming part of this whole situation was that Prem wasn't here with her. He was, with any luck, outside with the other first-graders, playing tetherball or four square.

Twenty minutes earlier, at the start of lunch, she'd been at the monkey bars with her best friend, Izzy, when she'd seen Prem across the schoolyard, sitting at the lunch table. Her younger brother, usually running around wild with his friends during this time, was cowering at the corner of the table, with an older boy hovering nearby. Karina crossed the yard and as she approached, she recognized Jake Potash from her grade.

"Man, that stinks!" Jake pinched his nose and pointed at her brother's stainless-steel tiffin, filled with rice and vegetable curry. "Get that crap away from me!" He kicked at the table, causing the tiffin to rattle and Prem, his face seized by fear, to slide farther down the bench.

Karina, fueled by rage and protective instinct, marched up and grabbed the tiffin off the table. "You bother my brother again," she spat out, "I'll kill you." The smirk lingered on Jake's face, so before she could think, Karina raised her arm and hurled the tiffin at him. Jake yelped as the sharp metal edge struck him square in the face, and curry was left dripping down his cheek. Karina stared as he wiped his face, and Jake must have recognized the anger in her eyes, because even though it was an absurd threat for a scrawny eleven-year-old girl to make against the school's biggest bully, he just spat on the ground and stormed away.

Before Karina could check on Prem, a playground teacher jogged over, breathless. "I saw that, Miss Olander. Throwing an object at someone? You are going to pay a visit to the principal's office." Before Karina could explain, the teacher took her by the upper arm and moved toward the building doors. Prem looked up at her from the bench, his face now streaked with tears. She touched her nose with the fingertip of her free hand as she was being pulled away and he did the same, the invisible thread that bound them.

When Prem had started kindergarten at Karina's elementary school last year, he worshipped his big sister and her friends by extension. Her parents were happy knowing they were at the same school, where Karina could look out for him. Prem was so nervous that first day as Karina showed him around, pointing out the playground where she would see him at lunch. "Look, you love monkey bars!" Prem smiled at her, then spontaneously threw his arms around her torso and squeezed tight. "Okay, okay," she said, unlatching him before anyone saw. "You're a big boy now." She touched him lightly on the tip of his nose. "You'll be fine. I promise." He nodded solemnly, placing his fingertip on his nose, then hers.

Karina had had a hard time adjusting at the school herself, mainly because there wasn't a single other person there like her. There were the white kids, the Chinese kids, the Indian kids and the Spanish-speaking contingent. But the combination of Karina's features—milky tan skin, dark eyes, thick wavy hair, prominent nose—made her feel like she didn't quite fit in anywhere. People were not unkind, but she sometimes felt like a puzzle to be figured out. The first time her father had picked her up from soccer practice, the other parents looked on with confusion when he waved from the car, trying to reconcile his pale, freckled complexion with hers. One mother intercepted her on the field to confirm Karina knew him before letting her go, making her acutely aware of how mismatched they looked. Her name only made things worse. Derived from *carus*, the Latin word for "love," it was also a Hindi name meaning "flower," "pure" or "innocent." Her parents were drawn to its meanings in different cultures; it appealed to their sense of their two ethnicities coming together in one child. When she was younger, Karina bought into their explanation, but now she resented having to repeat and spell her name for everyone.

Prem wound up with a different combination of features: his skin fair, his hair straight and fine, and his long, dark eyelashes looking as if they'd been curled and given a heavy application of mascara (totally wasted on a boy, in Karina's opinion). People were always surprised to learn they were brother and sister, and while there were moments when she wished they weren't, it still bugged her when someone expressed disbelief. Karina and Prem were the only two members of their club, even if no one believed they could belong together.

The school receptionist raised her head and looked at Karina now, peering over small wire-rimmed glasses that hung from a chain around her neck. "Your mother will be here in about twenty minutes, so just sit tight," she said with a stiff smile. Karina reflexively stopped swinging her feet for the few moments the woman addressed her, then started up again.

Karina had learned to be cautious of people, especially those who treated her with curiosity. Fortunately, she didn't need many friends; she had Izzy. Isabelle Demetri, a dark-haired, large-eyed girl, had found her in first grade, marching up to Karina at the swings and declaring they would be friends because of their identical purple lunch bags. Izzy was fearless, fun and didn't have much use for the boys who were always hanging around. Her passion was horses. She went to the stables to ride twice a week after school, sharing access to a pony named Mr. Chuckles, because her parents said buying one was too expensive. Karina loved going to the barn with Izzy and watching how her friend managed the large creature, the two of them engaged in a silent, gentle interaction of meeting each other's needs. But Karina had a special fondness for Dominick, the Demetris' charcoal cockapoo, who slept curled up at the foot of Izzy's bed, and who followed them patiently from room to room for no apparent reason other than to be close to them. Dominick seemed good and reliable in a way that was uncomplicated compared to many people she knew. Karina could trust Prem, her parents, Izzy and her animals, and that was enough.

Jake Potash had not been sent to the office, and Karina knew how the incident had looked to the playground teacher, so when she was called into the principal's office, she knew what to say. "Jake was picking on my brother. Prem's only six and I was sticking up for him."

The principal removed his reading glasses. "Fighting is not a way to solve disputes, Karina. Mrs. Kramer was right there; she could have helped you."

Karina nodded, looking down at her hands. She didn't mention Jake's comments or that he was only more brazen with his insults than other kids, whose questions could hurt just as much. At that moment, the door opened and her mother entered the office. When Karina saw her, with her blouse partially untucked from her pants and her forehead creased with lines, she felt her first pangs of regret about the situation. The principal asked Karina to explain the incident, while her mother sat, hands clasped in her lap, muscle pulsing in her jaw.

"This is her first infraction," the principal said, "so it will go on her school record, and she'll have to apologize to the other student, but we can leave it at that. And of course, she'll need to leave school for the rest of the day."

Her mother politely apologized and thanked the principal without ever looking at Karina. In the car, she drove with her hands tightly gripped on the steering wheel for several blocks before she spoke. "Karina, I don't know *what* is going on with you. Getting in fights at school?"

"He was making fun of Prem, Mom. That kid was teasing him for being . . . *different*." Even as she said it, she knew her mother wouldn't understand. Her parents were not part of the same club.

Her mother glanced in the rearview mirror and changed lanes to make a turn. "You should be proud of your Indian culture. Educate that boy, tell him everything Indians are responsible for—the invention of mathematics and chess, centuries of tradition, poetry, music."

Sometimes, when her father was traveling, eerie Indian music emanated from her parents' bedroom, illuminated only with a nightstand lamp. Mom sat with her eyes closed, moving her head in rhythm, looking more peaceful than she did in her daily life with them. This bothered Karina, as if her mom had to go somewhere else to be that happy, somewhere she couldn't take them.

"You don't understand," Karina muttered. "You *never* do."

"Excuse me?" Her mother turned around and shot her a piercing glare. "What did you say?" She turned her eyes back to the road. "You know I count on you to be a good sister to Prem, a role model for him. You can't be violent, Karina. You know better."

Karina remained silent, staring out the window as the shops and street signs went by. She knew her mother's approach of proudly defending Indian culture would only have stoked Jake Potash further. If the issue rose to the level that Mom deemed it important enough to share with Karina's father, he would have a different reaction. He would call up Jake's parents, tear into them with calmly spoken criticisms of their parenting, and threats to their child if anything similar ever happened again. Then he would meet with the school principal and file a complaint with the police. He would scorch the earth all around Jake Potash and the family from which he came, to isolate him in fear. That strategy could work, and if things got any worse, she might consider telling Dad.

But after that day of the incident on the playground, when Karina felt as if she'd been taken over by some external force, anger and energy coursing through her veins, Jake Potash never bothered her or Prem again.

2 | jaya

2008

Jaya pulled on her gardening gloves and handed another pair to Karina, who turned them over, exposing the ladybugs embroidered on each one. "Mom, these are . . . they're for little kids. Can I just use some normal ones?"

"They still fit, don't they? The other ones will be too big." Jaya bent down to lift a large bag of potting soil from the garage floor and hoisted it into her arms. "Grab a couple of those, honey." She nodded to the plant trays and began walking around the side of the house, toward the back-yard. "So, how was soccer this morning?" she called over her shoulder.

"Fine."

"Did you win? Lose? Who did you play against?"

"I don't know, some school. We tied."

Jaya placed the bag down near the flower beds and studied her daugh-ter, assessing the flat expression that frequented her face so often lately. At twelve, Karina was already beginning to take on the manner of an American teenager—the disinterest, the sullenness—about which Jaya had been warned. Suddenly, Karina didn't like anything Indian, not the food Jaya cooked, not the outfits she deemed scratchy and uncomfort-able, not even going to the temple. The experts said this kind of behavior wasn't personal, but how could it not be, when Karina was rejecting Jaya's very culture? It was hard not to miss the lively young girl who

7

had brought so much life to their family. Thank goodness, Prem, only seven, was still thoroughly childlike and curious about the world. Jaya had a few more years to bask in his boyish affection. There were some good things about having her children so far apart, despite the heartache it had caused. Jaya found the garden shears in the bucket of tools and sliced open the soil bag. "Must be tough without Isabelle on the team this season." This was what she did now, poked around delicately since she never quite knew what might be bothering her daughter.

Karina shrugged. "It's fine. It's not like I don't know all the other kids on the team. We've been together since first grade." She flopped down on the grass, cross-legged with her arms propped behind her.

"Yes, that's true." Jaya smiled and thought about how different Karina's stable upbringing was from her own. Jaya's father, a diplomat, was posted to a new country every few years, where Jaya attended top English schools and their home often hosted visiting dignitaries. While their family life was cosmopolitan, it had the effect of accentuating, rather than diminishing, how properly Indian they were. Jaya's mother knew how to prepare Indian delicacies from all over the country: thin crispy dosas from southern India and rich lamb curries from the north. Their homes were tastefully decorated with hand-carved furniture and sumptuous silk rugs. They subscribed to Indian periodicals and their dinner conversations revolved around current events back home. Jaya and her brother, Dev, were raised with the implicit notion that India, rich in its vastness and contributions to the world—raga music, great poetry and exquisite cuisine, to name a few—was superlative to whichever country they lived in.

"Okay, you know what to do," Jaya said to Karina, gesturing toward the empty flower bed. "Start digging the holes, then." Karina didn't move from her slouched position in the grass and shook her head slightly. "Where do you want me to put them?"

"Come on, honey. Same as always, eighteen inches apart for the front row, farther for the row behind. I think we'll need three rows total—flowering cabbage, kale, marigolds," Jaya said, pointing to each of the trays. "What are these?" Karina touched a plant with gray, velvety foliage that looked like underwater coral.

"Aren't they interesting? Feel the leaves. Those are called dusty millers," Jaya said. "Why don't you decide where they should go?" Jaya marked out spots for each of the rows in the flower bed and went to retrieve the garden hose. She took profound satisfaction in this act of planting flowers in the ground and watching them grow. Her mother had always kept beautiful floral arrangements in their houses, since they often had spontaneous visitors. But those cut flowers inevitably made Jaya sad, the way they began to wilt and smell rank within days. There was never the opportunity to plant a garden outside, with only one or two years in each place, often during winter, when the ground was frozen. So, Jaya learned to cultivate an inner life through her practice of classical dance, her own sense of grounding she could take wherever they lived. She had learned to be comfortable anywhere since home was nowhere.

Here, Jaya could finally grow her flowers in the earth, a way of rooting herself to this land she'd claimed for herself and her family. She and Keith had loved this house when they first saw it, a brick two-story on a quiet tree-lined street. They were both drawn to the sprawling backyard, though for different reasons. Keith saw the swimming pool as a symbol of success. He envisioned hosting summer parties and manning the grill while the children swam. Jaya prized the yard for the enormous canvas it provided to create a garden of her own, one that would include flower beds, rosebushes, herbs and vegetables, even a dwarf citrus tree that occasionally yielded limes. Karina was just a toddler when they bought the house, and Jaya had felt a deep energy connecting her to a place for the first time in her life, a feeling that had grown over the last decade. They could afford a bigger home now, in a nicer neighborhood, as Keith always reminded her when they drove past open houses on Sundays, but Jaya didn't want to leave this one.

Now, she scooped a trowelful of potting soil into each of the small holes dug by Karina, followed by a spoonful of bonemeal. "So, have you decided what you want to do for your birthday dinner? We could go to Benihana, or the Spaghetti House," Jaya suggested. "Maybe we can try that new ice cream place afterwards? Or do you want cake?"

"Mom, I don't see why I can't babysit for the Crandalls tonight. My birthday's not until tomorrow. Why can't we do dinner then?"

"Because your father's traveling tomorrow. His flight's at three o'clock," Jaya explained. "Besides, it's better to go out for dinner on Saturday, isn't it? No school to get up for tomorrow."

Karina rolled her eyes and jabbed her spade into the ground for a new hole. "It's not fair. I should be able to do what I want with my own time on the weekends. Izzy spends all day at the barn. Why can't I babysit for a few hours if I want to?"

Jaya looked up at her daughter and sighed. It was the same argument. Karina had started walking one neighbor's dog on the weekends, then another's. Now she wanted to babysit, it seemed, every Friday and Saturday night, cutting into their family time together.

"What else am I going to do with my time?" Karina said. "I'm already getting good grades, so you can't use that excuse."

"Karina." Jaya tilted her head to one side and smiled, hoping to defuse the indignation she could see brewing in her daughter. "Why are you so eager to do this? For the *money*?" She tried not to taint the word. The values bred into Jaya by her parents were crystalline: her first priority had been her studies; the second was dance. Nothing else was supposed to come into the equation as a child. In their culture, working for money was only for adults and beggar children.

"Everyone else at school does their own thing on the weekends. I just want to spend my time the way I want," Karina said. "And yes, earn some money—"

"You know we'll give you spending money for whatever you need," Jaya interjected.

"That's not the *point*!" Karina banged her spade onto the ground so hard it bounced some feet away and landed near a shrub.

Jaya looked away from the anger manifesting in her daughter, dug her gloved hands deep into the bag of potting soil and heaped it out in front of her. Keith felt differently about this. He thought it was good for kids to have a job, to learn responsibility and the value of a dollar. Perhaps this was another aspect of American culture that she just didn't comprehend. "I'll talk to your father about it, okay?"

Karina got up to retrieve the spade and returned to stabbing it in the ground, spraying soil all around her. Jaya reached for the tray of dusty millers and began wobbling one of them out of its sheath. They had started planting flowers on Karina's birthday as a special ritual years ago, a way for Jaya to share something with her daughter, as she had shared dance with her own mother. Jaya had studied the Bharatnatyam form of classical dance from the time she was five years old, right up until she left for university. It was her mother's way of ensuring she stayed deeply tied to Indian culture no matter where they lived. When they were in Delhi, Jaya studied with a leading teacher, but abroad, Jaya was taught by her mother, herself a dancer.

In every home in every country where Jaya's family had lived, there hung a series of five identically framed photos of her mother standing in full costume, in various dance poses: making a flute with her hands, her long fingers forming a flower, and so on. Each time they moved to a new house, these photos were the first items to go up. The whole family participated in the ritual of seeking out the right spot for them when they arrived in Ireland, Portugal, Kuwait. Jaya came to rely on those pictures, a symbol of constancy in their ever-changing homes, a sign of her mother watching over her. Jaya used to survey those images of her mother, with dramatically flared eye makeup and elaborate silk costumes, and wonder if she would ever grow up to be as beautiful and graceful. She had loved sharing something special with her mother. Unlike Karina now, who was like the little bunny in the children's storybook, always trying to run away from her.

"I'm not a baby anymore, Mom. I'm not a . . . *kid* like Prem. I can do things for myself. You don't let me do *anything*. It's not fair." Karina stood up and dropped her spade to the ground. "I don't even like this," she muttered. "I hate gardening." She shook her head and turned to walk into the house.

———

After finishing up the planting herself, and frankly grateful for the respite, Jaya entered the house to find Keith at the kitchen table, poring over his phone, as he'd been doing obsessively the past few weeks. He looked up at her, a deep furrow between his brows. "They're saying no bonuses this year. *None*, can you believe that? After busting my tail all year, they're going to take away my bonus."

"It's just one year," Jaya said.

"And what if it's not? First Bear, then Lehman. *Fuck!*" Keith said. "What's next? I mean, Brian had no idea what was coming down at Lehman until the last two weeks. No bonuses this year means we might be next. I might not even have a job next year."

"Well, we can deal with that if it happens," Jaya said, maneuvering around the stack of uncleared breakfast dishes in the kitchen sink to wash the dirt from her hands.

"I'm going to give Robbie a call. He might have something for me."

"Robbie *Weiss*?" Jaya said, looking over her shoulder. "The guy who started that bucket shop?" She found a brush and began scrubbing the crusted maple syrup from the dishes.

Keith nodded. "He co-founded a small firm, Duncan Weiss. They focus on middle market. We've worked on a couple of deals together. He told me to call him anytime I was ready to jump ship. I might be able to get him to pay my bonus if I come over before the end of the year."

"But you just said there are no bonuses," Jaya said, raising her voice over the running water and the clatter of silverware in the sink.

"Dammit, Jaya, do you have to do that right now?" Keith barked. "Are you even listening?"

Jaya turned off the faucet and spun around to face him with the dish scrubber in hand. *Who else is going to do it, and when?* she wanted to say, but forced herself to stay calm. Keith had been a bundle of exposed nerves since the financial markets crashed a few weeks ago. It was like someone had snatched the man she knew and replaced him with an overanxious imposter. "What are you saying, Keith?" Her tone came out accusatory despite her efforts. "You want to leave your firm because of one bad year to go to a . . . crappy upstart? To work for a guy you called, I believe, *ruthless*?"

"I am *trying* to make a living and provide for my family," Keith shouted. "The financial markets are in ruin and I'm trying to take care of you."

"Well, I don't *need* you to take care of me, not this way," Jaya snapped.

"What other way is there? You know my bonus is 80 percent of my income. We can't even cover the mortgage on my salary. And certainly not yours."

"I can go full-time," Jaya said. "We can get benefits through my job and cut back on our expenses until you find something—"

Keith laughed. "That's not going to make any difference, Jaya, and you know it."

"Can you just put your ego and male chauvinism aside for—"

"Okay, that's it!" Keith stood up, his chair scraping hard against the kitchen floor. "I need space to clear my head, before I say something I regret."

"Too late!" she called after him as the front door slammed. Jaya stood in place as she heard the rumble of the garage door and the squeal of tires. Turning back to the dishes in the sink, she thought she could hear a bedroom door close carefully upstairs.

3 | keith

"Poodle breeds are notorious for their intelligence and ease of train-ing," Karina read from the book in her lap in the back seat.

Keith glanced over at Jaya in the passenger seat. A small smile played on the edges of her mouth as she stared forward through the windshield. He looked back over his shoulder to his daughter. "Is that so?"

"Yes." Without looking up, she continued, "They are lively, active, fun-loving family dogs with a sense of the ridiculous." Karina closed the book and elbowed Prem. "See? Perfect for you."

A reflexive laugh escaped from Keith before he could stifle it.

"Hahaha, very funny," Prem said, with his signature snort. "Well, yes I am, thank you."

"We are just *looking*," Jaya said, removing her sunglasses to wipe the lenses. "No promises."

It was Saturday, one of the treasured days Keith had to spend entirely with his family. During the week, between long days at the office, client dinners and travel, he saw them only in passing. After the initial shock waves of the financial crisis had passed and it was clear no more invest-ment banks were collapsing, business was gradually starting to return to normal. Keith was glad he'd decided to stay at Morgan Stanley. Jaya was right: there was value in being at a name-brand firm in difficult times, where he'd built a reputation amongst his colleagues. The stock market was rebounding and the firm was on track to pay decent bonuses this year, easing tensions for him and at home. Jaya's return to full-time work seemed to make her happier as well, and she spoke enthusiastically about her projects. Things were a little more chaotic at home, but Keith tried to carry more of the load on the weekends since Jaya handled everything during the workweek. It felt good to have balanced the seesaw act of marriage and parenting over the past year without either of them crashing to the ground. He reached over and took his wife's hand as she gazed out the window; she turned to him and smiled.

The breeder in Watsonville, who had been recommended by the wife of one of Keith's colleagues, a woman who had the requisite free time for such research, was a reputable source for goldendoodles, Karina's top choice for a puppy. Her lobbying efforts to get a family dog had intensified over the past few months, culminating in a persuasive essay she wrote for English class, which Keith had to admit was quite compelling.

When they turned onto the long country lane leading to the farm, Karina began bouncing in her seat with excitement. Prem let out a long wolf howl. The rambling ranch house was surrounded by a large fenced-in yard. As soon as Keith parked the car, Karina and Prem jumped out and ran toward the kennels on one side of the yard, where a man in work clothes stood.

"Be careful, wait at the gate!" Jaya called out. As someone who hadn't grown up with pets, his wife had an instinctive fear of animals. Keith hadn't quite understood it when she'd explained: in Indian culture, dogs and other animals were considered dirty and would never be let inside the home. The only dogs she'd seen in India were the strays on the street, which she'd been taught to avoid as a source of disease and injury. Keith had grown up with dogs and loved them, so it took some effort to appreciate her view. Most of the time, he and Jaya were grounded by the values they held in common—hard work, planning for the future, creating opportunity for their children—but from time to time, there were these small reminders of their cultural differences.

Now, Keith noticed Jaya taking deep breaths, trying to keep her fear in check for Karina's sake. He had always admired this about his wife, how hard she worked to overcome her own fears. On September 11, 2001, two days before he was scheduled to fly to New York, Jaya had been heavily pregnant with Prem. As the news unfolded, she became hysterical, haunted by the notion that only a small accident of chance had kept Keith out of the towers that day. She didn't want him to fly, not just that week or the week after, but for months. It had surprised Keith, the appearance of this deep fear, a single imperfection in Jaya's otherwise unperturbable facade. His wife's self-possession was the defining characteristic everyone noticed. Years of living around the world and interacting with diplomats had given her a degree of confidence to fit into any social situation. He admired this quality, but it also left him feeling somewhat insecure in comparison. With his modest upbringing, Keith had struggled to learn about good food and wine, to develop the language of someone more cosmopolitan. Here, with this fear of Jaya's, was one small weakness with which he could help his wife, at last.

It took Jaya over a year to get on a plane herself, to visit her parents in Switzerland so they could meet Prem for the first time. She gripped Keith's hand tightly during takeoff, but he saw the resolve in her eyes before she closed them and rested her head back against the seat. He was filled with pride over how she could conquer something when she put her mind to it.

Now, Keith took Jaya's hand again and they walked together to meet the man who came to unlatch the gate for them. They introduced themselves and shook hands, the breeder first wiping his on his jeans.

"You guys want to see the new litter?" the breeder said to Karina and Prem. "Five days old. Cute as can be."

They followed him into the house, where a large crate on the living room floor held a mass of curly golden fur. As he drew closer, Keith could make out five very small puppies sleeping nuzzled into their mother, who warily eyed the humans as they approached the crate. The breeder knelt down and lowered his voice. "They were born on Tuesday. This is Daisy's first litter, so she's extra protective." He unlatched the crate and gently reached inside toward the closest puppy.

"Why aren't they outside with the other dogs?" Prem asked.

"They can't be around other dogs until they get their shots," Karina said. "Just in case they're exposed to something."

"That's right." The breeder looked impressed as he glanced up at Keith and Jaya. "Someone's done her homework." He held the puppy close to his chest and nodded toward Karina, who knelt down and took the tiny bundle from him as if she'd been handling puppies all her life. The smile on Karina's face was beatific. Even Prem was watching his sister with wide eyes.

"Three are spoken for, but I've got one girl and one boy left, if you're interested. That's the boy." He pointed to the puppy on the floor. "And here," he said, reaching into the crate with both hands and pulling out a tiny fur ball, "is the girl."

"The runt?" Karina asked, looking up at the breeder, who nodded back. Karina took the tiny puppy and held it close to her chest. "She's the smallest of the litter, so it's hard for her to compete for food and attention."

The breeder nodded. "The runt can be a little harder to care for and might have some issues. But Daisy hasn't rejected this one, so she's been growing."

Karina was whispering to the puppy, nuzzling the dog's head with her nose and smiling from somewhere deep within. Keith felt his heart catch in his chest, with this glimpse of the joyful child inside his often brooding teenage daughter. He glanced over to Jaya and saw her eyes brimming with tears. She met his gaze and smiled, and one tear spilled down her cheek. He squeezed her hand. The puppy reached out her pink tongue and began lapping at Karina's face. She giggled and the rest of them followed suit. Prem now had his chin down on the carpet, trying to get eye-to-eye with the other puppy, his face within biting or clawing range. Keith expected Jaya to warn him, but she just crouched down to the floor behind Karina. "What do you think, honey?" Jaya said. "Would you like to adopt one?" Keith's heart swelled with pride.

Karina nodded without looking away from the puppy in her hands. "This one."

"The little one? Are you sure?" Jaya asked.

Karina turned to them and Keith caught a hint of the same steely resolve in her eyes that he'd often seen in Jaya's. "Positive," she said.

"Normally, we let them go at eight weeks, but I would recommend twelve weeks for this little gal," the breeder said. "How's that sound?"

Jaya completed the paperwork and wrote out the deposit check. When they left the house a few minutes later, Karina was light on her feet with a limitless smile.

"Why is it called a goldendoodle?" Prem asked. "I mean, if you cross a golden retriever with a poodle, you could also call it a goldie-poo." He paused, thinking. "Or a poo-retriever. Ha!" He snort-laughed. "A poo-retriever, get it?"

Karina rolled her eyes and jabbed his shoulder as they climbed into the car.

"So, I'm not picking up any dog poo, okay?" Prem said. "Karina can train that intelligent dog to do it himself."

"Herself. She's a girl, dummy," Karina retorted. "And I already said I would walk her, feed her and brush her teeth. So, what should we name her?"

Embarking on the hour-and-a-half drive home, they stopped at a roadside stand to purchase three quarts of the strawberries for which Watsonville was known, and made a spontaneous side trip to Gilroy, the garlic capital of the world. At a family diner, they gorged themselves on garlic fries and played their drawing game on the paper tablecloth: one of them started a drawing, then each person added an element, taking turns until they ended up with some nonsensical figure, like a man with a tree growing out of his head, or a house with a cat face for a roof. Then they all proposed a name for the picture and voted on the best one. Today's picture ended up being a dog with a garlic bulb nose, and they decided "Gilly" was a good name for a puppy.

"Not the healthiest meal," Jaya said, as she continued plucking strawberries from the limp cardboard box on the drive home. "But we did manage to get in fruits *and* vegetables, so not all bad either." By the time they arrived home, the strawberry boxes were empty and stained and Prem had fallen asleep, his head resting on the back seat next to Karina, where she let him lie, undisturbed.

4 | jaya

MAY 2009

"Oh, this is heaven," Jaya said, falling back onto the plush canopy bed. Outside the hotel's picture window, the pyramid building punctuated San Francisco's skyline. "Absolute heaven. Forty-eight hours of complete freedom. I honestly don't know what to do with this much time."

Keith crawled across the bed toward her and straddled her body with his knees. "Oh, I can think of a few things." He kissed the tender hollow of her neck and made a trail around to her earlobe, nipping at it gently.

"Mmm." She held his head in her palms and kissed him deeply on the mouth, tasting the lingering flavor of his minty gum. "We don't even have to be quiet," she murmured.

"And we don't have to be quick." They slowly undressed each other and took their time exploring each other's bodies, familiar after twenty years together, but no less thrilling due to the unusual sense of abandon they felt in the privacy of the hotel room.

When they were finished, they lay next to each other, Jaya's head tucked under Keith's arm, her leg sprawled across his. There was such simple pleasure in feeling his bare skin against hers. Their lovemaking sessions at home had to be strategic and expeditious, while the kids were watching TV or after they had gone to sleep. It had begun to feel more like another activity that needed to be scheduled than the impromptu desire-fueled bouts of their early relationship.

At this moment, Jaya felt utterly content, knowing she and Keith could still be lovers as they'd once been, that those parts of them had merely been buried under domestic detritus, not extinguished by its weight. The rough patch they'd endured last year with the financial market collapse had been difficult, but they'd survived. Keith was calmer and happier now that things had settled down. Jaya traced circles on Keith's bare chest. "We should get your sister a really nice gift for doing this."

"Yes, so she visits again *soon*." He kissed her and glanced at the clock. "I made a reservation for dinner, but it's not till 7:30. You want to go down to the bar for a drink?"

"Seems fitting." She reached up and kissed him on the mouth, and he responded with a hunger that surprised her. They made love again, more briskly and rougher this time, unconcerned about the rhythmic banging of the headboard against the wall. Afterwards, they took a shower, soaping each other's backs and laughing about how decadent it was to stand under the hot water with no interruptions or deadlines.

———

Jaya had first met Keith in a London pub on a warm Friday evening in September 1990, where they had both gone after work for drinks with colleagues. She was surprised by the tall, sandy-haired man who sat on the stool next to her and took a long drink from his pint glass, draining nearly half of it before placing it on the table. He smiled at Jaya's widened eyes. "Long week," he said in a flattened American accent.

Jaya smiled, noticing the beginnings of his five o'clock shadow. "What do you do?" she said, intrigued by the crisp suit that accentuated his square shoulders, so unlike the men with whom she worked at the think tank, in their rumpled tweed blazers with elbow patches.

"I work at Canary Wharf," he said.

Jaya smiled and glanced up at the ceiling for a moment, as if deliberating. "Hmm." She raised an index finger. "Real estate, perhaps?" When he shook his head, she said, "Financial services?"

He grinned. "Clever girl." Jaya found herself annoyed that he'd called her a girl but pleased at the descriptor. She saw her colleague Anja, across the table, throw her head back and laugh heartily at something one of Keith's friends said.

"Can I get you another?" Keith asked, standing from his barstool and draining the last third of his pint glass. He gestured to Jaya's glass, still half full.

"Sure, Newcastle." She watched for the reaction she knew would come, the way his face broke wide open with that boyish smile.

"A true beer drinker," he said. "Impressive."

It was Jaya's father who had taught her to drink beer properly before she left for university. Her mother thought it was uncouth, but her father understood how things worked outside the delicate confines of diplomatic life, where women sipped champagne and men nursed crystal tumblers of single malt, and he wanted his daughter to be prepared. At first, Jaya detested the bitter flavor, but in time, she learned to identify the flavors of hops and barley until she could tell the difference between a blonde and a pilsner. She loved the rich, malty taste of Newcastle Brown Ale, but it was so heavy, she rarely drank more than one.

A second full glass appeared on the table before her. Jaya inclined her head toward the glass in thanks to him. "I'll have to pick up my pace."

"I'm in no hurry." He slid his barstool closer before sitting again. As Jaya learned in the conversation that followed, he was an investment banker with Morgan Stanley. Having spent the past two years in New York, he'd come to London for his third year with the firm, a temporary posting before attending business school back home.

"Why business school?" she asked, not expecting much of an answer. But Keith described the financial markets as a living, breathing animal with complex machinery. He explained how each part functioned: debt capital markets financed loans that made it possible for people to buy houses; corporate finance helped companies sell stakes to the public; and in his part, mergers and acquisitions, companies bought others to gain new business lines or divest themselves of parts that no longer fit. It was almost poetic the way he described everything working together to make people's lives more productive.

"Wow, that's quite an answer," Jaya said, reaching for the fresh glass of beer, noticing with a sideways glance that Anja and the other guy were still chatting and laughing.

"You like that?" Keith said, holding his glass up to clink hers. "I've been working on my application essays."

Toward the end of her second Newcastle, Jaya told Keith about her work at the Foreign Policy Centre, how she'd been fortunate to land such a coveted job after studying international relations and anthropology at university. Keith leaned toward Jaya to compensate for the increasing noise in the bar, his brow knitted in concentration as she spoke about water quality and constitutional reforms, trying to impress him.

When the bar became more crowded, Anja leaned across the table. "Hey, let's get out of here, go get some dinner?" The air outside was still warm and heavy as they deliberated over where to eat. Keith proposed going for a curry and Jaya wondered if he was just indulging her. Either way, she didn't care. They hopped into a taxi, a giggling Anja jammed in the back seat between the two men, while Jaya directed the cab driver to her favorite Indian restaurant.

She learned in time that Keith hadn't been pandering that evening with his choice of cuisine. He had a sincere interest in other cultures, and not in the exoticizing, appropriating way some men did. He genuinely wanted to learn to make paan himself, buying all the ingredients and even the stainless-steel tin filled with matching small cups. Her parents accepted him because their life experiences had made them broad-minded and his credentials were impressive: he was a top-tier investment banker, soon on his way to an Ivy League business school.

When Keith was admitted to Wharton after they'd been dating for only six months, Jaya assumed their affair would end with his departure. But he surprised her with a proposal on their one-year anniversary, which came with the blessing of her parents and a one-way ticket to America. At first, she worried about being far from her parents, but the distance from both their families turned out to be a blessing in the early years of their marriage, reducing the inevitable friction between such different cultures and upbringings. She and Keith were the sole meeting place of their respective histories; they could define their relationship without the baggage of her parents' cosmopolitan tastes clashing with his family's deep American roots.

That had been twenty years ago. Now, Jaya dressed in a sleek black dress with red heels for the evening. Keith chose a small table tucked into a dark corner of the hotel bar, where they sat close and sipped from tall flutes of champagne.

"Happy anniversary, babe," he said, nestling one hand between her thighs. "Even more beautiful than the day I met you."

"I love you," Jaya said, her eyes shining for the husband for whom her love had stayed constant and yet grown since they had met two decades earlier. Their differences had not proved a stumbling block, but rather an opportunity to forge a strong foundation for their marriage and their children, and it was this of which she was most proud.

5 | karina

JUNE 2009

The last few weeks of middle school were torture. Karina and her eighth-grade classmates were restless as their thoughts turned to long, lazy summer days. One day in the last week of the school year, a day like any other, Karina walked over to the neighboring elementary school to pick up Prem. During their fifteen-minute walk, Prem excitedly told Karina all about his day in third grade. Although she would never admit it to her parents, Karina enjoyed this time in their day, walking home together. Being alone with Prem was like being at rest. She didn't have to work to make conversation or wonder if she was saying the right thing. She could stop worrying about how her hair looked. Prem would do all the talking. Sometimes, he would take her hand or hook his arm through hers, which she would allow if no one else was around.

By the time they got home, though, Karina was ready to be done with Prem. She quickly dished out chocolate chip cookies and a glass of milk for him, then headed for the stairs.

"Hey, Kiki, you wanna go swimming today?" Prem asked, as he sat on the kitchen chair.

"Uh-uh," she said reflexively. She sometimes got into the pool with Prem, since he wasn't allowed to swim alone. But Karina's usual impulse was to say no to anything Prem wanted to do with her—play a game, do a puzzle, go to the park—and yes to anything he could do alone—read a book, watch TV. Those two precious hours at home without teacher or parental oversight were Karina's solace, two hours she could spend like a normal teenager. She felt her cell phone buzz in her back pocket with a message. "Do your homework and then you can watch TV," she said to him.

"Pleeease, Kiki?" He tilted his head to one side and pleaded with his big brown eyes. "It's so hot today, it's practically *summer*. And I want to try out the giant water shooter I got at Tommy's birthday party."

Karina shook her head and turned away, unwilling to expend any more verbal energy fending him off. Digging another cookie out of the jar and placing it on his plate, she made a silent deal with her little brother and went upstairs.

Her activities for the next couple of hours followed their normal pattern: she started her homework, then called Izzy to talk about it, which led to talking about the boys they each liked and analyzing every interaction they'd had with those boys in the past twenty-four hours. Karina tried on a few outfits, experimented with hiking up the hemline of her skirt and stretching out the neckline of her shirt. She practiced lightening her skin tone with cream foundation she'd borrowed from Izzy and pondered the results. Finally, she finished her homework, then went downstairs to check on Prem before Mom came home.

He wasn't in the family room watching TV, though he'd left the couch pillows all clustered on one side where he'd propped himself up. "Prem!" she yelled, plumping and redistributing the cushions across the couch, the way Mom would as soon as she saw them. Prem was not supposed to watch television after school. When he finished his minimal schoolwork, he was supposed to read or play with one of the educational toys in his room. In the kitchen, Karina brushed a pile of crumbs from the kitchen table into her open palm and dropped them into the sink. Where was the last kitchen chair? "Prem!" she called, getting annoyed. Mom would be home soon. She noticed that the door to the back patio

was ajar and tentatively touched the door handle, her mind beginning
to race before she threw the door open and walked quickly around to
the swimming pool.

Time stopped for a long moment as she took in the scene: the chair
propped up against the wrought-iron fence enclosing the pool, the still
diving board at one end, the crystalline aqua water with sunlight dancing on its surface, the oversized *Space Rangers* spaceship bobbing gently
in the deep end. With her heart pounding, Karina ran back inside to
retrieve the gate key, fumbled with the lock before flinging it open. As
she drew closer to the pool, she saw a thin arm, its edges whitewashed
through the water, dangling below the surface of the inflated spaceship.
Suddenly she was in the water, paddling furiously over to the spaceship,
yanking it out of the way to find Prem's body lodged beneath. She
choked on water as she screamed his name and tried to drag his body,
weightless yet heavy, to the side of the pool.

Somehow, Karina pulled them both out onto the deck. She recalled
the CPR training from her babysitting course and turned Prem's body
on its side so she could pound his back. His shoulder blades were so
small, so thin, and his whole frame seemed fragile. Placing him gently
on his back, she found the spot above his sternum and began to pump
with her fists, elbows straight as she'd been taught. Water spurted out of
his mouth like a fountain.

It was working. She could do this. She could save Prem and fix everything before Mom got home. After five compressions, Karina tilted his
head back, plugged his nose and put her mouth over his cold blue lips,
blowing with all her strength to push air into his lungs. She could do
this, she had to. She heard his voice in her head: *Kiki, please stay.*

"Prem!" Karina yelled as she tried pounding his chest once more.
She thought of running to call 911 but knew she could not leave him,
could not stop. "Damn it, Prem!" *Why won't he respond?* She screamed his
name until her throat was raw, then she began to cry. When she looked

up, she saw Mrs. Mandell from next door moving toward her, a phone to her ear.

Mrs. Mandell knelt down on the other side of Prem's body. "I called 911. How long has he been like this?" She picked up his hand and touched his wrist.

Karina kept counting as she pumped his chest. *Three . . . four . . . five . . . nothing.* Why wasn't he responding? Was he mad at her? Prem never got mad. It was only Karina who got mad at him. "I . . . I don't know. Ten minutes? Fifteen?" She met Mrs. Mandell's eyes and saw what she would later recognize as pity. In fact, it had been only three minutes since she had pulled Prem from the pool, according to the subsequent medical examiner's report, which also stated that Prem had been submerged in the water for at least twenty minutes, enough time for his lungs to fill completely.

"The ambulance is on its way, honey," Mrs. Mandell said. "Is your mother here?"

Karina shook her head. "She'll be home soon. Mom will be home soon," she said, choking on the words she said to Prem every afternoon as a directive, a threat. "Prem? Prem!"

The howl of a siren emerged in the background, growing nearer and louder. He had to wake up. He had to be okay. *Prem!* She could no longer tell if she was screaming out loud or just inside her head. The sound became woven together with the piercing wail of the siren. She saw Mrs. Mandell stand up and retreat. She felt someone pull her up by the shoulders, and she stumbled backwards as two uniformed men took her place at Prem's side. As they began to work, Karina was led inside the house and ushered to the kitchen table.

"Who lives here with you?" Another uniformed man stood before her, holding a small notepad. "Mother? Father? Both?"

"Both," Karina said, then in a whisper, "Mom will be home soon."

6 | prem

People want someone to blame after a person dies, especially when that person is a child. I was eight years old when I died, but I don't blame anyone, especially not Karina, even though she was the only other person there with me. She's the one people blame most, and they also say things like, "She was only a child herself, poor girl, so you can't really blame her"—but they still do. And I know Karina blames herself. Although she's never said this out loud to anyone, I know it's true.

Even when I was alive, I always knew what Kiki was thinking in her head, like *I bet if I give Prem four chocolate chip cookies after school, I can talk on the phone with my door closed for ten minutes before he comes to bug me.* Or *I really wish* Space Rangers *came on for a full hour, so this kid would leave me alone while I do my Important Things in the bathroom.* Kiki's Important Things were trying on makeup she wasn't allowed to wear to school, putting funny-smelling lotions on her arms and legs, and burning her ears with Mom's curling iron.

We spent a lot of time together, Kiki and I: every day after school until Mom came home from work. Mom always rushed in like she was late. She took off her work shoes and dropped her purse right at the door, then started racing around the kitchen, switching on lights, pulling things out of the fridge, turning on the stove. When I was little, I thought this was a game she was playing, to turn on everything super-fast, like in the Space Rangers' ship when they're trying to get liftoff, and I tried to help her by spinning the knobs for the oven and turning on the water faucet, until she got mad and told me to go to the TV room.

Mom is the other person people blame a lot for my death, right after they say it couldn't have been Kiki's fault because she was just a child. (By the way, when I was still alive, Kiki would have been really mad if someone called her just-a-child.) People blame Mom for leaving us alone together, but Kiki was already thirteen when I died.

Thirteen years old!

She was babysitting Mrs. Mandell's boys (who were younger than me) and helping old Mrs. Gustafson down the street by walking her dogs and watering her plants. Kiki was helping to keep alive six plants, two dogs and three little boys, not including me. She was practically the oxygen of our block. So, you really can't blame her, and not because she was "just a child herself, poor girl." She was NOT a child. She was my big sister, and even though she always hogged the TV remote and never wanted to play Space Rangers, I still love her the best of any person in the world.

I didn't know this until after I died, but it turns out Mom always felt bad about leaving us at home after school, even before all those people started blaming her. But I say, Forget That! Kiki and I loved hanging out together. We ate ice cream sandwiches right on the couch in the TV room, which was usually Not Allowed, except for special occasions like Guests or the Olympics. Sometimes, Kiki played dominoes with me or helped me build *huge* Lego towers. Sometimes, she let me snuggle up on her bed to read comic books while she did her homework. Those were the best times, so Forget That, Mom. I try to tell her, but I don't think she can hear me.

So, who is to blame then? If not Mom or Kiki, and not Dad because he was At Work as usual, then who?

Simple.

The water. The water decided to swallow me up that day, and if you've ever seen the Pacific Ocean or Niagara Falls, you know that when the water decides to do something, you can't stop it, no matter how hard you try. So, I definitely don't blame Karina, and you shouldn't either. She was the only one who kept me company while I was dying. She held my hand and kissed my forehead. She was the only one with me on the last day of my life.

7 | jaya

JUNE 2009

It was like no kind of sleep she'd ever had. Some might call it a dreamless sleep, but that made it seem unpleasant, as if it was lacking something vital. No, this was the best kind of sleep, the kind that transported her to another place. Sometimes, as she was waiting to succumb, she envisioned a giant pillowy cloud carrying her off into the sky, enveloping her until she was no longer visible. What she appreciated about this sleep was that it occupied both mind and body. She rarely woke before late morning, and she woke gradually, emerging from fog.

And then. And then, the beauty of that black vacuum dissolved, and the realization intruded. It started slowly, just an inkling, and then came crashing over her all at once, and there was no escaping it. This, too, took over her body and mind. Her eyes stung, the inside of her throat thickened, and the weight on her chest pressed the breath out of her. The dark haze engulfed her once again. In that darkness, she relived each important moment—was it to torture herself or to ensure she would never forget?

The first moment. Her phone rang as she drove home from work. The officer's flat, procedural voice came through the car speaker, the words he spoke incomprehensible. She felt anew the sense of dread and panic as she gripped the wheel. She pulled diagonally into the driveway and up onto a flower bed—she saw later—leaving the engine running as she ran around the house to where all those medics and police officers were standing: foreign bodies in her cultivated landscape. And then, the worst moment of all: the moment she saw Prem's thin body, lifeless and alone on the ground.

A police officer was standing in front of her then, saying something, more words that couldn't be computed by her brain. She stepped around him and moved toward her son. She touched his body and was struck by how cold he was. She took off her jacket and draped it over him, but that wasn't enough to warm him, and so she draped him with her body too. The police officer was still speaking to her, a hand on her shoulder, but she couldn't understand any of it, couldn't move her body away from her little boy. In that moment of disbelief suspended: police radios crackling in the background, the pool gate clanging, heavy footsteps treading around her. If she didn't open her eyes, if she just held Prem's hand in hers, if she kept singing his favorite song as she did when he was sick or had trouble sleeping, this moment would pass, and she could open her eyes to see her smiling, lively boy again. It would pass.

And for a second, she thought it did. The moment was interrupted by a cry, childlike and helpless, calling to her. *Mama. Mama!* She pulled back from Prem's body and called his name. His face remained unchanged, his eyes unopened, his body unmoving. But someone *was* calling her. She turned around to see Karina, running toward her from the house. The sight of her daughter in that moment was confounding, disappointing. How could this be?

Jaya stayed in bed until the realization suffused the sheets surrounding her, and finally she had to leave her bed to escape it. That was the only reason she ever left her bed: when it became a haunted space. Then, she turned to the shower, her no-man's land between sleep and waking, where the steady stream of water flowing onto her face and body washed away the haunting. When the hot water ran out, she occupied herself with all the meaningless rituals everyone was so desperate for her to resume: dressing, putting food in her mouth, receiving people. The longer she stayed in bed, the fewer hours she had to spend doing these things. At the end of the day, she returned upstairs to the freshly made bed, which showed no signs of the haunting. She could slip one of those small white caplets into her mouth, slide between the sheets, and wait for the sleep to take her again.

———

Jaya saw the way they looked at her: at the memorial service, at the temple, when they came to the house bearing fruit baskets and covered dishes and potted orchids. The pity—that was universal. They looked at her as if they were surprised she was still here on earth, still able to stand and walk and breathe. *I am surprised too*, she wanted to tell them. She was surprised every morning when she woke up. How could it be that the very being she had given life to, whom she had carried in her own body and manifested into the world, could be gone and yet *she* was still here? It was wrong. Jaya knew it and she saw in others' eyes: they knew it too. Often, they did not even meet her eyes, or they looked away when they did, as if her grief might be contagious.

And she felt their blame, the other women's. The mothers who stayed home with their kids, volunteering at school. The ones with high-powered jobs who hired expensive nannies to shuttle their children around to their rigorous schedule of daily activities. The crunchy-granola types who refused to use plastic containers or toys, who had rid their homes of dangerous shampoos. Jaya was none of those mothers. She was the mother who left her children on their own for two hours after school every day. She was the mother who had let her child die.

Who else could it be? Karina, responsible but still a child herself? Prem, innocent and inquisitive? There was no other alternative. So, she accepted their blame, felt it nest deep inside her. She had relinquished her maternal responsibility to a wrought-iron fence and the CPR skills of a thirteen-year-old. *Don't you think I know?* Jaya wanted to scream at them. *Don't you think I've already revisited every single meeting, every email I wrote, between the hours of 3:00 p.m. and 5:00 p.m. that day, and every day? I have asked and answered that question a million times,* she wanted to tell them. In their eyes, and in her own, she would always be the mother who had let her child die.

———

In her darkest moments, Jaya would wonder if Prem's life was tainted from the start, because of the way he'd struggled to come into it, and the world into which he was born. It had been difficult for her to get pregnant a second time, though Karina had been easy. Jaya knew they shouldn't have waited so long to start a family, four years after getting married, but Keith had an archaic male notion of being financially stable first. She would remind him of this delay many times as they tried to conceive, she was ashamed to admit. She would denounce "his misplaced obsession with money" and "his preoccupation with material success over what was important." Those words caused a wound Jaya could never erase, no matter how many times she apologized.

When she finally became pregnant with Prem, it was the turning point that gave them something positive to look forward to, to build from. A little brother for Karina, the first grandson in the family—he was their new beginning. She had been in her final month of pregnancy when she was awoken by a familiar discomfort in her lower back. Her eyes were adjusting to the still darkness when the phone trilled across the bedroom. She cursed and lumbered to reach it, praying Karina and Keith would sleep through the noise.

"Is Keith in New York?" Her mother's voice came through in a rush.

"What? No, he's right here, *asleep.* He's not going till Thursday."

Her mother let out an audible sigh. "Thank god. You've seen it on TV? *Horrible.*"

Jaya's hands shook as she exchanged the phone receiver for the television remote control on their dresser. Keith sat up in bed as the images unfolded on the small screen: smoke billowing from a hole in the high tower like a bleeding wound. They watched together in silence as the skyscraper began to fall in on itself and tumble, slowly, silently to the ground, sending up a giant plume, masking what had been there just moments before. Over a hundred stories of steel and concrete, engineering and human ingenuity disappeared in an instant, a magician's trick.

Jaya watched television all day and the following days, as Karina played with wooden blocks and tottered around the house in Jaya's high-heeled shoes, all permitted so long as she was safely out of view of the TV. Jaya watched through streaming tears as people posted homemade signs all over lower Manhattan, for boyfriends, sisters, fathers and room-mates who had gone to work on a clear Tuesday morning and had not been heard from since. Behind all these seekers and tellers, a gargantuan pile of rubble rose from the ground, smoke climbing from the wreckage while brave firemen trudged atop the mass in the vain hope of finding somebody, *anybody*.

Keith was alive only due to his arbitrary meeting schedule. She was only here in this country because of a chance meeting at a pub in London. Now the borders were closed, shutting her off from the rest of her family. All their lives were ruled by the whims of fate, and this realization made her feel powerless. This was the world in which they were raising Karina, into which their son would be born—this ugly, cruel, awful, dangerous world full of horror, where planes flew into buildings and people jumped from towers.

That had been eight years ago, when she recognized how the world was filled with dangers unseen and unanticipated. But this time, they had not been fortunate enough to escape the worst. And now, in her grief, her love for Prem had no home.

8 | karina

Two weeks after Prem's cremation ceremony, a period during which Mom had hardly left her bed, she finally wandered down to the kitchen, hair mussed and a sour smell trailing her. Karina was so surprised to see her that she just sat at the kitchen counter, watching as her mother opened the refrigerator and stared blankly inside before saying, "We don't have eggs?" No one had been to the grocery store in weeks. Dad had been sustaining himself on black coffee, and Karina on cold cereal.

Something sparked inside Karina with the simple query, something her mother might have said Before. "I . . . I'll go next door and get some," Karina said. "Be right back." She ran out the front door in bare feet and crossed the dewy lawn separating their house from the neighbor's. A few eggs. A few eggs would make things better, would make her mother happy, would bring normalcy back to their home. The guilt and shame that had been burning inside her for weeks abated for the first time as she knocked on the neighbor's door.

Karina returned a few minutes later with a full carton and set a pot of water to boil, rushing around the kitchen to prepare everything the way her mother liked, the way she and Prem had helped their father make it for Mother's Day—a hard-boiled egg, seasoned with salt and red chili pepper, buttered wheat toast and a sliced banana—the kind of breakfast she'd never seen at her friends' homes, filled with chocolate chip pancakes and waffles. She took the tray upstairs, but her mother had fallen asleep again, curled tightly into a ball, clenching a pillow to her chest like a child with a stuffed animal. Karina placed the tray next to the bed, where it sat untouched until her father later cleared it away.

———

"Karina was so good, so responsible," Mom said, placing one limp hand on Karina's knee, leaning toward her daughter. "She tried to save him."

"Mm-hmm," said the twelfth auntie of the week, sitting across from them on one of the dining chairs Dad had moved into the living room to accommodate the overflow of visitors who had been coming to pay their respects.

"We had that fence installed as soon as we moved into this house, to prevent just this kind of thing," Mom said, answering a question that had not been asked.

The auntie drew in her breath sharply and clucked her tongue. Karina hated these Indian ladies from the temple who came to the house in a steady stream, with their foil-wrapped dishes and fabricated concern.

Mom paused and took a sip of her tea. Then she gripped Karina's thigh tightly with her hand. "But Karina was such a good girl. The paramedics said she was calmly administering CPR when they arrived. She did everything she could to save her brother. She jumped right in after him." Mom turned to her, a pained smile on her face as tears welled in her eyes.

The auntie invoked God, as they all did, claiming to know that *Bhagwan* would take care. Karina felt her lungs grow tight with air she had trouble expelling. She didn't understand why they had to endure these visits, which left her feeling worse and didn't seem to help her mother. Karina thought she might have to cry out to relieve the pressure tightening in her throat. She quietly excused herself and went upstairs to the bathroom, the one she'd yearned to have to herself when she shared it with Prem. After locking the door, she leaned against the cool stone edge of the vanity and stared at herself in the mirror, her breath coming rapidly. She turned on the faucet and splashed cold water on her face, then rubbed it dry with a towel. She leaned closer to the mirror, taking in each blemish on her face: the dark patchy skin, the sprinkling of pimples across her upper cheeks, the hair sprouting on the bridge of her nose, beginning to knit her brows together. A sense of ugliness overwhelmed her, and strangely, it also somehow felt right. This was how people saw her from the outside: awkward, ugly, awful. And it reflected how she felt on the inside: rotten, undeserving of love or pride or anything good. She closed her eyes, longing to erase her image and replace it with a blank face that would fade into the background.

Her mother's words hung there, haunting her with their fundamental mistruth. The hurt in Mom's eyes, the sound of Dad crying from the garage at night, all the pain she had brought upon her family—there was nothing she could do to alleviate it. Karina opened the drawer of the vanity and rummaged around. There was no amount of mascara or eyeliner that would rehabilitate her ugliness, but she had been thinking about another way, waiting for the courage to try. The feeling of unease grew in her abdomen, infecting her from within until she thought she might have to throw up. She wanted to release it all, this pain that threatened to consume her.

When her fingers landed upon it, she knew. She retrieved the small blue Swiss Army knife she had given Prem, along with a compass, for his last birthday after he'd joined the Boy Scouts. She sat down on the bathroom rug and pulled out each of the tools: the blade, the screwdriver, the scissors. When she got to the nail file, she closed the others and slid the narrow metal tip under her fingernail until the pain in that delicate space intensified and began to throb.

And then, she felt a small rush of something else: a wave of relief.

Karina reopened the blade. She placed it in the same space under her fingernail and pressed down until the pain sharpened and she cried out. It felt as if the black cloud that had been surrounding her began to open up and rain down on her. She closed her eyes, leaned her head back against the cabinet and sank into that feeling: the pain and punishment for how bad she knew she had been. When she opened her eyes, there was a bright red line of blood spreading under her fingernail.

Karina heard her mother calling her from downstairs. She didn't like to be left alone with visitors for too long. Karina put her finger to her mouth and tasted the blood, its metallic flavor sharp and familiar. She rinsed her finger in the sink and rummaged through the medicine cabinet for a bandage. She could only find *Space Rangers* bandages, deep blue and undersized, for a child's hands. For Prem's hands.

Over the next few weeks, their house was frequented with visitors from the temple, the neighborhood, Dad's office, Mom's work and their school. During those visits, when she was expected to sit politely in the living room or the kitchen, Karina was always thinking about how to find a moment to escape to the bathroom upstairs that was now hers alone. Each time, as she climbed the stairs, she felt her heart beat faster. Behind the locked door, she would splash water on her face or brush her hair, but no matter how many ways she tried to avoid it, eventually she always found herself reaching for the Swiss Army knife at the back of the drawer. When she had bandages on a couple of fingers, she began to make the cuts on her inner thigh, where no one would see them.

She always felt the rush of relief, a release from all the poison that had been building up inside her. By the time she left the bathroom, the shame over what she'd done began to creep back into her mind, as she went downstairs to rejoin Mom and their guests for tea.

9 | keith

JUNE 2009

In the weeks after Prem died, Keith felt as if his body had been occupied by an outside force. He barely slept and his appetite dwindled; his eyes spontaneously filled with tears throughout the day. He hid away in the bathroom shower or sometimes in his car in the garage to cry, if not freely, then less self-consciously. He knew, intellectually, it was normal for him to cry. But the sound of it, to his own ears, undid him. He sounded like a child, like Prem when he'd fallen off his bike and scraped the entire length of his leg on the sidewalk. At the memory of Prem, and all the moments he would never have in the future, Keith cried even more.

Keith had never witnessed his own father cry, not once. He had grown up in a distant suburb of Philadelphia, in a Scandinavian Lutheran family that seesawed between newly prosperous and the verge of bankruptcy. His father was a serial entrepreneur, though not often a successful one. He always proclaimed to be on to the next big thing and started a series of businesses selling products, like car shammies and hand-crank flashlights, through late-night TV and mailbox flyers.

When a business did well (hand-crank flashlights took off during the cold war, as neighbors outfitted their basements for impending nuclear disaster), Keith's father took the family to fancy steak houses for dinner. He bought his dream car, a red convertible Thunderbird, and spent freely until another business (portable jump-starters to store in car trunks) went bust, as most of them did. Threatening red-lettered envelopes arrived in the mail and persistent phone calls from debt collectors rang in on call waiting while Keith talked with his buddies or tried to convince a girl to go out with him. By the time Keith left for college, the boxes of costly but useless inventory still lined one side of the garage, up to the ceiling.

Even at the lowest times, Keith's father never cried. Not when his businesses failed, not when the bank repossessed the Thunderbird (which by then had been sitting in the garage for six months, awaiting unaffordable repairs), not even when his own father died.

Keith had no sense of how to handle the grief he suffered in the wake of Prem's death. In the hospital, the social worker had given him the name of a grief counselor. "I think we should make an appointment," he said, sitting on the edge of their bed, next to Jaya, one evening.

She shook her head, a small but firm movement. "I don't want to. I don't want to talk to *strangers*. I don't want to talk to *anybody*, Keith. I just can't . . ." She bit down on her lip.

"Honey, the social worker said it's a good idea for the whole family to go. You know, to help Karina too," he said to appeal to her abiding maternal impulse.

"How is a complete stranger going to help our daughter? Help *anything*? Please, Keith, just let me be." She slid her body down under the bedcovers, reaching for the pillow behind her head. It was 7:40 p.m. "Can I just get some rest?" She began to cry, then turned away when he tried to comfort her.

Keith tried to broach the subject again the next day, and even called Jaya's mother to help convince her, but apparently, opening one's heart and soul to a professional was not part of the Indian culture, so he didn't garner much support. Jaya was strong, her mother reminded him. He remembered back to 9/11, when she'd been in her most vulnerable and emotional state, just a few days from delivering Prem. She had implored him to see what a dangerous place the world was, but Keith had seen it the opposite way: fate had given him a renewed lease on life. Losing friends in the World Trade Center that day made him want to go out into the world and not lose a single minute, not waste a bit of it. To go hang-gliding over the ocean, to run that marathon, to travel to beautiful cities like Istanbul and Beirut, even if they were dangerous. Yes, the world was unpredictable and wild, and also full of possibility and beauty he hadn't even begun to see. Outside of the year he'd spent in London, the city in which their divergent and unlikely orbits collided, he had seen so little of the world. He couldn't imagine doing what Jaya had in those dark September days, shrinking back into herself and making her world smaller, as if she could somehow keep them safe that way.

That trip they finally made to Switzerland was glorious. The children were spoiled by their grandparents, and he and Jaya spent a couple of romantic nights away at Lake Geneva, where they hardly left their bed. By their return flight, Jaya was back to normal, handing out snacks and coloring books to occupy the children during the long journey, while she read a novel. He'd been impressed with her courage then, and he needed to have faith in her now. This was what made their marriage work: drawing on their respective strengths.

Keith attended the first session with the grief counselor alone, out of obligation to the rest of his family. Going to a shrink, as his dad would call it, wasn't part of Keith's comfort zone either; he was in the habit of suppressing unpleasant feelings or using them as motivators for change. The counselor was a young woman, probably too young to be a parent herself. "Tell me about your son," she said when they sat down.

Keith shifted uncomfortably in his seat. Perhaps Jaya was right. How could a stranger who didn't know him, who'd never known Prem, help him grieve? Still, he started from the beginning. "He was an easy baby, always happy. We took him everywhere—restaurants, hikes, train rides—and he napped wherever and whenever." He explained that Prem had a lightness and joy that counterbalanced Karina's seriousness. "Prem always made us laugh, whether he was trying to or not. One time, he lobbied to have a water balloon fight *inside* the house." Keith laughed, recalling how Prem had unrolled giant garbage bags to cover all the furniture as part of his campaign.

He *laughed*. Eight days after his son's death. Immediately, he was flooded with guilt. Tears sprang to his eyes.

"It's okay," the counselor said. "It's normal to feel all kinds of emotions in the wake of a death, especially a sudden death. The death of a . . . child." She spoke the word cautiously. "Of course, you have happy memories of your son. That's the way it should be." She leaned toward him and placed a hand on the coffee table between them, as if trying to reach him. "At some point in the future," she told him, "when you think of your son, the happy memories will come to your mind before the tears come to your eyes."

Keith wasn't sure he believed her, but just to know such a thing might be possible, that there might be a day when he could smile before crying when thinking of sweet little Prem and all he had lost from his future, and all they had lost with him—there was some hope in that. It was the tiniest glimmer of hope, but Keith grasped on to it.

The next time, he brought Karina with him, and the counselor asked her some of the same questions. "What do you miss about your brother?"

Karina recalled sweet moments they'd had together, moments Keith was vaguely aware of but didn't remember himself. He'd been too inattentive; he'd missed so many moments. Tears welled up in his eyes. Karina cried too as she recalled Prem, wiping small tears from the corners of her eyes before they escaped. But when the counselor asked her about Prem's death, if she wanted to talk about that day, Karina firmly shook her head no, and Keith became protective. The police had already questioned Karina and he thought their questions had gone too far, had been almost accusatory. His daughter needed a safe place to heal and move on from the memory of that terrible day, not to dwell on it.

———

After many nights of rewarming casseroles brought by friends and neighbors, Keith tried to convince Jaya to go out for dinner, just to their neighborhood bistro a few blocks away, but she refused to leave the house. So, falling back on his earliest skill with women, he decided to cook something. Rummaging in the pantry, he found linguine, canned tomatoes, olive oil, capers, anchovies and chili flakes, and improvised a pasta dish. It felt surprisingly good when the steam from the boiling water rose to his face, to hear the satisfying crackle of oil in the hot pan as he prepared the sauce. He had forgotten this simple pleasure of preparing a meal, of throwing in pinches of salt and chili pepper until it suited him, an extra drizzle of fruity olive oil on top of the finished plate.

"Oh my god, Dad. This is so good," Karina said as they ate together at the kitchen table, with cloth napkins and a bottle of wine he'd opened. She twirled large forkfuls of pasta and ate them in one bite, then wiped the bowl with a crust of bread until it was clean. Jaya ate well too, finishing her plate and getting a second serving, and this brought Keith deep satisfaction.

A shared love of food was one of the things that had brought him and Jaya together after meeting in London. Unlike his wife, Keith hadn't grown up with fine food, and his appreciation of the gourmet was hard-won. When times had been tight in their household, Keith's mother had clipped coupons religiously and composed meals from an unlikely combination of ingredients that happened to be deeply discounted: grape jelly went into spaghetti sauce, canned corn into meatloaf. Keith never knew how haphazard this fare was until he went away to college and began eating with friends who hailed from New York and Boston. Only then did he experience the sheer bliss of eating food that was expertly paired, not unnaturally forced together in desperation. A delicate piece

of raw ahi dipped in soy sauce. A pungent leaf of basil on a slice of buf-
falo mozzarella. A drizzle of aged balsamic on fresh strawberries.

Once he'd stepped into that world, made infinite in Manhattan, there
was no turning back. He was determined to learn how to cook for
himself. By his junior year, when he shared an apartment, he was going
to Zabar's and blowing an entire week's food budget on the ingredients
for a slow-simmered Bolognese or coq au vin. These skills made it easy
for him to score with girls in college, who were easily won over by any
kind of home-cooked meal. Keith still loved to spend Sundays watching
football and drinking beer with his buddies, but he became infamous for
what he accomplished on Saturday nights with his famous linguine with
clams. Perhaps because attracting women suddenly came easily to Keith,
he found himself bored with most of them.

Jaya was the first woman Keith found himself interested in for more
than a few months; his attraction grew as he got to know her better.
He wasn't the least bit surprised—though he was intimidated—to learn
she'd lived in seven countries. Jaya picked up languages like passport
stamps, speaking four of them by the time she graduated from university.
They explored food and culture together throughout the great city of
London, trying out new cuisines like Afghani and Ethiopian, then seeking out special markets to replicate dishes in his flat's tiny kitchenette.

Now, in the oversized granite kitchen of their Los Altos, California,
house, Keith returned to cooking as a way to reach his wife. He wished
he could make her Indian food, the one cuisine he had ceded to her
expertise but that would bring her the most comfort now. Keith watched
how Jaya ate to gauge how she was doing. Some days, she ate ravenously;
other times, she just picked at her food. Reluctantly, he came to understand that how Jaya ate bore no relationship to the taste of the food or
any true appetite. She was eating purely for sustenance, when her body
reminded her it needed as much. Despite Jaya's indifference, Keith continued to prepare meals, hoping it would bring them all back to the table.

10 | karina

The calendar hung on the wall of Karina's bedroom, featuring photos of her and Prem every month. When she turned the page to July, she was confronted with a full-page image of her grinning, toothless brother, holding a dripping ice pop. He had lost both top front teeth a few weeks earlier and went around proudly showing off his "tunnel" for months. Probably taken with her father's primitive cell phone camera, the photo was of poor quality—it was grainy and Prem's eyes were half closed, as they often were when he was smiling big—but it captured her brother's essence. His goofy smile was so infectious, with that dribble of rocket pop blue at the corner of his mouth, that Karina couldn't help but smile back. She touched the tip of her nose, then placed her finger on his and let it linger there for a moment.

There was nothing marked on the page for July except the square for the fifteenth, on which she'd drawn a happy face and the name "Gilly." It was nearly time to pick up their poo-retriever. She smiled again, remembering how Prem had delighted in telling everyone at school about their new self-cleaning puppy. His third-grade teacher had relayed that story to her parents when she came to the memorial service and cried the entire time.

—

"We need to set up Gilly's crate and get everything ready," Karina said that night at the dinner table, as she spooned fragrant Thai coconut curry atop the jasmine rice on her plate. Some of Dad's efforts in the kitchen tasted better than others, and this was one of her favorites. She wondered when things would return to normal, with both her parents going to work and Mom rushing in to prepare dinner at night.

She saw her parents exchange a glance. "I can do it," Karina said. "It's in the garage?"

"Honey," her father said. She noticed he hadn't yet served himself any food. Her mother's plate held only plain rice, which she was pushing around with her fork. "Honey, we've been talking and"—he exhaled a heavy breath—"we don't think this is the right time to bring a puppy home. Maybe in—"

"What?" Karina said, turning to look at her mother. "No, we have to pick her up on July 15. That's the date."

"Honey." Her father reached out and put his hand on top of hers. "We can't handle it right now. In a year or so, things might be different."

"But . . . we *chose* her." Karina felt a prickling behind her eyes and she spoke louder. "*I* chose her. Gilly is ours. We decided."

Mom's fork clattered onto her plate. "Dammit, Karina. Do you care more about that stupid dog than your own brother?" Her eyes were deep black pools. "We canceled it. It's done." She picked up her fork and shoveled a pile of rice into her mouth.

Karina looked at Dad. It couldn't be true. He sat with his hands folded under his chin, unmoving. "I'm sorry, honey."

Karina shook her head and pushed away from the table. "I can't believe you did that. I can't . . ." And yet, it made sense. Why did she deserve a dog? She couldn't take care of anything, of anyone. "I'm not hungry." She left the table, breaking the family rule about staying until everyone was finished, which no longer seemed relevant. Karina ran upstairs to the bathroom and found relief in the one way that had become reliable: two thin vertical incisions on her left inner thigh. When she emerged from the bathroom, she sat at the top of the stairs and eavesdropped on her parents downstairs.

"There's no other choice, Keith," Mom was saying. "It's too much of a distraction. And my mother's coming next week. She's not used to pets. Can you imagine that thing peeing all over the house, chewing up shoes?"

Karina remembered that her grandmother was coming from India to stay at least through the rest of the summer. The voices dropped in volume. She heard some murmurs, then fragments in her mother's voice: "Do you really think . . . take care of . . . living being . . . ?"

So, that was it. This was her family. Dad spent half the day in the kitchen, preparing meals her mother barely touched. Mom was a smaller, meeker version of who she'd been, one who stayed in bed all day with the curtains drawn. Prem was gone, her grandmother was coming, and there wasn't room for anyone else. And she couldn't be trusted with anything. This was her family now.

Karina returned to her room, closed the door quietly and sat on her bed. She stared at her phone for a moment, then texted Izzy. She waited a few moments for a reply, but none came. She wasn't supposed to have her phone in her bedroom, a rule she had regularly broken when she and Prem had been home alone after school. With this thought, her anger was swept away by a fresh wave of guilt. Why had she made a big scene at the dinner table over a stupid *dog*? Everything was her fault, and now she'd made it even worse.

11 | jaya

JULY 2009

Jaya knew she only had to hold on until her mother arrived. She had called her parents, now retired to India, the night Prem died and her mother said she would come as soon as possible. With American expediency, Keith's family had all flown in from Pennsylvania for the memorial service and left a few days later. Jaya's mother hadn't rushed to be at the service—women in India usually didn't attend death rituals—but she wrapped up her affairs so she could stay with them for several weeks or even months, knowing that was when the real need would be, once the doorbell stopped ringing, the flowers stopped arriving and bags of food stopped appearing on the porch. When Keith brought her mother home from the airport, Jaya fell into her arms and felt herself revert to the child who could cry freely, her body shaking, tears and mucus running down her face. In the following days, she felt a deep comfort in the presence of her mother, who silently stepped into the role Jaya had vacated, caring for her and nurturing her family.

One morning, Jaya came downstairs after waking late and found her mother sitting cross-legged on the dining room floor in front of a small temple erected on an ottoman draped with a silk shawl. Her mother was chanting and counting on her prayer beads. Jaya moved closer and took in the scene. There was a small hand-carved sandalwood temple, four solid silver figurines of gods and goddesses, a stand for burning incense sticks, a silver dish holding a ghee-soaked cotton ball lit into a small flame, and a small silver bell—all of which her mother must have brought from India. Into this mix, her mother had placed a small orchid with bright purple blooms, which had appeared in the house along with so many other flowers over the past month.

"Ma?" Jaya said.

"Ah." Her mother sprang up quickly, still possessing in her sixties the grace of a dancer. "You slept?" She touched a strand of Jaya's hair, from the scalp down to the ends, then lightly circled her face with two fingers.

Jaya nodded slightly. "Do . . ." She looked at the improvised temple and the floor. "Do you want to sit on a chair or couch? Would you be more comfortable?"

Her mother's face flickered with confusion, then she smiled. "Hmph. You've become so American. Come join me—just take your bath first."

Jaya washed her hair and dressed in fresh clothes for the first time in days. When she returned downstairs, the scent of incense drew her in. She sat cross-legged on the floor next to her mother, facing the shrine. Without opening her eyes, her mother began singing a prayer song in low, even tones. The melody was familiar, one Jaya had learned as a child, and like a moving sidewalk, it pulled her along with its rhythm until she caught on to the words and began to sing. As her mother rang the small silver bell to keep rhythm, their voices harmonized perfectly and their two sounds became one.

Frail is the human being, with a million shortcomings. But you are omnipresent and you are merciful. Since you have given us birth, you will also bear our burdens. Jaya let those words wash over her, penetrate her, envelop her. A deep, visceral comfort emerged from falling into the rituals she had practiced as a child.

On the third repetition of the verse, Jaya felt her breath slow and deepen. She straightened her back and let air and prayer flow through her body and cleanse her soul. Her mind detached from its aura of pain and connected to something deeper, something outside of her. After two more repetitions, her mother slowed down on the final verse and they concluded with a resonant, *"Om shanti, shanti, shanti."* Peace. After a long moment, Jaya opened her eyes and saw the beautiful shrine before her, noticed intricate carvings in the wood and the detailed expression on the face of the Shiva figurine. She blinked a few times, uncertain what had just happened to make her feel lightness for the first time since she had lost her little boy.

———

Jaya began to join her mother at the shrine every morning, a reason to get out of bed along with the sacred obligation to bathe before prayers. The time she spent chanting and singing created a kind of numbness that buffered her from the anguish she otherwise felt in her waking hours. She spent more and more time in that state, drawn to the comfort it provided. As sitting on the floor came to feel natural again, Jaya reflected on her mother's observation that she'd become too American.

It used to be that every time someone asked Jaya where she was from, she had a difficult time answering. She'd explain that her parents were from India and she'd been born in Delhi but had lived all over the world when growing up. Earlier in her life, she might have described herself as European, having spent her adolescent identity-shaping years in Portugal and Ireland. Now she was considered American and expected to hyphenate her identity between the country where she began her life and the one where she now lived. But did that term, "Indian-American," truly capture her identity? Had she not met Keith that night at the pub, Jaya might have happily stayed in London for the rest of her life. Or moved to another country in the world, where her international policy work took her. Or even ended up back in Delhi when her parents resettled there.

"Indian" represented the most meaningful part of her—the culture and history she felt running through her blood; the language, food and music that made her feel at home. It was an inextricable, essential part of her; not just what she had been born with, but what she embraced. "American" represented the choices she'd made as an adult—the man she'd chosen to marry; the children she'd borne, Prem, with his love of baseball, and Karina with her stubborn independent streak. This was the place where she'd chosen to make a life, standing up and taking the oath of citizenship with tears in her eyes in a government building over a decade ago.

It was the nation where she'd felt personally violated when terrorists flew planes into buildings on a clear September morning, where that same day she went to the local hardware store to purchase an American flag and mount it outside their home, a small gesture of solidarity with her neighbors. Being American was woven into the fabric of her life— her connections with people, places, her family and the way she lived. Would she still feel as American, Jaya wondered, if she were to extricate herself from that fabric, to pick up and move back to India or some- where else? Would it simply travel with her like the habits she'd acquired from the places she'd lived, like eating dates after dinner in Kuwait? Or would America be eternally in her blood like India was?

———

When the small white pills ran out, Jaya found herself waking in the middle of the night, unable to return to sleep. One such night, she crept out of bed and downstairs to the kitchen for some herbal tea. It was an eerie feeling to be the only one awake in the house and, it felt to her, in the world. Her phone blipped with a message from her younger brother, Devesh, just starting his workday in London. She picked it up and read:

Meh

An expression of indifference; to be used when one simply does
    not care.
A: What do you *want for dinner? B: Meh.*
Do kids say this in America? Mine won't stop. Help!

Jaya smiled. Dev had been forwarding her daily emails from a website
called Urban Dictionary, part of his effort to better understand his children. Smita and Sachin were seven and nine, sandwiching Prem's age,
though they seemed more mature due to their urban upbringing. Dev
had met his wife, Chandra, at graduate school in London. Ironically, it
was the first time either of them had dated another Indian person, to
the delight of their respective parents, who nonetheless took credit for
the serendipitous pairing. Chandra worked as a mutual fund manager,
while Dev practiced law with a large firm. Jaya emailed him back a
smiley face and, almost immediately, her phone rang.

"You're up!" Dev sounded more delighted than concerned about her
insomnia. "It's so hard to call with the time difference." He carried most
of the conversation, complaining about the utter dullness of his role as a
junior barrister. But the next time she was awake at that hour, Jaya called
him right away, as it made her feel a little less alone in the dark house.
These days, she often felt suspended in time and space, recalling the time
she was ten years old and she and Dev were playing on a merry-go-
round. He and the other younger children sat atop it while they called
out for Jaya to spin it faster and faster. She ran in circles until she felt
as though she might actually fly into the air. And fly she did, when she
lost her grip on the metal bar, with the centrifugal force of the carousel,
landing on the hard ground and breaking her left arm in two places.

Jaya had always felt responsible for her little brother and served as
his counsel, being the first to reach all the major milestones of graduate

school, marriage, home and children. But now, she found herself comfortable with him in a way she only could be with someone who had known her all her life. They spoke conspiratorially about their mother, as they had when they were young, comparing notes on the meticulousness of her vegetable chopping and the way she shooed everyone out of the kitchen when she was cooking. Jaya now felt a deep ache for her brother and her parents, who all lived so far away. Some part of her imagined moving closer to them, feeling the urge to cling to the family she had left. Her mother and Dev offered the unspoken familiarity of her childhood, reminding Jaya of who she was at her core, before she'd formed this new life of hers, which now seemed to be splintering.

12 | karina

AUGUST 2009

The yellow roses were in full bloom. Karina had been watching the bushes for weeks, watering them in the morning and giving them special rose food from the carton in the garage. Normally, her mother tended the roses herself—it was the one area of the garden she didn't ask anyone to help with. Karina stroked one of the pale yellow petals to its base and was surprised by how firm and strong the flower bud was. Following the stem down with her finger, she landed upon the first thorn and lingered there for a moment. She pushed her finger into the tip of the thorn for a second . . . two . . . three. The release flooded through her, and her hand dropped away.

She leaned forward and inhaled the fragrance. Her mom would love these, she thought, reaching for the clippers. Karina arranged four stems at different stages of bloom in a tall vase and placed them at the center of the kitchen table, where her mother sat, drinking a cup of tea and idly flipping through a newspaper.

"Oh," Mom said when she looked up and noticed the roses. She reached out toward one of the flowers but stopped short and pulled back her hand. "Isn't that beautiful?" she said, turning to look at Karina. "From outside?"

Karina nodded, smiling. Her mother's gaze shifted to the window overlooking their backyard, and she seemed to stare at something invisible off in the distance. "It seems wrong for beauty to still exist in the world, doesn't it?"

———

The empty summer days left Karina with long hours to spend with her grandmother, with the occasional escape to Izzy's house. Izzy was the only one who treated her normally after Prem died. She didn't look at her with sad eyes nor did she avoid her, as did most kids. When Karina was in a bad mood or didn't feel like talking, Izzy let her be. Of all her friends, Izzy had known Prem the best, including all his funny little habits. Sometimes she would mention him, like when they ate ice cream sandwiches. Izzy recalled how Prem used to lick the ice cream out from between the chocolate wafers, digging his little tongue into that groove until it became deeper and deeper, holding it up proudly to show them.

Dad took Karina to the counselor every week, and afterwards he'd take her for frozen yogurt and ask her how she was feeling. Karina hated going to that office, which was just a room in the woman's basement, with its own entrance from the street. There was no natural light except from the window wells, which contributed to her feeling of being underwater. Sometimes, she had nightmares from which she would wake to think she was lost at sea on a small, sinking raft.

"When do you most feel the loss of your brother?" the counselor asked Karina.

There was no time when she didn't feel the emptiness where Prem used to be, the keen sense of imbalance in their family. "Mealtimes," she answered. There were four bodies at the dinner table again, but Prem's chair was half occupied by her grandmother getting up and down to retrieve warm food from the stove. Prem was not there to bore them with his accounts of entire episodes of *Space Rangers*, or to test out eight successive knock-knock jokes from his new book.

"And when there's no one to vote with me for Clue over Trivial Pursuit." Karina smiled. The sooner she could prove to this woman she was fine, the sooner she could stop coming here.

The counselor returned her smile. "What else feels different?"

"Well, we're not getting a dog anymore. We had one all picked out." Karina shrugged instead of trying to speak through the tightening of her throat.

"How do you feel about that?"

She shook her head. "It's fine. It makes sense. You know, we couldn't handle it right now. I can't really . . . I can't really take care of someone . . . something else. Maybe in a year or two." She gave the counselor a bright smile and glanced at the clock on the wall.

"You're going to be returning to school in a few weeks. How do you feel about that?"

Karina shrugged. "Okay. Fine. I mean, it's high school, so that'll be different. Bigger, I guess."

"Does that make you nervous, a bigger school with more students?"

"No. The opposite." Karina looked forward to being in a sea of people, most of whom didn't know her. There might not be more kids who looked like her, but at least there would be more kids and she could lose herself. Less chance that someone knew all about her family.

———

Two weeks before Karina started high school, the orchids began to die. There were five potted orchids in their home, one for every room downstairs. Each had been delivered at different times in the weeks after the accident, but, as if in collective protest, they all stopped flowering at once. The purple one in the dining room was the last to drop its blooms, standing defiantly after the others had wilted. During breakfast one day, her mother touched the barren stem in the small pot for a long time. Her grandmother was going to throw them all out, but Karina wanted to keep them, to see if she could coax them back to life.

High school began at the end of August, and Karina signed up for a full schedule of rigorous classes, despite the school counselor's warning for freshmen to give themselves time to adjust. She pushed herself in each of her classes, taking some pleasure in the depletion she felt each night when she crawled into bed, hours after her parents had gone to sleep. Though her father left her lunch money, Karina made her own breakfasts and lunches. She hitched rides to school with friends or rode her bicycle. There was already so much pain in their home that Karina wanted her parents to see only good things when they looked at her, to feel proud and happy; not to see in her the reason her brother was gone.

Karina spent much of her time after school at Izzy's house, doing homework and playing with Dominick. Izzy's parents often invited Karina to stay for dinner, and she always did. She was grateful for the relief the Demetris' spaghetti and casseroles provided from her grandmother's Indian cooking night after night.

———

Mrs. Galbraith, Karina's biology teacher, was grading papers one day after school when Karina went into the science room. "Hey, Mrs. G, do you have any books on orchids?"

"Orchids? Hmm, let me see." She crossed the classroom and started looking through the bookshelf, where Karina joined her. "Well, there's this." She held up a book on bonsai and chuckled. "Not quite the same. Why orchids?"

"Well, I . . . we have a few of them at home and they had flowers for a couple months, but now they've all dropped their blooms. I was wondering if I did something wrong."

Mrs. Galbraith leaned against the wall. "I know you're supposed to let them dry out between watering, since they're used to tropical environments."

"Yeah, I read that online," Karina said.

"Do you have a moisture meter?" Mrs. Galbraith ducked into a cabinet beneath the sink and pulled out a long metal rod with a green frog on the end. "I know it looks silly, but it's a copper probe." She showed Karina how to place the bright metallic orange tip into the soil so it would register the moisture well below the surface, near the roots. "You can borrow this one if you'd like." She held out the frog to Karina.

"Thanks. I'll bring it back."

"And I'll keep looking for orchid books," Mrs. Galbraith said.

When Karina returned the following week, she found Mrs. Galbraith standing at one of the tall lab tables, her gloved hands deep in a pot of soil. "Ah, Karina, I'm glad you're here. Give me a hand, will you?"

Karina dropped her backpack on the floor and joined her.

"This tree is going into that bowl." Mrs. Galbraith gestured with her chin to a ceramic bowl sitting across the table. "When I lift this up under the root ball, can you move the soil left in the old pot to the new one?"

"Sure." Karina pushed up her sleeves, slid over the bowl and scooped in the leftover soil. She examined the miniature tree in Mrs. Galbraith's hands. "Is that a . . ."

"Japanese maple bonsai." Mrs. Galbraith smiled at her. "Seeing that book got me thinking: this might be a good project for my students. I've had this one at home for years." She lowered the small tree into its new home and patted down the soil around it. Karina had never seen a bonsai tree, and it was oddly fascinating to see such a small replica.

Mrs. Galbraith took off her gloves and carried them over to the sink. "I have something for you." She opened a drawer and removed two books. "These should help you with your orchids. I haven't had a chance to read them, but there's good information in there about dormancy periods, which it sounds like yours might be going through. Take a look and let me know what you learn?"

"Sure. Thanks." Karina took the books, which both appeared brand new. "Turns out I was overwatering the orchids. That moisture meter went all the way to ten once I put it down below the surface. I'm letting them dry out now. Hopefully, a couple of them will come back."

Mrs. Galbraith shrugged. "Orchids are fickle. I never got the hang of them. Bonsai, on the other hand . . . very sturdy." She smiled. "Do you want to see how to prune this one?"

Karina watched as she trimmed the tree, and then tried it herself with the small scissors. She began helping Mrs. Galbraith with the bonsai after school and in the mornings whenever she had time. Once she'd learned what to do, she fell into deep concentration during these periods, using the tiny shears and tweezers to create sculpted branches and even layers of deep red leaves. A perfect miniature she could create entirely with her hands.

13 | keith

AUGUST 2009

Keith was grateful for Jaya's mother's presence. She managed the incoming visitors, tidied the debris of grief from their home and spent hours engaged with Karina. Every night, she prepared simple Indian meals, and though it was hard for Jaya to take much pleasure in food, Keith knew the familiarity of her mother's cooking brought his wife some comfort.

After weeks of feeling like a shell of a human being, emotions ready to be triggered at any moment, Keith needed a reprieve. The managing partner of his office had sent the largest floral bouquet he'd ever seen with a kind note, telling him to take his time. But Keith was up for partner this year; he knew his colleagues were using every chance to prove themselves and he felt pressure to do so as well. Jaya's mother encouraged him to return to work, and with her there to look after Jaya, Keith felt comfortable enough to start back slowly.

The day Keith returned to the office, he sat at his desk, surrounded by the Lucite mementos the bank produced to commemorate each completed deal. He had a bookshelf full of them, dozens and dozens of shapes that signified the work he'd done, valuable work. A career to be proud of. Keith flipped through the presentations prepared for his review and wrote notes in the margins, making useful suggestions about new ways of looking at the numbers. He even caught a couple of errors. He went out to lunch with Matt and Greg, guys he'd known since they were all new associates together after business school. They were awkward around Keith until he told them the best thing they could do was not treat him any differently than before. They both seemed visibly relieved and, from there, they quickly descended into familiar talk of clients who were assholes, who was hot in the new crop of summer associates, and which assistant Murphy was banging. By the end of the day, Keith felt better than he had in weeks. He continued working into the early evening, reviewing documents that could have waited until the next day. As he pulled into the driveway that night, Keith felt more hopeful than he'd been since Prem's death. He was back to work, where he felt competent again. He could return to normal. That's what he wanted.

And that's what he began to strive for, with what was left of his family. He still had a beautiful, intelligent wife in Jaya. He still had a smart and healthy daughter. They could still be a family. They still *were* a family. He had more than the department head, Bill Jeffs, and his high-powered wife in another executive suite, who collected expensive motorcycles instead of having kids. He had more than Chris Murphy, with his string of girlfriends but no one he deemed worthy of settling down with. Keith had a wife, a daughter, a home and a career. He had a family and a life worth preserving, and he was going to fight for them.

After several visits to the grief counselor, Karina said she didn't want to go back anymore. She was spending a lot of time at her friend Isabelle's house, which he understood to be a good thing. The counselor said that Karina reconnecting with her support network was important to her healing process. He didn't see much point in forcing her to continue seeing the counselor when she seemed to be doing fine on her own. Karina had always been tough. When she'd slammed her finger in the car door at the age of six, she wailed loudly, but by the time he'd run back outside with an ice pack, her tears had dried and she was ready to go to gymnastics class. Some kids were just built strong like that; they could withstand more than others.

———

His mother-in-law had been with them for eight weeks when she took Keith aside in the kitchen one morning and told him it was time for her to return to India.

"Of course," Keith said. "I'm sure your husband is eager to have you back."

"Yes, we have a family wedding to attend," she said. "But that's not the main reason."

Keith looked at her with curiosity. He'd never felt like he'd truly gotten to know this woman for himself. Jaya had told him many stories about her mother's talent as a dancer, her skills as a hostess, how rigorously she managed their childhoods. But with only a handful of visits over the past two decades, Keith didn't feel as though he knew her beyond the immaculate facade she presented. Now, she spoke plainly.

"My daughter is a very strong woman," she said, and Keith nodded in agreement. "She has the internal fortitude to get through this. But she will not discover that strength so long as I am here. It will be difficult"— her voice caught, and she cleared her throat—"to leave her like this, but I think it is best. She will learn to get back on her feet."

"Is she . . . talking to you . . . at all?" Keith was stumbling over his words.

"She seems to be finding some solace in her prayers," Jaya's mother said. "She sits there for an hour sometimes or more, and she seems calmer afterwards."

Keith glanced through the kitchen doorway to the makeshift temple his mother-in-law had set up in their dining room. He'd assumed she had brought it for herself, to stand in for the small alcove they had in their flat in Delhi, but if Jaya was finding some peace that way, he was relieved. He felt a surge of emotion swelling inside him. "She . . . *we've* been lucky to have you all this time. I don't know how to thank you."

She waved away his comment. Keith could hear the echo of Jaya's voice in his mind, explaining that you don't *thank* in Indian families; you just *do*. Help is given, without being asked for. He felt it now, the unwavering foundation of her support, holding him up, the way he had felt when wrapped in his father's strong embrace after Prem's memorial service. He hadn't relied on his parents for anything—financial or emotional—since he'd left home twenty-five years earlier. But he'd needed his father that day to help him stand upright.

"Jaya will find her way," she said. "You must look after yourself too." She peered at him. "And Karina. She acts strong, but she's still a child."

———

After Jaya's mother left, Keith hoped their lives would regain some normalcy. He was back to a regular schedule at work, and Karina had started high school, where she could ride her bike and buy her lunch in the cafeteria. But Jaya said she wasn't ready to go back to work yet. He worried about her, alone at home. Some days, when he came back, the house and kitchen looked just as they had when he'd left in the morning. Up in the bedroom, he found open sleeves of crackers and empty cartons of yogurt on her nightstand. Jaya was in the shower with the bathroom door locked. He suspected she stayed in bed all day, getting out only when she heard the garage door open.

Every night, he laid out takeout food on the kitchen table. When Jaya came down, wet hair combed back into a loose ponytail, she looked at the food with disinterest but always thanked him for bringing it. As she ate, she asked him about his day, listening to his answers with a glazed look in her eyes. When Keith asked her what she had done, she shrugged and her eyes grew sad. She shook her head and smiled apologetically, as if she had disappointed him. When Karina was home for dinner, they let her carry much of the conversation, telling them about her new high school classes, cross-country practices and band rehearsals. Sometimes, in the middle of the night, he heard Jaya downstairs on the phone, talking to her brother, Dev, in London in a low murmur he couldn't decipher. He was grateful she was talking to someone, yet felt hurt that it wasn't him. He was right here with her in the same house every day, wrestling with the same grief.

Keith tried again to get Jaya to see the grief counselor, but his efforts failed, so after a few more visits, he stopped going too. He knew they each had to mourn in their individual ways. Jaya was taking solace in prayer, and she often spent time in Prem's room. Karina carried around her brother's pocketknife and slept with it on her nightstand. Keith still couldn't bring himself to be in Prem's space, around his stuff. Who was to say therapy was the right way to process grief after all? Maybe they were all on their own parallel paths of mourning and would meet on the other side, intact or even stronger.

The only place Keith truly felt better was at the office. At work, he understood the rules and knew how to succeed. His colleagues treated him as they always had. Keith was surprised by how grateful he felt for the career he'd built. In college, he'd assembled a list of the highest-paid professions: cardiac surgeon, actuary, investment banker. He wasn't very good at science and only moderately so at math, so that ruled out the first two options. By the time he was a senior, Keith had narrowed his sights on Wall Street. He managed to collect three of those coveted offers, to the annoyance of peers who were struggling to find jobs in an economy still jittery from the 1987 stock market crash.

Keith had the grades, but what those white-shoe investment bankers really loved to hear was how he'd worked his way through college by holding down two part-time jobs during the school year and working with his father's enterprise in the summers. He left out the detail that his father had lost his college fund savings in the 1982 recession, forcing Keith to scramble for tuition money. He omitted the financial truth of his father's ventures, simply referring to him as a serial entrepreneur, which was technically true.

At Morgan Stanley, he worked day and night, crashing at the office as often as at home. In what little free time he had, he enjoyed the food and restaurant scene in New York in a way he hadn't been able to as a student. He realized his goal of becoming a top-ranked M&A analyst in his first two years, giving him his pick of where to spend his optional third year. By the time Keith was headed to London, the hub of M&A activity in Europe and a food capital of the world, he had already surpassed his parents in terms of professional achievement.

At the end of the year in which Prem had died, Keith was promoted to managing director, one of only four on the West Coast. He worried the position might have been a sympathy gift before remembering that no one in investment banking did anything out of sympathy. As a partner, Keith was expected to bring in new business and clients, and he discovered he loved the thrill of chasing a deal. The combination of his modest suburban upbringing, the entrepreneurial spirit bred into him by his father, and his name-brand MBA made him the kind of guy everyone could relate to. It brought him great satisfaction to know he'd brought in a big piece of a business for the firm, which would be reflected in his year-end bonus.

As the numbers accumulated on Keith's mental balance sheet, it became a security blanket he could wrap around himself and his family. He hadn't been able to protect Prem, he couldn't bring him back, and he couldn't spare his family the pain that had descended on them. But he could do this one thing—perhaps small or inconsequential—but he could at least do this and do it well. He could give his family a sense of financial security and well-being for the rest of their lives, something his own father had not been able to do.

14 | karina

Sitting at a school library computer, Karina smiled at her first semester report card and printed out the page to tuck into her backpack. She declined Izzy's invitation to come over after school and enjoyed her bike ride home despite the light drizzle in the air. She had worked relentlessly all semester, and to actually accomplish what she'd put her mind to filled her with hope. She was eager to share the news with her parents. Good report cards had always been a cause for celebration in their house; perhaps this was a chance to recapture something that had been lost. Her mother had been getting out more lately, usually to go to the Hindu temple. She'd also begun practicing new customs at home: praying before breakfast, lighting incense sticks, cracking open a coconut each weekend.

As they waited for their usual Friday night pizza delivery, Mom tossed a salad with dressing while Dad poured two glasses of wine and opened a bottle of ginger ale for Karina. Karina pulled the page out of her backpack and slid it across the kitchen island toward her parents. Her father picked it up and looked at her, a smile forming on his lips.

"Wow, look at this." He showed the paper to Mom. "Karina's report card. She totally kicked ass."

Mom gave him a weary glance but didn't remark on his language, then looked down at the page on the counter as she continued tossing the salad.

"Straight A's out of the gate in high school," Dad said, beaming now. "Who does that? Amazing."

"A-plus in biology." Mom made an effort to smile, though the sadness never really left her eyes. "That's great, honey."

Dad wrapped an arm around her. "I'm so proud of you, sweetheart."

When the pizza arrived, they ate sitting on barstools around the kitchen island. Without ever discussing it, they had abandoned the kitchen table after her grandmother returned to India.

"Mrs. Galbraith asked me to join the Science Olympiad team," Karina said, feeling the need to fill the silence with something. "It's usually just for sophomores and up, but she wants me to join now."

"Great." Dad poured himself some more wine. "You're going to do it?" He turned to Mom with the wine bottle poised over her glass, but she shook her head.

"Yeah, I think so. I mean, it's a commitment—a couple hours a week now, but a lot more the month before the competition."

"I'm sure you can handle it. You're already acing your classes. Don't you think, Jaya?"

"Hmm?" Mom said, looking up from the salad she was pushing around with her fork.

"Shouldn't she join the Science Olympiad team?" Dad repeated, pointedly.

"You've always been good at science," Mom said. She left unspoken what they were all thinking: Karina had always been good at science and math, while languages and arts had been Prem's domain. He'd had the most imaginative mind for telling stories; he even won the best essay prize last year for his comic strip featuring a superhero named WaterMan, who saved the world from impending drought. Now, Karina understood, she had to be everything, to fulfill all her parents' dreams for her and Prem.

Suddenly, Mom stood and reached across the island for her phone. "We should go to the temple tomorrow, to give thanks for your report card." She began dialing. "I'll call the priest to arrange a prayer ceremony." She was more animated now than she'd been all night, but not for reasons Karina wanted.

Karina looked at Dad with disbelief, but his expression was blank. Having been raised a half-hearted Lutheran, he was happy to leave the family's spiritual well-being to her mother. It had been a cursory education: Mom had taught them a few Hindu prayers, taken them to the temple for Diwali, obliged Karina to tie a decorative thread around Prem's wrist once a year in exchange for a coin. Now, Karina felt anger rise uncontrollably within her. She stood up and carried her plate to the sink. "God didn't have anything to do with it."

"What?" Her mother stopped, looking up from her phone.

"I said, *God* didn't have anything to do with my report card. And I don't want to go to the temple. I have a big history project to work on." It was the last thing Karina wanted to be associated with, that nonsense that swept her mother away from their family for hours at a time.

The atmosphere in the kitchen was tense as they silently cleared the dishes. Afterwards, her mother retreated upstairs for her evening prayers, and Dad proposed watching a movie. Karina offered to make popcorn while he got settled on the couch. As the din of the popping kernels waned, she heard angry voices coming from upstairs. Karina moved toward the staircase in the hallway and heard her father shouting, "You have to *do* something, Jaya. You still have another child—have you forgotten her?"

"And you *had* another child—have you forgotten him?" her mother screamed back.

A pause, followed by some words Karina couldn't make out, and her father's booming voice again: "You have to find a way to move forward."

"What does that mean, move forward? Go back to work? I'm home now, all the time. Nothing can go wrong. Isn't that what you want?"

"Why would you think that?" her father said. "Jaya, you have to stop blaming yourself."

"That's what you think, isn't it? It was my fault!"

Karina shut herself into the small bathroom under the staircase, the room where they were supposed to shelter in case of a natural disaster, the only room in the house with no windows. She switched on the fan and ran the faucet to shield herself from the sounds upstairs, then knelt to the floor and searched through the vanity cabinet, looking for something to take away her pain. She found a safety pin and used it to draw a thin line of blood on her inner thigh, relieved to feel the familiar sense of release. Karina sat on the cold tile floor, leaning against the wall as warm tears dripped down her face and the satisfying taste of salt reached her lips. This feeling, a reminder she was still alive.

Back in that basement office, the therapist had asked Karina about happy memories of her family, and she could recall many: riding bicycles together in Napa, where they'd traveled for a wedding; enduring a long layover at O'Hare airport with a marathon of Crazy Eights; padding around the house in fuzzy slippers on Sunday mornings as Dad kissed Mom on the back of the head and handed her a cup of tea. These fleeting images of contentment came to Karina in the weeks after Prem's death, when it seemed as if happiness had been torn away from them as a family, as if it was something they had always possessed, their lives an uninterrupted tapestry of joy.

But that was not true, Karina began to see now that more time had passed. When her parents began fighting more, it wasn't unfamiliar, just more exposed. Those little jabs had been there before. Karina remembered mornings in the kitchen when Mom and Dad avoided each other, clearly having fought the night before. She and Prem would try not to disturb the water, to keep their parents happy at those moments. At school, they heard kids of divorce talk about shuttling between two houses, the tense communication between their parents over swapping weekends. She and Prem agreed they had to do everything they could to avoid that fate, to prevent the dissolution of the family that was the only place the two of them belonged.

There was something Karina hadn't told anyone, ever: in those moments that felt like hours, after she pulled Prem from the water and tried to breathe life back into him, she offered to make a silent deal with God. He could have her parents, if only Prem could live. She and her brother could survive their parents' divorce, together. But without him, she couldn't endure anything. Having not believed in prayer or faith or miracles before that moment, she wasn't sure why she thought her wish would come true, the deal honored. Perhaps because it was her first show of faith, that she was willing to sacrifice something so important.

That had to be worth something, right?

Karina longed to tell her mother, as she now sat in prayer upstairs, that it was futile to appeal to God for anything. Had they ever been truly happy? She didn't know anymore. She knew only that any chance they had at happiness died along with Prem.

———

Toward the end of the school year, Karina came home one day to find a construction truck parked in the driveway and the sounds of a jackhammer coming from the backyard. She recalled her mother mentioning that the project would start this week: the swimming pool was being filled in and covered with a new patch of lawn. Her father had come into Karina's room and nervously asked her if it was okay with her. Inwardly, she was relieved. It may have been the first thing in the past year all three of them agreed on. Karina had found herself unable to walk by the pool, or even to look at it from her bedroom window, and had taken to keeping her window shades closed. Now, she followed the pounding noises to the yard and watched for a few minutes as the hollow shell of the pool was punctured, concrete and tile rubble littering its bottom.

Inexplicably heartened by this sight, Karina put down her backpack and dug inside the front pocket for Prem's small Swiss Army knife. She turned it over in her hand, noting its smooth, unscratched surface. She pulled out the large blade and pressed it gently into her finger pad. Then in a single, swift motion, she drew back her arm and flung the knife into the broken cavern.

15 | keith

Keith left the office early the day the crew began working on the backyard, knowing it might be a difficult day for Jaya. She had been singularly focused, almost obsessed, with removing the backyard pool before the first anniversary of Prem's death. As he entered the house, he heard voices upstairs and followed them. Jaya was leaning against the doorframe of Prem's room, watching a construction worker tear up carpet from the floor while another took a sledgehammer to the built-in bookshelves.

"What . . . ?" Keith said, taking in the scene before him. "What is happening here?"

"Oh!" Jaya turned to him with an excited smile. "There you are," she said, as if he was the one who had disappeared. "I've finally figured out what to do. It came to me when I was sitting in prayer. And these fellows were already here for the pool. So opportune!" She flipped through a small notebook she took from her pocket, stopping at a page with a pencil sketch. The drawing was of a full room-sized temple, dwarfing the small nook he'd seen tucked away in her parents' home.

Keith felt visceral pain in his chest as he heard the sledgehammer slam into the empty bookshelf. Where were Prem's things? His books, his toys, the pennants that lined the walls? He looked back to Jaya in

75

disbelief. "How . . . ?" *How could she do this?* he wanted to ask, but he was struck by the realization that she was dressed in a crisp salwar kameez, and her hair was freshly washed and combed.

"You know we've never had a proper temple in our home," Jaya continued, "and now we can have one, right here." She gestured at Prem's room, being stripped of all traces of their son. Keith looked from the notebook to Jaya, who smiled again. That smile looked like it was coming from some other person inside her. "It's perfect, isn't it? The perfect way to honor Prem."

"No." Keith shook his head. "NO. Tell them to stop. Stop!" he shouted at the workman with the sledgehammer. "Just stop!" He turned to the other workman, pulling up the carpet. "Please stop. Just, uh . . . knock off for the day, all right?" Keith stood guard in the center of the room against further destruction, until the men gathered their things and left the house. He ran his hand through his hair and looked around at the disarray. He took a deep breath and forced himself to speak calmly. "Don't you think we should have discussed this first?"

Jaya looked at him with genuine astonishment. "You never cared about this before, how and where I do my prayers."

"I care about this!" He gestured around the empty room, his voice rising despite his intentions. "I care about our son's room!"

Jaya's brow furrowed. "You've barely set foot in here for the past year—"

"Yes, but . . . " Keith sputtered in anger, feeling the sting of her words. He felt weak for being unable to go in there as she did, but he always assumed he'd still have the ability to do so. He hadn't expected her to destroy the place while he was summoning his strength. It was as if she saw right through him, to the most tender and vulnerable part, and stabbed a searing poker into it. Overcome with frustration, he banged his open palm against the doorframe. "How could you do this? You just got rid of all his stuff? His clothes, his furniture, his posters?"

"It's all boxed up in the garage," Jaya said, as if this made everything better. She touched the crook of his arm. "But those things don't matter. His spirit is still here."

"It does matter, *to me!*" Keith yelled, pacing across the room. "Can't you see that? Can you see anything past yourself? We are *all* hurting, Jaya. All of us: you, me, Karina." He shook his head. "I swear, it's like you don't understand me at all, and you don't even care to. You don't give a *shit.*" He turned and walked out of Prem's room. At the end of the hallway, he saw a glimpse of Karina as she disappeared behind her bedroom door. He turned back to Jaya. "She's home?" he whispered.

Jaya nodded. "Practice was cancelled."

"Christ, Jaya." Keith shook his head. Karina must have heard everything. "Jesus Christ." He ran down the stairs and grabbed his car keys from the front table. He would speak to Karina later, but right now he was too angry. Adrenalin pumping through his veins, Keith drove well over the speed limit on their suburban streets. By the time he merged onto the highway, where he could really let out the throttle, the lump in his throat had manifested into tears running down his face. He was no longer just angry; he was despondent. Jaya had moved so far away from him that she didn't even know him anymore. They were both good, loving parents, he still believed. It just seemed they couldn't be so together anymore.

———

By the end of the following week, the yard project was completed, with no sign there had ever been anything there but an expansive green lawn. It took six more weeks for the workmen to finish transforming Prem's room. When it was completed in June, the floors were cool marble and the closet doors had been removed to create an open alcove that housed three tall god statues, complete with silk garments and floral garlands, all imported from India. On the floor were three seat cushions embroidered with small mirrors and tassels. Standing alone in the transformed version of Prem's room, Keith could think of nothing else he could do to try to save his marriage and his family. He felt like he was losing himself.

The Hindu priest came to bless their new home temple with a private prayer ceremony. Jaya was animated in a way she hadn't been since Before, as if she had come back to life but as a different person. Keith numbly went through the motions: he and Karina wore what Jaya chose for them, stood and sat where she told them to, and followed the instructions she translated from the priest as they went through the steps of the ceremony. It eerily paralleled the service they'd had one year earlier to commemorate Prem's death, also in their home, with the same priest. Only this time, it was Jaya they had lost.

16 | karina

In the end, Karina lost both her brother and her parents. They divorced the summer she turned sixteen, two years after Prem's death. Given her father's schedule, her parents agreed she would live primarily with her mom, or at least this was how they explained it to her. Karina wasn't sure whether her dad fought to have her or not, but they settled on weekend visits when feasible.

After trying so hard to make her parents happy and hold her family together, Karina had still failed, so the only thing left to do was save herself. Now, beginning her junior year, she only had to hold on to her tenuous existence for two more years until she would leave for college. It would be a clean start. She could seek the place where she truly belonged, free from the baggage of her family. A shift occurred inside Karina, unnoticed by her parents but significant, as she redirected all her energy toward the one thing she could now control: her own future.

Karina took a leadership role on the Science Olympiad team, assisting the captain by running after-school meetings. With Mrs. Galbraith's help, she set up a peer tutoring program for younger students, which took up all her remaining free time. Her days were full and busy, but she liked having a sense of driving purpose—reasons to work late into the night, knowing exactly what to do when she woke in the morning.

"So, Karina." Mrs. Galbraith leaned against the lab table where Karina was sitting one day after school, stapling papers for the Olympiad quiz session. "Have you decided on your classes next semester? I'm teaching environmental science and I'd love to have you in my class."

Karina didn't look up. The class requisition form had been sitting in her backpack for a week, but she'd been avoiding the showdown with her parents. Ever since she'd taken an early interest in science, her parents had guided her toward medicine. At one time, this had appealed to Karina too, the idea of helping people feel better or even saving lives. She used to enjoy taking care of children and animals for her neighbors and the independence it conferred.

But all that had ended with Prem's death, along with many other things. The idea of being responsible for another living being had become too daunting. On the Olympiad team, she'd learned about earth science, geology, engineering. She saw how much diversity and richness there was in the field of science, with numerous paths that felt as equally noble and important as medicine. The abstract nature of environmental science felt safer, but she knew this discussion would result in another argument with her parents.

"Yes, definitely." Karina smiled at Mrs. Galbraith. That evening, she forged her mother's signature on the requisition form, feeling only a small flint of guilt as she did so.

———

"Truth or dare, Karina?" Maddie Kramer asked before taking a swig from the longneck bottle of Miller Lite.

"Dare," Karina said. They were in the basement of Maddie's home, as her parents and younger sister were out for the evening.

"She always chooses dare," someone in the circle muttered. "Make it a good one."

Other dares Karina had successfully executed were prank-calling for pizza, taking a swig from a liquor bottle, and downing a full spoon of red pepper sauce. Truth would have been easier, especially since she could always lie, but it wouldn't give her the same thrill. A joint was being passed around the circle, and Karina feigned taking a drag before passing it on.

Maddie, one of the popular girls at school whom Izzy knew from the barn, scrunched her forehead in concentration for a moment before a glint appeared in her eyes. "You have to spin the bottle, and whoever it lands on, you go into the bedroom with him for five minutes and take off your shirt and let him feel your tits." Maddie looked around to the rest of the group, who responded with whistles and catcalls.

Karina took a slow sip of her beer. She was new to this group. Many of the girls were paired off with guys, sitting between their legs or curled up with them under concealing blankets. Karina had not yet dated and, truthfully, hadn't even kissed a boy yet. Everyone was now watching for her reaction. She felt perspiration collect under her arms. "That's not going to take five minutes," she said, stalling.

"Well, then use the time however you like." Maddie grinned. "Or *he* likes!" Another round of whoops and whistles came from the group, as the guys disentangled themselves to sit in a circle around the bottle Maddie had placed on the floor.

Without allowing herself a moment's hesitation, Karina leaned forward into the circle and spun the bottle. After a couple of rounds, it landed on Kyle Derrick, a senior on the football team who had never spoken to Karina. Now, he smirked at her and rubbed his palms together. Again, moving against her fear, Karina picked up her beer and stood. Izzy shot her an anxious look, but Karina gave her a confident wink and smile, and Izzy reflected it back. One scream and she knew Izzy would come running. Kyle hopped up as his buddies slapped him on the back and wished him good luck. "Can I watch?" one of them called out, as they climbed the staircase leading out of the basement.

Karina chose the first bedroom, which, with its assortment of stuffed animals on the bed, must have belonged to Maddie's younger sister. Kyle followed her into the room and closed the door. Karina stood near the bed and pulled her mobile phone out of her jeans' back pocket.

"Oh, you wanna record it? Yeah, that's hot." Kyle grinned. "Didn't know you were so kinky." He took a step closer and extended a hand toward the hem of her shirt.

In a single, swift motion, Karina swatted his hand away. "Don't be an idiot, Derrick. You think I'm going to let you touch me?" She held up her phone, displaying the large digital numbers. "Four minutes, forty-five seconds. And counting. Go sit over there." She pointed to a pink fluffy beanbag in the corner of the room that looked like a giant's cotton candy.

"But that wasn't the deal."

"It's the deal now," she said. "Or I can go out there and tell everyone you couldn't get it up. Your choice."

"I can't tell them nothing happened in here. What am I supposed to say?" Kyle wore a little boy's hurt face.

Karina willed herself to not roll her eyes. "Nothing. You say nothing. I'll say nothing. Your buddies can come to their own conclusions. You get credit for being a gentleman—or I out you as a limp-dick." She held up her phone. "Three minutes, fifty-one seconds. Deal?"

Kyle threw his hands flaccidly into the air. He sighed and plopped into the beanbag, looking so pathetic that Karina almost felt sorry for him. She sat on the bed and took a sip of her beer. She'd felt a little woozy after drinking the first one too quickly but was now settling into a pleasant buzz.

"So, what's your story, anyway?" Kyle said, toying with a Rubik's Cube he picked up from the shelf next to him. "Not a lot of science geeks like to party. Shouldn't you be home, studying for the SAT or something?"

"Already took it," Karina said. "Beginning of this year."

"Bet you got a perfect score?"

"I did fine."

"Heh," he chuckled. "Not me, barely scraped four digits. But I still got signed to play for USC on a full ride."

"Congratulations." She was surprised to see that Kyle had solved the blue face of the Rubik's Cube. Karina's SAT score may not have been perfect, but it was pretty damn close. She was laying down the stepping stones to her future, and she wasn't going to let anything get in the way, certainly not the grubby hands of a cute, dumb jock like Kyle Derrick.

"So, you're what, Middle Eastern or something?" Kyle asked, still fiddling with the cube.

"No," Karina said flatly, offering nothing else.

"What then? You've got something different going on." He pointed his finger in a circling gesture around his own face.

Karina glanced up from her phone to glare at him.

"Hey, no offense. I'm one-eighth Navajo, even though I pretty much look white."

She waited for a moment before answering. "My dad's white, my mom's from India. But I'm pretty much white, like you." The alarm trilled on her phone. "Probably the only thing we have in common." Karina slid the phone into her jeans pocket as Kyle struggled to get out of the sunken beanbag, then followed her out the door.

———

"The school called today," Mom said when they sat down for dinner, the two of them perched on the kitchen stools next to each other. "They said you've missed some classes."

Karina put a forkful of green beans in her mouth and chewed. "Class. Singular."

"Don't be smart." Mom was watching her. "You think that's acceptable, just deciding not to go to some of your classes?"

"Mom, it's just P.E. Not a real class." The required P.E. uniform consisted of a gray T-shirt emblazoned with the school logo, and athletic shorts cut high on the leg—high enough to now reveal the series of cuts that had been extending further down her inner thigh. Karina had realized this a couple of weeks ago when she was changing in the girls' locker room bathroom. She begged off class that day by telling the coach she had bad menstrual cramps.

"Apparently, it's been happening for two weeks now. Is that right?"

Karina gave a small nod of her head. "It won't affect my grades, Mom. No one cares if I get a B in physical education." After being excused from that first class, the next time she wore her longer bike shorts. The coach let it go that day but told her she'd have to be in full uniform the next class if she didn't want to be marked absent. She considered covering the cuts with a bandage or wearing leggings under her shorts, but that would only draw more attention. So, she just decided to stop going to class.

"I care," Mom said, finally serving herself some food. "I care if you're not going to class when you're supposed to. First, it's one class, then another. And what are you even *doing* during that time you're supposed to be in class? Smoking? Drinking? Going off campus?"

"Mom! No. Nothing like that." Karina's fork clattered to her plate. "It's just one stupid class and the coach is bad, and I just don't like it. Why do I have to take P.E. anyway? It's an elective and Dad made me take it, but I hate it. *I hate it!*" she said, louder. "Can't you talk to him? I can still drop the class and use the free period as a study hall."

Mom lifted her water glass to her lips and took a leisurely sip. "You can talk to him about it this weekend. He's picking you up Friday after school. Don't forget to pack a bag."

Karina shook her head and stood up from the kitchen stool. "I'm done. I have homework to do," she said, leaving her half-eaten dinner behind.

Living with Mom was like living with a ghost who operated in her own ethereal sphere, making her presence known on occasion. It was no picnic, but Karina didn't love going to Dad's place either. He loved his fancy hotel apartment, but Karina found it depressing. All the units were identical, right down to the green and gold drapery. There were no other families living at the hotel, and it felt awkward to have her friends over. Dad had encouraged her to have a swim party there for her birthday, but she hadn't been in a pool since Prem, and went out of her way to avoid the one at the hotel. The last time she'd inadvertently passed it, when Dad had taken her to the gym, the smell of chlorine gave her heart palpitations.

On weekends with her dad, they followed a routine: dinner at a restaurant, room service for breakfast, and afternoons at his golf club, where he tried to teach her how to play. She didn't look forward to it, but the whole arrangement served her purposes, giving her the freedom to do what she wanted. Dev Uncle, on a recent Skype call from London, encouraged Mom to give her more independence. "Sachin and Smita are riding the tube to school by themselves, and they're only ten and twelve," he boasted about her cousins. "You can't constrain her, Jaya. You have to let her grow up." Karina didn't tell Mom that Dad went through a few bottles of wine every weekend, and she didn't mention to Dad that Mom stayed so late in Prem's shrine that Karina often made herself cheese toast for dinner. Everyone in her family had their secrets, and Karina became practiced at keeping them.

When the pressure inside her grew to be too much, Karina retrieved her supplies from the back of the vanity drawer, her anticipation building. She laid her materials out in the same way each time, this ritual itself becoming part of the process. There was a small towel, an unwrapped bandage, safety pins, tissues and a bottle of disinfectant left over from when she'd had her ears pierced. She always started with the small safety pin, unlatching it and lodging the clip under her thumbnail for the dull pain. Then she wiped the sharp tip with disinfectant and drew a thin line across her inner thigh, increasing the pressure until blood appeared. For a while, this one cut was enough to reach the feeling she was seeking—a flood of relief, even contentment. For a few moments after making the cut, her body felt right and her mind was at peace. She tried to make that feeling last as long as she could. Sometimes, one cut wasn't enough and she had to do it again. Eventually, she began to use the bigger safety pin with its thicker tip. It turned out it didn't matter that she had rid herself of Prem's Swiss Army knife, and now she regretted losing that last piece of him.

———

The last year of high school blurred with intensity and activity, and Karina relished the feeling of exhaustion that accompanied her schedule. As captain of the Science Olympiad team her senior year, Karina led them to the regional finals, where they brought home small trophies for third place and a great feeling of accomplishment.

Her father wanted her to go to a top college. He insisted on taking her to tour the Ivy League, and regularly bought her shirts from the Stanford bookstore. Sometimes, she felt like one of his employees to be managed, or an investment to be returned. Karina had a different goal: instead of a university with the best ranking, she wanted one that would give her the largest scholarship—something that could give her true independence from her parents.

As the end of high school drew closer, the sights of Karina and her friends narrowed. Izzy was determined to go to college on the East Coast. Karina knew there was little chance of them being near each other, since Izzy wanted to live someplace where she could experience winter and escape their comfortable suburban neighborhood. Karina admired her courage and, in Izzy's shadow, realized how little of it she had herself. She thought leaving Northern California was a big step toward independence. She applied to all the best colleges on the West Coast, while Izzy applied to only one token University of California campus for her parents. Karina knew throughout their senior year that graduation would be the end of them, but that understanding didn't make it any less painful when it happened.

17 | prem

Usually I'm the one in our family who can see something special, but sometimes it's Kiki.

She was the first to see something special in Gilly when she was just a little puppy. Gilly ended up being adopted by a family from the waiting list, with ten-year-old twin boys. When they went to pick her up, she had grown so much you couldn't even tell she'd been the runt, and they called her Maxi. Kiki could see from the beginning that Gilly would grow up to be strong, a little fighter who constantly nipped at everyone's ankles. I don't think I would have liked that biting part, but I would have put up with it for Kiki. Gilly would have made her really happy.

But I'm the one who could always spot the candy in its hiding place after Halloween every year. Mom kept the bucket on the top shelf of the pantry, and when she wasn't home, I would climb onto one of the kitchen chairs and stand on my tiptoes to try to reach it. When I was six and seven years old, no matter how much I stretched out my arm, I couldn't reach that shelf, and I had to ask Kiki to get it for me (which she did, but not the whole bucket, only a few pieces). Seeing my family now feels like that: each person is reaching, stretching their arms and wiggling their fingers as much as possible, but there are still giant gaps between them. And they don't have anyone to ask for help like Kiki helped me.

Sometimes I felt left out, when Kiki, Mom and Dad would talk about what color our new car should be, or which movie we could go see. They were all used to talking about things together for five years before I was born, and sometimes it was hard for me to push my way into their conversations. Most of the time, I could do it with a joke. Sometimes they laughed, and sometimes they didn't (even though I was *always* funny), but at least they heard me.

I always thought of myself as the clown in the family, but now that I'm gone, and I see what they're like without me, I know I wasn't just the clown, but the glue. I was the one who held them all together, whether they were laughing at something I did or annoyed with me getting in the way. They always had to worry about where I was, who would stay with me and who would drive me to T-ball practice. Without me to fuss over, everything fell apart.

Dad is back to spending all his time At Work, like Before. I never knew it, but now I can see he gets really excited when he's there. He feels the way I did when I played T-ball with my team on the weekends.

Mom is always in my room, which doesn't really feel like my room anymore. I like that she spends all day in there with me, even if all the fun things are gone, boxed up and moved into the garage. Mom said she couldn't look at them anymore, but she touched and kissed every single book and toy (even every T-shirt!) before she packed them up. No one was there to see her but me, so I know she really meant it.

And Kiki, poor Kiki, she's all alone now. It used to be the two of us, together always, and even though Kiki got annoyed with me, I know she loved our super-awesome power duo too. Now she has no one—no one who's like her, no one who understands her. She spends time with her friends, but she doesn't tell them anything important. They don't know the little secrets I know, like how she wishes she had straight hair like Izzy, and how she actually likes those dinosaur-shaped chicken nuggets dipped in ketchup, just like me.

Kiki spends too much time in the bathroom, but not just trying on makeup like before. Now she does things she thinks no one else will see. And she's kind of right, because Mom and Dad don't see her anymore, not really. They don't see *inside* her to all the pain and hurt she feels, the swarm of snakes coiling around in her belly when she's awake, and in her mind when she sleeps. She hurts herself just to drown it out, but it never works for very long. I want to bang on our bathroom door, like I used to when I really had to pee in the morning and she was still doing her hair. I want to bang and say, *Stop, Kiki, stop!*

I want to pull her from our bathroom and pull my mother out of Not My Room Anymore, and pull Dad away from his office, and pull them all together, close the giant gaps between them and join their hands and say, *There! Now don't let go of each other. Don't you dare let go!*

But I can't pull them together. They can't hear me. And they can't hear each other.

So, I knew what was coming when they all went out to dinner at Alfredo's just before what should have been my eleventh birthday. It was two years since I died, and still no one could reach one another. They were floating away in different directions, each in their own orbit. Kiki didn't seem surprised either, when Mom and Dad explained they were getting a divorce. She didn't even cry, not then in the restaurant. Only later, alone in bed that night.

When we used to get bored on long car rides, Kiki and I would play the Worst game, trying to imagine the worst thing we could eat (worms), the worst thing we could wear (skunk skins), the worst job in the world (portable-toilet cleaner for me, slaughterhouse worker for her). Divorce was the worst thing that could ever happen to our family, we always agreed.

I should have been more careful. I should have tried to stay longer. I didn't know I was the glue.

AWAY

18 | the olanders

Keith emerged from the shower to see Courtney still asleep in his bed, tangled in the steel-gray sheets with her long hair spread out across the pillow. He glanced at the time and realized he was going to have to get her up and out. He pressed a button on the remote control to raise the window shades and another to tune the bathroom TV to Bloomberg, though markets were closed today. Courtney didn't stir. *Ah, to be in your twenties and sleep like that.* He raised the TV volume and ran the bathroom faucet to shave. By the time he finished and was patting his face with a towel, Courtney had rolled over to face the bathroom door.

"Hey there," she murmured. "You're up early."

"I have to get going at eight, remember?" He slammed the bathroom drawer, his anxiety mounting about the day ahead.

"Mmm," she said. "Too bad. I thought we could get room service and stay in bed all morning." She gave him a sly smile, which did not have its intended effect.

"You should get up. It's seven forty-five." Keith left the bedroom with a towel wrapped around his waist, hoping his departure would propel her out of bed. In the kitchen, he poured himself a cup of coffee that had been brewed to perfection by the espresso machine, which had also ground the beans while he'd been in the shower. The elaborate machine had been a splurge, one of the few items he'd chosen for himself in this condo; the rest was standard issue with the furnished unit he'd purchased a year earlier.

Shannon, a young woman he'd dated briefly last year, had tried to make the place homier by adding personalized touches, like photos of the two of them in places they'd traveled. Keith asked her to remove them, the first argument in their ostensible relationship, which led to a discussion about their future and their inevitable dissolution. Keith had already had a picture-perfect family and lost it; he didn't expect a second chance, at least not with someone new.

For reasons he didn't want to explain to Shannon or Courtney or anyone else, Keith liked feeling as if he was living in a hotel (which in fact he was, on the residence floor of a luxury hotel that had newly opened in the heart of Silicon Valley to accommodate the influx of global visitors). It felt more like he was traveling for work, as he did often, and less like a sad single guy's apartment. The whole condo had been a splurge after the divorce, when he was contemplating the expense of two households and Karina's college tuition ahead.

He'd finally made the move to Duncan Weiss, after avoiding it for so long because of Jaya's voice in his mind. The move had taken some adjustment; policies and procedures were not as established there as they'd been at Morgan Stanley, but he was acclimated now. Culturally, the smaller bank felt more comfortable than his previous blue-chip firm ever had. He may have had an Ivy League diploma, but at heart, Keith was a scrappy entrepreneur's kid from Philly. Most importantly, as a bigger fish in the smaller pond of Duncan Weiss, he took home a larger share of the bonus pool. With his first-year bonus, he'd paid off the modest mortgage on their family house so Jaya and Karina could live there without worry. A year later, he bought himself this condo, justifying it because of how hard he worked. When his parents came out to visit, they were awestruck by the heights to which their son had climbed in the pecking order, as he knew they would be.

Courtney walked up behind him in the kitchen and wrapped her arms around his waist, sliding one hand down beneath his towel. She nibbled at his ear. "Sure you don't want to come back to bed for just a few minutes?"

Keith put his coffee cup on the counter and refastened the towel around his waist before turning around to meet her expectant face. He summoned patience: he was desperate to get her out of here now, but she would be nice to come home to in a couple of days. He cupped his hands around her face. "Next weekend, we'll order room service and stay in bed all day. Promise." He kissed her deeply, in a way he hoped would satisfy her. "But right now, we've gotta go."

He patted her ass before returning to the bedroom, where he spent an unreasonable amount of time deliberating over which shirt to wear. As he tucked a pale blue linen shirt into his jeans, he caught a glimpse of himself in the mirror. How could he be old enough to be taking his daughter to college? There were still times when, putting on a suit, he felt twenty-five years younger, dressing for his first job at Morgan Stanley in New York. The time had passed in an instant. And yet, when he thought about it, the weight of those years and all that had happened had left their mark.

Courtney kissed him goodbye at the entrance to the parking garage, and by the time he reached his car, she'd already sent him a sexy text message. He deleted it without replying, irritated at her frivolity, her obliviousness to the import of the day. It had been over four years since Prem died, and Keith still keenly felt his absence. What would his son be doing today? How would he be feeling? Would he be sad to see his sister go, or happy to come out from her shadow? Keith was always accompanied by the ghost of an eight-year-old boy frozen in time, a son he would never teach how to shave, tie a necktie or drive.

Keith had learned to live with the things he couldn't control, starting with Prem's death and ending with the dissolution of his marriage. Jaya had been determined to pursue a path without him. Her resolve, always formidable, became unnerving once it was turned against him. When they emerged from that rawest period of grief, Jaya had built a wall around herself, blocking out everyone, including him. In the end— once he understood that she no longer wanted to live the same life with him—what lingered was this: she didn't seem to value what they'd created together. He wanted her to acknowledge that they'd had it all, and she'd chosen to squander it.

Keith put the car into top gear for the one short stretch of highway on the route to the house and lay his head back against the headrest, trying to settle his nerves. Without knowing why exactly, he'd gotten a haircut yesterday, feeling more like he used to in the early days of his and Jaya's courtship than in the later years of their marriage. At Karina's graduation party at a Mexican restaurant a few months earlier, he and Jaya had stood off to the side together with their margaritas and watched Karina and her friends dance in sombreros. He and Jaya basked in the lovely young woman their daughter had become, and Jaya smiled and laughed most of the night. He always hoped for that version of his ex-wife, but she didn't materialize often.

Keith had learned to focus on the things he could control. He'd maintained a good relationship with Karina and given her the opportunity to pursue anything she wanted in high school, to go anywhere she wished for college, regardless of expense. He'd hoped she would dream a little bigger than UC Santa Barbara. His own education had undoubtedly opened doors for him. But those doors were now open for his daughter as well, who had reaped the benefits of a good neighborhood and schooling, and he did take some comfort in her staying in state, just a few hours' drive away.

Mostly, what Keith could control was his work. Duncan Weiss truly valued Keith and gave him more freedom. He'd risen to become the top producer on the West Coast, bringing in more fees than any other partner. With no family life to come home to, Keith preferred to work hard and travel frequently, which helped foster his success. He'd learned that winning wasn't always so much about survival of the fittest as it was about just *survival*—simply outlasting everyone else. He had a strong network of clients with whom he dined and played golf, people he genuinely enjoyed. His network became his competitive edge: he was so closely intertwined with his clients' businesses that when a transaction came up, he was right there; they never considered calling another banker. And the rush he got from doing this work hadn't diminished at all through the years.

As he neared the house, he found himself slowing down as he always did, remembering the times he'd pushed Prem's bicycle down this open street, noticing the big oak tree in Mrs. Gustafson's corner yard that Karina used to climb. Jaya casually talked about selling the house after Karina left for college, but Keith had insisted she keep it. It was the one thing connecting them all to the life they'd once had.

From her bedroom, Karina heard the low growl of Dad's car pulling into the driveway and called out to her mother as she ran down the stairs to meet him. She was determined to make this a good day, the first full day the three of them had spent together in years—probably the last full day they'd have together for who knew how long. The thought launched shivers of excitement and fear down her arms.

When Dad leaned down to embrace her, Karina lingered in his strong arms for a moment. He kissed her on the forehead and stepped back. "Hi, darling. Ready?"

"Yup! It was quite a puzzle getting everything to fit in the car." She gestured across the driveway to the new VW Jetta he'd bought for her, its rear seat filled to the roof. "Can't open the trunk till we get there, because it might all come bursting out."

"Oh, I could have helped you with that. Why didn't you tell me?" Dad removed his sunglasses and perched them on his head. "I can put some stuff in my car."

Karina detected the familiar note of regret in his voice. He always wanted to be told when he was needed, not understanding that it didn't work that way. To assuage him, she cocked her head and laughed. "Dad. Really? In that thing?" She looked pointedly at his two-seater Porsche 911, which housed its engine in the rear and had a small storage compartment under the front hood.

"What? You know, it can fit six—"

"Yes, six bushels of apples in the front compartment. You've told me." She laughed again. "I'd like to know how many Porsche drivers have apple farms. Actually, you can take all the food Mom's packing for me. I told her not to bother, but she's afraid I'll never eat again."

"Well, she worries about you." Dad tousled her hair and pulled her close, wrapping his arm around her one more time. "Come on, let's go see what your mother's cooked up for you."

———

Jaya looked in the mandir room and saw that the *diya* flame and incense were still alight. She couldn't leave the house until they were finished, and she wouldn't risk the bad luck of extinguishing them early, not today. This morning, she had woken before dawn to begin her prayers for the momentous occasion. She prayed to Saraswati, the goddess of learning, to guide her daughter's education, and Durga, the mother goddess, to watch over her child. But Jaya found that her mind and her prayers this morning were repeatedly drawn back to Prem. The prospect of letting her firstborn go into the world reminded her inescapably of the child who had left her unnaturally four years ago.

Jaya had survived those years by developing a deep spiritual practice.

She could see now that before Prem's death, she hadn't been living in harmony with God and the universe, challenging fate to bring her misfortune. While she'd thought her job at the Policy Institute was meaningful, it had really just been secular work: dealing with human beings and situations of their own making. The life she and Keith had created—and the persistent pursuit of money to fund that life—was a false belief, to an insignificant end. She was ashamed to realize that the home she'd created, with paint colors and furnishings she'd carefully selected, held no shrine before her mother came to visit. Western life had become so much a part of Jaya that she'd neglected the most important part of life itself. But with Prem's death, she had a chance to realign the way she lived.

Jaya returned to her bedroom and put the last few items into her overnight bag, zipped it up and carried it down the stairs. As she descended, she saw Keith and Karina in the front foyer.

Now that she was living in accord with her spirituality, there was little friction in her daily existence. She prepared modest vegetarian meals and no longer expended energy on sensorial pleasures: she wore simple clothes, cut her hair short, wore no makeup. She hadn't bought a lipstick in years. Jaya found solace in her *mantras*, her prayers, and her knowledge that her life now honored God, keeping her and those she loved safe. It was better now, for both her and Keith, though he didn't seem to accept this truth as she did. She wished she could be free of the pull of guilt she still felt from him.

"Here." Keith leaped up the stairs to meet her. "Let me get that." He reached for her bag. "Thanks." Even during the divorce, when they were drawing a line through their life, separating their belongings, their friends and their memories, Keith had remained decent toward her, more heartbroken than angry. Jaya knew then that whatever else had gone wrong in her life, it had not been a mistake to marry him. Karina and Prem were the good things that had come out of her marriage. And her rediscovery of faith was the one good thing that came from Prem's death. Everything had a purpose, once you appreciated the spiritual laws of the universe.

"The food still needs to be sealed up," Jaya said, heading into the kitchen. "Karina, what fruit would you like to take? I have apples, pears, grapes—"

"Mom, I don't need that much food. I have orientation events for the first three days. I probably won't even be in my room much."

In the kitchen, Jaya sealed the plastic containers holding the food she'd prepared: rice, chapatis, dal and Karina's favorite vegetable curries. At least her daughter would eat well for the first few days until she got settled.

Keith came into the kitchen. "Last bag's in the car and I have space for the food. All set?"

"Yes," Jaya said, washing her hands as Karina loaded the containers into a bag and handed it to Keith. "I just need to get one more thing. I'll meet you outside."

Jaya was taking a statue of Saraswati on their journey, a smaller replica of the one standing in the shrine upstairs. The goddess of learning would bring blessings to Karina as she began her university career, and Jaya planned to say some extra prayers on the drive. She had specially procured the idol a couple of months ago and tucked it away for safe-keeping. *But where?* she thought as she rummaged through the house. It wasn't in her dresser drawer, though she came upon the solid silver Ganesha figurine to send to Devesh and Chandra in London as a blessing for their new home. It wasn't in the temple room, although she saw that the *diya* and incense had finally burned out, so she took a moment to clean them up. She couldn't very well leave a mess in the temple for two days while she was gone. Just imagine what kind of calamity she might invite.

"Mom!" Karina called from downstairs. "We've got to get going or we'll hit traffic."

As if traffic was the worst thing that could happen on this important day. Let her make the journey without the Saraswati, and they would see how much misfortune could befall them. She could hear Keith's loud car engine starting up outside. *Ah!* She remembered suddenly and went to the closet in her bedroom, where she retrieved the Saraswati from the top shelf. She slipped it into her handbag and headed downstairs. *Good.* Now, she was ready.

———

After ten minutes of waiting in the car with the engine running, Karina finally saw her mother emerge from the house. Karina reminded herself, as Mom climbed into the passenger seat, to stay calm and cheerful today. She had grown accustomed to her mother's living in her own head, being late, forgetting things, and she had learned to compensate, but it still annoyed her. Her parents were cordial with each other in her presence; their marriage had seemed to fade away rather than explode in fireworks the way other kids described. Yet she still felt the need to be their bridge; she was keenly aware of being the one thing that still joined them to each other. Would they even see each other anymore, after she left? Would they still talk?

Following her father's car through the neighborhood, Karina expected to feel some nostalgia. But instead, she was ready to get out of this life, to leave behind the memories of Prem and her parents' divorce, the house that felt empty with half her family missing, the school where everyone looked at her with pity. The only people from school she would miss were Izzy and Mrs. Galbraith. She and Izzy had spent nearly every weekend night over the summer at each other's homes, collecting clothing and dorm room furnishings to pack for college. Izzy, ever confident as she headed to Brown, had already declared her major as English and was plotting to get a publishing internship in Manhattan next summer.

Karina's insides clenched at the idea of being so far away from her one true friend. She knew Izzy would easily find new friends and an exciting new life.

Karina only hoped the same would be true for her. She had chosen the University of California Santa Barbara because it had a strong science program, its large student body offered anonymity and her significant merit scholarship would limit how beholden she was to her father for financial support. He'd been disappointed when she wasn't admitted from the Stanford wait list, but Karina was secretly relieved. Stanford was too close to home and the thought of staying there suffocated her. But from UCSB, L.A. was a stone's throw, and the beaches of San Diego and the thrill of Tijuana were just a short drive farther south. Las Vegas and Palm Springs were a few hours to the east, and from there, the entire country lay. There was a great swath of the country that she hadn't yet seen: nearly forty states, according to the map above her desk at home, which had stopped acquiring thumbtacks after their last family trip with Prem, to the Grand Canyon.

College would be a fresh start for Karina. She had even left under her bathroom sink the kit in which she stored her safety pins and razor blades, buried in a shoebox full of makeup that her mother had relinquished to her a few years earlier. Karina was leaving all that behind too, in hopes of new friends and a new life, where she would not feel the urge to cut herself anymore.

19 | karina

The dorm orientation meeting was at 7:00 p.m. and Karina found herself pacing around her empty room in anticipation. Her roommate hadn't yet arrived, and her parents had left after taking her out for an early dinner. She had been looking forward to this moment of pure independence, but now found herself nervous. Happy sounds of laughter and chatter came from the other rooms down the corridor. Karina changed her T-shirt three times, trying to achieve the unattainable right look.

At 6:40, there was a commotion at the door and Karina jumped up to open it. On the other side stood a girl with a pillow under her arm, dragging a large suitcase behind her. "Hi," she said. "I'm Stephanie. We must be roommates."

"Great! I'm Karina. Do you have more stuff downstairs? I can help you bring it up. There's a dorm meeting at 7:00." She heard herself speaking quickly and tried to slow down.

"Nope, this is it." Stephanie plopped down on the bare mattress. "My dad dropped me off and had to turn around and drive back to Redwood City for work tomorrow. He's on a big construction job right now. New office building, six stories, all glass," she said with pride.

"Wow, that's . . . that's a lot of driving." Karina thought of the luxury hotel room in downtown Santa Barbara where she and her parents had stayed the night before.

Stephanie shrugged out of her backpack, leaving it on the mattress. "Ten hours in one day." She smiled wearily. "Most time I've got to spend with him all summer. He works so hard." Stephanie Cortez, Karina would later learn, was a first-generation American, the first in her extended family to go to college and imbued with all their hopes.

"Yeah, mine too." Karina's words, though true, rang hollow to her own ears.

"Should we go downstairs?" Stephanie said, glancing at her watch. "It's almost seven."

In the spacious dorm lobby, Karina was struck by how many of the girls gathered there looked similar, with long, pin-straight hair, mostly blond—the kind of hair she'd always coveted, the opposite of hers. Karina caught bits of conversations about beaches, bars, sorority rush, parties later that night. Some of the girls seemed to know each other already. She looked around for a familiar face, though she knew that no one from her high school had enrolled at UCSB. They sat through a rundown of the dorm's rules and procedures, then the meeting concluded with an icebreaker: they were supposed to talk to as many people as they could in five minutes and share one unique fact about themselves with each person. As soon as the bell rang, an Indian girl Karina had noticed on the other side of the room made a beeline for her.

"Hi, I'm Priya Patel. Pre-med. And no, my parents don't own a motel." She smiled conspiratorially. "That's two facts. How about you?"

"I'm Karina, from Los Altos."

"Huh. I'm from Fremont. I've never seen you at the ICC." Priya frowned when Karina looked confused. "The Indian Community Center?" she said, with a touch of sarcasm. "Haven't you been? God, my family practically lives there on the weekends." Priya glanced down at Karina's name tag and winced. "Oh . . . sorry, I thought . . ."

"I'm half Indian. My mom," Karina said. "But I've never been to the ICC."

"Consider yourself lucky," Priya said. Just then, the bell rang, indicating that only one minute was left. "Well, nice to meet you."

Karina felt both relieved and disappointed when they parted. The next girl she turned to had that sleek blond hair. "I'm Jessie," she said to Karina. "Short for Jessica. And I'm the youngest of seven." She nodded and smiled knowingly. "Yup. Three brothers and three sisters. I'm the caboose. My folks are counting the days till their last tuition bill. How about you? Any siblings?"

"Oh, I . . . I'm Karina, from Los Altos," Karina said, as her mind raced. She was accustomed to being around people who knew her whole story and avoided the topic entirely. "I'm an only child, actually." She knew she didn't owe anything to a stranger, and yet the words felt disloyal out of her mouth.

"Oh. Sometimes I think that would be *nice*," Jessie quipped, but a flicker of pity seemed to cross her face.

Karina made her way through the crowd back to Stephanie, who was speaking lightning-fast Spanish with another girl. She stood awkwardly by until the bell rang again and the meeting concluded. Stephanie and her new friend hugged and promised, in Spanish, to see each other soon. Karina returned to her room with Stephanie, who seemed nearly as out of place in that sea of girls as she did. Nearly, but not quite. Karina's club of two in the world had been reduced to one, and suddenly she felt very alone.

———

Karina felt a disquieting discomfort that first week as she wandered around campus, trying to wean herself from the map folded in her pocket. She expected to meet more people once classes started, but after every class, everyone scattered like the marbles she and Prem used to play with. They'd lie on their bellies in the family room and line up marbles in their sights before taking a shot. It seemed improbable that she missed Prem even more now, four years later, and yet she longed to share what she was experiencing with her little brother, whose face she envisioned with its shadow of facial hair lining his upper lip. It brought her some consolation to picture him accompanying her across campus, as she imagined how she would describe everything to him. She saw him at the end of her bed with a book when she studied, his gangly thirteen-year-old legs bumping into hers. He might not have understood what she was going through, but it still would have brought her comfort to tell him. Who else could she tell about her renewed sorrow? The only thing more unbearable than suffering alone was the idea of having to share it with one of her parents, where it would multiply.

Even with a hefty scholarship, Stephanie was working both on and off campus to pay her way through college, and she only came back to their room late at night. Karina got into the habit of waiting up for her to return from her second job at a Chinese buffet restaurant near campus.

"By the end of my shift, I can't stand the smell of that food anymore, but hey, it's free." Stephanie smiled as she unwrapped cartons full of white rice and plain noodles, which she proceeded to transform with ingredients brought from home. They sat together in the common kitchen of their dormitory, slurping bowls of soup made with rich chicken bouillon, canned beans and dried chilies.

"I don't know how you do it, working so hard all the time," Karina said. After their shared late-night meals, Stephanie would often stay up studying after Karina went to bed.

Stephanie scooped a spoonful of brothy rice into her mouth and shrugged. "I'm used to it. I've worked since I was fourteen." She wiped her mouth with a paper towel. "I'd rather work harder now than take on a lot of debt, you know?" Stephanie spoke about her mother, who cleaned houses, her father in construction, and her two little brothers, who aspired to be a soccer player and an Air Force pilot. As her roommate described caring for her younger brothers, Karina almost mentioned Prem, but something held her back. Stephanie made her brothers quesadillas after school and helped them with math. She was responsible. She was good.

One night, Karina surprised Stephanie by cooking up a batch of rice noodles from the restaurant with Indian spices and ghee that her mother had insisted on packing for her over Karina's protests that she'd have nowhere and no reason to cook on campus. The noodles were edible, but not tasty. The more spices Karina tried to add, the more muddled the flavor became, until they both had raw throats and running noses.

"Let's leave the cooking to me," Stephanie teased. "You can take out the trash or something."

Karina agreed, laughing.

Since Stephanie wasn't around much, Karina tried to get to know other girls in her dorm. She struck up conversations in the bathroom, tagged along with groups going to the cafeteria, and spent evenings studying in the common room. Her days were full those first months on campus, but it was hard for Karina to get into gear. That desire she'd had to roam and explore, that curiosity to discover all that was different from what she'd known, began to recede a little. Karina found herself missing the comfort and familiarity of her life at home, as imperfect as it was. When she saw signs appear around campus for the Indian Students Association, she heard her mother's voice in her head and went to the first meeting. She saw Priya from her dorm there and hoped they might sit together, but Priya was already ensconced with a group of friends. Karina sat through discussions of a bhangra dance competition, throwing colors for the Holi spring festival and monthly Bollywood film nights. There was the temptation to fill her social calendar here, with events every weekend. But she couldn't keep up with the conversation over which films to select and knew nothing about bhangra. Other than food, her

familiarity with Indian culture was limited to her mother's classical dancing and prayers—which she preferred to forget. She realized she wouldn't
fit in here any better than amongst the dorm girls.

Before coming to campus, Karina had imagined it would be very
freeing to be someplace where no one knew her or anything about her.
Instead, it felt like a burden she was carrying: who she really was inside,
that person and those truths only she knew. She didn't know how to be
the person she was and also someone new here at college.

———

A few months into her freshman year, comfortable with her classes and
earning good grades across the board, Karina was eager for some additional way to occupy herself. She approached her biology professor,
Dr. Choi, knocking tentatively on his open office door.

"Hi, Dr. Choi. I'm Karina Olander. I'm in your—"

"Advanced Biology class. Yes, Karina, what can I do for you?"

"Well, I was wondering if there might be any way of earning extra
credit?"

"As I recall, you're already doing quite well in my class. You want to
bump your A to an A-plus?" He smiled at her as he slid his pencil behind
his ear.

"Well, I . . . it's less about the grade, I guess. I'm just looking for some
way to get more involved on campus, and I've always loved plant science,
environmental science. I helped my biology teacher with projects in
high school. I thought you might have some ideas?"

Dr. Choi reclined in his chair and studied her for a few moments.
"Yes, in fact, I do," he said at last. "I cross-teach in the Environmental
Science Department, and I usually ask a few students to work in our
Botany Lab over there. Four hours a week for a half-unit of credit. Some
students do it their whole four years. Sound interesting to you?"

"Yes, it does." Karina smiled, feeling the first ray of sunshine in weeks.

When she showed up at the Botany Lab the following Friday as instructed, a half-dozen other students were there. Dr. Choi matched Karina with Claire, an effortlessly pretty freshman from Pasadena, and tasked them with grafting stems for a hybrid breed of tomatoes. Karina hadn't worked with vegetables since her mother gave up gardening four years ago, but she recalled intuitively how to pluck suckers from tomato plants, and the earthy scent on her hands felt good and familiar.

Claire was bubbly and talkative, and when they finished up, she proposed that the whole group go out to a Thai restaurant, where they drank beer and shared heaping bowls of noodles and curries. The other lab kids, four girls and two guys, were all science majors of some kind. They were studious; their workload was heavy and their tastes fairly tame. Claire, who seemed like she could be friends with anyone, for some reason took Karina under her wing and invited her along everywhere. Outside the Botany Lab, the group studied together, ordered pizza to their dorm rooms, and occasionally went to a keg party, but rarely had more than a couple of beers. So, it was at the lab that Karina found her first group of friends.

It was nice to have the companionship of a social pack, a group of people to travel with on the large campus. Karina finally felt as if she had a place to be, without awkwardly looking around at everyone else. She felt her old sense of confidence returning. Karina shared the bare minimum about her family life with her new friends: she was an only child, her parents divorced when she was in high school, her dad was a banker who worked a lot, her mom stayed home. All these facts were accurate. It was not the truth, but it was enough to satisfy her friends.

They were all now discovering, at eighteen, the people they wanted to be, unconstrained by who they'd been before. Karina held out hope that she too could be someone new, that she might have a fresh start.

Karina laid eyes on James as soon as she entered the first session of the Environmental Policy seminar, a class intended only for upperclassmen, which she'd had to lobby her adviser to take. James was sitting in the far-right corner of the rectangular table, a goatee and John Lennon glasses camouflaging his youthful face. As the professor explained how the seminar would work, she stole glances at him, conveniently seated in front of the room's only clock.

The seminar would culminate in a group project to be presented at the end of the semester. The professor encouraged them to form groups that reflected different disciplines and strengths. Karina looked around the room and wondered if it had been a mistake to push so hard to be there. What did she have to offer her classmates other than one semester of basic college courses? She glanced up at the clock, and John Lennon caught her eye and gave her a small lopsided smile. When her stomach lurched, she knew she would stay in the class, no matter how unprepared she felt.

The day of the next class, Karina spent twenty minutes choosing her outfit and another twenty minutes blow-drying her unruly wave of hair. She still arrived at the classroom five minutes early and was pondering where to sit when a voice behind her made her jump. "Decided to come back, huh?"

She turned around to find herself eye to chin with John Lennon. "Yeah. Why wouldn't I?" she asked, sounding more defensive than she intended.

He raised an eyebrow and the corner of his mouth curled into the beginning of a smile. "It's a tough seminar. Some people drop after the first class. I'm glad you didn't." The smile spread across his perfectly shaped lips. "I'm James, by the way."

She held her palm up and made a stupid little wave. "I'm Karina." Then she walked around to the middle of the table and took a seat, and James sat down next to her.

His scent was pure, clean—soap mixed with fresh cut grass. From the corner of her eye, she saw that he wore hiking shoes, athletic socks, khaki shorts and a worn, soft-looking red T-shirt with a faded logo. Distracted, she barely noticed when the professor asked them to form groups. The girl on the other side of James turned to him and Karina's heart started to fall, but she tapped James on the shoulder. "Hey, you guys mind if I join you?"

James's face broke into a wide smile. "I was just about to ask you the same thing. I'm a poli sci major and Sophie's econ."

"Perfect. I'm enviro sci," Karina said, though she was technically still undeclared.

They decided to meet at the library two evenings a week. Outside of those meetings, Karina daydreamed about James, imagining his fingers in her hair as he kissed her. She was sure he could see right through her attempts to sound intellectual. One evening, after Sophie left early for a sorority meeting, Karina and James stayed until the library closed at 10:00 p.m. James had his bicycle but she was on foot, so he offered to walk her home. Their discussion along the way drifted away from the seminar, to his summer plans to hike and repair the Pacific Crest Trail, and hers to work at an organic farming co-op in Ecuador. In the darkness across the street from her dorm, James held his bike steady with one hand, and leaned down and touched his lips to hers. Karina immediately felt goosebumps rise on her skin, and a sharp, tingling sensation on her tongue, zapping down to her stomach. She put out a hand to steady herself on his bike frame and wobbled it instead. The bike crashed toward them, digging a gash into Karina's leg. She yelped in pain before trying to regain her composure.

"Oh, no. I'm so sorry." James knelt to the ground to look at her wound. "That's pretty deep. You have to clean and bandage it well. I'll come in and help you."

"No, that's okay." Karina, humiliated, forced a smile. "I'll be fine." She limped off by herself into the night, feeling as awkward and unlovable as James had now seen her to be. There wasn't a single bandage in her room; she was too superstitious to have any of her old supplies around. Stephanie went to the residence assistant to borrow the first aid kit, then cleaned and bandaged Karina's wound.

"Wow, girl." Stephanie smiled. "Where I come from, if you come back from a date with blood on you, we send a posse out for the guy."

"It wasn't a date." Karina grimaced as she climbed into bed. Her phone buzzed with a text message from James: *Hope you're feeling better* ☺. Despite the pulsating, searing pain through her leg, she felt a flutter of excitement.

———

The next morning, when Karina was leaving for class, James was standing in the same place she'd left him the night before.

"Still hurts, huh?" He grimaced as he saw her hobbling across the street.

"It's not bad," she lied.

"Liar." He pushed his bike alongside her on the sidewalk. "Well, at least we'll have a good story to tell one day." His smile sent something warm flowing through her body. As they parted ways on campus, he said, "Dinner Friday?"

"Sure," Karina said. "Should we ask Sophie?"

James paused before stepping onto his bike. "No, just us."

———

On Friday evening James picked her up, walked her to his car and opened her door. She assumed they would go to one of the casual places just off campus, but he drove them downtown to a nice Italian restaurant where they were the youngest patrons by at least a decade. He smiled at her in the yellow glow of the candlelight warming the table. "You look nice," he said, admiring the dress she'd spent an hour picking out from Claire's closet.

"Thanks, so do you," she said reflexively.

"No, I mean it," James said, holding her eyes with his, not looking away when it was uncomfortable for her. "You really look beautiful."

Karina felt herself flush and gave him a genuine smile before looking down at her menu.

Over salads and pasta, James told her about his family. He and two brothers had grown up outside San Diego, in a pleasant suburb called Carlsbad. His father was a patent attorney with a big firm, and his mother was a special education teacher. She taught at the high school James and his brothers had attended and drove them all together. James described how embarrassing it was to be hanging out with his buddies, worrying his mother might walk by. Karina sympathized, but really she wondered if it would be that bad to have your mother so present in your daily life that she wouldn't miss anything, much less everything. James's older brother had followed in their father's footsteps and was attending his first year of law school at UCLA. His younger brother surfed obsessively, and alternately threatened to drop out of high school or join the Marines instead of going to college. James spoke about his brothers fondly and referred in passing to their family vacations skiing or camping. The fabric of his life was clearly solid without holes in the center, without even so much as fraying at the edges.

When it was her turn to talk about her family, Karina said she'd had a brother who'd passed away when he was young, and she didn't like talking about it. James looked sympathetic and didn't ask for more. She felt comfortable with him, despite their differing backgrounds, or perhaps she loved his world so much, she longed to be part of it. That night, when he walked her to the door, patient with her slow pace, he kissed her again, longer this time.

The next morning, Karina woke early, desperate to talk to someone about the night before. It was Stephanie's one day to sleep late, so Karina crept into the hallway to call Izzy on the East Coast. It turned out that Izzy was dating someone too, a med student from Spain.

"Alvaro studies all the time, like literally every waking hour, so he's a good influence on me. And *I* make sure he takes study breaks." Izzy giggled.

Karina then recounted every detail of her evening with James. "And the kiss . . ."

"Well? Does he kiss as well as he talks?" Izzy teased.

"No." Karina paused. "Better." They dissolved into laughter for a few moments. "But I don't know, Izzy . . ."

"Why, what's the problem? He sounds perfect for you!" Izzy said.

Karina knew something was holding her back, her fear that she didn't really deserve someone like James. He didn't *truly* know her, and if he did, he might not feel the same way. "I haven't told him everything. You know, my family and stuff."

"Well, you just met," Izzy said. "Give it time. Do it when you're comfortable." When Karina didn't respond, Izzy continued. "K, it'll be fine, trust me."

Karina spent the rest of the weekend alone, not even responding to Claire's calls to join the group for dinner. She went running, read, ate by herself and wrote in her journal. By Sunday night, she'd made the conscious decision to allow herself to fall in love with James, to trust him. She fell hard, free-falling, weightless and airy, with all the courage it took to believe she would not hit the ground.

––––––

As a junior, James lived off campus in an apartment he shared with a friend. On weekends, Karina spent afternoons with him lying on his luxuriously double-sized futon or on the small, grassy hillside behind the complex, studying, reading books or just talking. They went to the farmers' market, bought fresh strawberries that dripped sugary juice down their chins, warmed up frozen organic pizzas in the oven for dinner, tossed salads with bottled vinaigrette. Karina loved playing house, falling asleep in James's arms at night and waking in his bed in the morning.

Karina had told James she was a virgin in an awkward exchange not long after they met, when he'd surprised her by slipping his hand down her pants while they were kissing on his bed. "What?" he asked softly as she turned away, uncomfortable. "No one's ever done that to you before?" She shook her head and felt his chin on her shoulder from behind, his arms wrapped around her.

"It's okay," she whispered. "It's just . . . I haven't done . . . that." And then, like an idiot, thinking he didn't understand her, she felt the need to explain further. "I'm still a virgin."

He kissed her hair, her ear, her neck. "Yeah. I thought so," he said, and she felt her heart sink, her lack of worldliness exposed.

Then he whispered softly into her ear, "Me too."

James explained how he'd never had a serious girlfriend before. "Of course, my parents told me to wait until marriage, and there were years sitting in church, hearing about sin. Now I figure, I've waited this long, the first time should be special." He leaned down and kissed her ear again. "With someone special. Like you."

Karina's reasons for remaining a virgin didn't have much to do with morality. She certainly could have found a way to lose her virginity in high school at one of those weekend parties when her parents weren't paying attention. Joanie Teager had been so desperate to "get it over with" that she lost her cherry in the back seat of her parents' Lexus sedan. "Those leather seats were so annoyingly sticky," she had said to Karina and Izzy later, leaving the impression that was the most lasting impact of the whole experience. "I mean, I had to peel my ass off of there afterwards."

Now, Karina felt justified in waiting. All those awkward school dances when she didn't have someone to hang on to, cute Kyle Derrick with his exploring hands at that party—something had held her back all those times, and she'd thought she was just a prude or self-conscious. But now she knew why she'd waited, and it was worth it.

———

On the Monday morning after that weekend, two months after James had first walked her home from the library, Karina made an appointment at the Student Health Center, from which she left with a nondescript paper bag containing her first four weeks of the birth control patch. In her dorm room, after showering, Karina stared at her naked figure in the mirror and contemplated where to apply the patch. It seemed like a monumental decision. Her only other such rite of passage had been starting her period at age thirteen, three months before Prem died.

Karina had been terrified when she'd first seen the blood on her panties in the school bathroom that day, then excited, then terrified again. She was uncomfortable all day, with a wad of toilet paper jammed between her legs. When Mom came home that evening, she sat with Karina on her bed and matter-of-factly showed her how to wrap the wings of a pad around a clean pair of aqua blue panties from her dresser. Mom whisked away the dirty panties and scrubbed them clean, then stocked the bathroom vanity with boxes of pads in various sizes. Karina returned to school the next day reassured, grateful for her mother.

The supply of liners and pads under the bathroom sink lasted six months. By then, her mother had retreated to Prem's room for her daily prayer and meditation sessions, and she could not be reached for anything—not for something important, like where they would scatter Prem's ashes, so certainly not for something as mundane as Karina's dwindling supply of feminine products. By then, the casseroles and pies from neighbors and colleagues were depleted, and Karina and her dad were making weekly trips to the store on Sunday nights. They fell into the habit of stocking up for easy-to-prepare meals: cereal and milk for breakfast, turkey or peanut butter sandwiches for lunch, frozen lasagnas and pizzas for dinner.

Karina had to give Dad credit for trying to make the new weekly ritual fun for her. He would send her off to buy whatever she wanted for breakfast and didn't care if she came back from the bakery with frosted pastries, which Mom would have scoffed at. On one such expedition, Karina ducked into the pharmacy section for a box of feminine pads and stowed it in the cart under the glazed donuts. Though she was certain Dad saw it, he never said anything. Not then, not later when she put it on the conveyor belt at the checkout, and not when she pulled it out of the grocery bag at home and took it to her room. Nor did he say anything when Karina bought pink Gillette Daisy razors and shaving cream (the same brand Izzy's mom had chosen for her) and baby fresh deodorant in the months to come.

Staring at herself in the mirror now, it was hard to believe five years had passed since then. She traced her fingers lightly over her inner thigh,

where her smooth skin held no visible memory of the cuts they used
to bear. She peeled the clear backing off the matchbook-sized patch,
shaded to match someone else's skin color, and pressed it onto the right
cheek of her ass. *Cheers, Joanie Teager*, she thought.

————

Karina waited a few days to tell James, enjoying her secret in the interim.
The next time they were together, she allowed him to remove all her
clothes down to her panties and bra. Their kissing had grown more pas-
sionate, their touching more desperate, and it felt unnatural to stop short
of where both their bodies wanted to go.

Karina had mistakenly thought that she would immediately be pro-
tected by the force shield of the patch, not realizing it would take a full
month for the birth control to become effective. At first, it didn't seem
so long—after all, she'd waited nineteen years for this, what was thirty
more days?—but now, feeling James's hot breath on her neck, his hands
on her hips, it felt impossible. She took his hand and guided it to the
patch. He pulled his head back a little. "What's this?" he whispered as
his fingertips encircled the outer edge of it, sending a tantalizing shiver
down Karina's leg.

She smiled at him, suddenly feeling shy. "Birth control patch."

James's eyes grew bigger and an incredulous smile spread across his
face. "Really?"

"Really," she said, meeting his eyes. "I'm ready too."

It was equal parts torture and excitement the following twenty-seven
days as they dutifully waited for the oversized bandage to do its job.
Karina came to understand what people meant when they said half the
enjoyment of something was in the anticipation. The underlying tension
of what was coming permeated their daily interactions, their frequent
text messages. She and James discussed how to make their first time

special, to infuse it with the meaning it deserved, and finally decided on an upcoming weekend when they were invited to a friend's family beach house. There would be grilling on the deck, boogie-boarding in the ocean, a keg of beer and the requisite drinking games. And James and Karina would make love for the first time, losing their virginity together.

———

The first night at the beach house, after the evening's festivities, Karina showered and returned to their room, where James was waiting for her. He slipped her robe off her shoulder and leaned in to kiss her collarbone, then pulled her over to the bed. As James untied her robe and rolled on top of her, Karina reached to switch off the bedside lamp. She breathed in the salty flavor of his skin. In the dark, they groped and bumped into each other like two inept dance partners. Eventually, they found a rhythm. She was trying to understand this new sensation, of having him inside her, when he opened his eyes and looked at her.

"I love you," he said softly. It wasn't the first time he'd said those words to her—and she'd said them too—but they nonetheless took on new meaning that day. They slept naked and entwined. When they awoke, sunlight was falling through the window shutters and across the bed, and James's arm was wrapped around her shoulders. It felt to Karina like a perfectly happy moment.

"You should really come boogie-boarding today," James said. "Those waves were awesome yesterday."

Karina drew in a slow breath and let it go. "My brother's name was Prem," she said softly. "He called me Kiki."

James raised his head slightly from the pillow to look at her face. She didn't turn around, but she clasped his hand under hers. "He was eight years old. He drowned in our swimming pool." She heard his sudden intake of breath.

"Is that why you don't swim?" he asked cautiously.

"I can swim. I love the ocean, actually. I just . . ." Although she still went out of her way to avoid swimming pools, she felt comfortable at the ocean. When she thought about its expanse and driving currents, its inherent danger, her feelings didn't seem rational. This was one of many things she didn't understand about the way her mind worked. She had stopped trying to make sense of why cutting herself felt good, or why she didn't feel like a blend of her parents, but like something apart from both of them.

Now, James nuzzled his nose and mouth gently into her ear and tightened his arm around her body. She rested her chin on his forearm and closed her eyes, still feeling the narrow rays of sun across her face.

"I was the one, who found him," Karina said. "I tried. To save him." She told James about her failed attempts at resuscitation. She described how her mother had retreated to bed for weeks and later emerged with the elements Karina had loved about her scraped out like the innards of a squash, only a hard shell remaining. A new person had grown in her place, who sat all day in the shrine she had built to her only son, who would never come back.

Hot tears slipped down her face and onto James's arm. She tasted salt as they ran over her lips, and she wiped her face against the bedsheets. "It changed me too. Made me more independent. I learned to cook and do my own laundry. I got really focused about school and college. And that's when I grew really close with Izzy and her family."

James kissed the top of her head. "You must think about him all the time."

She nodded, her chin against the forearm he wrapped tightly around her. "He'd be thirteen now, the same age I was when . . ." She hesitated, unsure if she should share the next thought with him. "Sometimes I picture him . . . sitting next to me in the front seat of the car when I drive home to Los Altos. I explain how to drive, how to merge onto the

highway. He loved understanding the mechanics of how things worked."
Was it crazy that she had imagined him growing up alongside her, a way
to recapture all the moments they had lost together?

"I'm glad you told me," James said, nuzzling her head before drifting
off to sleep again.

There it was, Karina thought as she lay awake in his arms, listening to
his breath grow heavy. Izzy had been right. She'd told him the worst of
her past, the worst of her truth, and he still loved her. He loved her, and
she was worthy of his love.

———

As the end of the school year approached, Karina found herself dreading
the separation she and James would have to endure. For nearly three
months, they would be thousands of miles apart and, because of the
remoteness of their locations, would have limited ability to communi-
cate. James would be working with a trail repair crew along the Pacific
Crest Trail, covering some 600 miles by truck and by foot. Karina was
going to Ecuador for an internship with the Fair Coffee Co-op, a pio-
neer in organic farming, recommended by her professor, Dr. Choi. The
prospect was exciting and scary, but Stephanie had bolstered her. "I
would go in a minute, if it paid anything. And you might even lose that
gringo accent," she teased.

In the last week of school, after they'd both finished their final exams
and papers, James surprised her by driving them out to a lake about
twenty minutes from campus. There, under a tree, he laid out a plaid
blanket and a spread of picnic food. After they'd enjoyed a languid meal
of cheese, bread, grapes and wine, they lay back on the blanket and
snapped a selfie of themselves. Her head rested on James's chest, her hair
splayed out like an ink blot around her face. James's face was the best
part. That's what her eyes always returned to. He looked blissful.

She revisited that photo daily during the time she was in Ecuador. She spent her days teaching classes to the employee-owners in Spanish and writing a report documenting the co-op's successful practices. At night, she lay in bed listening to love songs with her headphones, waiting for sleep to come. At the end of the summer, when Karina said her goodbyes, part of her felt guilty for having spent some part of the past ten weeks counting down until this moment, when she could return to the familiarity of home, of James.

21 | keith

Keith was squeezing in one last meeting before Karina came home tomorrow for the summer. He had arranged to take off the entire week she was to stay with him before she spent the second week with Jaya, an arrangement they had confirmed a few nights ago. They still spoke every few weeks, usually about Karina, the house or other administrative tasks they shared, and caught up on the outlines of their lives. Occasionally, Jaya brought up an anecdote she'd remembered about Prem and they would laugh about it. Other times, when she claimed to actually sense Prem's spirit in someone else, Keith grew so uncomfortable he'd find a way to end the call.

When they'd spoken a few days ago, Jaya had seemed particularly distracted, as if she was eager to get back to something else. Could she be seeing someone? She could, of course, and she had every right to. Keith had been dating freely—though only for casual recreation—for years now. What he and Jaya had had together was irretrievably gone, and he did want her to be happy. Still, the thought of another man being with her was difficult to stomach, and somehow felt like a final failure of the life they'd shared.

Now, sitting in the reception area of Machtel Industries, the world's leading semiconductor manufacturer, Keith glanced at his watch and noted there were still ten minutes before his meeting with the CEO, Jeff

123

Erstine. It was Keith's policy to be early for meetings like this, a regular check-in to stay abreast of his client's needs; it signaled he knew the CEO's time was more important than his. Humility was rare in investment banking and it went a long way with these entrepreneurial guys. His phone buzzed and his sister's name flashed on the screen. As the sibling who'd stayed near their hometown, it fell to her to check up on their parents. He was grateful for this and sent her extravagant birthday gifts and money whenever she even hinted at a need. But he had to bolster himself for her phone calls, which inevitably detailed their mother's crippling arthritis and father's descent into frailty. He muted his phone and slipped it into his pocket.

"Be right back," Keith told the receptionist, then showed himself to the restroom. He knew his way around this office, built three years earlier from the proceeds of the secondary offering he'd led. It was his first huge fee for the firm, eighty million dollars. He'd celebrated by buying a box of authentic Cubans for Jeff and the Porsche for himself. As Keith walked down the corridor, he saw, through the ten-foot glass walls of a conference room, a group of suited Asian men packing up their things. He slowed his pace and looked more closely, spotting what he thought was a familiar face. In the bathroom, a quick check on his phone confirmed who he'd recognized: John Cho, scion of Korean semiconductor maker HyunCom.

Keith's mind began churning. What was going on here? Was Machtel considering acquiring HyunCom, or entering into some kind of manufacturing or distribution partnership? That would make damn good sense. Machtel had the North American and European markets cornered, and HyunCom was the leader in Asia. Together, they would be a powerhouse and drive all the smaller players out of the market, taking their share. It was such a good idea, *dammit*, that Keith was disappointed he hadn't proposed it himself.

Who was Jeff working with on this? Was there another bank involved?

That would really gall Keith, to not even have been given a chance to compete for the business. Shaking off his annoyance, he walked briskly back to the reception area, where a smiling young woman was waiting for him in a narrow skirt and clingy blouse. She introduced herself as Rachel, Jeff's second assistant, and appeared to be at least two decades younger than the assistant Keith knew.

"I'll take you back, Mr. Olander. Would you like anything for lunch? I just brought in a sandwich for Mr. Erstine."

"No, thank you," Keith said, a little flustered by what he'd just seen, and now by this woman. How did Jeff concentrate with a nymph sitting right outside his door? He collected himself before entering Jeff's office.

"Keith!" Jeff walked out from behind his desk to shake his hand and gestured for Keith to take a seat at the table, where his lunch sat, wrapped. "Sorry, have to make this a working lunch. Crazy day. Can Rachel get you something?"

"No, thanks. She already offered." Keith gave a friendly wave in Rachel's direction and watched as she left the office. He tried not to be rankled by the implied downgrade of their business relationship from their usual high-priced restaurant lunches.

"So, what's going on?" Jeff asked, unwrapping his sandwich.

Keith was wary of asking directly about the HyunCom executives. Instead, he asked Jeff some detailed questions about the business and industry, for which he'd been prepped by his research analysts. How was quality control out of the new plant? Where did orders stand compared to last quarter? When did he expect the design for the new chip to be finished? In between bites of turkey sandwich, Jeff answered by simply repeating statements from the last quarterly earnings call. Growing impatient, Keith found himself unable to stay away from what he'd seen. "Do you have any major partnerships in the works? I have a couple M&A ideas I'd like to run by you. If you acquired one of the Asian market leaders, for example, you could really dominate the whole space."

Jeff chuckled and shook his head as he tossed his crumpled sandwich wrapper cleanly into the trash can. "Keith, I'm just focused on running the business I have, maintaining quarter-over-quarter growth, and keeping our recruiting yield up in this market. We can't hire people fast enough to support our growth."

"Well, I hope if you ever have needs in that area, you'd come to us, at least give us a chance to help you out." Keith hated sounding like he was groveling. "You're a very important client to the firm, you know."

"Yeah, for a half-point cut." Jeff grinned at him.

"Well . . ." Keith shrugged, feeling like a schoolboy who'd been called to the principal's office. "Yes, but I hope you feel we've given you excellent service for your fees. Like I said, you're a very important client."

"Absolutely, Keith, absolutely. And I appreciate everything you've done." Jeff stood up, Keith's cue to do the same, not even forty-five minutes after he'd arrived. "Let's definitely keep in touch."

"Yes, will do," Keith said. "Next time, I'll take you to my club for a real lunch. Get you out of this office for a break."

Jeff smiled, they shook hands, and Keith headed for the door. As he passed her desk, Rachel called out, "Bye, Mr. Olander."

Keith stopped. "Call me Keith."

"Okay. Keith," she said, tilting her head and smiling at him.

Keith leaned in a little closer. "So, Rachel, since I didn't manage to eat any lunch, would you like to grab some dinner tonight?"

———

Rachel didn't hesitate to drink three strong cosmos on a weeknight, prompting Keith to wonder how long she would last as Jeff's second assistant. By the time they ended up at his place, she had told him about the international flights she'd booked for the executives from Seoul and the teams of attorneys that had taken up residence in their conference room over the previous weeks. A deal was going down, no question. Keith was annoyed with himself for not thinking of it, irate that his firm had been cut out.

He fumed about it all week, his mind rattling with the news and its repercussions. When his colleagues learned he'd missed out on the deal, it would look like he was losing his edge, not to mention the big payday. Keith did what he often did in times of stress: he spent many hours late each night reviewing his investment portfolio, assessing his returns and making a few key stock purchases to rebalance his asset mix. The only thing that kept him from decompensating entirely was having Karina there with him for the week. She talked endlessly about her classes, her dorm and her new friends at the Botany Lab. She divulged that she had a boyfriend at school, and Keith had a cocktail of emotional reactions to this news. He was pleased that she'd confided in him. There were some things he'd just relinquished to the mother-daughter domain, types of conversations he assumed he would never get to have after losing his son. Still, he warned Karina not to get too serious about James, who was probably, at some level, like all guys his age. "Just be careful, honey. I don't want you to get hurt."

"I know, Dad. Don't worry." She smiled, threw her arms around his neck and kissed him on the cheek.

Keith couldn't remember when he'd seen his daughter so light and happy. It was heartening for him to know that after everything she'd been through, Karina seemed to have landed on her feet.

22 | jaya

Jaya had purchased her tickets as soon as they'd gone on sale three months earlier, when it was announced that the Guru was coming to town. He was scheduled to speak at the San Jose Convention Center for five days—full days, from ten in the morning until eight at night. Now, as she shuffled along slowly in the entry line that wrapped around the convention center and into the parking lot, she felt her excitement, which had been building over the past couple of weeks, climb to an intensity that took her by surprise.

Her cousin in India had sent Jaya a CD of the Guru's lectures a few years back, after Prem died and Keith moved out, but she hadn't opened it until after Karina left for college. Once Jaya started listening, the Guru's words captivated and lifted her. Human life was full of suffering, and all suffering was caused by attachments; this was an essential truth in the Gita and many other scriptures. In pursuit of simplicity over the past few years, Jaya had shed the things with power to hurt or distract her: her work, her husband, her friends. She could focus exclusively on connecting to the higher spiritual force guiding the universe when she sat in Prem's ashram and find solace there. But once she left that room to rejoin the outside world, with its attendant perils and reminders, her fears and guilt returned. She felt compelled to do everything in exactly the right way—from her prayer rituals to her Ayurvedic food preparation—to avoid the disaster and penance she always felt lurking. Jaya realized, after listening to the Guru, that she had simply exchanged one form of suffering for another. He explained how it was possible to not just numb her pain temporarily, but to rise above it. His words guided her gently through an exploration of her grief, probing her feelings as an inner witness who was present and yet could stand apart from them. Jaya was eager to continue this process of detachment, from not only external pressures, but those internal feelings as well; to reach the higher plane of consciousness of which he spoke.

The Guru's words brought her peace when she thought of Prem. All our lives on earth were fleeting, connected to who we were before and everything that would come after, he explained. In this way, she was never really separated from her son. Jaya had been acquainted with reincarnation since she was a child—the cycle of birth, life and death repeating itself over time, throughout the ages—and believed it to be true in a nebulous way. But now she found herself looking for signs of Prem everywhere: his smile on a newborn baby, the joyful squeal in a younger child scrambling across a hanging rope bridge. At times, she felt his presence so strongly, it was as if he was right next to her, telling her something funny to make her laugh out loud, guiding her gently away from the dark abyss of sadness. Other times, it felt like an effort in vain, like she was trying to recapture something that was forever gone.

Up ahead, there was a small scuffle in the line as a group of ladies tried to cut in to join their friends. Voices were raised and some elbows thrown to block the line-cutters, but eventually the host organism flexed to accommodate the invaders, and the slow procession of the line resumed. Jaya carried a tote bag with only a floor cushion, a water bottle, and her car keys. A simple vegetarian lunch would be served in the middle of the day.

As soon as she entered the building, Jaya joined the throngs of people ahead of her who began walking faster, even running (those who were physically able, for many in the crowd were in wheelchairs or walkers) to secure their seats in the large open auditorium. Jaya skirted around the edge of the crowd and found herself a good spot toward the front, directly facing the stage. It helped that she was alone, as most people had come in groups.

Sitting cross-legged on her floor cushion, Jaya closed her eyes and began to do her *pranayama*, deep breathing exercises. The sounds of thousands of people moving and speaking built to create a buzz around her. She was not accustomed to being in crowds of this size. After some time passed, a sudden hush fell over the crowd and Jaya opened her eyes. The Guru was walking onto the stage, escorted by a woman in a white sari, the color of widows and religious devotees. He sat on a raised plat-form, on a floor cushion just like the rest of the audience. It was com-pletely silent in the large auditorium, and even this moment of absolute quiet felt holy. The Guru put his hands together and bowed his head. The audience did the same, some prostrating themselves on the floor.

He began to speak in a mellifluous voice that hadn't come through on the CDs. He told the story of Lord Ram, from the Hindu scripture Ramayana, which everyone in the audience surely already knew. The Guru started with Ram's boyhood, described his home and the land on which he was raised, his ambitions and altercations with others, and finally his exile to the forest. Along the way, the Guru departed from the story to explain how the events in Ram's life mirrored our own. When Ram was confronted by others who challenged him, he reacted first with pride and anger. He battled with others because of his ego, and it wasn't until he was banished to live alone in the woods for years that he understood the fault in his ways.

Before Jaya knew it, the white sari–clad woman had returned to the stage to assist the Guru from his seat, and an announcement was made that lunch would be served. Jaya unfolded her tingling legs and stretched them out in front of her. Glancing around, she was almost surprised to see so many others, two thousand people in all. She had forgotten the crowd as she listened. She had been so singularly focused on the Guru's words, she didn't realize three hours had passed.

During the afternoon session, when the Guru described Ram losing his wife, Sita, and spoke about how we all lose those we love and this was a great unifying truth amongst humans, Jaya began to cry. Tears rolled down her face and she tried to discreetly wipe them away with her sleeve. Then, she heard sniffles and muffled cries from those around her and realized she was not alone. The woman sitting next to her, an elderly woman with a small gray bun, reached over and took Jaya's hand. She felt the strength from the old woman seeping into her, stabilizing her, drilling deep into her core. At the end of the evening lecture, Jaya felt welded to her spot on the floor. She watched a cluster of people surround the Guru as he left the stage.

"Those are the disciples." The old lady nodded toward the stage. "They travel with Guru and live with him at his ashram in India." She stood up, tucking her cushion under her arm. "This is your first time, seeing Guru?" she said, and when Jaya nodded in response, she wobbled her head before departing. "Tomorrow, then."

The next day, Jaya was eager to see if the Guru's lecture would inspire the same intensity of feeling in her as before and was surprised when it did. By the end of the week, she felt like a different person, who had seen a new, undiscovered land. And she did not feel ready to be done with the Guru. She wanted to follow him to the next city he was visiting, Sacramento. Even if he repeated the same lecture, she knew her understanding would continue to deepen. What would it be like to be one of the Guru's disciples, in his presence at all times, traveling with him, sharing meals, having private conversations?

Alas, she was not able to follow the Guru to Sacramento next week. Karina had just arrived back from Ecuador, and after spending a week with Keith, she would stay with Jaya before returning to campus. It was striking to think of how little she saw Karina now: two weeks in the summer, two weeks over the winter holiday and a few scattered weekends. After dividing that time with Keith, it amounted to just a couple of weeks each year. It was reassuring, of course, that her daughter was grown and independent, pursuing her own life and dreams. And that left Jaya with more freedom to pursue her own. Although she couldn't go to Sacramento, she had already checked the Guru's website to see the rest of his itinerary.

23 | prem

My family reminds me of the math lessons I had in third grade with Miss Gaither. First, everyone divided: three of them separated into three individual worlds. Now, they've each multiplied by two. Each one of them is part of a new pair.

When I was alive, I liked being a pair with Kiki during our after-school time. I liked walking back from school and hanging around home with her, even if we were doing different things. That's the best part of being a pair, isn't it? Just being with someone and feeling better that way, even if you're not doing anything together or speaking. Being part of a silent pair can feel really, really good.

Sometimes, I was a pair with Dad, when he took me to the car wash and let me sit in the front seat while the world outside the car turned soapy white and magical. We would pretend we were in a snowstorm, shivering and hiking over the mountains, and we'd point ahead to a warm house we spotted on the horizon. Or, Dad turned the music up really loud and we played drums on the dashboard in rhythm with the spraying water.

When I was really lucky, I was a pair with Mom, and she read me stories of Akbar and Birbal in bed at night, from those books she had gotten from India. Akbar and Birbal were a pair too: Akbar, the great Mogul emperor in India, and Birbal, his wise counselor, who always had a clever solution to his problems. Birbal was very smart and also very funny, sort of like me (even Mom said so). I loved all those stories, but my favorite was "The Tale of the Tough Question." An important visitor to the king's court, eager to make Birbal look bad, asked him if he would prefer a hundred easy questions or one tough question. Birbal asked for the tough question and the visitor said, "Which came first, the hen or the egg?" and Birbal replied, "The hen." When the visitor asked how that could be, Birbal said he'd already asked his one question and was not allowed another. So clever, that Birbal!

Mom packed up almost everything in my room when she changed it into Not My Room Anymore. But after putting that *Akbar and Birbal* book in the cardboard box, she took it out again. She flipped through the pages and smiled, then she put the book aside before she taped up the cartons and moved them to the garage. She keeps that book in her bedroom, on a small bookshelf next to the comfy chair. Sometimes, when she can't sleep, Mom turns on the small lamp, sits in the comfy chair and reads one of the stories from the book.

Her favorite story is different than mine: "The Tale of the Most Loved Possession," in which the king fights with his queen and banishes her from his palace, telling her she can take only her most loved possession. The heartbroken queen consults Birbal, and the next day, she packs up her young son to leave. When the king realizes that the boy is her most loved possession and she's willing to leave behind all her jewels and riches, he changes his mind. Mom reads the story in a soft voice, but loud enough for me to hear. She always feels better afterwards, and so do I. I loved being a pair with Mom, and we get to do it now even more than Before.

Everyone seems to find their pair. Now, Dad has a girlfriend most of the time. She changes a few times a year, and they always go to fancy restaurants—even fancier than Alfredo's or the Spaghetti House, but without the crayons and paper table covers. Instead of playing tic-tac-toe or our drawing game while they wait, Dad and his girlfriend drink wine and talk about movies they've seen or trips they're planning. He never does any of the things he used to do with us, though. He never takes her to the car wash.

Mom has her Guru, and even though she doesn't talk to him directly, he's still her pair. She listens to his words in the car and she hung his picture in Not My Room Anymore. I didn't know it could work that way, that someone can be your pair even without knowing you. In that case, I would have chosen the captain of the Space Rangers' ship to be my pair. We would have had so much fun! Anyway, Mom is a lot more peaceful now that she's paired with her Guru. She cries less and leaves the house more. She seems calmer than she's been since I died. I wouldn't have guessed the Guru to be her pair, but I'm glad she seems happy.

And Kiki has James. James is with her all the time, in real life and also in her head and her heart. He's replaced the snakes that used to coil inside her. James likes playing basketball and he really loves to be outside in nature, which might be why he and Kiki make such a good pair. I think I would like James if I met him, and I hope he would like me. I would even let him win at basketball. I'm pretty sure Kiki and I would have stayed friends when I grew up, because of all those little secrets only I knew as her brother. But if she can't be a super-awesome power duo with me anymore, I'm glad she has James.

When my family was still together, we switched up our pairs all the time. Now, everyone is in their own worlds and drifting farther apart. Kiki hasn't introduced James to anyone, Dad keeps his girlfriends to himself, and nobody but Mom has met the Guru. It seems impossible for them to be a group of six. The closer each person gets to their pair, the less they remember our family. They each seem happy, but I know they're each still sad about missing me. That's the thing about pairs. Even the best ones don't last forever.

24 | karina

Karina had been back home from Ecuador for only a couple of days when she made up her mind. The plan was to spend two weeks with her parents, one week at each home, before returning to campus. But James was making a trip to Santa Barbara over the weekend to clean out his apartment from his subletters, and she was going to drive down to surprise him. Even if it meant driving five hours one day and back the next, there would be one glorious night in between. Her new apartment wasn't ready yet, but when Karina told Mom she was making a quick trip down to campus to pick up her keys and move a carload of stuff, her mother was surprisingly accommodating.

Saturday morning was bright and warm. Karina loaded up her car with boxes of clothes and books that she would keep at James's until her own place was ready. She had convinced her father that the added expense of a private apartment was worth it, as it would afford her better studying conditions for her more intense course load this year. "But won't you be lonely?" Dad had asked. She'd just smiled in response, because the real reason for the solo apartment was to allow her and James more privacy. Karina thrilled to the idea of them spending nights and mornings there, undisturbed. She pictured plants on the windowsill, the two of them cooking together in the kitchen, lying on the couch to study, her feet in his lap.

During the five-hour drive down Highway 101, Karina sang to music on the radio and imagined her reunion with James. Her skin had taken on a warm glow in the Ecuadorian sun, and her calf muscles were toned from climbing the hilly terrain. She visualized how James now looked, with his longer hair and more freckles from being outdoors all summer. When she got to his apartment, she parked her car next to his and popped a mint into her mouth. She picked a handful of wildflowers from the blooming bushes outside and found the fake rock where James and his roommate kept their hidden key.

The front door creaked as she opened it into the living room, which was empty except for several full garbage bags. Karina walked down the hallway toward James's room, where the door was ajar. Her heart quickened with excitement until she heard a sound: a female voice, laughing. Karina froze. After a moment, she continued moving down the hallway, a quiet dread growing in her chest. In his room, on his bed, was James—his tousled brown head of hair, his broad pale back, his narrow butt, a body she would recognize anywhere—on top of another body. The sounds of laughter and soft words skimmed past her ears.

Karina's throat tightened and a twisting energy gathered inside her. Each of her hands reaffirmed their possessions: the bunch of wildflowers, which dropped to the floor; and her car keys, which she raised above her head and, in one smooth movement, flung toward the bed. Tracing a beautiful arc through the air, the keys smacked into James's neck with a metallic twang and bounced onto the floor.

"What the . . . ?" James touched his neck and turned his head, his face turning blank when he saw Karina. He rolled off to the side, exposing the naked figure of the girl underneath.

The girl screamed as if she was in a horror movie, then pulled the bedsheets over her. "What the fuck? Who the fuck are *you*? And what is she doing here? James?"

James grabbed for his boxers. "Karina? What? What are you—"

"What am I doing here?" Karina hissed, leaning down to retrieve her keys from the floor. "Don't worry, I was just leaving." She turned and marched out of the room.

"Karina," he called after her as she threw open the front door and ran down the half set of steps to the sidewalk. He caught up to her and pulled on her arm from behind. She whipped around, dislodging his hand, and shot him a look that warned him not to try again.

He retracted his hands in a gesture of surrender. "Look, Karina, I'm sorry you had to see that, I really am. I was going to talk to you when you got back . . . I just wanted to do it in person." He was stumbling over his words and she stayed silent, letting him. "I've just been thinking . . . it might be good for us to take a little break."

A break? Isn't that what they'd just had for three solid months? "When did this start?" Karina asked. "Over the summer? Last year?"

"What?" James looked wounded. "No, of course not. Just recently." His shoulders sagged. "Karina, look, we've just been moving so fast, you know? And we're still young. I think it might be good to spend some time apart, a few months. Maybe we can make a date for New Year's or something." He offered up a weak smile.

Karina felt something leave her heart, flutter outside her body and away. "New Year's?" she asked.

"Yeah, sound good?"

Karina tilted her head at him. Had he ever really known her? "No, not really. How about when hell freezes over? Does that work for you, *James*?" She spat out his name and turned on her heel, forcing herself to hold on, digging her nails into her palms as she returned to her car.

Karina drove a few blocks before pulling over on an empty street. She turned off the engine and rested her head on the steering wheel. The tears did not come right away. Probing her fresh wound, she envisioned James's back and shoulders moving, the girl beneath him. Then the tears came, fat and ugly, accompanied by a raw moaning sound she almost didn't recognize. She had cried this way only once before—the day Prem died—and it didn't change anything, nor did it make her feel any better. Her father had come into her bedroom to try to console her, and the helpless, wounded look in his eyes made her nauseous. Over the years, Karina had learned to tamp down tears; they did her no good.

Now, with a carload of belongings and no place to keep them, Karina tried to think of what to do next. Finally, she texted her Mom: *All done here! Mix-up with keys. Heading home tonight.* She drove to the drugstore, where she grabbed a king-size Snickers bar, a bag of barbecue potato chips and a large Diet Coke for the drive home, as well as bandages, antiseptic and razor blades. The simple act of walking out of the store with that bag began to make her feel more in control.

The week spent at her mother's house was thankfully full of activity. Izzy was still home on summer break, so Karina had someone with whom to share her heartbreak. She could cry in front of Izzy and express all the hurt and pain she felt without worrying how it would affect her. They went to the barn together to visit Mr. Chuckles, who was now old and sick with cancer, but still exuded a sense of serenity. As Karina stroked the side of his long, elegant head and brushed out his mane, she tried to breathe deeply and think of an entirely new future without James that she could endure.

When it was time for her to return to Santa Barbara, Karina almost asked Mom to come down with her, to help her move into her empty apartment, hang posters on the wall, fill the fridge. But she just climbed into her car and drove off, wiping away tears. A certain numbness came over Karina as she returned to campus, walling herself off from memories as she passed the lake where she and James had had their picnic.

As she began her sophomore year, going through the familiar motions of student life, Karina was able to piece together what had happened. UCSB had gone from feeling like a huge campus to a more intimate one as she and James had narrowed their circuit to certain sections of the library and their favorite off-campus eateries. Now, when she went to those places, she sometimes saw them together: James and his new girlfriend. With her clothes on, she was recognizable as the leader of a Saturday-morning yoga class on campus. Ironically, it had been Karina's suggestion that she and James try the class at the end of the prior school year, in the last week before finals, when they needed a study break. Karina had never done yoga before, but even she knew that the way Yoga Girl pronounced words like *chakra* and *asana* was all wrong, and it grated on her, this girl trying to appropriate Indian culture. But wasn't Karina a phony too? It's not like she knew where all her *chakras* were.

Now Karina saw her everywhere. She recognized her ponytail from behind as she walked next to James's bike. She saw her cute little red Fiat parked in front of James's apartment on the weekends. Karina knew she should avoid places where she might run into them, but she found herself drawn there instead. And yet, nothing relieved the deep ache in her chest or the long hours crying. She lost trust in herself for having placed her trust in James. When she returned to her empty apartment, it felt like solitary confinement instead of the cozy home she'd planned to share with him. Everything she did reminded her that she was alone, and James was not. Although the campus now felt familiar, she no longer felt like she belonged there.

Karina had let her friendships with Claire and her other Botany Lab friends lapse last year, as she spent all her time with James, and now she was ashamed to admit they had broken up. She had staked everything on it—the love she suspected she didn't deserve in the first place, and now she knew she had been right. And so, she found relief from her pain as she always had—by herself, alone on the bathroom floor, coaxing out the deep crimson drops along her inner thigh, where now, no one would ever see her again.

———

With a gaping hole at the center of her life where James used to be, Karina began spending more time at the Botany Lab alone, helping Professor Choi rework the irrigation system before the lab group started up again. On a Friday afternoon three weeks into the fall term, to avoid returning to her empty apartment, Karina was still at the lab at five o'clock.

"Karina, you shouldn't still be here!" Professor Choi bellowed when he came around to lock up. "Come on, it's the weekend—go have some fun!"

Karina cried all the way home as she rode her bike into the wind, tears splattering across her face. After getting home, she sent Claire a message: *Hey, what's up?* A moment later her phone rang.

"Karina!" Claire squealed. "How was your summer? I need to hear all about it. Summer school was *so* boring. This place was a ghost town. I couldn't wait for everyone to get back. How's everything? How's James?"

Karina felt the tears prickling behind her eyes. "Gone. We . . . broke up." She began to cry again, biting down on her lower lip.

"Oh, Kar, I'm sorry. Guys can be such assholes," Claire said, making Karina smile. "What are you doing tonight? Come out with us. Patrick and I and some friends are going out for cheap pitchers, then dancing. We can pick you up in an hour, okay?"

Karina was relieved and even a little excited as she spent the next hour washing and blow-drying her hair, applying makeup carefully and choosing her favorite pair of skinny jeans and a flowy blouse that fell over one shoulder. She could be attractive when she made the effort, she told herself as she examined her final image in the mirror. Had she stopped making an effort? Is that why James lost interest? As she put on dangly earrings, she banished all thoughts of him for the night.

When Claire arrived, she gave Karina an extended hug, then intro-duced her to Patrick, whom she'd begun dating over the summer. At the bar, they met up with Patrick's friends and some of their Botany Lab group, who all greeted Karina warmly without asking where she'd been the past several months. Patrick was a life-of-the-party kind of guy, always telling funny stories and refilling everyone's beer glass. He didn't seem like the boyfriend type, but he was clearly enamored with Claire. Karina couldn't be sure how many glasses of beer she consumed, due to Patrick's constant refilling, but she soon felt lighter and happier than she had since returning to Santa Barbara a month ago, or maybe even since leaving campus the spring before. All that heartache and pining all summer! Where had that gotten her?

"So, why'd you break up with your boyfriend?" Henry, one of Patrick's friends, leaned toward her. Henry had been relatively quiet this evening, at least compared to Patrick's boisterous behavior. Karina turned to him: he was cute, with sandy brown hair and warm eyes. He smiled at her, a boyish, flattering smile. A smile that said he was interested in her answer.

"What?" she asked, cupping her ear to block out the din of the bar. She'd heard him but didn't know how to answer.

"Claire said you just broke up with your boyfriend and need to have a good time tonight." Henry's impish smile was tickling some-thing inside her.

"Ah," she said, nodding. The way he'd phrased it made it sound like Karina had had a choice in the matter, as if she'd made the decision that devastated James's life, rather than the other way around. She liked this version better. "Yeah, well." She paused, shrugging the shoulder from which her blouse fell. "He was an asshole."

"Enough said." Henry grinned at her. "Sounds like you need to do some celebrating. I'll be right back."

When he returned to the table, he was holding a round bar tray loaded with half-full shot glasses. "What's this?" Patrick boomed, sliding glasses across the table until everyone had one in front of them.

"In honor of Karina's independence," Henry said, holding up a glass. Karina looked around the table of people, all of them holding a shot glass, wishing her well. A warm feeling of belonging engulfed her. She intended to drink the shot in a single gulp as Patrick did, but she could only manage half the liquid (tequila, she later learned), which burned her esophagus and immediately made her dizzy.

"Bottoms up, Karina!" Claire yelled. "You've gotta finish it all or it's bad luck."

Karina lifted the glass to her lips and threw back her head, guzzling the rest of it down to hollers and cheers of approval.

———

Karina awoke the next morning in her bed, uncertain how she'd gotten home. She craned to see the alarm clock and was shocked to find it was nearly noon. Moving her head just that small amount was painful, as if heavy bricks were clanging around in her skull. She closed her eyes and tried to keep her head still so the pain would subside.

Some of the night before came back to her. The bar, the pitchers of free-flowing beer, the tray of tequila shots, then another. How many shots had she had? She could still taste tequila in her throat, that sharp, astringent flavor, the burning sensation on her tongue. Her stomach suddenly lurched and she barely made it to the bathroom before vomiting, realizing as she knelt in front of the toilet that she was naked. Grateful, for once, for her own apartment and bathroom, Karina rinsed out her mouth, splashed water on her face and found a bottle of Advil behind the mirror, which reflected her smeared eye makeup. She moved slowly back to bed, stepping over her purple blouse and skinny jeans inside out, entwined with her panties.

Images flickered through her mind: Henry's face above her, him unbuttoning her jeans, her slapping his hand away, pushing his shoulder, writhing and twisting underneath him. Oh god, what had happened last night?

She *did* know one thing that had happened, by the familiar burning sensation in her vagina. *Oh god.* She reached around to her lower back and touched the smoothness of the patch, right where it should have been. Thank god for that, so familiar it had become a part of her body. She had applied the last patch out of habit, before realizing she might not need it anymore. Karina closed her eyes and fell back asleep for a while, until she was awoken by her phone ringing. She reached down to the floor and pulled it from underneath her jeans.

"Well, good morning!" Claire's chipper voice came through the line. "You certainly were the life of the party last night. I didn't know you had those dance moves."

"Mmm," Karina moaned. "Claire?"

"Henry was sweet to take you home. He is *cute,* girlfriend. And such a good guy. Patrick's known him for ages. We're all going to that diner near the highway for pancakes. Five bucks for a tall stack. You in?"

Karina clenched her eyes closed. "I can't," she said. "I have a big paper to work on."

"Okay," Claire said. "We'll miss you. Especially Henry." She giggled. "Hey, next weekend we might go out to the harbor waterskiing. You should come."

Karina murmured something to get Claire off the phone and turned off her cell before tossing it on the floor. Why hadn't she said anything? And what was she supposed to say? *I can't remember what happened last night because I drank too much? I think Henry might have forced me to have sex? I lost control of myself and everything that makes me* me? Claire might not even believe her, given her loyalty to Patrick and her impression of Henry as such a good guy. And she'd seen Karina doing those tequila shots, flirting with Henry at the bar. Maybe Karina was also to blame. Had she led Henry on? Had she really told him no? She rolled over onto her side, folded her knees up to her chest and cried quietly until she fell asleep again.

When she woke again mid-afternoon, the pounding in her head had subsided. She took a long, hot shower, scrubbing every part of her body until she felt clean. Afterwards, she took her supplies from the bottom drawer of the bathroom vanity, lay everything out on the counter and took extra care to swab all edges of the razor blade with disinfectant. The release she felt as the blade cut into her skin was immediate, and she remained sitting on the closed toilet seat, a trickle of blood down her inner thigh.

She fell asleep on the couch Saturday night and woke panicked the next morning, recalling fragments of a bad dream. She'd been in the middle of an ocean, swimming from island to island, trying to find a place to hold on, but each island dissolved into sand when she reached it. After Prem's death, Karina had stopped worrying about something bad happening to her, since nothing could ever be as bad as losing her brother. This was faulty reasoning, she now realized: Prem's loss had damaged her so irreversibly that she had never found her equilibrium again. Every loss she suffered now hurt her more, not less, stealing more of what little remained of her. But still, there was something left, something worth preserving. On Sunday evening, Karina pulled out a notebook and turned to a fresh page. She needed a plan.

Should she tell someone what had happened with Henry? She recalled the presentation at freshman orientation about the dangers and temptations they would face: fraternity hazing, alcohol poisoning, sexual assault. Karina, like most freshmen, heard little of it. It was like trying to feed broccoli to a group of children peering into a candy store. They might have choked it down, but only to get on with the real reason they were there: freedom, independence, a chance to make their own choices and chart their own lives forward as adults. Karina had heard the stories of girls who had come forward on campuses all over the country to report sexual assault. They carried mattresses across campus, they were called sluts, they had to tell their stories over and over, losing some of their dignity and privacy every single time, to a bunch of adults who only cared about their endowments and football stadiums.

Her mother didn't even know about James or that she was sexually active, so this would definitely be too much for her. Dad understood that college kids drank and might have sex, but he would get angry, vengeful, lash out at the school and Henry and make a big deal of the whole thing, which was not what she wanted. What she wanted was for this to go away. She wanted to forget it ever happened, to have no lasting effects on her life of this one bad night, this one lapse in judgment, this one reduction in her defenses.

"Izzy," she wrote at the top of the page. She would call her tomorrow.

"Student Health—STDs," she wrote next. *Shit.* She'd been so careful her whole life, holding off through high school, waiting until she found someone she loved, someone who loved her. A tear dropped onto the page and she brushed it away.

"Job," she wrote last. She wanted what her old roommate, Stephanie, had: a schedule so busy she barely had time to study and sleep. No free time to go to bars or pancake houses or waterskiing. No downtime to think. No empty hours to fill.

Night came quickly, and though she was tired, Karina had trouble sleeping. Every time she was close to dropping off, images of Henry ran through her mind: him laughing with her at the bar, pushing her onto the bed, dancing up close to her at the club, her elbow banging into the wall as she tried to squirm away. Finally, she took her duvet out to the living room couch and slept there all night.

The next morning, on her way out, she dropped a bag containing her favorite jeans and purple blouse down the incinerator chute.

25 | karina

Karina's phone rang and her father's smiling face appeared on the screen. She deliberated for a moment before sending the call to voice mail. She wouldn't be able to avoid him forever, but right now, it seemed like the only thing to do. Her mid-term grades had just been posted and they were the worst she'd ever received: one B, two C's and a D. She had a tougher course load this year, and she'd been struggling to focus in her advanced science and math classes since the term started, falling further behind. Yesterday, she'd received a notice reminding her of the minimum requirements to maintain her scholarship. If she didn't pull her grades up by the end of term, she would be on probation, and after the next term, her scholarship would be revoked. The thought of having that conversation with Dad was something she just couldn't face.

Karina's scholarship covered her tuition each semester, but she had to call her dad every month for money for her other living expenses. He always transferred the funds right away, but he waited for her to call first so he could talk to her once in a while. During her freshman year, she'd enjoyed those conversations. When she was done with an exam or paper, she would lie on the bed to call him and spill out all the details, in sheer exhaustion and relief of being done. Once she began to spend all her free time with James, those calls morphed into what her calls with Mom had always been: short, obligatory conversations providing assurance

that everything was fine and her grades were good. This year, after the
breakup with James and the incident with Henry (as she now thought
of it, unwilling to give it more import in her life), she'd been avoiding
calls with Dad altogether, trying to get by with text messages and email.
If she had to hear that thin layer of concern in his voice, always there just
below the surface, she was afraid she might crack. Karina was trying to
form a new life, a new skin over the scarred one; she had to be protective
until it grew strong enough to shield her.

Something else had happened in the last few weeks: she had lost
Prem. She could no longer picture him growing older alongside her.
Either she had reached the limits of her imagination, or she had crossed
over some threshold into adulthood and left him behind. Whatever the
reason, losing him again was a rekindled pain that bore fresh guilt.

———

After a few weeks of looking through online ads and biking to inter-
views, Karina found a part-time job at Natural Foods Market, a store
about two miles from campus that sold organic produce, whole-grain
foods, and other natural products. It was a quarter of the size of a typ-
ical grocery store, and the produce department, where Karina worked
two evenings a week and Sundays, was the star. During her shifts, it was
Karina's responsibility to ensure her section was stocked with fresh and
appealing produce. She encouraged customers to smell and touch the
fruit and offered free samples. It was one of her favorite parts of the job,
to pull out a small knife, like the one she'd once given Prem, from her
apron pocket and slice a perfectly ripe pear or a fresh, tangy apple. The
customer was unfailingly pleased by the gesture, and usually impressed
enough with the flavor to make a purchase.

This was the first time that Karina had done any kind of work that
engaged her body more than her mind, and she found some relief in it.

Time passed quickly at work and left her with little energy for anything but her studies. She began to feel like a visitor on campus, going there only to attend classes. She eschewed the library, campus eateries, anywhere she might run into James, Yoga Girl, Henry or even Claire, who had texted her a few times to invite her out again. Once in a while, she met up with Stephanie to study, but with few other friends left, Karina no longer socialized and the penance of this felt appropriate. She cycled between her classes, her job and her apartment, where she continued to sleep on the couch, still unable to return to her bed.

Karina had originally sought the job to stay busy, but the money turned out to be an additional boon, enabling her to fund her own living expenses and avoid calling her father. She used her employee discount to stretch her two-hundred-dollar weekly paycheck to buy groceries and was learning a lot about food preparation at NatMark, like how to roast marked-down overripe tomatoes and blend them into a rich paste for sauces and soups.

One day in the break room, some other team members were trying to convince her to join their Sunday night potluck. Karina felt warm in their camaraderie, so when her phone rang and it was Dad, she answered impulsively. "Hi, Dad." It had been several weeks since they'd spoken live, only exchanging text messages during that time.

"Honey! Hi! I was beginning to wonder if you'd been swallowed up by the library."

"Yeah." She smiled into the phone. "Sorry, it's been really busy."

"How's that calculus class going, still tough?"

"Well, yeah," she said. Calculus was trending at a D. "I think I'm going to drop it. I'm the only sophomore in the class and I think it's just too advanced for me."

"What? No, honey, don't drop it. We'll get you a tutor. Do you want me to find one?"

Karina paused, annoyed by his intrusiveness. "I don't want a tutor, Dad.

I don't want to take the class. I just . . . it's just not the right class for me."

Her father chuckled, which chafed her more. "What do you mean, not the right class? It's the next math class in the series, right? You've always been strong in math. Maybe you just need a little extra help this time."

"Dad." Karina spoke through clenched teeth. "I'll figure it out for myself. Okay?"

The pause on the other end of the line brought her some satisfaction, as she imagined him recoiling. "Gotta go, Dad. I'm in the library and can't be on the phone."

"Okay. Bye, honey, I—"

She ended the call and jammed the phone into her back pocket as she left the break room to begin her shift. A few minutes later, a text appeared from him: *I trust you know what's best for you. Just here for you, whatever you need. Also, sent bank transfer this morning. Love you.* Karina shook her head and replied with a quick smiley face emoji.

————

A month after she began working at NatMark, one of her colleagues went on an African safari, and the store manager put Karina in charge of receiving deliveries in the back and ensuring all the produce on the floor was in good condition. Karina enjoyed wearing the rubber coveralls over her clothes and dealing with the forklifts and pallets in the back, so different from the cerebral work her parents did, which she'd always been expected to do as well. Though her grades hadn't improved much, Karina asked for additional hours at NatMark, gravitating more to her job and the feeling of being good at something and valued for it. As her earnings increased with both her promotion and hours, Karina became intrigued by the possibility of gaining full independence from her parents.

One day, as she was stocking a new shipment of navel oranges, Karina felt someone watching her. She looked up to see a man standing about ten feet away. He was older, maybe early thirties, with wavy brown hair and a rugged complexion.

"Oh, can I help you with something?" With the back of her gloved hand, Karina brushed away the loose hair from her ponytail.

He smiled at her. "My neighbors have a tree of oranges with the most amazing zest—intense flavor and aroma. Have anything like that?"

"Hmm. Well, I've never had that question. I can tell you the best orange for juicing." She held up one of the navels she was stocking. "Or . . ." She took a few steps over to the clementines and held up a pair, joined by their leafy stems. "The most popular for lunch boxes and picnics."

"How about these?" He held up a Sumo Citrus. "These look kind of like my neighbors'."

"Ah, Sumos are delicious," she said. "My personal favorite. But you have to get past how ugly they look."

"Oh, that's definitely not it," he said. "My neighbors' oranges taste like absolute shit."

"Well, I'm sorry, sir," she said, laughing, "I don't think we carry oranges that taste like that."

His laugh, like his voice, was deep and resonant. "Okay, don't call me sir." He pointed a finger at her. "I'm not *that* much older than you. I'm Micah." He extended his hand.

"Karina." She took off one of her industrial rubber gloves to shake his hand and felt an electrifying warmth from his open palm.

"Karina," he repeated. "The beautiful girl who loves the ugliest orange." He tossed the Sumo into the air and caught it.

The spark of attraction she felt, the first since meeting James, caught her off guard and she looked down to mask her reflexive smile. "Would you like to taste one of those?" she asked, pulling out her knife. "It does have a thick skin, so it might give you that zest you're looking for."

"Sure," he said, holding her steady with his eyes. "I'd love to."

———

The next Sunday afternoon, Micah appeared again, at the end of her shift. He and Karina discussed the flavor properties of different colors of asparagus, and how disappointed he'd been the first time he cooked the purple variety and its unique color leached out. The following weekend, he told her about growing his own rhubarb, and how his near-perfect lettuce crop had been decimated by a family of rabbits. "I was going to put up a wire fence, but I knew they'd just try to jump over it and hurt themselves on the sharp wires. A lost head of romaine is one thing, but a bleeding rabbit wouldn't rest well with my conscience, you know?" He laughed, and Karina searched for something interesting to say to keep the conversation going, to keep him there with his rich eyes and warm smile.

Each week, she anticipated seeing him, and they had longer and more involved conversations. "What are you studying at school?" he asked her and seemed genuinely interested as she described her interdisciplinary environmental science major. He inquired about her seminar water systems project, and when she explained the conclusions, a fleeting thought of James passed without emotion. Micah seemed fascinated by the things she described, admiring of what she knew. Karina told him about her work at the Botany Lab, breeding new varietals of heirloom tomatoes and pole beans.

"So, what do you grow in your own garden?" Micah asked her.

Karina shook her head. "I don't have a garden. I live in an apartment near campus. No outdoor space, unfortunately."

"What? A young woman full of knowledge about fruits and vegetables and no garden of your own?" Micah cocked his head.

Karina smiled and shrugged. "Well, I get all my produce here."

Micah studied her face for a moment. "There's something very special that comes from growing something of your own. Starting with the tiniest seeds, the seeds left over from the tomato you ate for lunch. Burying them deep within the soil, invisible to the rest of the world. You water them and watch and wait. And one day, the first green shoot appears. And you know *you* did that. *You* nurtured and created life." Micah selected a tomato from the bin—deep red, perfectly round, skin unblemished—and held it up. "And then, you taste it." He closed his eyes and brought the tomato closer to his nose, inhaling deeply.

Karina watched with intense curiosity. She had the sensation he was going to bite into that tomato like an apple, and she had an inexplicable desire to do the same. But, after a long moment, he simply opened his eyes and held the tomato toward her. She leaned forward to smell it, closing her eyes to take in the aroma, fruity and earthy at once. When she opened her eyes, Micah's proximity and strong gaze took her by surprise. Karina felt the quick heartbeat in her chest and took a step back.

"I share a plot with some friends at Rancheria Community Garden. Do you know it?"

She shook her head.

"Why don't you come by sometime? We could use someone like you. Our peppers and tomatoes are thriving, but our herbs and lettuces are getting feasted on by critters. If we can't turn things around soon, we'll be doomed to eating ratatouille all winter long instead of salads. Saturday morning, around nine o'clock?"

Karina watched as he walked away, uncertain whether she should go, yet impatient that Saturday was still six days away.

26 | karina

When she got home, Karina looked up the Rancheria Community Garden and learned it was one square block of city land designated for individuals who lived in multi-resident buildings or otherwise didn't have access to outdoor space for gardening. People like her. She was nervous about going alone, so she called up Stephanie, who still lived on campus in their old dorm. "Hey, Steph!" Karina said, happy to hear her friend's voice for the first time in weeks. "You free next Saturday morning?"

By the time she and Stephanie arrived, Micah was already there with two friends, who both looked older, in their mid- to late-twenties. "Karina!" he called out, and any apprehension she'd felt about coming faded. Karina introduced Stephanie; Micah introduced them to Ericka, a petite part-Asian woman wearing overalls and a purple bandana wrapped around her brown pixie cut, and Jeremy, with a faded T-shirt and a heavily stubbled chin he kept rubbing. Music was playing from a small wireless speaker. Micah poured them coffee from a large thermos and walked them around the garden, pointing out someone's rainbow chard and another person's Romanesco cauliflower.

"That's Mrs. Godfrey's patch." Micah pointed to some wilted carrot tops. "She hasn't been here since her hip surgery. Looks dry." He pulled a garden hose over and trained it on the center of the box. "Gotta take care of things while she's gone—she lives for this garden, sweet old lady."

The area Micah and his friends were working on was actually four individual plots that they had pooled to work collectively, and it was planted with tomatoes, bell peppers, zucchini, lettuces, and several herbs. Stephanie leaned down to a plant bearing large dark-green chilies. "Ah, poblanos. My mom makes the best mole when these are in season."

"Take them," Micah said, smiling at her.

"Really?" Stephanie looked at him. "I'm going home next weekend. She'd love these."

"Absolutely! Your mom will make much better use of them than we can." Micah handed her a canvas bag. "Here, take them all." Stephanie grinned as she took the bag.

Micah continued to walk Karina through the garden. "Lemon verbena?" Karina pointed at a patch. "What do you use that for?"

Micah smiled and shrugged. "Not sure yet, but we're gonna have a lot of it. If you have any ideas, let me know." He led her back to the tool bucket and handed her a pair of gloves. "Karina," he said. "From your name, I'm guessing you're Indian." He held up one finger and continued, "But not entirely. Perhaps Caucasian too?"

"Uh, yeah. That's right," Karina said, taken aback. "How . . . ? You can tell all that from my name?"

"Your name. The almond shape of your eyes. Your skin tone." Micah smiled at her. "I studied a little Sanskrit, believe it or not."

"What? No, you're kidding."

"Yeah, I have one of those brains for language. I pick them up easily."

"How many?"

"Seven or eight." He smiled, shrugging. "I've traveled all over the world, so I've seen a lot of different people and combinations in my life. What's it like, being from two cultures? Do people always try to peg you to one or the other?"

Karina looked at him, trying to read his face. "People don't know what to make of me."

"How does that feel?"

Micah was exploring questions she'd never been asked before, much less answered. Karina was grateful for the sunglasses and baseball cap shielding her face. "Unmoored, I guess. You know, I'd love to just walk into a place and feel like I'm with my people. But that doesn't happen. *Ever.* I tried the Indian Students Association on campus and it was kind of a bust. Not Indian enough. Everywhere else, a little too different to fit in."

Micah smiled and murmured sympathetically. He dragged a bag of manure over to the tomato plants. "It's human nature, to want to categorize things in a way we recognize. But people don't realize it's in the mixing that greatness happens. Rock 'n' roll came from the confluence of R & B and country music. Hybrid tomatoes, like these"—he paused to snap a sucker from the tomato vine—"are the most delicious. And children of two races combine the best features of each. Always the most beautiful."

Karina's smile came involuntarily, though she told herself he hadn't complimented her directly. She was struck by how it felt to be truly seen by Micah. He didn't think of her as a novelty, like some people, or look past her differences entirely, as James had.

"Wait till you meet August." Micah smiled at her. "He's got at least four kinds of blood in his veins. And he's a beautiful human being, inside and out. That's what it's all about: how you feel inside, no matter how people perceive you. That's the only way you can truly belong anywhere. What does it mean, by the way?" Micah asked. "Karina?"

Karina shrugged. "Not much to me, except being saddled with a name no one can spell." She smiled and told him an abbreviated story of her name's significance to her parents.

Afterwards Micah, nodding, said, "That was the name given to you; doesn't mean you have to bear it forever. Perhaps it's played its role in your life and it no longer serves you."

Karina kept her eyes trained on the tomato plants, reaching to snap a large sucker off the vine as she considered Micah's comment. Prem had never called her by that name anyway. He had started calling her Kiki because he couldn't pronounce her name when he was a toddler, and never stopped. She'd loved this private nickname, though she never let on. When Prem died, that name died with him, and nobody had spoken those two syllables to her since.

Stephanie came over to join them, beaming as she held up the bag full of poblano chilies. "What can I do?" she asked. "Put me to work." Micah handed her a pair of work gloves and a spade to spread manure around the base of the plants. As they all continued to work together, Karina observed that Micah, Ericka and Jeremy had an easy way amongst them. Ericka had a tiny frame, maybe five feet tall, and everything about her seemed compact until she laughed, a tremendous laugh that startled. Jeremy was quieter, very muscular, and jumped up whenever there was a need to haul giant bags of organic soil across the garden.

Micah asked Karina to take a look at the irrigation system they had set up in the plot, mostly drip hoses on timers. She noticed that the drip holes were too far apart and several of the hoses were kinked. "Hey, you guys should hear this," he said, calling over the others. "Karina's an expert on growing crops efficiently in drought-like conditions."

"Which we definitely have here." Ericka slipped the bandana off her head to wipe her forehead and neck. "Whew."

Only then did Karina become aware of the sun beating down directly overhead and a low grumble in her stomach. She looked at her watch and saw that three hours had passed.

"Getting hot out here, huh?" Micah took a long drink from his water bottle. "Maybe we should hang it up for the day."

Yes, it was hot, and Karina's T-shirt clung to her with sweat. She had manure under her fingernails, she was sure she smelled rank, and she was starving. But she didn't want to leave this place, or these comfortable, kind people she'd only just met. She felt a veil of melancholy descending as she helped wash off the tools and bang soil from the gloves.

"Hey, Ericka," Micah called out, "let's pick some of those lettuces and herbs and take them by Mrs. Godfrey's place on our way home. I bet she could use some fresh food and visitors." He turned to Karina. "She's so active, for a septuagenarian. Probably going crazy being laid up." Micah raised his sunglasses onto his head, revealing his warm eyes. "Thanks for coming, Karina, Stephanie. I hope we'll see you again next Saturday?"

"I usually work on Saturdays," Stephanie said, disappointed. "But I'll try to bring back some mole after next weekend for Karina to bring you guys. Thanks for the chilies."

"Bye, Karina!" Ericka pulled her into a tight hug. "Great to meet you!"

Karina and Stephanie walked across the street toward the car. "You didn't mention he was *super* good-looking," Stephanie said, with a coy smile.

"Is he?" Karina said. "I guess he's kinda cute."

"Yeah, and *nice*. Smart, charming," Stephanie continued. "Not like those immature frat boys on campus."

———

Karina continued to attend classes and study during the week, but she began to really look forward to Saturday mornings, when she faithfully went to the community garden. Micah was there every week, sometimes with Ericka or Jeremy, sometimes with a woman named Zoe with long blond dreadlocks, or August, a guy with an olive complexion and spiky black hair. They always brought a thermos of hot coffee and played eclectic music, making the hours pass easily.

On Sundays, when Karina worked at NatMark, Micah usually came into the store around noon. One afternoon, she pointed out the new rainbow and Chioggia beets that could be eaten raw, thinly shaved, because they were so tender.

"You know, I never tasted a beet until I was twenty-five," Micah said. "Or eggplant, or avocado. Growing up in the Midwest, my entire vegetable universe was potatoes, corn, carrots and peas." He laughed at Karina's involuntary facial expression. "Yeah, and half the time, those were out of a can. How about you? Where did you grow up?"

"Bay Area."

Micah raised an eyebrow. "Hmm. Fancy."

"Well, not really, but I did eat everything. My parents are both foodies and my mom's Indian, so lots of vegetables you've never heard of."

"Sounds like a pretty great childhood." Micah watched her, then changed the subject, to her relief. "Where are these from, do you know?" He held up one of the beets.

She checked the tag. "Oregon."

"Hmm." Micah strolled past the beets and toward the parsnips. "Wouldn't it be amazing if we could meet all our own needs with home-grown, organic produce? Band together and do it all ourselves, rather than outsource the most important part of our health to commercial factories?"

"Might get a little boring, wouldn't it?" She smiled. "All that lemon verbena and no tomatoes?"

Micah threw his head back and laughed that deep, resonant laugh that made her warm with pleasure. "Really, with our year-round climate here, there's no reason we can't make it work. In fact"—he took a step closer to her—"it's already happening. We have a piece of land." He lowered his voice. "*Eight acres*, with a nine-thousand-square-foot house, plenty of space for everyone. Ericka and Jeremy moved in a few months ago."

"You all live together?" she asked.

Micah nodded. "Twelve of us. There's space for maybe one or two more, but that's it. We're being very careful about who joins us, because it's a very special thing we're creating. A new way of living harmoniously, with the earth and with one another."

"Like . . . a commune?" she quipped, expecting him to laugh.

Micah's expression remained serious and he cocked his head. "Well, that's one label. There's a reason this idea has persisted for centuries and across cultures. Commune, kibbutz, collective, cooperative—call it what you want; it's a beautiful concept. At our core, human beings need to live together, to share our burdens and challenges, to celebrate the fruits of our labor and our victories. Extended families used to live together— grandparents, parents, aunts and uncles, dozens of kids—and in some countries, they still do. But these days . . . Well, I don't know about you, but I don't exactly have a big family to share my life. So, we're creating a family. A family of sorts."

Karina envisioned herself in her lonely apartment in Santa Barbara, Mom in their house in Los Altos, Dad's condo in Palo Alto, his family back east, Mom's in India—the fragmented shape of her family. Every important step she'd taken in her life—her efforts in high school, her college scholarship, James—was with the hope it would propel her further from the dysfunction and sadness of her family and give her somewhere new to belong. And yet, nothing had done that.

"I'd love to see it sometime." The words were out of her mouth before she could consider them.

Micah smiled and grabbed a bag of rainbow carrots for his basket. "I'll ask the others."

When Karina showed up at the community garden on the third weekend in November, a dozen people were gathered there, the largest group she'd seen. Ericka, Jeremy, August and Zoe all greeted her with hugs, then Ericka linked her arm through Karina's and introduced her to the others. There were several milk crates and plastic bins stacked in the center of the cluster of people and, oddly, Christmas music was playing.

Micah stepped up onto a wooden bench. "What a beautiful morning!" He held out his hands toward the sky. "Today," he continued, "is the culmination of many months of hard work. Today we harvest the crops we've been tending since September. Can you believe," he said, spreading his arms wide and looking around, "that in September, none of this was here?"

With a pang, Karina thought back to September, when she had made the drive from Los Altos down to Santa Barbara, anticipating her reunion with James. She swallowed hard and trained her attention back on Micah.

"And now, we have zucchini, tomatoes, beets, Brussels sprouts, broccoli, and much more." Micah looked around at the group. "Each one of these plants is here because you took care of it." When he said "you," his eyes met Karina's. "You nurtured it, watered it, weeded it and helped it grow.

"All endings turn into new beginnings," Micah continued. "Today, we harvest our beloved community garden for the last time and transition our energies to the Sanctuary. After we celebrate and give thanks on Thursday, we will begin planting our new fields there Friday."

Karina's parents had been asking whether she was coming home for Thanksgiving. When she was growing up, the holiday had been a muted affair with just their immediate family. There was no squeezing extra people around the dining table, none of the antics of a large, boisterous family coming together to fight over politics or laugh at old jokes. It was always a challenge to find a turkey small enough for just the four (or later, three) of them. Her mother hated leftovers, and all the small birds seemed to get bought up early, so she had taken to getting their turkey a month before and stowing it in the freezer, where it took up half the compartment. Karina and Prem would have an ice cream binge the day Mom brought home the turkey, to make room for the bird. That was often the best part of the holiday, and it was what Karina missed most about Thanksgiving after Prem died.

Her father had insisted they celebrate the holiday together throughout Karina's high school years, even coming over to the house with bags full of groceries after he had moved out. But somehow, with just three of them, something essential was missing, like the salt in their food. Her parents had perfected their menu over the years and took pride in the way everything tasted. But despite the creamy mashed potatoes with chives, the port-wine gravy, the delicate haricots verts with toasted almonds, the Thanksgiving feast had never quite managed to leave her satisfied.

Karina didn't have anywhere to go in Santa Barbara, but part of her didn't want to mark the occasion at all, to feel the absence of what should have been there, like her tongue returning to a lost tooth. It was tempting to just stay in town to study and work. She knew she could pick up extra shifts at NatMark, since Thanksgiving week was busy.

"So, grab a bin and let's get started," Micah said, clapping his hands together. There was a cheer from the crowd and a few claps.

Karina wandered over to the bin holding work gloves and crouched down next to August, who was rummaging for a matching pair. "So August, do you live at the . . ."

"Sanctuary?" He looked up at her. "Yeah, moved in about six months ago. It's a beautiful place, truly." August's voice caught. "Sometimes, I think Micah saved my life with that place." Before she could ask what he meant, Micah came over and gave Karina a warm hug in greeting, his arm lingering comfortably around her shoulders. "Want to work on the beets with me?"

They knelt on the ground at two adjacent corners of the plot. Micah pulled up one of the plants by its greens, revealing a lumpy rose-pink bulb. "Candy-cane varietal," he said. "Red-and-white striped inside. So beautiful when you slice it open." He rubbed the beet vigorously against his shirt and bit into it.

"So, you're not going to be coming here anymore?" she asked, trying to filter the anxiety out of her voice.

"Yeah, that's right," Micah said, as he dug his spade into the soil to pry up another beet. "It's exciting, what we have planned, Karina. Eight acres of beautiful land we've cleared and improved with soil amendments and fertilizer. There's a well on the property we've hooked up to an efficient drip irrigation system, and we're ready to start planting our first crops. At full production, we'll have even more than we need, so we can donate to food banks."

She laughed. "A well? Where is this place, anyway? Out in the countryside?"

Micah shook his head. "Rancho Paraiso, less than twenty miles from here," he said. "Paradise Ranch, as named by the early Mexican settlers. Today, it's a super-wealthy community with massive homes on huge lots, all geared toward maximum privacy."

Karina took a deep breath. "Actually, I . . . I'll be here over Thanksgiving," she said, her heart thumping loudly in her chest. She held up a beet plant by its greens. "And I make a mean roasted beet salad."

"You know, it's okay to feel that way," Micah said.

Karina looked at him, wondering at his meaning.

Micah continued. "To not want to go home to your family. It's okay. Thanksgiving is a loaded holiday. So many expectations about how you're supposed to feel, how everything's supposed to look, who's around the table." He put an arm around her shoulders. "You can join our family this year."

27 | karina

The community of Rancho Paraiso featured single-lane roads wind-ing through gently rolling hills surrounded with thick foliage. Every so often, there was a driveway leading to an imposing gate marked with pillars, but no houses were visible from the road. Eventually, Karina came upon the right address and followed a long gravel driveway, bordered on both sides by lemon trees. At the top, a roundabout with a tiered foun-tain sat in front of a sprawling two-story house with a four-door garage, where several cars were parked.

Stepping out of her car, Karina tugged at the hem of the sweater-dress she'd chosen to wear with her favorite tall boots and approached the house's towering front doors, thick slabs of wood against which her knuckles barely made a sound. The door swung wide open to reveal Micah, more dressed up than usual in a collarless long-sleeve white shirt and dark blue jeans. Karina held out the bunch of sunflowers she'd brought.

"Karina." Micah opened his arms wide and took a few steps back-wards to allow her to enter. Behind him was an enormous picture window with a striking vista of the pool and gardens, with rolling hills in the distance. "Welcome to the Sanctuary, our little piece of heaven." He took the bouquet with an appreciative bow and led her into the house. "Come on in."

They entered the largest kitchen Karina had ever seen, with an expansive island around the perimeter and a dozen people who were all working but greeted her warmly. Ericka wiped her hands on a kitchen towel and came over to give her a hug before returning to her green beans.

"That's Chef Guy at the stove, doing the heavy lifting," said Micah, pointing to a plump black man in an apron.

Guy smiled widely as they approached. *"Salut, ma cherie,"* he said in a distinct French accent as he leaned in to kiss her on both cheeks.

"Can I help with something?" she asked, aware of the busy hive around her.

Micah handed her a glass of white wine and gestured to a counter stool. "Relax a bit first. You've been running around all morning, am I right?"

Karina nodded as she sat. "I helped open the store this morning. Feels good to get off my feet for a minute." The wine was crisp, not too sweet, and made her feel very adult. The only times she'd tasted good wine like this were when she had a few sips at special dinners with her parents. The kitchen was fragrant with pungent herbs, garlic and turkey roasting in the oven. Karina took in the scene: knives scraping against boards, people laughing and chatting as they reached past each other, mismatched aprons, and assorted wineglasses scattered along the long granite countertop. The space was filled with people who represented a mix of complexions and races. It felt messy and delicious and warm and festive.

"When you're done," Micah nodded toward her glass, "I'll show you around the property." Karina warmed at the prospect of some time alone with him. She took one last sip and stood up. As they walked through the main hallway, Karina found herself continually surprised at the scale of the house: the ceilings were soaring; the dining room housed an enormous round table set for fourteen; the family room sported a television screen the size of her bed.

When Micah led her outside, Karina averted her eyes from the swimming pool at the center of the backyard. She spotted a grove of lemon
trees off to the side and detoured in that direction. "How many trees are
there?" she asked, leaning closer to smell the fruit.

"We have about a hundred left. We had to clear a lot of them to make
space for all this." Micah waved his arm toward the field of dark soil
lined with irrigation tubes and pointed out where they connected to the
underground well. "We're almost finished with the composting system,"
Micah said, leading her up a slope. "I want to put in solar panels on this
hillside to generate all our electricity, but that's a big investment—sixty
grand—so I'm still trying to collect the money. Eventually we'll be a
closed loop system, taking nothing from the earth we don't put back in
some way. Imagine, if everyone lived like this, how many problems we
could fix—climate change, water shortages . . ."

"Did you know 70 percent of freshwater use is for agriculture?"
Karina said. Her mind traveled back to the seminar that had brought
her and James together, the hours they spent in the library poring over
journal articles on drought, water delivery systems, desalinization plants.
"And food production will need to grow by over 60 percent over the
next twenty years, just to keep up with population growth?"

"Yes, and that's why what we're doing here is so important. We're
creating a model that can be replicated in communities across the country, then around the world." Micah pointed out to where the ocean was
visible on the horizon. He leaned over her shoulder and she felt his
warm breath on her neck. "You know the first time I saw the Pacific
Ocean? I'd never been outside the Midwest, never seen anything but
corn and wheat fields. Then I drove cross-country when I was eighteen
in a beat-up Chevy Cavalier with no AC." He chuckled. "And when I
arrived in Santa Cruz, California, I thought I'd landed in paradise. I took
off my sneakers, sat down on the boardwalk and dangled my feet in the
water. For the first time in my life, I felt as if I belonged somewhere."

Micah smiled at her. "I tossed those sneakers in the trash can; I knew I was never going back."

"What did you do then?" Karina asked, trying to conjure images from her childhood visits to the Santa Cruz boardwalk with her family.

Micah shrugged. "Odd jobs—construction, food service. My favorite was being a carnival barker on the boardwalk."

Karina laughed. "You were?"

"Hey, I was good at it!" Micah touched her arm playfully as they continued walking. "I had a nose for those things. How to get someone to pony up for a prize: when a guy was trying to impress a girl, or parents needed a break from their kid."

"So, basically, you pawned off a lot of giant stuffed animals?" Karina teased him.

Micah shrugged. "Once you understand what makes people tick, you can help bring them into brighter lives. If all human beings lived like that, the world would be a different place. One day, I was sitting on the beach in Santa Cruz, my bare feet in the sand, gazing out over the blue water, and I just had this vision of a world where every organism functioned together and every human being strived for full potential." He looked wistful. "Ever since then, I've been working toward building a place like this."

"Have you looked at hydroponics?" Karina asked, excited. "I could show you a few things we set up at the Botany Lab if you want to try them in a greenhouse or indoors."

"That's exactly the kind of expertise we need." Micah smiled at her as they came upon a large screened shed, a chicken coop with a dozen birds clucking about inside. He stopped and turned to her. "Let me ask you something, Karina. Are you satisfied with your life right now, truly satisfied?" Micah looked directly in her eyes. "Do you feel like you're living up to your highest potential? Are your relationships meaningful? Is your work rewarding?"

The mention of relationships turned a wrench in her stomach. Karina considered her answer. She enjoyed her job at NatMark and she was good at it, but was stocking potatoes meaningful work? She thought of her father, who worked all the time, who prized work above leisure time and hobbies. But her father believed in work of the mind; she knew he would be dismayed at the thought of her doing manual labor over advanced calculus.

"I . . ." Karina hesitated, unsure how to admit what felt like a weakness. "I don't think so. I feel like I'm just going through the motions, but I'm not sure what it's leading to. I think . . . I *hope* . . . there's more out there."

"There is," Micah said in quiet declaration. "There is, Karina." He handed her a wire basket and opened one of the henhouse doors, where two pale blue eggs sat nestled in the straw. "Sitting in a classroom can feel good, but reality is very different than school. The opportunity to make an impact is right now, every day, in the way you live and work." He placed one of the eggs in her open palm and she felt its warmth. After collecting a dozen more, they continued walking down the path and through the grounds, as Micah pointed out the sand volleyball court, putting green and tennis court. They approached the horse facilities and were greeted by the familiar smell that took Karina back to visiting the stables with Izzy.

"Isn't he a beauty?" Micah said as they reached the stall that housed a stately chestnut horse. "He's a rescue. I took him in after the wildfires last summer displaced a lot of large animals. Unfortunately, no one here knows much about horses. But I did get him this guy for company." He pointed to a black and white goat in the neighboring stall.

Karina stepped up on the railing and held the back of her hand out below the horse's nostrils for him to smell her. She was captivated by the enormous eyes that gazed serenely at her, and in that moment, she felt a strong pang for Izzy. She wanted to call and tell her all about meeting Micah, the community garden and her new friends. But their calls had trailed off over the past couple of months, mostly because Karina couldn't quite bring herself to tell Izzy the full truth of what had happened that night with Henry. She had gotten as far as telling her she'd been with a guy, the first since James, and it hadn't felt right, only made her sad. She was too ashamed to admit the rest, and ever since then, the thought of talking to Izzy, who knew her so well and would know something was wrong, became harder and harder to deal with.

"He likes you," Micah said, as the horse nuzzled her hand.

"What's his name?" Karina stroked the side of his head.

Micah shrugged. "You want to give him one?"

"He needs a good brushing." She ran her hand over the tangles in his mane and the matted nap of his coat. "If you have brushes, I can do it."

Micah laughed. "Okay, I'll find a brush for your next visit."

Karina looked over and smiled, comforted by the thought of returning. She stepped down off the railing and gave the horse one last pat on his elegant neck.

"We're planning to have cows too," Micah said, as they walked away. "Fresh milk, maybe cream and butter. Have you ever tasted the fresh stuff?" He shook his head. "So good."

When Micah turned and began walking toward the house, Karina voiced a question she'd been holding on to for some time. "August said you saved his life. What did he mean by that?"

Micah watched the ground as he walked, his hands tucked into his back pockets. "We all have demons, Karina. Every one of us. We all have something that haunts us, that prevents us from reaching our true potential. I just helped August untie himself from those demons. He might be grateful, but I only showed him the way. He did all the hard work. Any of us can have that." He stopped and turned to her. "You too, Karina. You can do extraordinary things with your life, if you choose."

Karina nodded as he spoke, intrigued by a future where she could be free of her own demons, the shame she carried for wrecking her family and her body. What might she achieve if she could leave behind all the terrible misjudgments that led to Prem's death, James's betrayal, the incident with Henry? She allowed herself to imagine this as she and Micah walked in silence back to the house.

———

There were eighteen of them for Thanksgiving: twelve people who lived in the house and six others, including Karina, who didn't. Some of the guests, she learned, were surfers from a beach that Micah and August patronized. A couple of others had a fresh juice stand at the farmers' market nearby. The atmosphere in the house was joyful and relaxed, and the buffet was abundant, with at least two dozen dishes: Thanksgiving favorites like stuffing, cranberry sauce and pumpkin pie, as well as less traditional options. Chef Guy had baked a tarte tatin instead of a traditional apple pie, Zoe had made Cajun-style red beans and rice, and everyone cheered when Ericka pulled a pan of Korean short ribs from the oven, still sizzling. As Karina made her way through the buffet line, she noticed a bowl of cumin-spiced roasted cauliflower, which reminded her of one of her mother's Indian dishes.

Micah stood in the archway between the dining and living rooms, where they all sat, and spoke about how deeply moved he felt to be building a new type of community that reflected their values. He said a few words of appreciation about each person present, then held up his glass toward Karina. "And I want to thank Karina for joining our family today. She is incredibly knowledgeable and isn't afraid to get her hands dirty. But, most of all, she has a beautiful energy that's wonderful to be around."

Karina felt tears well in her eyes as Micah expressed gratitude for healthy food cooked with love, the fresh air outside, and spending a special day with people to whom he felt a deep connection. She was emotional because she felt it too. As she looked around the room at the mash-up of skin tones and cultures, for once she didn't feel like an anomaly. She dared to believe that they saw something in her: a better version of herself that she could nurture into the light. Karina knew then, for the first time in as long as she could remember, perhaps the first time in her life, she was where she belonged.

The Sunday after Thanksgiving, Karina dressed up a bit for her shift at NatMark, in a new pair of flattering jeans, a thin gold chain at her neck, a touch of eyeliner and lip gloss. It was a slow day at the store and time crawled as she looked for Micah. She had practiced what she planned to say, but almost lost her nerve when she saw him, pushing an overflowing cart. "Wow. Leave something for the rest of us." She grinned.

Micah's face broadened into a wide smile. "Our fridge is *empty*. We took our leftovers to the homeless shelter downtown Friday and served lunch to about two dozen people. Ericka had to go buy more pumpkin pie so we wouldn't have an uprising."

Karina noticed they seemed to weave these good deeds into almost everything they did, as if it was part of their DNA. She took a deep breath. "Thanks for having me over, Micah. I really loved it."

"Well, everyone loved *you*, Karina," he said. "I mean, *really* loved you. You fit right in. I think Ericka believes you're her long-lost sister." His eyes shone.

Karina smiled, relieved that they felt the same way she did, and hoping Micah was included in that sentiment. "I've been thinking about your question, what I want from my life? I really believe in everything you're doing at the Sanctuary, and . . . I want to be part of it." She took another deep breath and exhaled. "I'd like to come join you . . . to live there." She held her breath, waiting for the response that would mean everything, whether or not she could finally usher her life down the right path.

Micah nodded slowly. "What about school? It's pretty far from campus."

"I realized you were right," Karina said. "The classroom isn't the real world. I want to get out and make a real impact now. I want to do this."

Micah watched her speak and a small smile played at the corner of his mouth. After what felt like an interminable time, he spoke. "I'll have to talk with the others; we do everything by consensus. But personally, I'd love to have you join us."

28 | the olanders

DECEMBER 2014

By the second week in December, a stressful frenzy had descended on the UCSB campus with the imminent end of term. The library was suddenly full, every table occupied by anxious students. Karina went through the motions of going to class, studying for finals, working her shifts at NatMark and returning to her empty apartment, but her thoughts always drifted back to the Sanctuary and the life she envisioned there.

Micah finally got back to her, two weeks after Thanksgiving. "We're going to convert the theater upstairs to a bedroom for four people," he said when he called. "Eventually, we'll invite three more people to join us, but it was unanimous, Karina. You're our first choice to move in. It'll take us a couple weeks to get ready, so you can think about—"

"I don't need to. I already know." Karina felt her whole body quivering. "I'm so excited. Thanks, Micah."

Everything was falling into alignment. In the past weeks, since the warning letter about her scholarship and Thanksgiving, the importance of college had receded further in her mind. The Sanctuary was a place where she could live amongst people she respected, who respected her. Whom she could trust, even if she drank too much tequila. Who didn't promise love one moment, then take it away. Forget about doing analysis or reading policy statements or breeding plants in a lab or writing papers to save the earth. She could actually *do* it every day, as she lived.

Karina informed her academic adviser that she would be taking the next semester off to earn money, an excuse he readily accepted. Her current term grades would put her on probation for her scholarship, but she would have a year to re-enroll and complete her graduation requirements. She gave her landlord notice she would be vacating and began packing up her belongings. She asked her manager at NatMark if she could work more shifts, feeding him the same story she'd told her academic adviser. She told Stephanie, Claire and a few other friends that she was studying abroad for the next semester, returning to Ecuador. She wanted to cut off ties completely, wanted them to stop calling and inviting her to do things.

It was remarkably easy to pull all this off, because no one knew her very well at college, other than James. One of the appeals of leaving the bubble of the UCSB campus entirely, of traversing twenty miles and a world away to Rancho Paraiso, was that she would never have to see him or Yoga Girl again. It was easy, too, because Karina realized she was quite a good liar. She had become so practiced at holding back truths about herself, offering lies of omission. Telling her mother she and Prem had spent the entire time after school doing homework, but neglecting to mention that Prem did his in front of the TV while she got some privacy in her room. Telling the counselor she had no feelings about Prem she wanted to discuss. Telling the rest of the world, friends and neighbors and teachers and her father: *Yes, she was fine. No, there was nothing they could do.* Omission. Omission. Lie. Lie. Lies.

So, now she could do it again one last time: tell a story people were willing to hear. And the people who should have known her best, Mom and Dad? To them, she would say nothing, at least not right now. They knew she was busy and couldn't come home as often. As long as she maintained regular communication, they'd have no reason to suspect a thing. Once she was settled and happy in her new life, she could tell them more. Karina headed home for winter break, excited about what waited on the other side of it.

Keith's nerves were rattled as he sat in his attorney's office. Last week, the SEC had informed him it was investigating his sizable stock purchase of HyunCom, weeks before its acquisition by Machtel Industries was announced and the stock rose 30 percent. At first, Keith was inclined to cooperate with the investigation, despite his attorney's advice that it might not be in his best interest. Keith didn't think he'd done anything wrong, either at the time of the purchase or now. Although compliance was a little looser at Duncan Weiss, he'd had extensive training on securities fraud and insider trading laws at the beginning of his career. He knew the rules. You couldn't trade on your own deals, or other deals at the office. But the Machtel-HyunCom deal *wasn't* his. That's what chafed him. Jeff Erstine hadn't told him anything. Keith had bought the stock on a hunch; he was a good investor with strong intuition and market knowledge. It's not like he made a rational calculation at the time; his emotions had gotten the better of him. But he still thought it was harmless, and small dollars too.

However, when Carl, his attorney, explained the fact pattern as the SEC saw it, it painted a different story. Keith had exclusive access to Machtel's office, an opportunity to spy on the company's non-public activities. He had probed a former employee (as he'd expected, Rachel hadn't lasted very long as the CEO's second assistant and was now cooperating with the SEC) for more non-public information about the acquisition and traded on it a week later. Keith agreed to let Carl try to find out how strong the SEC's case was, and if there was a settlement to be made.

"It doesn't look good, Keith." Carl sat behind his imposing wooden desk. "Even if it wasn't what you intended."

Keith shook his head. "But I'm a small fish. We're talking less than a million. Surely, the SEC won't go to the mat for a case like this." It was a petty revenge bet, for god's sake. "They must be willing to settle." He tried to keep the desperation out of his voice.

"That's my hope, Keith. But there's no predicting when the SEC wants to make an example out of someone. And the U.S. attorney is completely independent, so even if we settle the civil charges, there's still the possibility of a criminal indictment—which could mean a trial, conviction, prison time."

Keith felt his vision blur, the leather-bound books lining the wall behind Carl swimming before his eyes, colors mixing. These were possibilities Keith couldn't bear to consider, upending the man he believed himself to be. He had started investment banking in the era of Boesky and Milken, two men repeatedly held up as cautionary tales in his early years. That kind of thing would never happen at Morgan Stanley, he'd told Jaya, where the rules were hammered into them and abundant precautions put in place. He thought Jaya had been overcautious when she'd warned him against moving to Duncan Weiss years ago, and he'd since felt vindicated in his choice, in part because of how much he'd earned. But reward rarely came without risk, as he knew. Jaya's absolute moral compass had always kept him away from the gray zone. Perhaps he'd gone adrift without her—another thing he'd lost, along with his wife and family, without even realizing it. Now, she seemed to operate in a different sphere, where the things that occupied him—the things that used to occupy them both—no longer figured into her life.

Keith had to make all this SEC trouble go away, quietly. He tried to flush those other possibilities from his mind as he drove home to meet up with Karina, home for winter break. She'd been here all week, and it was one of the best visits they'd had. They went ice skating at the mall and drove over the Bay Bridge to see the city lights at night. He took her to the driving range a couple of times and gave her some pointers on her swing, which had deteriorated after not playing for so long. "You live in Santa Barbara," he said. "How can you not make it onto the golf course once in a while? It's right on your campus!"

Karina explained she'd been busy with classes and a research project at the Botany Lab that might lead to publication, which would be great for her graduate school prospects. He bought her a thick GRE prep book and she seemed interested, flipping through it every day. She even had a few prospects for summer internships near campus. On her last night with him, they got pizza from their favorite spot and he poured himself a nice cabernet, as well as a touch in a second glass for Karina.

"You seem really happy, honey," he said. "I trust that young man's treating you well?"

Karina shook her head. "James and I broke up."

"Oh," Keith said. "Well, this is the most . . . ," he paused while he searched for the word, ". . . contented I've seen you in a long time." He smiled at her, placed his hand over hers and squeezed.

"Thanks, Dad." Karina smiled back. "I am really happy."

"Good, you deserve it," he said. "And I'm sure that *James* didn't deserve you." He winked at her. "Listen, before you go to your mother's tomorrow, I want to give you a head's up on something."

Karina sat back and took a sip of her wine, looking more like a woman than he was prepared for. Keith took a deep breath. "Your mother has been following a guru—one of those self-proclaimed holy men from India who travels the world giving lectures and attracting followers. Probably harmless," he assured Karina when he saw her eyebrows rise in inquiry. Keith had been alarmed at first, when Jaya had mentioned the whole thing to him a few months ago, but he'd since noticed a positive change in her. She sounded calmer when they spoke, less anxious.

"Seems legit, from what I've read," Keith added. "She's not giving him money, I don't think, or not much. She went to his lecture when he passed through San Jose, and she listens to his CDs at home. It's given her a bit of a community, actually, getting together with these other . . . *devotees*, I guess she calls them." He exhaled heavily. "To each his own, I suppose. Anyway, just wanted you to know so you're not taken by surprise."

————

"His name is Guru Brahmananda." Jaya proudly showed Karina his framed portrait, adorned with a fresh floral garland, in the mandir room.

"He looks like Dev Uncle," Karina responded.

Jaya squinted at the portrait, trying to spot any resemblance to her brother. Other than graying hair and their approximate ages, she could see nothing in common. Did all older Indian men look the same to her daughter? It troubled Jaya that their families saw each other so infrequently, given the distance and schedules. Their children had only met twice before Prem had died; the cousins were little more than acquaintances with foreign accents. Jaya pushed aside that disturbing thought.

"I wish you'd been here when he came through to give his lectures," she said. "He is so wise. And the way he puts his ideas into words . . . It's like poetry, so beautiful. I went for five days and never got bored or uncomfortable, even sitting cross-legged on the hard floor. There's just something . . . peaceful about hearing him speak." Jaya smiled broadly, remembering that first magical experience, which had since been replicated in four more cities to which she'd traveled to see the Guru speak. How could she explain it? His talks were so moving because he didn't preach but used the power of personal stories to transform. "I have some CDs, if you want—"

"Mom!" Karina said, peering closer at Jaya's face. "What happened to your tooth?" She pointed to her own cheek.

"Oh, that," Jaya said, waving it off. "One of my molars was causing so much pain, the dentist took it out a few weeks ago."

"But . . . what?" Karina became very animated now, waving her arms around. "Took it out? Can't you get it replaced? You can't just walk around with a big hole in your mouth!"

Jaya smiled, not understanding why Karina seemed so upset about such a little thing. She waved her concern away. "It doesn't bother me, so who cares?" She would have liked to help her daughter see that those things she concerned herself with—branded clothes, expensive mascara, that blue lampshade for her new apartment—none of that mattered. But Jaya had learned that they were each on their own spiritual journey in this life, and she couldn't push Karina to be receptive to her ideas any more than Keith could push Jaya. She had to meet Karina where she was, to find some common ground with her daughter as she grew older and further away.

"Come," Jaya said, taking Karina's hand and walking her out of the mandir room. "Come see the box of tulip bulbs I got at Costco. Maybe we can plant them tomorrow."

———

A few days later, Karina made an excuse to drive back to campus early to register for some new classes. She found it hard to believe that Mom once worked as a policy analyst, evaluating research studies and analyzing data; she seemed almost gullible now. It still struck a nerve, the feeling that her mom was indifferent to her, as if her parental concern was a finite resource that had been fully drained by Prem. But Karina had come to rely on her mother's credulity; it facilitated Karina's independence, so she did not question it.

Karina arrived back in Santa Barbara the evening of December 30, which gave her the following day to clear out her apartment and move. She was circumspect in choosing what to bring. She stared for a long time at the bag in her bathroom vanity, where she still took pains to hide her supplies, though she lived alone. As she removed and considered each item—the razor blades, the cotton squares, the bandaging tape she'd graduated to due to the length of her cuts—she thought of the relief these things brought her. At first, she tucked the bag away in one of her cartons, then she removed it and walked it down to the incinerator chute before she could change her mind. Tomorrow was a new day, a new chapter. A new life.

29 | prem

The most beautiful place I ever saw was Hawaii, when we went there on vacation. Even though it touches the same ocean as California, it felt like another planet. The sand was soft like velvet under my feet but became as hard as clay when I mixed it with water. Kiki brought me pailfuls, because they were heavy and she was twice as old as me, as she always liked to tell people. It was the only time in our lives that would be true, when I was five, as I reminded everyone. Every day on the beach, I built an enormous sandcastle, and every night after we left, it was washed away. I didn't mind; I built the castle bigger and better every day, with fortress walls, lookout towers, moats and drawbridges.

While I built my castles on land, Kiki loved being in the ocean. She stayed in the water for hours and hours, floating on her back and looking up at the sky. When the water was the same temperature as the warm air, she said she felt *amphibious* (a word she'd just learned), moving comfortably between land and sea. On the long plane ride home, I drew a picture of Kiki as a mermaid with green scales and long flowing hair. Then, because it wasn't quite right yet, I added a superhero cape. And that's how I sometimes think of her even now, with a touch of magical powers.

Grown-ups believe there's a big difference between magic and the real world, but I'm not so sure. In the comics, the villain and the superhero are always clear, but in real life, it's harder to tell. If you see yourself as the hero of your own story all the time, like Dad, sometimes you're not even sure what's right and what's wrong anymore. It may seem impossible for the hero to act like a villain, but I've seen it happen more than you'd think.

Sometimes, like Kiki, you're not even sure what's true anymore, and if you think about it long enough, you can convince yourself that something did or didn't happen. Even if you believe in magic, like Mom, you might think that it's possessed only by certain special people and that you need them to share it with you. But no one can really give you magic. Everyone knows you have to find it in yourself.

Just like the Space Rangers hovering in outer space, looking out at the planets, you can see the real world doesn't look at all like you expected: everything seems smaller, simpler, quieter at a distance. The real world is all an illusion. It's all in how you see it.

SANCTUARY

30 | karina

Micah arrived with Jeremy and August the next morning to help Karina move. As they all carried boxes down to the parking lot, Karina recalled how different it had felt in September, lugging her stuff alone after James's unexpected betrayal. She realized with satisfaction that New Year's Eve had just passed without even a thought of James or his proposed reunion. When the apartment was emptied, Karina felt no nostalgia as she left her keys on the kitchen counter. Before they drove off, Micah said, "We should do something special to celebrate Karina moving in. How about we drive down the coast to that cove with the awesome burrito shack and catch some waves?" He turned to Karina. "Have you ever surfed?"

Karina shook her head. She had spent short periods of time at the beach over the last few years: at a freshman orientation party, a field trip with one of her environmental science classes, the weekend she and James lost their virginity together. She had always stayed on shore to be safe, though she enjoyed the sensation of her feet pressing into packed wet sand and the water lapping at her ankles.

Micah opened the van door. "I'll teach you. You'll love it."

Karina tried to fight the nervous energy building in her chest as she followed the van in her car, but by the time they arrived at the cove, she was on edge about what was to come. The roar of the water filled her ears. The guys stripped down to their shorts and Micah untethered the surfboards that were always tied to the top of his van. "I'll just watch this time," Karina said. "I don't have a suit."

Micah dusted sand from the boards. "You can wear my wet suit." He tossed it to her, turned to face the ocean, closed his eyes and inhaled deeply; then he hoisted the board under his arm and began running toward the beach. August and Jeremy took off after Micah with the other board. Standing there alone, Karina stepped into the wetsuit, feeling herself caught between the attraction that drew her toward Micah and the fear that held her back. She took a deep breath and followed them down to the water's edge.

August and Jeremy got into the water while Micah stayed on the beach to explain the basic principles of surfing to Karina, drawing out a phantom board with a stick in the sand. He showed her where to position her feet when she stood up and how to balance her weight; he had her practice "popping up" from the face-down paddling position to standing. All this required concentration and core strength, and she found herself perspiring in the sun.

She grabbed his arm after ten minutes of practice. "Micah, why don't you just go? I'll wait here, really."

Micah stopped, looking at her. "You can swim, right?"

"Yes, but . . ."

He placed his hands on her shoulders, looking into her eyes. "Fear is the biggest thing holding you back in life, Karina. You'll feel so much stronger once you do this. Trust me?"

She nodded, wanting to believe him.

"Good. I'll be right there with you the whole time."

She told herself this was not a stupid thing to do as Micah tethered the board strap to her ankle and led her toward the water. He stayed right next to her, coaching her as she entered the ocean, jumped over the waves and paddled out beyond the break. The familiar sensation of being buoyed by the surf reminded her why she'd loved the ocean so much as a child. As she lay face-down on the board, Micah treaded water as they waited patiently for the right wave. "I'll count to three and push you in front of the wave, then you pop up, just like we practiced, okay?"

"Okay," Karina said, taking in the expanse of open water in front of her. In her mind, she saw the image of herself as the mermaid super-hero that Prem had drawn in Hawaii. Micah counted, "One . . . two . . . three!" She felt the board thrust forward, as if powered by motor. Hearing Micah's instructions, she reflexively jumped into a crouch-standing posi-tion. The board skimmed the surface of the water like a seagull. Karina felt a split moment of exhilaration, air rushing past her ears, before she lost her balance and tumbled off the board, plunging into the water.

When she got her feet beneath her, August was running from the beach to take the board from her. He carried it out of the water and she sat down, coughing from the salt water in her lungs. Her nose and eyes were burning and goosebumps rose on her skin from the cool air, but she was astounded at what had just happened: she had flown across the ocean, like she belonged there.

Micah had swam toward shore and was now walking toward her, beaming. "You did it!" he yelled. "How do you feel?"

Karina coughed again as August draped a thick beach towel around her shoulders. She pulled it closer as she shivered. "Like . . . I was flying."

"You're a natural." Micah shook his head. "You know how hard it is to get up on the board the first time?"

"Yeah, you looked *fluid*," August agreed.

"Until I fell." Karina laughed.

"We all fall," Micah said. "You should see the wipeouts I've had." He pointed to a small white scar over his left eyebrow. "Got this one at Bondi." He extended a hand to help her up. "I'm really proud of you."

They had a quick lunch at the burrito shack, and Karina enjoyed the feeling of warm sun on her body, her toes digging into the sand, even the roar of the ocean nearby. She hadn't been immersed in water like that since their swimming pool in Los Altos, and had forgotten the pleasure of it, having been haunted for so long by its other associations. As they ate, Karina watched other surfers riding waves, amazed that she had done what they were doing: moving effortlessly in the water, defying gravity and her fears.

"Thanks, Micah," Karina said as they walked away from the beach. "You were right, about how that would feel."

Micah smiled at her. "Everything you want is on the other side of fear, Karina."

———

After arriving at the house, Micah took Karina upstairs to the theater room. "Isn't it beautiful?" he said, pointing out the ornate gold-leaf ceiling. "People used to sit here in the dark, staring at a screen instead of connecting with each other. I'll let you get settled before dinner." Before leaving, he leaned over and kissed her on the forehead. Karina was startled, then delighted, and finally told herself it must have been a platonic gesture, even as she wished it was something more.

There was a knock at the door and her heart quickened, thinking it was Micah again. But when she opened the door, she found Ericka, who leaned forward to hug her. "So glad you're here! We're neighbors." She gestured to the room across the hall. "Need help?"

"Just figuring out where to hang my clothes, since there's no closet in here."

"Put them in our closet, mine and Zoe's."

"Oh, I don't want to bother you when I need something," Karina said.

"What?" Ericka giggled. "Door's open all the time. Micah must have told you, right? We all keep our doors open, instead of walling ourselves off."

"Yeah, right," Karina said, though she didn't recall hearing this. "If you don't mind." She picked up a stack of clothes and followed Ericka to her room.

Ericka made space in the closet. "Help yourself. Zoe and I share everything. We don't need much, just a few outfits each."

In the closet, Karina noticed a richly saturated red kurta sewn with tiny mirrors, a more decorative version of the ones her mother wore. "Yours?" She touched the sleeve. "From India?"

"I wish," Ericka said. "I got it in Artesia a few years ago. I've always wanted to go to India, though, to a yoga retreat or meditation center. I've always felt a little Indian in my soul. Does that sound crazy? Have you been? What's it like?"

"Not since I was young," Karina said, still fingering the detailed embroidery of the blouse. She had visited her grandparents all over the world, her cousins in London. Her only connection to India was through Mom, her idols and prayers, her music and dance costumes, the food she prepared. Karina continued to mull this over as she finished unpacking in her room: how half-Korean Ericka could feel Indian in her soul while Karina didn't know how to feel about it. She tried to match Ericka's spirit of simplicity, taking out only the items she needed to live, and leaving the rest stashed under her bed before returning downstairs.

"Hey," Micah said, putting his arm around her shoulders and drawing her into the kitchen. "We have a special dinner to welcome you." He pointed to a large roasting pan just out of the oven, holding chickens nestled amongst carrots, parsnips and turnips.

"Looks amazing," Karina said.

"And that," Micah pointed at the phone in her hand, "you should leave at the front door. We all do. Phones go in a basket in the front coat closet." He smiled, his warm brown eyes crinkling at the corners.

Karina hesitated, accustomed to feeling her phone in her back pocket all the time.

"Try it," Micah said. "I bet you'll like it as much as the rest of us. If not, you can always take it back. But you should make the effort to really *be* here, with us."

"All right." Karina walked toward the front closet. It was true, she hadn't seen people using their phones much around the house, nor at the community garden. Maybe that was why time seemed to slow down here. She gingerly placed her phone into the basket with the other phones, wallets and key rings. By the time she returned to the kitchen, dinner was ready. Her mouth watered as she spooned wild rice onto the center of her plate, topped it with chicken and drizzled some sauce from the pan. The aroma of thyme and lemon were heavenly. Her mom's cooking had become increasingly bland since she'd decided, under the guidance of Guru Brahmananda, that garlic, onions and chilies were not good for her spiritual being.

They squeezed around the dining table while reggae music played throughout the house. Micah motioned for her to sit next to him. "To the newest member of our family, Karina!" he said, holding up his glass until she picked up the glass of red wine in front of her and clinked his. "I knew as soon as I met you that you were a good person, with a good heart. Now you're surrounded by good hearts."

Ericka held her glass in the air. "Karina, I loved you from the first time you came to the community garden. You're super-smart and really fun to talk to and hang out with. Welcome, sister!"

Each person around the table said a few words, welcoming Karina, complimenting her, telling her what they loved about her. She had a sip of wine with each toast and soon found herself feeling emotional. August was the last to speak. "Karina, I was really impressed with your moves on the surfboard today." Laughter broke out around the table. "Seriously, it takes a lot of courage to try something new. You are *fearless*, girl! Can't wait to see what you do next." He held up his glass and everyone did the same, toasting her, and Karina felt the warmth of red wine slide down her throat.

31 | karina

Her first morning at the house, Karina woke to a deep resonant gong. She felt weighted to her bed from the physical toll of moving and too much red wine the day before. But the sound continued, so she crept out to the hallway. Through the window and the darkness, she saw Micah standing outside next to a large gong as a crowd gathered on the lit patio.

Behind Karina, a door opened and August hurried past her down the stairs. "Morning meditation," he said. "Don't want to be late."

"What time is it?" she said, self-conscious in her thin T-shirt and shorts.

"Six. Don't worry, you'll get used to it." The gongs increased in frequency. Karina was reluctant to appear out of step with the group, so she trailed August down the stairs.

Outside, the chilly air raised bumps on Karina's arms. Everyone was seated in a grid-like formation, cross-legged with eyes closed. A stick of incense burned on the patio table, releasing a sweet fragrance into the air. Micah, standing at the front of the group, pointed to an open spot in the front corner of the patio, where Karina took a seat in the same position as the others.

"Close your eyes," Micah intoned in a low voice. "Follow your breath as it enters and leaves your body, making each breath deeper and longer than the last." Karina tried to focus on his instructions but found herself straining to discern which way he was moving, when he was close to her. The breathing of those around her was audibly heavy.

"Breathe." Micah modeled a long, deep breath. "Breathe in . . . breathe out." Karina tried to follow his rhythm. "Pay attention to your thoughts." He spoke in a voice that seemed to be right on her. Karina shivered again as a light breeze passed over her. She straightened her spine and pushed her shoulders back. "If there are intrusive thoughts, gently push them away," Micah said, from somewhere farther away. "They are not productive; they will not serve you."

Scattered, random thoughts entered Karina's mind: skimming the top of the water on the surfboard, the delicious burrito on the beach, her vacant apartment, James, Yoga Girl and her high ponytail, her little red Fiat, the photo of Karina and James at their picnic, the lizards and coconuts in Ecuador.

She was startled by the deep, reverberating sound of the gong again, as it rang three times. After its last echo faded away, she opened her eyes, feeling like a failure. The sun was rising now and the view of the distant hills was beautiful, with a light mist on the horizon. Micah nodded toward her as he sat facing the group. She folded her knees in front of her and wrapped her arms around them, mindful of her immodest attire.

"Karina," Micah said, "your first time meditating?"

She nodded. "I'm not very good at it."

He smiled. "You'll get better. It takes daily practice, to calm your mind and direct your thoughts. You'll have your breakthrough, and it will be beautiful when it happens." Micah turned to the group. "Does anyone else want to share thoughts about this morning's practice?"

August cleared his throat. "It helps . . . it helps center me. I find, on the days I can really focus during the morning meditation, it helps with the cravings."

Micah nodded as August spoke. "It helps you avoid thinking about getting high?"

August rocked a little side to side. "Not stop thinking about it, exactly

. . . but stop *wanting* it so much. It gives me strength to resist, I guess is what I'm saying."

Zoe watched him speak, a hint of a smile on her face. After everyone murmured approval for his confession, Zoe reached for his hand and squeezed it.

———

After meditation, Karina was desperate to crawl back into bed. But as Micah finished speaking, Zoe walked to the front of the group and began passing out yoga mats. Karina reluctantly unrolled one. She hadn't taken a yoga class since the one with James and Yoga Girl on the quad last year, and images of their two bodies intertwined kept coming unbidden to her mind as she stumbled through the next hour, trying to follow Zoe's guidance.

After yoga, Karina followed the others into the kitchen for breakfast. Chef Guy made two big pans of soft scrambled eggs, and Ericka ran a full loaf of whole-grain bread through the toaster. Karina offered to help, but when no one took her up, she poured herself a cup of coffee and sat down, yawning widely.

"Tired?" August asked, joining her with a plate heaping with food.

Karina nodded. "I think I need a nap."

"You'll get used to it." He chuckled. "I used to need nine or ten hours when I was gigging every night. Never got up before noon." He gestured to the pink- and red-streaked sky. "Missed all those beautiful sunrises for years. Here, it's so peaceful, I get by with five hours."

Karina found that hard to imagine, but if it was true, she supposed it would be helpful. After breakfast, Micah ran through the day's projects: weeding a field of crops, spreading fresh mulch in the citrus grove, mowing the front lawn, raking out the chicken coop. Karina approached Micah. "Hey, did you get those horse brushes? Maybe I can do that today?"

"Not yet. Maybe later, we can go together," Micah said. "Why don't you work on weeding today? You have a great eye for those little insidious ones."

It was eight o'clock when they began working outside, and except for a few water breaks, they worked straight through until after noon, when Karina began to feel hungry. "Should we . . . stop for lunch?" she asked Ericka.

"We don't usually," Ericka said, without looking up from the soil. "We don't stop during our work periods, so we can maintain focus and self-discipline."

Karina wasn't sure what to make of this, but she was reluctant to go back to the house alone when everyone else seemed content to keep working. She drank more water and tried to keep her mind off the gnawing in her stomach. Thankfully, by four o'clock, they were finished. Several people got into the pool to cool off, and Karina went inside to take a shower. She was still wearing the clothes she'd slept in, now covered in perspiration. All she wanted to do was get into bed and sleep for the night, but she was too hungry for that.

When Karina came back downstairs, the scent of grilling meat greeted her. She strategically took a seat with her back to the pool, where some were still swimming. A bowl of guacamole sat on the table and she dug in hungrily with a tortilla chip. Micah, holding a beer bottle, was monitoring lamb chops on the barbecue. Karina knew she should offer to help with dinner preparations, but she was too exhausted. They ate outside, everyone milling around, in casual conversation.

She turned to Micah to excuse herself, but before she could speak, he put a hand on her shoulder and said, "Karina, tonight you get to experience one of the most special things we have here, the Music Salon." Karina followed the others down the hallway, toward the sound of an electric guitar tuning up. The living room featured a large leather sectional, a drum set in the corner, guitars propped on stands and large amps on the floor. Unsure where to sit, Karina perched on one of the couch's wide leather armrests.

August was playing the electric guitar, and he moved from tuning up right into a solo. His left hand slid up and down the fingerboard while his right hand twanged on the strings. Karina didn't recognize the melody, but his virtuosity was clear. As August trailed off with a single blazing vibrato note, he nodded to Micah, standing behind the keyboard, who began to play, fingers dancing up and down the keyboard. August joined back in on the guitar, then Rufus, another resident Karina had met at Thanksgiving, blended into the harmony on bass. They all played together for a while, until finally Micah led several dramatic chords to close. Karina clapped along with the others but still found herself fading. The loud music was compounding her exhaustion and her head began to ache again.

Ericka leaned close to her and whispered, "Do you play anything?"

"Not really," Karina said. "A bit of clarinet when I was a kid." The clarinet her parents had bought for her twelfth birthday still sat on the top shelf of her closet back home. She'd been excited at first; it felt important to have a musical instrument of her own to carry back and forth to school, her name emblazoned on the case. She forbade Prem to touch it and yelled at him once when she found him on the floor of her bedroom with the clarinet in his mouth. "That is so gross!" she screamed, tearing it out of his hands. "Now I have to sanitize the mouthpiece and throw that reed away!"

Her father encouraged her to continue with band practice when their lives resumed after Prem's death. He dutifully drove her to school early, and though she went through the motions, she couldn't hold the clarinet without remembering the hurt look in Prem's eyes and the yelp that escaped from his throat as she pulled him across the room. When she told her dad that she wanted to quit a few weeks later, he didn't protest.

Micah called Zoe up, and she took a seat behind the drum set in the corner, sticks poised in the air. When the music picked up again, Karina managed to slip out of the room unnoticed. Feeling a strange brew of disappointment in herself, she settled into her bed. After having slept on the couch for so long, she'd forgotten the comfort of a bed, which felt safe again in this new space. Still, as she lay alone in the theater, Karina felt surrounded by a sea of the unfamiliar, struggling to figure out the daily routine and norms of her new home. As the music from below pulsed through the floorboards, Karina hoped it wouldn't take long to find the sense of belonging she had expected.

———

When Karina awoke in the middle of the night, the absolute darkness of the theater was unsettling, and it took a moment for her to remember where she was. Her head was aching and she desperately needed water. As she walked down the hallway, all the doors were open and the entire structure of the house was silent, asleep, breathing together. She crept down the staircase, gripping the banister carefully. In the kitchen, she drank a full glass of water and poured herself another. As she passed the living room again, half-lit by moonlight through uncovered windows, she was startled to see two figures lying on the couch, fully nude and entwined, with a kaftan blanket draped across their legs. One body was olive-toned and muscular, the other very fair. Neither face was visible, but she recognized Zoe's blond dreadlocks. Shaken by the sense that she was intruding, Karina returned quickly to her room and climbed into bed, only later remembering she'd forgotten to leave her door open.

32 | karina

It felt like she'd only been back asleep for a few moments when the gong sounded the next morning, and though she was still tired, Karina didn't allow herself to linger in bed. She quickly got dressed so she was prepared to join the others on the patio, determined to do better today. As she sat in meditation with her eyes closed, the fragrance of the incense coiled into her nostrils, bringing her back to childhood. She tried to concentrate on Micah's guiding voice as her mind rebounded between various thoughts. By the time Micah rang the gong again, Karina realized she had not truly heard anything he'd said and had again failed at meditating. Was this what it was like for Mom, when she sat in Prem's shrine for hours of prayer? How did she maintain her concentration all that time? Karina felt a new appreciation for her mother, for all those hours she spent in what had looked like nothingness but now seemed unattainable.

After a breakfast of Greek yogurt with homemade spicy cinnamon granola, Ericka said, "Hey, Karina, Micah said you know how to take care of the horse. Will you show me?"

The two of them walked down the path to the stables. "When did you come live here?" Karina asked.

"End of last summer, about four months ago," Ericka said. "It was a godsend, this place. Micah. I needed a safe haven and I'm so lucky I found it."

Karina glanced sideways at her as they approached the stables, where the horse was chewing on the front bar, eager to be let out. When she opened the stall, he ran into the field with a loud whinny. "How so?" She grabbed a rake from the tack wall and began shoveling out what appeared to be several days' droppings from the stall.

"I was in a bad situation. I'd been living with this guy—the love of my life, I thought." Ericka shook her head. "It was good in the beginning, but after a few months . . . He didn't treat me right. He had a temper." She looked at Karina. "It was bad. But I didn't have anyone to turn to. Not really on good terms with my family, know what I mean? And I know it's not smart—everybody warns you not to do this—but I grew apart from my girlfriends after being with him for a while. It was just so *intense*. It took all of me, you know?" Ericka offered to take the rake from her and continued cleaning out the stall.

Karina nodded, knowing too well that feeling of being all-in; how it could destroy you when the thing you'd handed yourself over to suddenly vanished, leaving a giant void in its place. She felt reassured that she wasn't alone in that, but also an unexpected flicker of gratitude that James had been decent, at least until the end. Karina opened a bag of fresh shavings to scatter on the ground.

"I was working at a juice bar on the beach where Micah and his friends surf sometimes, and they'd come in afterwards with their wet suits off to their waists, like half-peeled bananas." Ericka giggled. "The boss always made them sit outside so they didn't drip all over the floor. When things got worse at home, I started working at the juice bar more—for the money, and also just to get away. One day, Micah came to pick up his carrot-ginger juice, and he just stopped and looked at me, *really* looked at me. And he asked me why I was so sad." Ericka's voice cracked, her eyes shiny. "I burst into tears, and my boss was so freaked out, he told me to take the rest of the day off." She took a deep breath and exhaled. "Not really comfortable around too much estrogen, you know?"

Karina smiled as she refilled the water bucket.

"So, I took off my apron and sat outside with Micah and Justin and Cameron. Have you met Cameron, from the bike shop?"

Karina nodded, remembering Cameron had been a guest at Thanksgiving. At the time, Karina had been proud to be the first of that group to move in. Now, tossing fresh hay into the stall, she was ashamed of her pettiness.

"It was like this black storm cloud that had been hanging over me just lifted away a little bit. They were so kind. They made me laugh. I came to the Sanctuary that night for dinner." She looked over at Karina with a smile. "The next morning, I waited till he left the apartment, then I packed up my one bag and left. After two years of living together, it turned out to be just that easy. New home, new friends. Even took on a new name." Karina looked incredulously at her. "First, it was so he couldn't find me." Ericka stroked the horse's long neck. "But sometimes, when the answer comes easy like that, you know it's right. I'm telling you, Karina, this place is magic. Just let go and see what happens."

Late that afternoon, standing in the middle of the fields, Micah called out to them, "Group circle in an hour, folks."

"What's that?" Karina asked August, who was working near her. He'd rolled up the long sleeves of his shirt, revealing forearms marked with bold tattoos: a thick ankh symbol on his left arm, a bass clef on the right. She recognized that his was the body she'd seen entangled with Zoe the night before.

August raised an eyebrow. "Group circle? We do it a couple of times a week. Kind of a collective therapy session—a chance to keep ourselves honest and clear the air around here."

An hour later, they sat on the grass so that everyone was able to see one another. Micah plucked a fresh lemon from a nearby tree and held it in the air. "Same ground rules as always. Only speak if you have the lemon. And speak with complete honesty." Micah had told her that one of the cardinal rules at the Sanctuary was to ask a question like "How are you?" only if you genuinely had the time and desire to hear an honest answer. Similarly, you should not blithely say "nothing" or "fine" in response, as you'd been used to doing before.

David, one of the older guys in the house at almost forty, held up his hand and Micah tossed the lemon to him. He turned it over in his hand for a moment, then looked directly across the circle. "Justin, I feel like you're shirking your responsibilities in the field. You help a bit with the weeding or fertilizing, then wander off somewhere on the property and come back when the work is nearly completed. I had to say something, man, after today." David looked around at the others to explain. "He was taking a nap under that big oak tree on the other side of the hill. We can't be doing that."

"Speak directly to Justin," Micah said gently, "and speak only about your own feelings."

Justin held up his hand and David pitched the lemon at him. "I felt really violated today, man. You invaded my privacy. I feel like you're trying to control me, to impose yourself—"

"Remember to use 'I' instead of 'you,'" Micah reminded him.

The discussion escalated as David grew angry and impatient, and Justin became defensive. Karina was uncomfortable watching what felt like a private altercation between two people along with a gallery of observers, though there was also a bit of a voyeuristic thrill in it.

Ericka, who was always cheerful with everyone, spoke up. "Justin, I was disappointed when we went to the grocery store last week. You left me to go wandering through the produce section, tasting samples and chatting up the staff." Ericka's tone was nonconfrontational. Micah was nodding. "I was just disappointed you weren't really my partner." After she spoke, Justin's posture changed. He sat on the floor with his knees folded, his arms wrapped loosely around them, staring at a spot on the floor. Justin was the newest person in the house other than Karina, and his discomfort at this moment became hers. She made a mental note to be more helpful around the house with meals and cleanup, even when she was exhausted.

"Justin, how do you feel, hearing that?" Micah asked.

"Feels shitty, man." Justin scratched at his sideburn and shook his head. "I don't mean to be a free rider here, but I guess that's what I've been doing." He looked up now, around the circle. "It's no excuse, but it's just nice to be in a place where I can count on people, you know? Where everybody"—Karina was surprised to hear a crack in his gruff voice—"everybody takes care of me." He sniffed, brushed his nose roughly with his thumb. "I never had that before, you know, growing up with a drunk mom and no dad. Nobody ever gave a shit about me."

Karina felt her throat swell as Justin's voice caught, recognizing that sense of feeling alone, if not as neglected as he'd been. He cleared his throat and continued. "I'm not used to being able to count on people. I guess I was taking advantage of that." He hung his head and spoke the next words softly. "I'm sorry, people. I'm genuinely sorry. I'll do better."

Karina looked around the group, unsure how to react. To her surprise, it was David who stood up and crossed the circle. He reached a hand toward Justin, pulled him to his feet and gave him a bear hug. David braced his strong hands on each of Justin's shoulders and said, "I just want you to be the best you can be, man." Justin nodded, then Ericka stood to embrace him. Karina wondered if they were all expected to repeat this gesture and readied herself to stand, but Micah spoke up. "Let's take ten minutes and meet back here."

Micah, David and Justin huddled together, and Karina walked over to the patio and found August lighting up a cigarette. "Is that allowed?" she asked. August smiled wryly and shook his head. "Not usually, but I get a reprieve during group circle. So tense sometimes, I need something to take the edge off, you know?"

Karina nodded. She had just witnessed something remarkable transpire. Such honesty and self-revelation were foreign to her, and perhaps this was why she found herself so intrigued by it.

August turned his head to exhale. "Three cigarettes a week is still better than the pack and a half I used to smoke every day. At this rate, I'll be weaned completely by summer. I never liked to smoke in the summer anyway."

"Ah," Karina said, "so you're more of a seasonal smoker?" She smiled at August. It was a relief to discuss something light after the emotional intensity of group circle. "By the way, you were really great at the Music Salon last night."

August smiled and shook his head. "You know, Micah is like a musical *genius*. He plays four instruments totally by ear. He doesn't like people to know this, but he went to Juilliard for a few years before he moved out here."

"He did? Why wouldn't he want people to know that?" Karina asked.

August shrugged. "You know, Micah doesn't believe in labels. They get in the way of your authentic self. It's one of the reasons he started the Sanctuary, where we can all just be our best selves. Without all the crap out there." He nodded out to the horizon, encompassing the world outside their property.

33 | the olanders

FEBRUARY 2015

Keith entered the hotel ballroom shortly before the event was to begin and saw the event planner rushing from table to table, adjusting centerpieces. He couldn't help but notice her shapely figure in the snug black dress as she leaned over.

"Oh!" She stopped bustling when she noticed him and came over, breathless. "Everything looks good. The AV guys were here an hour ago and we double-checked all the equipment. The laptop's hooked up to the screen and . . . what else?" She glanced around the room, decorated with platinum tablecloths, elegant white and green floral arrangements and strategically placed up lights that created a soft, sophisticated glow. Large commercial cameras on tripods stood in the corners of the room, and glittering silver stars hung from the ceiling. Lining the entrance to the ballroom was a replica of the Hollywood Walk of Fame, with a star emblazoned with the name of each person on the company's management team.

"Looks great," Keith said. Brittany . . . Brandy . . . What *was* the girl's name? He'd only spoken with her a dozen times over the past few months as she organized this closing dinner for one of the firm's top clients. Vida had become the number one player in video editing software with its acquisition of a competitor, a transaction Keith had led and closed.

"Brianna?" one of the hotel's catering staff called out. "Do you want the cupcake tower set up before guests arrive or after dinner?"

Brianna. That was it.

———

Hours later, after two glasses of champagne and an earthy burgundy, Keith stood at the podium and praised Vida's CEO and management team for their visionary leadership and shrewd business acumen. After he showed a short film that satirized Vida's laborious acquisition process and generated much laughter and applause, the CEO replaced Keith at the podium.

Mack raised his glass. "I want to start out by thanking Keith Olander for closing this transaction, against many obstacles. Not only is he great at his job, but he's truly one of the good guys." Mack took a sip and everyone else followed suit, and the room resonated with the clinking of glasses and people calling out Keith's name.

One of the good guys. What did that even mean? In this crowd, the bar was pretty low. Keith wasn't an adulterer, he was generous at bonus time and he didn't yell at his people. But did all that add up to make him *good*?

What would happen if people found out about the SEC investigation? The reputation he'd worked so hard to build would be tarnished in an instant. Jaya had always warned him to be extra careful with every expense report, in every interaction with subordinates who might be sensitive to criticism. He'd always believed that she just didn't understand the culture of investment banking and the people who populated it—the crude language, the yelling at analysts like it was military boot camp, the punishment of long hours and work overloads that simply came with the territory. He hadn't yet told Robbie Weiss, his boss and CEO of the firm, but he would need to soon if the investigation proceeded. With heaviness settling in his stomach, Keith recalled his father's words: "Don't pre-worry. Deal with it when it happens." This had been his mantra every time creditors came calling or a business started heading south. And where did that advice get him? Keith always thought it made his father a coward, the way he shirked from his impending failures, but he supposed that depended on how you defined success.

———

Later, over drinks at the bar, Mack and the team ribbed Keith about the attractive bartender who kept flirting with him. Mostly married themselves, these guys loved to live vicariously through Keith, whom they imagined bringing home a different woman every night. They had no idea how it really felt to be alone in a hotel room, flipping aimlessly through TV channels to fill the few hours between work and sleep, knowing that no one was waiting for a good-night phone call from him or would anticipate his flight home the next day. These guys envied his freedom, but they didn't understand how draining dating could be—the dance of figuring out someone new, the mishaps of expectations and communication that inevitably arose. And it didn't sit right with him, to be seen as a swinger rather than a husband and father. It was a reminder that he'd failed at his most important life roles. Without satisfying the guys' prurient interests, Keith excused himself for the night on the pretext of his early morning flight.

Alone in his room, Keith stretched out on the bed and closed his eyes, trying to put his finger on what had left him feeling so unsettled. He wanted desperately to talk with someone about what was going on. Perhaps if he just shared the bad news, voiced his darkest fears, he would feel better. He couldn't tell anyone associated with his work, of course. Keith picked up his phone and began scrolling, realizing how few people on his VIP list weren't work related. He scrolled past his lawyer's name, Karina's (obviously not), and hesitated when he reached Jaya's. She was in India right now, but he wished he could speak to her as he used to. It had been four years since their divorce, but the aching loss of her in his life still felt nearly as strong. He shook his head. That person he was remembering was gone now. He didn't know how this Jaya would react, with her newfound sense of piety and righteousness. She may not have room in her mind anymore for the gray zone of Keith's life and work. She certainly didn't have room in her heart.

Approaching the end of his list, Keith's eyes alighted on his father's name, next to the same phone number he'd had as a child. There were so many numbers he used regularly now that he didn't know by heart, but this one was carved into his memory. He dialed and, predictably, his father picked up on the third ring.

"Hi, Dad," Keith said. "Did I call too late?"

"Nah," his father answered. "Just watching the Phillies in extra innings. How are you, son? Everything good?"

"Well, actually, not all good, Dad." Keith proceeded to explain, in layman's terms, what was happening with the SEC case. He admitted that he'd probably behaved rashly and made a mistake in conducting the trade, but he hadn't meant harm, hadn't been trying to commit large-scale fraud. Keith wasn't sure what he'd expected from his father, but it wasn't the uncomfortably long silence that followed his explanation.

When his father finally spoke, the first thing he said was, "You have a good lawyer, son?"

"I . . . yeah, I do. Carl's got a lot of experience in these cases." Keith fumbled through a response. "And I've already put aside a trust account for Karina, so she won't have to worry about paying for college or grad school." As soon as he said it, he felt himself petty for making this point with his father, as if to prove some superiority. "Listen, Dad. It'll be fine." Keith found himself trying to placate his father. "Anway, I know it's late there. I'll let you go."

After they said good night, Keith laid his head back against the pillows, feeling more unsettled than before. He tried to console himself that his father wasn't sophisticated in these matters. Keith shouldn't have expected him to understand. But another thought occurred to him, which he ventured to examine instead of instinctively pushing it away. His father certainly had his faults, as a man and a father, but he'd always been honest, if not always successful. In that aspect, perhaps, Keith had not matched his father's achievements at all.

———

In the five days since arriving in Pune, India, Jaya hadn't had one decent night's sleep, though she wasn't sure if this was due to the ten-hour time difference, the spartan cot on which she slept at a fellow devotee's home, or the fourteen hours a day she spent at the Guru's ashram. She woke each day at dawn when the pigeons began their guttural clucking outside and was so consumed with anticipation for the day ahead, she couldn't return to sleep. She had planned to come down here for a week after visiting her parents in Delhi, but had now extended her stay by a few more nights, thanks to the generosity of her host, Aparna.

Aparna was a widow only a decade senior to Jaya, though she looked much older. She had a slender frame, wore all-white saris and had long stopped coloring her hair, which she wore in a braid or bun. She had moved to Pune several years ago from Mumbai, after her husband had passed away, to be closer to the ashram. Her modest bungalow was a half-mile away and she spent most of her days at the ashram, sometimes traveling with the Guru's entourage to lectures in other regions of India. She was a cheerful and composed woman who seemed more inwardly fulfilled than many.

"Everything changed once I came here," Aparna told her. "Everything fell into line. My days, how I spend my time, the people who come into my life, like you."

"How . . . how do you support yourself?" Jaya felt awkward asking, but she was curious, and Aparna didn't seem to mind.

"I have a small stipend from my husband's pension," she said. "Everything else, God takes care. Guru takes care." She bobbed her head side to side. "Everything is taken care." Jaya was fortunate, she realized, to be able to come here without any financial sacrifices, thanks to Keith's support.

The ashram served simple vegetarian meals twice a day, not only to devotees but to visitors who stopped in. Some days, the Guru gave a lecture, but every day people streamed in to pay their respects and make offerings. There were large donation boxes bolted securely to the ground at each entrance, which were cleared out each night. The Guru's books and recordings of his lectures were sold from a small shop inside the ashram, as well as framed photographs like the one that hung in Jaya's temple room back home. It was all very pragmatic, the need to fund Guru's considerable operations.

For Jaya, being here in the wellspring of his energy was a powerful experience. Everyone at the ashram, from the floor sweeper to the Guru's inner circle, seemed to reflect and compound his radiant presence. Here, sitting for hours in prayer and meditation, not alone but surrounded by others of the same mind-set, Jaya felt she was reaching new heights of spirituality that went far beyond the rote religious rituals she had practiced as a child. It was remarkable to her how, after a few days living amongst these new people in Pune, she could feel bolstered in a way she hadn't when she'd lived with Keith for twenty years.

She no longer had to look for Prem reincarnated in other individuals; his spirit simply inhabited her. Jaya felt his presence so strongly at times, it was as if he was right next to her, telling her something funny to make her laugh out loud, guiding her gently away from the dark abyss of sadness. She marveled with his childlike wonder at the tendrils of the jasmine blossoms that flowered outside the ashram. Her days were unhurried, full of the small pleasures he used to enjoy while the rest of them bustled around him—an unexpected sun-shower, a comfortable pillow, a midday nap. In the wake of Prem's death, her abiding love for her son had had no home. Now she had found one, and he was with her everywhere. She felt blessed to have Prem in her life for eight years, and even after his death, she was still learning from him.

When Jaya returned to her parents' home in Delhi, she was eager to share with her mother everything she'd experienced. "Next year, I want to go back for a whole month. Maybe you can come?" Jaya expected her mother, who'd always been spiritual, would love the idea.

"Ah, I don't know, Jaya." Her mother sighed. "After so much shifting around my whole life, I just want to stay in one place these days. Besides, I have my bridge club, my embassy docent tours, my dance lessons for the little girl downstairs. My life is so full, how can I leave everyone for that long? How can *you* do that?" Her mother looked at her with an expression of concern, lines furrowed deep between her brows. "I worry this is getting to be too much, Jaya. It's one thing to have daily prayer in your life, as we've always done. It's another to dedicate your whole life to it like this. It's not . . . balanced."

"It brings me peace, Ma," Jaya said. "And it's not my whole life. I have other things."

"What else do you have?" her mother asked. "No work, no husband, and you've barely talked about Karina this whole trip."

Jaya felt the words like a slap across the face. Is that what her mother truly thought of her? After all, it was her mother who had reintroduced her to spirituality. "Karina's fine," Jaya said. "She's . . . busy with her own life; she's basically an adult now. She doesn't need me anymore."

Her mother smiled and reached out a hand. "Don't fool your-self, darling. She will always need you." She squeezed Jaya's forearm. "I'm not saying you have to stop your spiritual journey. I know it has brought you some peace. Just don't make it *everything*. You deserve to have more in your life. Look at Dev: he has a family, a career, a whole *life.*" Jaya felt herself shrink from the comparison to her brother, who had made different choices, marrying an Indian woman, living in a cosmopolitan city. How would her life have been different if she'd made such choices? Would her marriage have survived? Would they have had more family support? It was never far from mind that Dev had more than she did, with his two children and solid marriage, but now it struck her with force.

On her way home from India, Jaya stopped over in London to spend a few days with Dev and his family. Her niece and nephew were teenagers now, straddling the age Prem would have been. It was a painful reminder, but Jaya pressed herself to face the feeling, and gradually, she felt its grip on her loosen. They were a delight, these sprightly young people who navigated their way around the city by tube. Dev and Chandra returned in the evening with take-away from one of the restaurants a few blocks away: Chinese, kebabs, and the best curries Jaya had tasted outside India. Their lives weren't perfect: their jobs were stressful, and Chandra's elderly parents, with their traditional Indian expectations, lived nearby. But there was an abundance, an overflowing richness to their lives that made stark the contrast her mother had pointed out.

It wasn't until the plane ride back to California, as she reflected on her mother's words that Karina would always need her, that it struck Jaya her mother might also have been referring to their own relationship, that Jaya would always need her mother, and this seemed to ring true.

34 | karina

After a few weeks, Karina grew accustomed to the pattern of her days at the Sanctuary. Every morning started at 6:00, with meditation guided by Micah, followed by yoga with Zoe. Despite her initial resistance to the practice of yoga, Karina grew to enjoy Zoe's classes. The ritual of saluting the sun each morning as it rose over the serene terrain; the conscious work with her body, becoming aware of both its strengths and limitations; the floral aroma of incense, reminiscent of the temple where her mother took her and Prem for special occasions—all these components resounded in some deep, untapped part of her that had been hibernating in her core since childhood, since birth. The culture of her mother's country was, for once, relevant to her: the sense of unity in body, soul and nature aligned. Karina realized what she had been missing before, the utter rightness that came from a whole that fit together as it should. At the Sanctuary, she could be herself for the first time, not hide parts of herself or try to make up for what she lacked.

The daily meditation sessions, however, continued to be difficult for her. The more time she spent sitting quietly and thinking, the more her mind was troubled by disturbing memories she had long ago buried. She saw the swimming pool with the inflatable gray raft floating in it, and Prem's thin brown arm extending from underneath. She heard the screaming of her own voice, the ringing in her ears. She felt the

211

cold, clammy skin of Prem's arms, his fingertips wrinkled and white. She felt the crack of his thin ribs as she pumped his chest, his damp cheek against hers as she tried to convey life from her body to his. She felt the raw, burning sensation in her throat from screaming. And she could not forget the sight of her mother draped over Prem's lifeless body, nor the disappointment in her eyes when she looked up and saw her. The meditation sessions left Karina feeling vulnerable in a way that didn't seem to lessen over time. She found herself pondering how long it had taken her mother to learn to sit silently like this. What did she reflect upon, all those hours in Prem's shrine room?

Fortunately, the rest of the day was always so busy, she could push those thoughts aside. When she wasn't scheduled at NatMark, she worked with the others at the Sanctuary, rotating through the outdoor tasks of tending to the chickens, the beehives, the vegetable crops and the fruit trees, and churning the compost pile. Twice a day, she went down to the stables to care for the horse: brushing him, feeding him, cleaning his stall and turning him out in the field. And, with thirteen residents and assorted visitors, the house chores of cooking meals, cleaning and laundry seemed never to cease. In comparison, working at NatMark felt leisurely, even though she had taken on busier daytime shifts now that she didn't have a class schedule to work around. The six or eight hours passed quickly, and she was proud to bring home groceries with her employee discount. August whooped when she walked in one day with a ten-pound bag of navel oranges that were marked down, and Chef Guy loved the knobby Jerusalem artichokes and seasonal persimmons she managed to find.

Throughout each day, Karina moved from one task to the next until she was physically and mentally exhausted. She was used to feeling tired all the time and fortified herself with coffee many times a day. Accustomed now to skipping midday meals while she was working outside, she loaded up with a big breakfast as the others did. The only time of day she was alone was in her theater bedroom, during those short windows between falling asleep and waking up. She knew she would soon share her room with others—as everyone else in the house did except Micah—when new residents were invited to join. Still, she loved being part of this community, of feeling as if she belonged. There was always someone to share meals with, to work alongside, to speak openly with. She had nearly forgotten what that sense of closeness was like, with her family Before.

Karina called her parents every weekend while she took a long walk around the grounds. She always had some "facts" about the past week to share: test scores in chemistry, the paper she was writing on *Hamlet*, the new jicama slaw in the cafeteria. She didn't feel she was being untruthful, just reflecting the life they wanted for her, as she had always done. In high school, she hadn't told them she found relief in the tiny slices and punctures on her inner thighs. To keep the peace between her parents, Karina had also learned to keep their secrets from each other. Her real life, her real heart and experience, bore little resemblance to the persona she created for them. This dissonance, Karina told herself, was the price of living the life she chose.

———

"Karina," Micah called from outside one evening. "Come out here, you've got to see this." She went to join him on the back patio. It was late evening, but the glow outside was brighter than usual. Up in the dark sky, the moon was whole and seemed to be right upon them, its striations visible. Half the night seemed lit from its incandescence.

"Wow," she breathed. "It's beautiful."

"Full moon," Micah said. "We should do something to commemorate it." He looked around, his eyes panning the horizon and the grounds. "Come on, let's swim," he said, taking her by the elbow to lead her toward the pool.

August and Zoe had come out of the house to join them and were chiming in about the beauty of the moon. "Yeah, man. Let's swim under the stars. Under the full moon."

A cold fear flushed through Karina's veins. She shook her head at Micah. "I don't like swimming. You go ahead. I'll sit here." She wondered if she would even be able to watch. Nearly every morning in meditation, she found her mind returning to Prem's accident, exploring her role and the shadow of guilt that came with it. The memory of Prem had almost become closer to her now than in years past, when she had deliberately blocked it out.

Micah leaned against one of the stone pillars that marked the edge of the patio and pushed off his sandals. "Come on, I saw you surfing in the Pacific! You have to banish that kind of negative talk, Karina. It doesn't serve you."

She felt herself trembling and tried to calm her mind. He hadn't led her astray so far. And he had helped her get into the ocean. Perhaps it was time to do this, finally. "Okay," she said, turning back toward the house. "I'll get changed."

"What?" Micah laughed, pulling her by the hand toward him. "Seriously? Don't do that. It's so beautiful to swim naturally." He smiled, dropped her hand and pulled his T-shirt over his head.

It didn't have to be a big deal. Skinny-dipping wasn't a capital offense. The marks on her inner thigh had faded to the point they wouldn't be visible from a distance. Karina followed Micah down the steps toward the swimming pool. She stood next to a lounge chair in the far corner of the patio and undressed as slowly as she could. Zoe bundled her dreadlocks on top of her head, standing buck-naked by the side of the pool. August ran past her from behind and cannon-balled in, generating a splash that nailed everyone. Justin threw a beach ball to August, then jumped in himself. Karina rolled her clothes into a ball to hide her undergarments and turned to face the pool.

"Come on in!" Micah said. "It's not cold once you get used to it."

Karina sat on the edge of the pool, arms wrapped around her knees. A whiff of chlorine reached her nose and she held her breath against it. Her brain and nerve endings felt like they were on fire. She was shivering and fighting the desire to flee when she spotted Justin floating face down in the center of the pool. Her heart began to beat faster as she watched for what felt like several long moments. She tried to scream Micah's name, but no sound came out of her mouth. Terror began flooding her chest cavity. She stood up and stepped down to the first stair of the pool, then the second. The water level was up to her mid-calves when Justin spontaneously stood upright and shook his head rapidly, spraying water like a lawn sprinkler. "Dead man's float," he said to August, standing next to him. "Totally meditative."

Karina froze in place, her brain flooded with a potent mix of relief, fear, anger. Her breath came hard; tears were ready to burst forth. She turned quickly and climbed back up out of the pool. A distant part of her mind heard Micah call, "Karina, what?" but she didn't look back as she grabbed a towel, wrapped it around herself and ran toward the house, leaving her carefully wrapped clothes behind.

She ran up the stairs and into the bathroom, where she locked the door and ran the shower at its hottest setting. Her breath was still coming fast, her heart racing. The bathroom filled with steam; when she took in a big, deep lungful, she began to cough. She ran cold water from the bathroom faucet and drank directly from the tap. When she looked up, the mirror was covered in condensation. She drew a big heart on it with her finger. "You're okay, Kiki," she said to her partial reflection, then dropped the towel and stepped into the hot shower.

She scrubbed at her body with an orphaned loofah and every bath product that lined the shower wall, until the chlorine on her skin was replaced by mango, kiwi, coconut and cocoa butter. Eventually, the water ran tepid, then cold, and she reluctantly turned off the faucet, feeling as if she was breaking a spell, and this made her cry all over again. Her eyes burned, her head throbbed and the pain of it was the only thing that stopped her from crying more.

She cracked the bathroom door open and, hearing loud music coming from the salon downstairs, felt relieved she wouldn't have to face anyone. She crept quietly down the hall to her room and pushed open the door. Inside, a single lit lamp illuminated Micah's figure lying atop her bed, his legs crossed at the ankles and hands clasped across his chest.

"I was worried," he said, without turning to look at her, and she was grateful for this small mercy. "What happened out there?"

She sank down on one of the plush velvet chairs that had formerly populated the room, several feet away from the bed. "Nothing," she said, then caught herself just as Micah turned his head toward her. She sighed. "I just didn't think that was funny, what Justin was doing."

"Floating in the pool?" Micah asked.

"Dead man's float, he called it," she said, unable to control the sharp edge in her voice. "It wasn't funny."

"I don't think he meant it to be funny," Micah said. "He was just doing something that felt good to him. Meditative, I think he said."

She snorted out a rude chuckle and shook her head. Then, to her horror, she started crying again, big fat tears rolling down her cheeks like children racing down parallel slides at a playground. She was gulping for air, her breath ragged and punctuated by cries coming from low in her throat. Then she was rocking, forward and back, putting a hand on her forehead, because a hand needed to be there, but it wasn't cool like her mother's, and brought no relief. She felt her hand replaced by Micah's, soothing against the fire that raged inside. Micah pulled her out of the chair and onto the floor, where he held her, his arms wrapped around her, rocking with her. When she stopped crying, they were still in this position, lying sideways on the floor.

And she told him about Prem. This time, she shared everything. Not only that she was the one to discover Prem and could not save him, but her slow-motion realization that she had caused this unspeakable thing to happen. She was the one who had neglected her baby brother and his innocent pleas to go swimming that day. She was responsible for the pain that transformed each of her parents in their own way and led to the ultimate dissolution of her family.

"You've been punishing yourself ever since, haven't you?" Micah stroked her hair from behind.

Karina closed her eyes. "I used to do things to . . . hurt myself. And that actually made me feel better for a while. Isn't that fucked up?" She gave a wry laugh.

"Look at me." Micah turned her around to face him. She expected to see his pity but met only compassion in his eyes. He placed his palms on either side of her head. "It wasn't your fault."

She shook her head, tears streaming down her cheeks.

"It wasn't your fault. You were just a kid."

"Then whose?" She had never voiced this before, the unyielding blame she'd absorbed.

"Well, your parents for one, for putting you in that position," Micah said. "And for neglecting you afterwards. That's why they can't help you with this. They have their own pain consuming them. But you have me. You have all of us now." He held her in a tight embrace, and she allowed herself to stay there until her tears ran dry.

"You've crossed an important barrier, Karina," Micah said. "You allowed yourself to look at the pain in your past, to look at it head on and say, *You don't have power over me. You don't define me.*" He looked deeply into her eyes.

She nodded, holding his gaze.

"You know why that is? Because you've opened yourself to the message, to the power of being here and living in this way. You know you deserve something greater than what you've had until now. You're destined for it."

He stood up and walked past her, closed the door to her bedroom and locked it. He leaned his back against the door and, as if by magnetic force, she was drawn to him. "I know what you're feeling," he whispered, reaching out to caress her cheek with the lightest touch. "It's undeniable, between us." They kissed, and soon they were on her bed, the culmination of so much heat simmering between them. Micah was confident as his hands moved over her body, yet gentle as she knew he would be. Afterwards, she began to cry again, but it was from a rush of emotion and gratitude. Karina did feel as if she had crossed a threshold, leaving behind Henry, James, college, her razor blades and everything else that had plagued her. Before they fell asleep, she rose to open the door, but Micah told her to leave it closed. That night, as she lay watching him sleep, she was struck by her fortune: to have met Micah when she did, to have the power of his love and presence in her life.

———

The next morning, Karina woke to find Micah gazing at her. "Serotina," he said.

She looked at him quizzically.

"*Serotina*," he repeated, "is the Latin word for 'late-flowering.' You see it associated with a lot of fruit trees—plum, wild cherry. I was thinking it's a beautiful name. For you."

"For me?" Karina laughed. "I already have a name."

"You have to be brave about crafting your own life now, your own story, not just accepting one that was given to you. You're moving on from the past, from that person who suffered such trauma." He tucked a strand of hair behind her ear. "And 'late-flowering' has such a lovely connotation. It means: be patient, the best part's still coming. It's very pretty. Serotina." He smiled at her. "Maybe Sero for short, like Sara."

Karina smiled back at him. She had, of course, spent years as a child wishing for an easy American name. "Okay, I'll think about it."

———

The next afternoon, during group circle, Micah sat across from her and held her eyes. "Today, we're going to talk about pain," he said to the group. "Each one of us carries pain around inside. And the more we hold that pain in, the more it corrodes us. But it doesn't have to be that way. Today, Karina is going to be very brave and share her pain with us." Micah smiled and nodded toward her.

She took a deep breath and began.

By the time she finished, she was crying. But so was Micah, and so was every other person around the circle. Ericka and Zoe sat on either side of her, clasping her hands in theirs. Across the circle, Justin stood up, walked over and knelt down in front of her. "I'm so sorry, Karina," he said, and leaned forward to embrace her. With his touch, a flood of emotion rushed out of her and she wept in his arms until she was ready to let go. Looking around the circle, she saw everyone around her feeling what she was feeling, sharing her pain. They were celebrating Prem's presence in her life and mourning his loss from it. They were dividing and diffusing and diluting her pain, the pain she had carried around with her for so long. She had mistakenly thought that if the people who knew and loved her best—Dad, Mom, Izzy (indeed, the same people who had known Prem best)—if *they* couldn't help lessen her pain, then no one could, ever.

But, as Micah had explained to her the previous night, the Sanctuary was here for her, not only to share food and work and joy, but to share pain and grief as well. She didn't have to feel guilty for reminding them of something so painful. She didn't feel like she owed them a certain kind of signal so they could stop worrying about her. They didn't want or need anything from her, except to hear and honor and share her pain, to lift up the community as a whole.

———

The next day, she and Micah worked together on caging and supporting tomato plants that had grown to be over five feet tall. "I'm really proud of you for sharing yesterday," Micah said. "How do you feel now?"

"I feel . . . lighter," Karina said. "I didn't realize I was carrying so much around with me, all these years. And now, I just feel unburdened."

Micah handed her the roll of twine. "Told you."

"You did." She smiled, snipping the twine with clippers. "I've been thinking. I am ready to leave all that behind—the person who carried that story and all that pain for so many years. I'm ready to leave it all. Even my name."

Micah smiled, took the twine and clippers from her hand and dropped them to the ground. He pulled her close and put his lips near her ear, kissing it through the brush of her hair, and whispered her new name, Serotina. And as he spoke it, it became hers, wholly.

35 | prem

I'm not sure why Kiki finally decided to tell everything. Maybe she needed all those people around her to soak up the hurt she felt. Or maybe she just got tired of carrying it around inside her for so long. She thinks these people she's living with are special. She never gets annoyed even though she's with them all the time, day and night. And she's much nicer about sharing the bathroom with them than she ever was with me. But as far as I can see, they're just like everyone else: they still worry about fitting in with the group, and the guys still fart in their sleep.

Kiki doesn't really seem like the sister I knew. I'm not sure I like this new person, but the truth is, everybody else in the world keeps growing and changing while I stay the same. I don't know how I would have changed during the past six years if I was still alive. Maybe I'd have glasses, or braces, or I'd even be publishing my first graphic novel now. This makes my family the saddest, when they think about all the what-ifs and how I would have turned out. They imagine only the best things happening to me, and feel cheated.

But as I watch my friends grow up, I know it might not have turned out all good for me. I could be like Tommy, who punched a hole in the wall and got sent away to military school. Or Brendan, whose parents yell at him every time he gets a B, so he chews his fingernails until they bleed. Or I could just be like everyone else my age, embarrassed about my pimples and nervous around girls, and frustrated when no one understands what it's like to be me. It's not right for my family to play the what-if game, so I don't either.

Even though I don't grow any older, I watch everyone else and I've learned a lot. Dad still thinks of me as being eight years old, and Mom looks for me everywhere. Karina was growing me in her mind for a while but now she's stopped.

I don't get what's so important about growing up anyway. All that worry and work. Maybe I'm kind of lucky I get to stay my favorite age forever.

I try to imagine how we would all be together as a family if I hadn't gone swimming that day. The thing I loved best about my family was the togetherness. Like the time we went to a drive-in movie for an old-fashioned experience (according to Dad). The radio was crackly, and Kiki and I were fighting over the pillows in the back seat, and I spilled vanilla milkshake all over myself and was sticky the rest of the night. All those things went wrong and we *still* had so much fun. I remember laughing at the movie and resting my head on Kiki's shoulder when I got tired, and Dad carrying me out of the car and up to my bed. Those times the four of us were together, that's what I miss the most.

We are all alone now. Mom, Dad and Kiki each have their own lives. They don't see each other much. They hardly ever talk, not about anything important. Kiki doesn't tell our parents the truth about what she's doing, and the truth is growing bigger in the background, like the giant alien ship looming behind the Space Rangers captain. She doesn't ever talk to them about me. In a way, I have it the best, because I can still be with each of them when I want to, but they can't really be with me. And they've stopped really being with each other.

I don't know about this new group of friends, but maybe Kiki is finding togetherness with them. Maybe they can be like her family since ours is gone.

36 | serotina

Micah was poring over some paperwork at his desk while Sero waited for him in bed. "Anything I can help with?" she asked.

Without looking up, he said, "Not unless you have an extra 30K lying around." He closed the file folder and shoved it into the desk drawer. "I was really hoping to get those solar panels installed before summer, but it's not looking good."

Sero had been contemplating how she could contribute to the Sanctuary in a meaningful way, beyond purchasing groceries at NatMark with her employee discount and caring for the horse. "I have some money in my savings account," she said as Micah joined her. "My security deposit, plus what my dad gave me for this semester—about ten thousand dollars. It's not enough, but it's a start?"

Micah, his arm around her shoulders, pulled back to look at her. "You would do that?"

"Sure," she said. She didn't need that money for school anymore. Though now she was reminded that she would have to, at some point before summer, tell her parents about withdrawing from college. She pushed that thought away. "I don't pay for much, other than groceries. Maybe the others can chip in too and we can get enough?"

"They already have. That's how we collected the first half for the down payment," Micah said. "You know everyone with outside jobs contributes their paychecks to our collective living expenses. And that's just enough to get by, truthfully. Some months are a little tight."

She noticed the lines on Micah's brow and thought for the first time about the mechanics and finances of managing this place. Not everyone in the house had regular paying jobs. August and Zoe were in a band that played gigs on evenings and weekends. Others, like Ericka, had shown up without a penny, and now worked only at the Sanctuary. They grew most of their own produce and had the chickens. David went to the local farmers' market most Sundays to sell their extra organic eggs and produce at a steep markup.

"I've been working on another idea, to bring in some additional income . . ." Micah trailed off.

"What is it?" she asked. Micah remained silent, stroking her bare shoulder with his fingers. She looked up at him. "Tell me."

He studied her for a few moments, as if he was trying to decide something. Then he sat up. "Sero, I'm going to share something with you, because I trust you. I *can* trust you, right?"

"Of course," she said.

He nodded. "Put your clothes on."

She followed him through the quiet house, out the back door and down a few stone steps to an exterior door she hadn't noticed before. He drew a key from his pocket to unlock it and led her into a brightly lit basement. It was a cavernous space separated into a few rooms, empty but for two folding rectangular tables, the kind her parents had kept in the garage for backyard parties. On each table were a dozen potted plants. Sero took a few steps closer, examining the distinctive leaves. "Is that . . . ?"

Micah smiled. "The purest, organic medical-grade marijuana."

She looked at him, unsure if he was serious. "That's your income idea?"

"What you see there, fully grown and harvested, will go for about twenty thousand dollars. Imagine if we converted this entire space into a grow farm?" He spread his arms wide. "It could be ten, twenty times that. The previous owners used this as a wine cellar, so it already has its own temperature and humidity controls."

"Don't . . . don't you need a license for that?" Sero felt her heart beat quickly and leaned against one of the support pillars. "Yes." Micah pointed at her with his index finger, as if she'd landed on an important point. "Yes, we do, and we'll have one. It's in process." He put his hands in his pockets. "So, what do you think?"

She hesitated, unsure what to say or think. "I . . . suppose it's a good idea . . . if it's legal?"

"Well, it is legal in California now." Micah plucked a leaf from one of the plants and rubbed it between his fingertips. "These are absolutely top-grade premium seedlings from a reputable source. I got them in December. Should be flowering soon. But, Sero, you can't say anything about this. I trust you, but no one else knows."

She nodded. As they returned to his bedroom, the secret and the fact he had entrusted her with it filled her with pleasure.

——————

The next evening, after mulling over the idea all day as she worked outside, she went to Micah with the questions that had been edging into her mind.

"Tell me again why you like this idea? Aren't you worried about the risks?"

"Well, first off, it's no riskier than growing and selling any other crop, now that it's legal," Micah said. "Growers and dispensaries are licensed, product is tested at independent labs, everyone pays taxes—a totally legitimate industry.

"Second, it's a lot more profitable than any other crop. That vision we have, of building a zero-impact community that can be replicated as a model around the world? Well, fueling a big dream costs money. We have to fund those solar panels, drill another well on the property, all of it." Micah tilted his head and smiled. "And that is where your expertise comes in. Hydroponics and low water usage."

"And we have a license?" she asked.

"Yes, I told you. It's in process." He kissed her gently on the lips. "What, you don't trust me?" he said playfully. He kissed her again, pressing her mouth open with his tongue, and Serotina felt the effect of this vibrate through her body. She thought of how he'd helped her to get into the ocean and open up in group circle with her darkest secrets. Of course, she trusted him. "You worry too much," he whispered. "You have someone to catch you now."

———

The next morning, after meditation, yoga and breakfast, Serotina went upstairs to get dressed for her shift at NatMark while everyone else went outside to work. Before showering, she retrieved her laptop from under her bed, where it remained most of the time. She began to research growing cannabis plants, jotted down some notes and continued to think while she worked at the grocery store. By the time she saw Micah again that evening in his room, she was eager to share with him what she'd learned. "You said those plants are about six weeks old?"

Micah nodded. "I've been keeping the lights on eighteen hours a day, turning them on before meditation and off before I go to sleep."

Serotina flipped through her notes. "So, if we switch to a twelve-hour light cycle, they should go into flowering state and be ready to chop down and dry in a couple months. And if we add thousand-watt bulbs to that space, we can increase the yield." She looked up at him. "If our yields are as high as I've been reading, we can generate a half-pound from each plant . . . What does that translate to?"

"Premium grade sells for over a hundred dollars an ounce, so that's . . ." Micah reached over to the nightstand and pulled a mobile phone out of the drawer.

"Almost a thousand dollars a plant, and . . ." Her mind starting blurring with the numbers.

Micah tapped at the screen for a few seconds and turned it toward her. So many zeroes. "How many do you think we could fit down there?"

"I'd have to measure the space, but we should be able to fit a lot if we're methodical about it," she said. "Can we get more?"

Micah smiled. "As many as you need, darlin'."

"Since the full cycle is four to five months, we should probably have multiple cycles going, so we always have some maturing at different times, a steady supply." Her brain churned as she thought through the growing cycle and the systems from the Botany Lab she could put in place. For a moment, her mind registered that it was crazy that she was thinking all this about *marijuana*.

Micah leaned forward, took her face between his palms and kissed her. "You're amazing, Sero. I knew you were the right person for this."

"We can get the solar panels." She smiled.

"We can get the solar panels," Micah repeated. "And the dairy cows. And another composter. And maybe some heavy-duty farm equipment. We can get it all." Micah closed his eyes for a moment. "You'll have help," he said. "Jasmine can help you set things up and take care of the plants. Rufus is building a website to start processing orders as soon as we're ready."

"I thought no one else knew about this?"

"Yeah, just the three of you. Jasmine hooked us up with the seedlings from her cousin near Sacramento who's been growing for years. And Rufus is our computer whiz. But I still want to keep it quiet for now. I don't want any hurt feelings because I chose you to lead this." He kissed her lightly. "We're under some time pressure, though," he added. "We made a big investment getting the Sanctuary off the ground and we have a lot of bills to pay. I'm counting on you." He closed her eyes with his thumbs and kissed each of them in turn. When Sero opened her eyes, Micah was looking at her as if she was the most important person in the world—the *only* person in the world—and the feeling stirred in her was one she wanted to preserve for always.

The basement could only be accessed by the side door on the exterior of the house, so it wasn't hard to be discreet. Serotina designated one room of the basement to house the existing plants through their flowering state, which required a twelve-hour light cycle. The second room would house new seedlings through their six-week vegetative state with eighteen hours of light. She and Jasmine calculated how many new seedlings they could accommodate and placed an order for the first two hundred with her cousin, who would drive them down the following weekend in exchange for cash payment from Micah.

On her days off from NatMark, instead of working the fields outside, Sero drove for hours to hydro stores in outlying areas and purchased special lights, irrigation tubing, timers, feed drums and other supplies for their operation, using the credit card her father had given her. If he asked about her purchases, which he never did, she would tell him they were supplies for the Rancheria Community Garden she'd mentioned. She spent fourteen-hour days researching, driving and working. Her arms and back ached from hauling bags of cocoa fiber and equipment, but she felt propelled by the importance of this project for Micah, for *all* of them.

After the shipment of new seedlings arrived, she and Jasmine meticulously set up the tables, overhead timed lights, and drip hoses for irrigation and feeding solution. "This is amazing," Micah said when he saw the setup. "*You're* amazing." He pulled her toward him and kissed her hard on the mouth.

Bolstered by his praise, Sero went down to the basement to inspect the seedlings every morning after meditation and yoga. She checked the soil with a copper probe and measured the air humidity, making any necessary adjustments before going upstairs to breakfast. She charted the plants' growth so she could plan growing cycles and predict yield for the whole operation. It was an unexpected joy to be working with plants again, the way she used to at the Botany Lab, and to use her mind in a way she didn't realize she'd missed at NatMark. Her days began to have greater purpose, as she felt like she was truly contributing in a meaningful way to this place she believed in so strongly.

37 | serotina

After a tiring shift at Natural Foods Market, Serotina turned her car into the long, climbing driveway that always helped her transition to the mind-set of being back home at the Sanctuary. As she parked, she saw Jeremy and Micah standing at the edge of the drive, each holding a large shovel. She pulled two grocery bags out of her trunk and, drawing closer, saw they were digging up the interlocking paver stones that composed the driveway. A patch of about ten square feet had been cleared, with dirt, stones and grass tufts scattered everywhere. Underground pipes were exposed beneath the surface.

"What's going on?" she asked.

"Problem with the plumbing," Micah said, with a smile. "We're trying to find it."

Jeremy lodged his shovel under a stone and pried it up. "Tree root probably made its way into a pipe."

"We had to shut off the water for a while," Micah said. "But there are buckets inside.

"No problem." Sero headed into the house, impressed with their resourcefulness.

In the kitchen, Chef Guy kissed her on both cheeks when she handed him a paper bag of fresh wild mushrooms. As she was helping to prepare dinner—grass-fed beef tenderloin with a sauce made from the mushrooms, scalloped potatoes and grilled asparagus—water suddenly sputtered out of the kitchen faucet, then began to flow freely. Everyone in the kitchen cheered.

With some time before dinner, Sero walked down to the stables. "Hey, Buddy," she said as the horse greeted her with a low nicker. She'd been using "buddy" as a nickname but decided it was as good a name as any, so she'd made it official. She took out the curry comb and brush she'd purchased earlier in the week, stepped into the stall and began grooming his thick coat. She thought again of calling Izzy, but Sero didn't know where to start explaining her new life, and she wasn't sure Izzy would understand. Instead, she just snapped a photo of her with Buddy and sent it to her.

That night at dinner, Sero clinked her wineglass with a fork and waited for the conversation to settle down. She had grown into the role of Micah's right hand, whether because of the confidential project with which he had entrusted her, their romantic relationship or both, and it was a responsibility she relished. Sero held up her glass. "A big thanks to Micah for fixing our plumbing problem."

"Yeah, I had no idea you were so handy, Micah," August said. "Plumbing *and* keyboards, man, that's a unique combination."

Micah smiled, shaking his head. "Well, it's not fixed, unfortunately. I'll have to let the landlord know. Hey, at least it's nothing important, right? Not like we need water to survive." Sero smiled at how positive he always seemed to be, even in the face of adversity.

———

After nine weeks under the twelve-hour light cycle, the first few plants Micah had originally shown Sero had grown to full height, finished flowering and were ready to be dried. She and Jasmine cut them down and hung them from the basement ceiling. Sero impatiently checked the plants every day, but just as she'd read, it took a full two weeks until they were completely dried. She trimmed the first plant herself, using small clippers to separate the buds from the stems and leaves. The largest buds could be sold at a premium price, while the smaller ones could be rolled into cigarettes, and the leftover clippings used in edible products. After she showed Jasmine how to trim, it took both of them the rest of the day to finish the batch, and Sero's neck was sore and her fingers cramped. But she felt proud of what she'd created and hoped Micah would be too.

He came down after dinner to join Sero, Jasmine and Rufus in the basement and, with great ceremony, pulled rolling papers out of his shirt pocket to roll the first joint. Sero had tried smoking weed a couple of times at high school parties but hadn't really enjoyed it, as it usually just made her sleepy. At college, her lab friends weren't into pot and neither was James. Now, watching Micah inhale deeply and with pleasure, she was intrigued to try it again. They passed the joint around; the first drag made Sero cough, and the second went straight to her head. "A1 quality weed," Micah declared, and they all shared high fives and hugs. After the others had left the basement, Micah said, "I'm so proud of you, Sero. You're making a real difference to this place. I don't know what I'd do without you." Sero flushed with pride and slept heavily that night, her dreams vivid and fantastic.

———

The next morning, she still felt a little high, and perhaps this was why she found herself deep in concentration during the morning meditation session. "Every element of our life is within our control," Micah said. "Just take the example of nourishment. We can choose not only what we eat and how much of it we eat, but also how quickly we eat and with whom we eat. We can even choose whether or not to eat. The practice of fasting teaches us to tolerate discomfort. It shows us the value of disciplining ourselves. That's why we don't break from our work outside to eat a meal. Fasting for periods of time helps focus the mind and our commitment."

Sero considered this. She enjoyed food greatly, but did she always stop to taste each bite, or to consider how the setting in which she ate affected her perception of the food? She might also be guilty of eating without forethought and indulging in the hedonistic pleasure of the food. As she resolved to try to think more consciously about this, she was startled by a ringing sound. She cracked open her eyes and saw Micah's legs moving swiftly through the group and into the house behind them. On the second ring, she recognized it was the doorbell, which was hardly ever heard since the door was always unlocked and someone was always at home.

Distracted from her meditation, Sero gave up and opened her eyes. She heard the front door open and Micah exchange harsh words with someone. A few moments later, Micah returned, continuing his discourse on the value of self-discipline. Sero snapped her eyes shut.

Later that evening, when Sero brought up the subject of that morning's meditation, Micah was curt with her, unwilling to engage in further discussion. "I'm sorry, Sero, I'm just tired," he said. "I have a migraine and I haven't been sleeping well. I think it would be best if we slept in our own beds tonight." He kissed her gently, holding her shoulders.

"Okay, sure. I hope you feel better," she said, wondering why he seemed so unsettled. As she was leaving his room, she turned back with a thought. "Hey, who was at the door this morning?"

"Hmm? Oh, nothing. No one," Micah said, uncapping a medicine bottle on his nightstand. Then, seeing her dubious expression, he added, "It was the plumber. He came by unannounced and I told him he'd have to make an appointment to come back."

"Oh." She smiled. "Well, let me know if I can help. I can meet him when he comes back." Sero returned to her room, reassured it was just the tedious responsibilities of the house troubling him, nothing to do with her. She wished she could share and lighten his burden, the way he had for her.

———

The next day, Sero was helping to prepare dinner when August walked into the kitchen with a pile of mail and handed it to Micah.

"Want some help?" August sidled up to Zoe, who was shucking corn.

"Thanks, babe," Zoe said, a mountain of fresh ears of corn piled in front of her. "We're grilling it with mayo and spices, Mexican style."

"Mmm." August nudged her shoulder with his.

Sero liked seeing August and Zoe happy and flirtatious together, especially compared to that first awkward time she'd caught them sleeping on the couch.

"Goddammit," Micah muttered under his breath, reading a letter he'd just opened from the stack.

His tone was barely audible, but Sero was acutely tuned into his frequency. She walked over to him. "What's wrong?" she asked softly, leaning forward.

Micah shook his head and she noticed the deep crease in his forehead. She found herself feeling angry at the piece of paper that had made him feel this way.

"Damn neighbors." He flung his right hand toward the sliding glass doors. "Creating problems again, complaining to the landlord. First, they wouldn't let us get dairy cows on our property, a full six acres away from their house, just in case some 'unpleasant odors'"—he put the offensive phrase in air quotes—"drifted over to their precious outdoor party space. You know *they* are the sole reason we can't produce our own dairy products? Those two people force us to go to the store every week to buy milk and yogurt!"

"They can do that?" She craned her neck to see the paper.

"And now," Micah said, shaking the paper in his hand, obscuring her ability to read it, "they're complaining about the roosters crowing too early in the morning, creating"—he modeled air quotes again—"'noise pollution' in an otherwise bucolic setting known for its peace and tranquility." His hands fell to the table.

Zoe glanced over at them with an inspecting look, as if Sero had done something to cause Micah's anger. Feeling uncomfortable and responsible—if not for his mood, then for not being able to improve it—Sero put her hands on his shoulders and began to knead gently.

"Do these rich folks even know what a real bucolic setting is?" Micah seethed, ignoring her efforts. "It's one that includes animals, with all their *sounds* and *odors*, for god's sake. What is *wrong* with these people?"

"Come on," Sero said, unsettled by her inability to calm him. "Let's go take a walk." She grasped his hand and led him outside. "Maybe we can move the coop somewhere farther away from the neighbors, so the noise doesn't reach them?" she offered, as they began walking.

Micah shook his head. "Sometimes I feel like that gladiator who has to run through a gauntlet, you know? Everywhere I turn, there's another obstacle. When we moved in, it was the oppressive community board not letting us get rid of the citrus trees, can you believe it? That total water-hogging grove, because it had 'local historical value.'"

"So, what did you do?" Serotina asked.

"I calculated the grotesque amount of water those citrus trees used and I mentioned that I'd spoken to a reporter at the *Union-Tribune*, who said it would make for an interesting story." Rancho Paraiso had been in the news the year before as the highest per capita consumer of water in the entire state during the unprecedented drought.

"See?" Serotina smiled at him. "You outsmarted them. And we've replaced all that with drought-tolerant plants and drip irrigation, which must translate to half the water usage, or less, right?"

Micah shrugged. "Then, that asshole landlord hounds me relentlessly every time the rent check doesn't arrive exactly by the first of the month. Can you believe that?" He looked over at her. "I mean, who decided the first of the month is fair anyway? Why should we be forced to pay for the entire month in advance? The rent check always gets there by the end of the month." Micah shook his head as Serotina tried to think of a response to this. "He's not very intelligent, that's the problem. Even after I showed him how the whole solar investment would pay for itself in five years, he didn't get it. He doesn't understand sometimes you have to spend money to make money. And there are more important things than money anyway, like taking care of the planet.

"Now," continued Micah, pointing over the hill to the property fence, "it's that damn neighbor who doesn't want us to have our chickens! What does he know, with his gas-guzzler cars and his fancy, wasteful mansion? Two people living alone in an eight-thousand-square-foot, three-million-dollar house, and he's trying to tell *us* how to live? We represent the opposite of everything that guy stands for. The Sanctuary houses thirteen people, soon *fifteen*."

Serotina wanted to ask about this—her room was the only one in the house with open space—but didn't want to interrupt. Micah seemed more animated now, his mood lifting.

"The Sanctuary is full of joy and life and warmth. We'll be water-efficient and carbon-neutral if we could just get rid of all these other obstacles." Micah stopped on the path. He turned to face her, resting his hands on his hips. "It takes a toll, you know. On me." He looked down at the earth, kicking it with his shoe. "I know everyone here is counting on me, and my body just absorbs all that responsibility."

Sero could see it, the weight of the burden in the lines etched into his brow, the twitching at the corner of his eye. She wrapped her arms around his waist, trying to dissipate some of that tension from his body.

His voice dropped to a whisper. "I wake up in the morning with an aching jaw, from grinding my teeth all night. I've never done that before now. And this." He pulled up one of his long sleeves to reveal a chalky white rash covering his arm. "Caused by stress."

"What can I do?" Serotina asked, interlacing her fingers with his. "Let me help you. I want to help."

"I know," Micah said, leaning forward to kiss her forehead. "I know everyone here will sacrifice when called upon, just like I am now. That's what keeps me going. We're going to win this, Sero. We're going to fulfill our vision here at the Sanctuary, together."

Sero smiled, believing him with all her heart. It wasn't his temper she'd seen just now; it was his passion. The same passion that had helped grow four hundred pounds of organic produce at the community garden, that had helped August overcome his addiction, that had helped Ericka leave her abusive relationship, that had helped her release the guilt she had been carrying since Prem's death six years before. His passion had made so many good things possible, and she felt honored to be witnessing it. She promised herself she would do whatever she could to help the Sanctuary succeed, to be the confidante and support Micah needed.

38 | the olanders

The only thing left for Keith to do was secure Jaya's signature on the transfer documents. His accountant had asked him repeatedly if he was certain about this; it was unusual to transfer a large quantity of assets to an ex-spouse without any court order to do so. Jaya would be able to do as she wished with the money, the accountant advised: spend it all, run off with a new man. Keith laughed at that proposition. Clearly, his accountant had never met a woman like Jaya. Yes, Keith was certain. As soon as Jaya signed those papers, he could take some solace from knowing that whatever happened to him, she and Karina would be taken care of in the future.

Establishing the accounts, orchestrating the transfers and completing the associated legal and tax paperwork had given him something productive on which to focus the past several weeks, as his attorney learned more about the SEC's case against him. Keith had, as his lawyer had advised, already set aside the requisite assets to cover the stock gain, potential penalty and legal fees.

"I'm trying to sit down with the SEC to discuss the civil charges, but they're taking their sweet time," Carl said. "The good news is the DOJ doesn't seem too interested in pursuing criminal charges, Keith. Lucky you're in Silicon Valley. They'd probably make you an example if you were in New York, but in California they're more focused on border crimes—drugs, immigration."

Keith felt hot shame at the mention of his fate in the same breath as those offenses. He hadn't thought about how he would explain the asset transfer to Jaya, whether he could bring himself to admit to her his questionable behavior. His *criminal* behavior. She had always thought him too ambitious and driven by money, and now she'd be proven right. And yet, he wished he could talk to the woman he remembered, who was smart, thoughtful, grounded. He missed having her insight and perspective in his life. But that woman was gone, and Jaya now seemed, at best, indifferent to him.

Keith couldn't even imagine telling Karina about this. She didn't have to know anything yet, and hopefully never would. The last time he'd seen her over winter break, she'd seemed happier than ever. She was bubbly and full of stories about the classes she'd finished, the community garden she shared with her friends, new recipes she had been trying out. He missed hearing from her as often now, but other parents had told him to expect this; it was all part of the normal development process, a sign that she was truly ready for life on her own.

———

Jaya sat across the table from Christophe, who had arrived only three weeks earlier from his native Ivory Coast. "Any work, I will do any work," he was saying earnestly. Christophe was thirty-eight and trained as a physician in Africa. But with three children and a wife to support, the modest savings with which he'd immigrated were quickly being depleted. He had applied to drive a taxi with every company in the Bay Area. Christophe was wearing a suit and tie, as he always did, though Jaya had told him he could dress casually for their meetings.

"Your first job is always the hardest to get," Jaya said, as she'd told many other new immigrants at the Refugee and Immigrant Support Center, where she volunteered. After returning from India, with her mother's reproach in mind, Jaya had decided to get involved in some new pursuits. *Seva*, service to others, was one of the pillars of the Guru's mission, to strengthen communities by supporting the most vulnerable members of society. Alongside other devotees, she tried working at a soup kitchen and a homeless shelter. It was uncomfortable interacting with strangers and making small talk after living in a world of her own making for so long. But then Jaya heard about RISC on the radio and sought it out on her own. She'd felt an immediate connection the first time she came here, and she became a regular volunteer.

"Missus, where are you from?" Christophe said, finally comfortable enough at this visit to ask her a personal question. "You are not from here, a . . . native American?"

Jaya smiled and did not correct his use of the term. "No, I'm a naturalized citizen, originally from India." After years of struggling with this question, she had decided that the definition of who she was and where she belonged was far broader than any one nationality. Jaya's true home was her inner consciousness that traveled with her everywhere. It was inside herself that she either felt at home or out of place. At first, she'd found this an unsettling thought, that her inner demons would follow her everywhere; but gradually, she came to find comfort in the idea. If she invested the time and energy to follow the Guru's teachings and progress along the path toward a higher consciousness, it was something she would always have, that could never be taken from her. Her essential humanity was untethered to geography, place, even to people. In this way, she had made some peace with being so far from her parents and Dev's family, and even took strength in knowing her lattice of support was as expansive as the earth.

At RISC, Jaya helped individuals acclimate to the United States, navigate the systems of government they needed to use and get settled in a new life. The work she did here wasn't complicated: filling out leases and driver's license applications and other essentials of American life. It was, as they used to call it in her previous role at the Policy Institute, small-scale work—serving one person at a time. The institute hadn't funded programs like this because they were not scalable; their growth was restricted by the supply of individual volunteers like her. Jaya's previous job had been to seek out effective programs that could be expanded to serve larger populations quickly, through technology or grassroots efforts. In that world, she'd tried to solve problems on a systemic level. But all systems are, after all, made up of people, and most change fails because of them—through corruption, politics, egos. That work was illusory, drawing her away from what was real.

She had come to understand that the trials she faced on earth were meant to help her connect to the pain and suffering of others—to practice universal love and kindness, to be less connected to earthly concerns and more connected to the spiritual sphere. It was hard work, but it was a world view that made sense and felt gratifying to her. She endeavored to make each of her interactions authentic now, to touch others personally as she had been touched. At RISC, Jaya was making a real impact, a true and meaningful difference to actual people. God had created human individuals, not systems. When you lost that connection with personal touch, you lost what made us essentially human.

"Let's practice some interview questions, shall we?" Jaya said, keen to help build Christophe's confidence before his next interview.

"Okay, missus." He straightened his back and tugged at the lapels of his jacket. "I am ready."

"At this pace, we should be done with the whole batch in two weeks," Serotina said to Micah. She and Jasmine had been working long days to trim the first harvest of plants they had grown from scratch. "And our total yield will be about ten pounds."

Micah grinned. "Fantastic. Hey, Rufus, come over here. Bring the laptop."

Rufus joined them and placed his computer in front of them. "Presenting . . . Greenfields, the web's finest purveyor of licensed medical-grade marijuana." On the screen was the brand name with a logo featuring the cartoon image of a smiling sun in sunglasses. "For our website. And I'll print it on our package labels."

"Ooh," said Jasmine, leaning on Rufus's shoulder to see.

"Looks cool, man." Micah slapped him on the back. "Bringing a smile to faces everywhere. Sero says we'll have ten pounds ready in two weeks, so let's turn on the website and get this show rolling."

The next day, orders began coming in. Rufus started preparing the shipping labels and packages, while Sero and Jasmine continued to trim the buds.

"We're sure this is all legit, right?" Jasmine asked.

"Well, in California," Rufus said, "medical marijuana has been legal for over a decade. To place an order on our website, people have to upload a doctor's prescription, and we require an adult signature for the UPS deliveries. So, I'd say we're being *extra-super* careful."

"And we have a dispensing license," Serotina added, confident about this from her conversations with Micah.

Every evening after dinner, Sero took Micah down to the basement to update him on their progress. The entire batch had sold out in the first week, generating almost twenty thousand dollars in revenue, and he was eager to get it shipped so they could collect. "How long until the next batch is ready?" he asked Sero as he licked a rolling paper to seal a joint.

"Twelve weeks," Sero said, flipping through the crate of labeled shipping envelopes on Rufus's table.

"No way to do it faster?"

Sero shook her head. "Unfortunately not. Hey—" She paused at one of the envelopes, then flipped through a couple more. "New Mexico?" She looked up at Micah. "And Montana? Can we do that, legally?"

"Listen, Sero." Micah smiled at her as he leaned back in his chair. "There's *legal* and then there's *right*. Something may be legal, but it's not right. And something can be right but might not be legal. I believe in applying our intelligence and sense of right and wrong to situations, not just blindly following the letter of the law like a lemming. You agree?"

"Well, I think it depends—"

"Okay, let me give you an example," Micah interrupted. "You might not know this, because the girl is tough as nails, but Ericka has two severely herniated disks that cause her chronic back pain. She's entitled *by law* to get a handicapped placard for her car. You know how helpful that would be, when we go to the farmers' market or the nursery, to be able to park close when we're loading those heavy trees and soil bags? Yeah, super helpful. But is it right? Does she need that spot more than someone else? Probably not. So, she doesn't use the placard and we park far away. If we took a handicapped spot—legal, but not right."

"Okay," she said, "but in that case, she's not doing anything wrong either way."

"Now, another situation with Ericka: Over-the-counter painkillers don't work for her; they don't put a dent in her suffering. And she doesn't want to use prescription meds, because of the risk of getting hooked. You know what does help her? Smoking marijuana, once in the morning, once in the evening. That's it. Two joints a day and she's a perfectly functioning member of society. She doesn't get addicted. Everyone's happy, right?"

She nodded. "Yeah, but medical marijuana is legal, and she can get—"

Micah held up a finger and spoke over her. "Now, what if Ericka lived in Wyoming? Exact same situation, same medical condition, same solution, same ethics, right?"

"Right," she admitted.

"Right," he echoed. "But Wyoming has different *laws*. You know why? Dick-fucking-Cheney, that's why. Let's look at the options available to a person in Wyoming." Micah held up one finger. "Get hooked on opioids and end up on the street or dead." He held up a second finger. "Become a debilitated member of society on disability." Now, he held up three fingers. "Knock off Dick Cheney." He grinned at her. "Or . . . order a package from us and hurt no one else. Perhaps not *technically* legal by Wyoming's outdated laws, but definitely *right*, right?"

She didn't respond as she considered his argument, which did seem to make sense.

"The same has been true throughout history. Slavery was legal for centuries, but not right. Women didn't have the right to vote in this country until they fought for it. Gandhi stood up to the British and was thrown in jail. Just a few years ago, marijuana was illegal and now the laws are changing everywhere. We're ahead of the curve, Sero. Don't you want to be on the right side of history?"

She did, of course. That was why she had come to the Sanctuary in the first place, to live in a better way, according to higher ideals. It was legal to pillage the earth, after all, even profitable, but it didn't make it right.

Micah pulled a lighter from the pocket of his jeans and lit up the joint. "Besides, the cops don't give a shit about weed now that it's legal. They're more focused on the tons of cocaine smuggled over the border. Trust me, I've got friends on the force." He held out the joint and Sero took it from him, allowing herself a long drag and the satisfaction of helping their cause.

———

The next day, around noon, Sero saw Micah in the kitchen, coming in from his long morning run. Apparently, he'd had competitive times in several marathons in his twenties, though he never boasted about it.

"All done packing up the first shipment," she said.

"Great," Micah said, guzzling a can of coconut water. He touched her shoulder as he walked past, and she felt a tingling heat sensation as his hand trailed down her back. Since they'd begun sleeping together, he sometimes touched her like this, but always subtly, never drawing too much attention. "I'll drop it off this afternoon. Want to come along? There's a feedstore near the shipping office; you can get that new lead rope you wanted for Buddy."

"Sure," Sero said. "I'd love to."

They spent an entire glorious afternoon together, trying out a new smoothie bar, strolling around, buying supplies for Buddy. When they arrived at the shipping office, there were no parking spots out front, so Sero offered to carry the bin of packages inside while Micah waited in the car, double-parked on the street. Afterwards, as Micah drove back to the Sanctuary, Sero found the contentment she'd felt all day begin to dissipate. She loved being alone with Micah and hardly ever had the chance—only two or three nights a week in his bedroom. The other days, she missed that connection. And having so many other people around the house had started to feel stifling. Her time alone was limited, between meditation, yoga, group circle, shared meals and chores. Even with seven bathrooms in the house, there were busy periods with thirteen people trying to shower and brush their teeth, and sometimes the hot water ran out for those at the end of the line.

That night, there were two visitors at the Sanctuary for dinner: Tommy, the mushroom grower from the farmers' market, and a Brazilian girl named Cerise who worked at the hardware store in town. Cerise was petite with rosy cheeks, black hair cut in a straight bob and wore a small silver ring in her nose. She did not look like someone you would go to for advice on home repairs, but Micah and Jeremy raved about her knowledge of plumbing fittings and valves. The guests sat on either side of Micah at the dinner table, and as Cerise laughed and answered their questions about power tools, Sero found herself feeling particularly uncharitable.

"Hey, Micah," Justin asked at dinner. "What's happening with the driveway, man? It looks like a construction site out there." The front driveway was still dug up, necessitating all of them to park tandem in front of the garage instead of using the circular drive. A large pile of paver stones had accumulated on the front lawn, many of them now broken. Fortunately, the water in the house had not been affected since that first day they had shut it off to start digging. Sero had been hesitant to ask Micah about it, but Justin apparently wasn't. "Seriously," he continued, looking around the table, "when are those pipes going to be fixed? It'd be nice not to have to climb over that pile of rubble every day." Micah stood up from the table to carry his plate to the kitchen and gave Justin a withering look that ended the conversation.

40 | serotina

APRIL 2015

Serotina worked tirelessly on Greenfields through the spring. Another hundred pounds of product in the cycle would be ready for sale in a couple of months. "We should order the next batch of seedlings," Sero told Micah one evening in bed. "Our mother plants aren't big enough to generate their own yet."

"Okay, I'll arrange it. Listen, Sero." Micah propped himself up on his elbow and looked at her. "I think it's time for you to stop working at NatMark. You're much more valuable to us here, working on Greenfields full-time."

"What about my employee discount? That makes a big difference to our food costs, doesn't it?" Sero had conflicting emotions about the idea. She liked getting out of the house, having some time away from the group. But she also liked feeling indispensable to Micah; she hoped he wanted her around more not just for Greenfields, but himself.

"Well, pretty soon, we'll be self-sufficient for food. And in the meantime, don't worry about the groceries." Micah leaned down to kiss her. "Anyone can do the shopping. We need you here. *I* need you."

———

On the morning of the community board meeting to address the chickens, they held a special meditation session on the back patio. With her
eyes closed, Sero followed the mental images Micah painted, of the future
utopian Sanctuary, where they not only grew all their own fruits and
vegetables, but also produced their own milk, made their own yogurt,
butter and cheese, baked their own bread. Solar panels and water wells
would minimize their impact on the earth. She meditated on what this
place would feel like, the pride that would come from knowing they
were self-sufficient, that they were not taking from the planet but taking
care of it. When Sero opened her eyes afterwards, she was not the only
one wiping away tears. The sun was rising over the hills in the distance,
the birds were chirping, and she had never felt so sanguine about her
future than at that moment.

Micah proposed that the entire Sanctuary family undertake a one-day
fast, to demonstrate solidarity and resolve for their mission. "You must
decide what you're willing to sacrifice for the greater good of this community," he said. "Are you willing to give up a few meals that your body
doesn't even truly need? It's not much of a sacrifice when you think of
it that way, is it?"

Everyone readily agreed, so after yoga, they all went directly to their
work, while Micah left for the meeting. The day seemed to drag on
forever. Sero hadn't realized how much time was normally passed in
preparing, enjoying and cleaning up from breakfast and dinner. She
grew hungry a few times, but her appetite passed, and she found herself
acceptably satiated with tea and chewing gum. The true deprivation was
not having Micah around.

When he walked in the door, six hours later, one of his shirttails was
untucked and his hair was disheveled—the way he looked after a late-
night jam session. He dropped his binder of materials on the table with a
thud. Sero felt her stomach twist with anxiety. She had listened to Micah

rehearse his presentation last night, in his bedroom. She'd thought he was very persuasive and told him so.

"Friends, we have a formidable enemy over there." Micah stretched out his arm and pointed outside. "But today, we prevailed." His face brightened with a smile, and enthusiasm crept into his voice. "I made our case for the chicken coop and the board agreed we have a right to keep the birds on our property."

Ericka and Zoe started cheering. "All right, Micah!" Rufus called out. "That's my man!" Sero felt a silent pride gathering within her chest.

"So, I've decided we should get a dozen more chicks and expand the coop. And beginning tomorrow, I'm going to start looking for two calves. Finally, there will be milk at the Sanctuary!" At this, everyone applauded. August held two fingers to his mouth and let out a long, high wolf whistle.

"They approved the cows?" Sero beamed at him, the hunger pangs in her belly all but forgotten. "Not yet, but they will. Right now, we need to send a message to that neighbor, to the board. We aren't going to be subject to power and control by others. We came to the Sanctuary so we can live free. We didn't escape the oppression of our dysfunctional families or our abusive relationships or our addictions just to be subject to more unjust rules, did we?"

"No!" they said back in unison. "No, we didn't!"

"We came together to live a better way. We don't need permission for that. We're getting closer to our dream, friends." Micah smiled.

———

The next morning, Sero came down to the kitchen to find an enormous pile of assorted citrus heaped on the island: oranges, grapefruits, tangerines. Chef Guy was slicing and working the fruit through a commercial juicer, filling up a big pitcher. "What's all this? From our trees?" Sero asked skeptically.

"Nope." Rufus grinned as he peeled an orange. "Courtesy of our fine neighbor. We're showing him: he can't control what we do with our land, or we'll control his."

"You just took all this? Does Micah know?" Sero asked, as Ericka and Zoe joined them in the kitchen.

Rufus looked up at her, one eyebrow raised. "Whose idea do you think it was?" He popped a slice of orange into his mouth. "Mmm, these blood oranges are awesome! Try." He offered some to the three women.

"No, thanks," Ericka said. "I'm fasting a little while longer."

"Still?" Sero asked.

"Me too," Zoe added. "It was such a high yesterday, and our focus really worked, you know, to support Micah?"

Sero skipped breakfast to go along with the others, but by noon, her hunger got the better of her and she came up from the basement to get something from the kitchen. Rummaging through the fridge, she found a package of pre-sliced cheese. The wrapper bore the name of the monster chain with new stores deceptively called "neighborhood markets," but which still sold the mass-manufactured food they shunned at the Sanctuary. Curious, she pulled out a slice and nibbled on the corner. It was flavorless and had the texture of smooth plastic. Where had this come from, and why was it in their otherwise wholesome kitchen?

Looking around, she found more anomalous grocery items: blueberries and apples that weren't organic, bottles of vinegar and almond butter from the same mega-market. She took the vinegar bottle in hand, intending to find Micah and ask him who was doing the shopping, but then reconsidered. He was under so much pressure these days. Some nights, he laid his head on her shoulder in bed and confessed that the problems with the house and landlord were weighing heavily on him. Sero wanted to continue to be his place of refuge, not another source of worry.

———

Ericka began to lead regular fasting days at the Sanctuary every Sunday. After meditation and yoga, when they would normally eat breakfast, she instead led them through a visualization exercise to imagine all the energy their bodies normally expended in food preparation and consumption being redirected toward building their vision of the Sanctuary and out into the universe toward the collective good of others. "We can sustain ourselves on much less than we do. Don't be greedy in taking from the universe. Teach yourself to step back, take less, leave more for others. Self-restraint will make you stronger."

Serotina grew accustomed to the fasting days, especially since she had not been eating lunch for months now. She knew there would be a wall of hunger in the late morning, and another in the late afternoon, and she pushed through them by steadily drinking black coffee and tea. She found it remarkable that her body could go an entire twenty-four hours without food, when all her life she had fed it every few hours without even thinking about it. Sometimes she felt drowsy or a little dizzy in the sun, but it was nothing she couldn't handle.

After a couple of weeks, Ericka began fasting on Wednesdays as well. Some people in the house joined her and others did not. While Serotina had come to appreciate the feeling of discipline and cleansing she had on Sundays, she found a second fasting day too difficult to endure. On Wednesdays, she ate breakfast furtively and felt guilty whenever she did so in front of Ericka, who remained cheerful as she worked hard all day.

———

At the end of April, Sero noticed that about a quarter of the cannabis plants in the flowering room had developed mold on their leaves. She tried to nurse the damaged plants back to health by pruning them, but when that proved ineffective, she isolated them to stop the mold from spreading to the other plants. Climbing the steps out of the basement, she wondered how she was going to break the news to Micah that they needed to procure new plants, mature ones, which would be costly, if they wanted to fulfill their existing orders on time.

Walking through the house to look for him, she heard the sound of a guitar strumming from the living room. She followed it, picking up the distinct tenor of Micah's deep voice, and the undertones of someone else's. Something made her walk quietly toward the room and approach from the side where she wouldn't be seen. Her stomach fell as she saw Micah sitting behind Cerise, holding a guitar on her knee, her hair falling into her face. His left hand was on top of hers, instructing her where to put her fingers on the fingerboard. She'd heard a rumor that Cerise might be invited to move into the Sanctuary but had brushed it off since no consensus vote had come up yet. The only open space in the house was in Sero's room, which for the past four months had been hers alone. But now, as she watched Micah brush Cerise's hair from her eye, she wondered if she'd missed something. Cerise giggled when she managed to play a chord. Sero backed away quietly from the living room and returned to the basement.

During the next morning's meditation session, she reflected on the scene with Micah and Cerise. Why had it bothered her so? He was just showing her how to play the guitar. Micah was a kind-hearted, generous soul. That's why everyone loved him. That's why *she* loved him. And he loved everyone. He told them all that, individually and collectively, all the time. She chided herself for her own small-mindedness.

———

"We need to talk about who's moving in next." Justin opened up the group circle discussion. They were in the living room, sitting on the large leather sectional and the floor. "Cameron's been waiting since Thanksgiving, man."

"There are some concerns about Cameron," Micah said gently. He stood up and began walking around the perimeter of the circle, hands clasped behind his back. "Cerise and Daphne are moving in this Friday. They'll be joining Sero in the theater, so we'll need everyone to help get them situated and prepare a welcome meal."

"When did we decide on that?" Justin said. "I don't recall voting for them."

"I don't know, you must've missed that group circle, Justin. Maybe you were napping."

Sero thought back to the group circles she'd attended and those she might have missed for work, because she didn't remember voting on Cerise and Daphne either.

"When are we voting on Cameron?" Justin asked. "I'd like to know what the issue is. He's a totally stand-up guy, I can vouch for him."

"We don't have space right now," Micah said. "Also, the dairy cows are arriving soon and we need to figure out a milking schedule—"

"Don't change the subject," Justin interrupted. "Cameron can bunk with me. We can squeeze another futon in the room."

"Justin!" Micah snapped. "We'll discuss it later, you and me. Okay?" He stared Justin down. Sero felt her stomach curdle with anxiety. No one spoke back to Micah, not even in jest.

"Nah." Justin shrugged. "Let's do it now." He rolled his head to look around the circle. "In front of everyone. That's the way it's supposed to be, right? Everything out in the open. So, here's what I think, Micah. You like bringing in more girls, especially *your* type of girls—"

"The dairy cows will need regular—" Micah interrupted in a raised voice.

"What happened to consensus, huh? Or even democracy? It's a

fuckin' dictatorship. Should we even be getting cows, with all the meth-
ane they release—"

"ENOUGH!" Micah bellowed from deep in his throat, an outburst
that shut down Justin and took everyone else aback. Sero glanced around;
the others looked as shocked and frightened as she felt, averting their
eyes from both Micah and Justin. "Group circle's over for today. We have
a ton of work to do. It looks like shit out there. The beans need trellises,
the strawberries haven't been watered in forever, and the damn citrus
trees have some sort of pest infestation. Don't you care about this place,
guys?" When no one responded, he yelled, "Let's GO!"

Everyone scrambled to their feet and moved outside. Micah and
Justin remained behind, and that was just as well. Sero was so disturbed
by Micah's anger that she didn't want to see him right now. The mood
in the fields was tense, as everyone busily pulled out work gloves and
tools and worked quietly.

"I think Justin's tried to hit on every woman here," Zoe said at last.

Not me, Sero thought, unsure how to feel about this.

"And he always does a half-ass job washing dishes," David added.

"Well, it *would* help to have regular hot water in the kitchen," August
said, chuckling. "How long till the plumbing's finally repaired?"

Sero tried to tune it all out, the negativity and the bickering. She
walked over to the citrus grove by herself and tried to figure out what
was wrong with the trees. Some type of pest had been eating tiny holes in
the leaves and leaving a viscous white layer on the fruit, which couldn't
be scrubbed away. It would require some research to find a solution,
but she was preoccupied with Greenfields and the moldy plants, about
which she still hadn't told Micah, and now she was even more reluctant
to do so.

Sero was uneasy the rest of the day. She and Jasmine went about their
work at the Greenfields farm—mixing the feed in large tubs, replac-
ing burned out bulbs—without discussing what had transpired during

group circle that morning. Was she the only one who thought something was wrong? She kept dwelling on Justin's accusations. Is that why
there were so many ethnicities in the house? Was the very thing that had
made her so comfortable here all to suit Micah's taste—all the petite,
attractive, tan-skinned women? When their work for the day was done,
Sero returned to the house and headed for the front closet to retrieve
her phone, craving a conversation with Izzy.

When she reached the foyer, however, she heard loud banging sounds
coming from outside and glanced out one of the windows beside the
front door. Micah was out there alone, swinging a pickaxe over his head
at a new patch of paver stones near the unearthed pipes. She watched
for a few moments; the wild, violent way he swung was disturbing. Sero
grabbed her phone and ran out the back door toward the stables. She
slowed to a walk when she was a comfortable distance from the house,
and dialed Izzy's number. Voice mail. She texted her mom, who was now
back from India and had shared pictures of her grandparents and their
flowering oleander bushes.

When she reached the stables, she stroked Buddy's head for a few
moments before entering the stall. She raked up the floor, refreshed his
bucket of water and put out some fresh hay, even though the last batch
was barely touched. The horse was uncharacteristically quiet, his tail
hanging limply as she moved around him. "Hey, Buddy," Sero said, picking up the body brush and turning her attention to his coat. She noticed
a lump protruding above the corner of his mouth and touched it gently.
"What's wrong, huh?" Buddy remained staid, unresponsive even when
she tried to lead him out of the stall for a walk. Not until she was back at
the house did her phone buzz in her pocket. Surrounded by the others,
she reluctantly sent Izzy to voice mail.

It was a small group for dinner that evening, as Ericka, Zoe and a few
others were on their Wednesday fast. The big group dinners that Sero
had loved so much didn't happen as often at the Sanctuary anymore, and

this saddened her. Micah joined them late in the dining room, but Justin did not show up. "What happened?" Sero whispered to Micah as they ate. "With Justin," she added in response to his blank look.

"Gone," he said, reaching for his wineglass.

"What? For good?" She felt an unsettling in the pit of her stomach.

"Yes, for good. And it really is. His choice, but good for all of us." He looked at her with a smile and took a long sip of wine.

41 | serotina

APRIL 30, 2015

The next evening, after dinner, Micah called for a group circle. They sat outside, around the large firepit, each person's face either aglow or shadowed, depending on the angle.

"We have to get serious here, friends." Micah took a plump grapefruit from a nearby tree and rolled it into the center of the circle. "As you all know, Justin left yesterday. After his outburst during group circle, we had an open discussion, and I decided it was time for him to leave."

Sero replayed his words from the night before. Hadn't Micah told her that Justin had chosen to leave on his own?

"But his stuff is still in our room," Jeremy said. "You sure he's not just pissed off, the way he gets sometimes, and he'll come back in a few days?"

"He's not coming back. I asked him to leave and that's final. He didn't want his belongings. You can use them or toss them," Micah said. "As we all know, the Sanctuary is a special place. Many of you pointed out that Justin didn't honor our values all the time, so it was best for him to leave. For the good of the group." Micah glanced around the circle. "This is an important juncture, friends. Cerise and Daphne are joining us tomorrow. We're on the verge of great things. Each of you should ask yourself right now, at this moment, whether you really believe in our vision." It sounded like a rhetorical question, so Sero remained quiet, but she saw several people nodding. "Do you?" Micah extended his arms out in front of him.

257

"Yes," David said.

"Yes!" Ericka echoed. And a chorus of voices called back to him.

"What are you willing to do to make those beliefs a reality?" Micah's voice rose. "It won't be easy. We have obstacles and challenges in many forms. There are those, like Justin, who try to break us down from the inside. And there are those out there"—he pointed out behind him—"who are threatened by what we represent. I want to show you something." Micah stood, walked a few feet away from the firepit, and came back carrying a newspaper bundle. "This is an example of what we have to contend with." He placed the bundle down on the ledge of the firepit and delicately began to unwrap it.

Jasmine screamed, her hands flying up to cover her face.

"Oh my god," Ericka said.

"What the hell *is* that?" Rufus muttered.

Sero craned her neck to see. Nestled in the center of the crumpled newspaper was a grotesque bloody mess of matted white feathers, tiny entrails, and what appeared to be a small orange beak.

"That," Micah said, pointing to the bundle, "is what's left of our dozen new baby chicks, courtesy of our neighbor's dog."

The rest of the group shook their heads in disgust. "Oh my god, what a sick fuck," Rufus muttered.

"He's doing this because he's threatened by us, but we're not going to let him win," Micah said. "Tomorrow, I'm going to get *two* dozen new baby chicks, and we're going to install barbed wire around the coop, in case that dog comes back."

"I'll teach that fucking dog a lesson," Rufus said, slamming a rock onto the ground. "Eye for an eye, man. Life for a life."

Sero looked over at Micah, expecting him to defuse Rufus.

"Ah." Micah pointed at Rufus. "The ancient Mesopotamian saying, from King Hammurabi's Code: 'to make justice visible in the land.'" He held one fist in the air. "I'll tell you what *I'm* willing to do for our

vision. I'm willing to work, night and day. To write as many letters as it
takes and go to as many meetings as I have to. I'm willing to take on the
worries and stresses for every person here, to carry them and solve them,
so that you"—he pointed around the circle, capturing each of them in
his sweep—"you can all focus on making the Sanctuary the best place
it can be."

"I'm going to make sure our new chicks are safe and grow up to be
great layers," Zoe called out, and Micah beamed at her.

"I'll go to the farmers' market twice every weekend," David offered.
"Different markets, Saturday and Sunday, to bring in more money for
our produce and eggs."

"Does it help, Micah, when we fast?" Ericka said. "It feels like we're
all in solidarity behind you, but does it help?"

Micah smiled at her. "It does, Ericka. It really does."

"Let's do it tomorrow, all of us. We can fast for twenty-four hours,
until the welcome dinner," Ericka proposed, and others agreed. "I might
go for two days this time." She beamed at Micah.

———

Sero moved restlessly around her bedroom that night. After dinner,
Micah had said that group circle had given him another migraine, so she
was alone in this room for perhaps the last time before her new room-
mates arrived. Sero hadn't lived with anyone since Stephanie Cortez
in her college dorm. She felt a small pang for their tiny room and the
camaraderie they'd shared, eating bowls of spiced-up noodles and rice
late at night as they shared stories of their families and lives. The last time
she'd seen Stephanie was on that first visit to the community garden,
with the windfall of poblano peppers. That moment, branching to her
current life at the Sanctuary, seemed so long ago.

Suddenly, she remembered the fast she'd be doing the next day and realized she was hungry now. How was Ericka going to fast for two full days? She had the bone structure of a bird and was barely a hundred pounds as it was. In the last month, her face had been losing the apple roundness of her cheeks and had begun to look chiseled. But she seemed so happy and dedicated that Sero had refrained from saying anything to her.

She had mentioned to Micah a few days earlier that maybe Ericka was becoming too lean, but he countered her. "Sero, you're just so used to seeing obese Americans. Eating fewer calories is actually better for you, helps you live longer. It's been scientifically proven." And it was true, Sero discovered when she later looked it up on her laptop. In many studies, calorie restriction was associated with increased life span and health. This discovery just increased Sero's confusion and guilt over not fasting as often herself.

Now, by the light of the fridge interior, Sero grabbed a package of sliced cheddar and an apple from the fruit bowl on the island. She retrieved her cell phone from the basket in the front hallway, careful not to make too much noise, and walked outside and down into the Greenfields farm. She sat on one of the folding chairs at the table where they usually packaged orders and bit into the apple, then folded a square of cheese in half and stuffed it into her mouth. She pressed the voice mail button on her phone and Izzy's voice came pulsing through the speaker. "Karina! Girl, where are you? It's been so long. Call me back. I have news." Serotina smiled, not expecting the spark of sentiment she felt at hearing that name. She touched her screen to call Izzy back.

"K!" Izzy answered the phone. "Where've you been? How's school? How's everything?"

Sero didn't know where to start. "Good. What's going on with you?" she said, sidestepping the question. "What's the news?" She folded another slice of cheese in half, then in quarters.

"Let's just say it has to do with Alvaro's house in Spain this summer, and a certain invitation to meet someone's parents."

"Get out!" Sero was now breaking the cheese squares into crumbs, then squeezing them back together between her fingertips.

"I know. Alvaro *really* wanted me to meet his family. I think this could really be it, Karina."

"I'm so happy for you, Iz," she said. "So, when do I get to meet this guy?"

"Come to Spain!" Izzy squealed. "Meet me in Barcelona after I go to his house. He's interning at a hospital there all summer. We can travel around the Costa Brava and fly home together. *Please*, we'll have a blast. And your Spanish is *so* much better than mine."

Sero rolled a thin rope of congealed cheese under her fingers, unsure what to say. Her life didn't operate on a school calendar anymore. In past years, she'd worked diligently to fill her summers with internships or activities, but now her life was the Sanctuary. "Yeah, maybe. That sounds fun."

"I'll send you my flights. I have to be back for my internship in July. My English professor recommended me to this literary agency and they hired me. For *free*, of course." Izzy giggled. "Anyway, enough about me. What's going on with you? What's new? How's that horse you sent me the picture of?"

Sero twisted the stem of her apple until it snapped off. "Buddy. Yeah, he's . . . actually, I'm not sure. I think something might be wrong with him. He hardly eats anything and he's got this big lump near his mouth."

"Hmm. Sounds like when Mr. Chuckles got a tooth abscess. We knew something was wrong when he stopped eating." Izzy chuckled. "Call the equine dentist. If you don't treat those, the pus pocket can go up to their brain."

"Oh god. That sounds serious." Sero collected the pile of cheese curds in a tissue and tossed it all in the trash.

"I gotta go, K, but promise me you'll think about Spain, okay?"

Sero sat scraping at the apple core with her fingernails, digging out the small dark seeds and recalling the biology lesson in which she'd learned that benign-looking apple seeds contain arsenic. She was truly happy for Izzy, but she felt a sadness cloaking her, remembering how easily James had let her go for the summer to Ecuador, and afterwards. She hadn't found the kind of love that Izzy had with Alvaro, and she wasn't sure she had it now with Micah either.

———

The next morning, she went to see Micah in his room. "Hey, can I come in?"

"Uh, sure." Micah was sitting on his bed with a towel wrapped around his waist, fresh from the shower. Sero forced her eyes away from the broad expanse of his shoulders, to focus on what she needed to say.

"I think Buddy needs to see a vet. He's acting strange and hasn't been eating at all."

"Maybe he's fasting with us today." Micah smiled.

"I'm serious. He might have a tooth abscess."

"He'll be fine. He's a hearty animal. Besides, we don't have the money for a vet right now. We have to invest every dollar into Greenfields. And now we have some extra expenses, don't we? To replace the plants you lost?" There was a smirk on his face at her startled expression. "Yeah, I heard about that. You thought I wouldn't?"

"No, I . . . I was going to. You just seem so stressed that—"

"You know what stresses me out, Sero? When I can't trust someone."

Shaken, she tried to steer the conversation back to Buddy. "Okay, what if I paid for the vet? Or can I borrow the money I put into the solar fund?"

"The money in the solar fund has been paid as a deposit for the solar panels. That's the way these things work." Micah's voice was harsh and condescending. "If you want to waste your own money on a vet, that's up to you. But if you have extra money, I hope you would contribute it to our collective fund, where it can be invested for our collective benefit."

Sero knew she should stop before he lashed out at her as he had at Justin. As she turned to leave, her eyes fell on the nightstand, upon which sat a mobile phone and the familiar crumpled brown wrapper of a Snickers bar. She paused, taking this in. Then she turned around and said, "Micah? How do you know those chicks weren't killed by a coyote? I see them out there in the early morning all the time."

"I *know*, Serotina"—Micah pronounced her full name slowly—"because that asshole neighbor told me at the last meeting that he would sic his dog on our chickens to teach me a lesson." He stood up, adjusted the towel around his waist, and walked into his closet, making it clear he was done with the conversation.

———

The fasting was difficult for her that day, so by the time Cerise and Daphne arrived in the late afternoon, Sero was cranky. She helped them get settled in the theater room and, despite her reservations about losing her privacy, invited them to share the clothes in her dresser. By the time of the welcome dinner, Sero was famished. She served herself two portions of pan-seared halibut with lemon-herb crust, wilted greens and French lentils, and found herself spooning one bite after another into her mouth, without slowing down to think about the food. She just enjoyed the flavors and the fullness it brought to her, and soon this made her feel guilty. Compounding her sense of guilt was the presence of Ericka and Zoe, still in good spirits, who had decided to extend their fast to a second day.

After dinner, Micah stood up with his wineglass. "Cerise, you have already saved my hide several times with your amazing expertise in all things technical." He bowed in her direction and Cerise's dimples appeared. "I'm excited for everyone else to be around your beautiful energy." Sero again felt an unjustified enmity toward Cerise, so didn't even register what Micah said next about Daphne. They went around the table, everyone saying some nice words about Cerise and then Daphne, and when Sero's turn came, even though she didn't know either of them very well, she knew to do the same.

<hr/>

The next day, Serotina helped Chef Guy prepare a batch of spinach and cheese omelets for breakfast and handed a plate to Ericka, but she insisted she was still fasting and consumed only one cup of black coffee. Out on the patio, Cerise and Daphne ate heartily as they laughed and talked with the others. Seeing them, Sero was reminded of the fresh excitement she'd felt months ago when she first moved in. She placed the extra omelet on the table between them. "Go ahead, we have an extra," she told the girls.

Daphne happily divided the omelet between their two plates. "Thanks, Sero. These eggs are delicious." Sero knew they would need the energy for the long day ahead of them. She had been fortunate to work mostly in the basement the past few months, a respite from the hard outdoor labor. In the past week, the weather had turned summer-like, with the sun beaming down from a cloudless sky, and a stillness to the air. After breakfast, they all went out to the fields to join Ericka and Zoe, who were clearing old kale and chard. Some of the plants had grown to the size of car tires, with thick and tenacious roots.

Ericka was squatting, wrestling one particular plant from the soil. When it finally broke free, she fell backwards on the ground. Sero looked up as Ericka began laughing. She got back up to her feet, but wavered for a moment before falling again, sideways, her knees buckling under her.

Sero ran over and crouched down next to her friend. There was a bright scarlet trickle of blood down Ericka's forehead, where she had come into contact with a sharp branch on the way down. "Ericka? You okay?"

Ericka's eyelids fluttered and she mumbled something that sounded like, "Just dizzy." She rested her head on her outstretched arm and her eyes drifted closed.

"Ericka, what's wrong? Did you hit your head?" Sero looked over her shoulder and spotted Jeremy a few rows behind her; she shouted for him to come over. He lifted Ericka's tiny frame in his arms and carried her back up to the house, where he laid her on the couch and went to find the first aid kit. Sero got some orange juice from the fridge and brought a glass over. She tilted the glass to Ericka's lips, but she shook her head. "Just have a sip," Sero coaxed. "You'll feel better. You must have low blood sugar or something."

"No," Ericka said, pushing the glass away so it splashed both of them. She hoisted herself up to a sitting position. "I'm fasting all day. That's what I promised Micah."

"What?" Sero said. "Ericka, you just passed out."

"I'm fine," Ericka said. "Just a little dehydrated. Maybe some water?" Sero returned to the kitchen and washed the sticky residue of juice from her hands, confused and angry. Jeremy bandaged the cut on Ericka's forehead and Sero brought her a glass of water, which she drank down. "Thanks, guys." Ericka smiled at them. "Go back out there. I'll come soon."

After Jeremy kissed Ericka on the forehead and left, Sero sat on the edge of the couch next to her. "You have low blood sugar, or low blood pressure, or something, Ericka. You really need to eat something."

"I'm fine," Ericka reassured her. "Just have to build up my strength. I need to be stronger for—"

"Micah wouldn't want you to do this," Sero said, cutting her off. "Want me to go ask him?"

"Not just for Micah. For the group." Ericka gave Sero's hand a limp squeeze.

Sero shook her head and returned to the kitchen, where she took out a loaf of bread and the new jar of unnatural peanut butter that didn't belong in their pantry. She made a pile of sandwiches, left one on the table next to Ericka, who'd drifted off to sleep, and took the rest outside. As she returned to the fields, she heard low voices coming from the fruit grove. Glancing back over her shoulder, she saw Micah and Zoe, heads bent toward each other. Maybe they would be able to talk some sense into Ericka and get her to eat.

42 | keith

MAY 5, 2015

Keith swirled the Barolo in the bulb of his wineglass and sipped. He nodded approval at the sommelier, who filled the rest of his glass and the one across the table where Jaya would be seated. Keith had taken the liberty of ordering the wine; she'd always deferred to him on this, and he needed a drink to calm his nerves before she arrived. He had to be careful not to have more than one glass, though; he had planned what to say and needed to stay sharp.

Jaya floated into the restaurant ten minutes after the hour, dressed in an unassuming, crisp cotton Indian outfit—not overdressed, yet out of place amongst the cocktail dresses and suits. A demure smile graced her face when she spotted him, and he stood up to greet her, touching her shoulder and leaning in to kiss her cheek. She smelled faintly of green apple and roses, a familiar scent. They took their seats and Keith gestured at her wineglass. His palms were moist and he wiped them on the cloth napkin in his lap.

"How was India?" he asked.

"Wonderful," she said. "I'm planning to go again next year, make it an annual trip."

When was the last time she'd described something as *wonderful*? "And your parents?" Keith asked.

"Good, fine," she said, in the moderated way he was accustomed to. "Have you spoken to Karina lately?"

"It's been a week or two," Keith said, as he thought back. "We've exchanged text messages, but I haven't actually talked to her live."

Jaya laughed lightly and he watched her entire face brighten. "I know what you mean," she said. "Sometimes we exchange ten text messages in five minutes, and I think, *Wouldn't it just be easier to pick up the phone?*"

The waiter arrived to take their order, and Jaya glanced briefly at the menu before ordering the only vegetarian entrée, while Keith asked for his regular salmon. After the waiter left, Keith took a deep breath and placed his wineglass on the table. "Listen," he said. "There's something I want to talk to you about."

Jaya's expression turned serious, mirroring his.

"There's some trouble at work. I . . ." Keith clenched his teeth, preparing himself for her judgment. "I . . . I made a mistake. A pretty big one."

Jaya leaned in a little closer and placed her folded hands atop the table. Keith felt frozen, his voice caught in his throat. He still cared a great deal, he realized, about what she thought.

"I conducted a stock trade last year that was . . . it turns out . . ." Keith exhaled heavily. "It wasn't entirely above board. I was privy to some insider information, which tainted the purchase. I didn't . . . I didn't *think* I was doing anything wrong at the time, but I shouldn't have done it." Now that he had admitted it, he felt a rush of relief and the words continued rolling out of him. "I should have just played it safe and stayed away from the company entirely." He ran one hand through his hair as he shook his head, then dropped his hands on the table.

To his surprise, Jaya reached across the table and cupped her hands around his. He forced himself to meet her eyes and saw that, unexpectedly, they were full of understanding. She nodded gently for him to go on.

"The SEC started an investigation into the trade, and . . ." Keith looked at her and shrugged, his throat tight. "I have a good attorney.

We're hoping to settle the case and pay a fine." He desperately needed a sip of water, feeling the perspiration under his shirt, but he didn't want to break the grasp of Jaya's cool and calming hands around his.

"So, if you settle, you pay a fine and no . . . prison, or anything else?"

Keith nodded. "That's the hope. That's what usually happens in minor cases like this. But, Jaya, it may be a pretty significant fine. It may change . . . everything."

"What would it change?" Jaya said softly.

"Well, I may have to sell the condo, and . . . I'm not sure what else. That's why I wanted to put aside money for you and Karina, for your future needs, so you don't have to worry." His voice cracked a little. "I'm not sure it will be enough, but . . ." He shrugged again, his throat clamped shut.

"Okay. I'm not worried." Jaya smiled and sat back in her seat, releasing his hands.

"Okay?" Keith asked. "That's it?"

"Well, if you learned from your mistake, and you're going to be okay, the rest is just money and things." Her face glowed as the smile spread to her eyes. "We can handle that, whatever it is."

A small cry escaped Keith's throat as relief flooded his body. *We.*

"I can sell the house. I don't need it, or the new account you established," Jaya continued. "So, you can count on that for your settlement too."

"No," Keith said, shaking his head. "The house is in your name—"

"Keith," Jaya said. "I don't need any of that. I can live with very little. I already *am*, just inside a big empty house with a big bank account I barely touch."

Keith blinked rapidly, trying to keep her in focus as tears welled in his eyes.

"I appreciate what you've done all these years," Jaya continued, "keeping the house while Karina was here and securing her education—"

"Well, you know our daughter, she's done most of that herself,"

Keith quipped, prompting a smile from Jaya. For the first time, he saw her pronounced lack of material need as an intrinsic quality, not an indictment of his value in their relationship. He'd never understood it this way before and he felt a surge of gratitude along with profound regret over the loss of their marriage. The waiter returned with their entrées. Jaya never had an appetizer, claiming she didn't need all the courses restaurants pressured you to order, and tonight, Keith had unconsciously done the same to parallel her. How many dozens of ways had he changed shape to accommodate her when they were together? He missed the counterbalance of her in his life.

"And I appreciate what you've done for me," Jaya continued. "Without the means, I wouldn't have been able to do what I've done these last years. It's important to me, so I'm grateful."

Keith hadn't expected this reaction. They were no longer married; she didn't owe him any kindness, and yet she had offered it, unsought. Jaya had shown him more understanding and support than even his own father had. Perhaps she'd never been as one-dimensional in her judgment of his ambition and materialism as he'd always thought. Perhaps her view was more a reflection of her personal values and less about him. Her reaction tonight was grounded and calming, and he felt its effect spreading to him. *The rest is just money and things*, he repeated silently to himself as he drove home from dinner, more settled than he had felt in a long time.

43 | serotina

MAY 16, 2015

Rufus shook his head at the computer screen. "Can't get these damn invoices to print," he said, punching at the keyboard. They were all on edge, trying to fulfill their current Greenfields orders. The new seedlings had arrived to replace the molded plants they'd disposed of, but they were behind on their output. "I guess I can send them to the printer in Micah's office upstairs."

"I'll run up and get them," Serotina said, eager for the chance to catch a moment with Micah. He'd been so distracted lately and disappeared for long periods of time behind his closed door, where she could hear him on the phone. Questions accumulated in Sero's mind. Small things, like the cell phone in Micah's room and the junk food when he was supposed to be fasting, she could excuse. She'd even tried to overlook the mass-manufactured food in their kitchen. Micah might not even know about the groceries, since he rarely helped with meal preparation. Chef Guy was the right person to ask about that. But other things were harder to ignore, and Justin's accusations hung in her mind with a truth she recognized. Micah was a *good* person—the kind of person who took care of an infirm woman's garden and fed the homeless after Thanksgiving. But his compassion didn't seem to extend to a suffering creature like Buddy or to the neighbor's potentially blameless dog. If she was wrong about Micah, what would that mean for her now? Her world had come tumbling down with the realization she had been wrong about James.

"Thanks, Sero," Jasmine called out as she left.

Outside, she spotted Ericka and Zoe working in the fields in the distance. Zoe was always recognizable with her mass of dreadlocks, but Ericka looked increasingly diminished, her shirt hanging off her bony frame like adult's clothing on a child. Sero swallowed back her concern and entered the house. Upstairs, she found Micah's bedroom door open and wandered into the closet office, which was empty. Trying not to feel upset by this small disappointment, she picked up the paper sitting in the printer's output tray.

It wasn't an invoice; it was a letter addressed to someone named Joe Petrosyan. The letter was short, and Micah's name was at the bottom, awaiting his signature.

> Pursuant to California Civil Code 1941.1, landlord has breached warranty of habitability in the residential lease. The house is uninhabitable due to ongoing plumbing issues since March 2015 that impede the regular supply of water to fixtures, which materially affects tenant's health and safety. After landlord failed to address multiple requests for repair, tenant properly issued notice that rent payments would be withheld until such time as conditions are made habitable. As such, California Civil Code 1942.5 prevents landlord from evicting tenant for 180 days after repair request was made. Tenant kindly requests that landlord cease and desist from sending eviction notices and furthermore provide immediate reimbursement for the $20,000 tenant has incurred in his efforts to have the plumbing problem repaired.

Sero stared at the page, trying to make sense of the words. Eviction notice? Running low on hot water occasionally hardly qualified as uninhabitable. If Micah was withholding rent payments, where was the money from the household fund to which they all contributed? If there was truly a problem with the pipes, why had he turned away the plumber that day? And how did they still have water flowing in the house and the fields? She would have known immediately if there had been any interruption in the Greenfields farm, since those plants needed a steady supply of water to grow on their aggressive timeline. She recalled Micah swinging the pickaxe maniacally at some invisible ghost under the ground.

Serotina stood in the center of the closet office and looked around at the piles of papers and envelopes. She walked over to the picture window in Micah's room, the largest in the house and the only one occupied by a single person. Out in the fields, everyone was scattered throughout the rows of crops. She spotted Micah standing with Cerise, his arm around her shoulder. Then his hand drifted down her back and rested on her jeans' back pocket. Sero returned to the closet and began looking through the piles of folders. She found one titled "Solar" and opened it up to find assorted color brochures from solar companies. There were no contracts, no deposit receipts, nothing. In another folder, untitled, she found several unopened letters from the IRS, addressed to a name she didn't recognize.

Feeling increasingly frantic, Sero found a folder labeled "Greenfields," and opened it, desperately hoping to see the license she'd attested to. It wasn't what she expected, what she saw inside that folder, but it was strangely familiar. Receipts from the purchases she'd made for Greenfields: lights, feed, irrigation. The detailed manifest for the first shipment, with her signature. And a photocopy of the front and back of the credit card her father had given her, which resided in her wallet in the front hall closet.

She stood in place, closed her eyes and tried to think. The printer stopped and the invoices she'd come upstairs to retrieve sat in the output tray. Sero looked at the mess of papers around her. She carefully replaced the folders and papers she'd taken out, took the Greenfields invoices and walked back downstairs, a sinking feeling in her chest.

44 | jaya

Dev and his family were visiting from London, and Jaya found the additional energy in the house unexpectedly refreshing.

"Come on, Jaya Auntie, look up at me and smile." Sachin, her fifteen-year-old nephew, held his phone up above his head, angled down toward her as she chopped vegetables at the kitchen island. Jaya brushed her nose with the back of her hand and shook her head with a smile.

"Not like that!" His sister, Smita, shrieked as she lunged toward him, reaching for the phone. "Cooking in the kitchen? You trying to attract the hopeless traditional men?" She clucked her tongue, sounding older than her thirteen years. "We need a picture of Auntie out on the patio, in a pretty dress with the sunlight glinting off her hair."

"Eh, you've been reading too many romance novels." Sachin held the phone out of her reach. "Time is of the essence. Twenty thousand people join Match every day. Her perfect partner could be out there right now, just waiting for her to pop up on his feed."

"I'll write your profile, Auntie." Smita turned toward Jaya, an excited smile on her face. "Trust me, I'm *really* good at this. Can I pick out a dress from your closet?"

"What's going on here?" Dev entered the kitchen, chuckling. "Are my children hounding you again?"

Jaya smiled at him. "Not at all, they're being perfect angels."

Dev threw his head back and laughed in that boisterous way Jaya had always loved. "Well, now I *know* you're lying," he said, as each of his teenagers pummeled his shoulders from opposite sides. "Yes, it seems the tables have turned in 2015, and now children pressure the adults to get married instead of the other way around."

"Who pressured you to get married?" Dev's wife, Chandra, joined them in the kitchen, one eyebrow arched and a yoga mat tucked under her arm.

"No one, darling." Dev put his arm around Chandra's shoulders and kissed her. "And it was the best decision of my life."

"Damn right." Chandra slapped him on the ass. "Are you coming to Bikram or not?"

"I'd love to, but I already promised Jaya I'd stay here and help her with the cooking."

Chandra shot Jaya a knowing glance. "Okay, just don't complain when your back feels stiff tomorrow." She waved her fingers over her shoulder as she turned to leave.

"Really?" Jaya said. "That's your excuse? Now she'll expect you to make dinner when you get back home."

"Ah, no risk of that. Chandra has tasted my cooking." Dev grinned. "We have a deep mutual understanding of my limitations."

"You're very lucky, you know?" Jaya said, tossing green beans in a colander. "That she puts up with you." Seeing Dev, his family and their life in London had been a revelation for Jaya. How many different ways there were to live in the world. The choices Jaya had made only represented a single path, one that made sense at the time and place she'd made them.

"Hey," Dev said, feigning offense. "I'm a catch. Speaking of which, how's Keith?" He winked at her. Dev had always liked Keith for being whip-smart and winning his way into their parents' hearts. "We're not an easy crowd to keep up with, especially for a Yankee," he'd always said of his brother-in-law.

"He's fine, some stress at work, the usual," Jaya said. She hadn't told anyone what was happening with Keith, trying to safeguard his privacy and reputation until they knew more.

Having Dev here made her feel safe and comfortable. She loved the warmth and lightness she felt in the presence of her niece and nephew. How she would have liked to have them around all the time, not just on the phone or for sporadic visits, but integrated into her life. In the beginning of her marriage to Keith, Jaya had thought it was easier to be far from both their families, free to establish their own rituals and norms, but perhaps the fabric of their life was weaker for it, leaving them untethered when adversity struck.

Sachin's phone rang and he left the room to answer what was, no doubt, the daily call from the girlfriend he was trying to downplay. Smita had already gone to rummage through Jaya's wardrobe. Dev took a cutting board and knife from the drainboard and motioned for Jaya to pass him some of the green beans she was dicing into small pieces. "I'm not completely useless, you know. I can do menial labor." He smiled at her. "So, are you really going to do it?"

"Do what?" Jaya dropped a handful of bean trimmings into the compost bin.

"Start dating again." Dev eyed her. "Smita will have you up and running by tonight if you agree. Actually," he said, wobbling his head, "she's not really one to ask permission, so maybe even if you don't."

Jaya didn't take her eyes from her cutting board, watching the wide cleaver cut precisely through a dozen beans at once. "I don't know, Dev . . ."

"Well, I think you should, for what it's worth," he said. "It's been *years* since Keith, and you're all alone now that Karina's gone." He raised a palm in proactive defense. "I know, I know, you're not *alone*; you have a very full life and spend time with lots of people."

But Jaya hadn't been about to say those things this time. She enjoyed how full and happy her home had been this week, and she found she could carry on her daily prayers, her service work, her life, without feeling conflicted as she used to. Perhaps it was that she'd become more practiced at her spiritual work, more centered and less prone to distraction than she had in the beginning. Whatever the reason, she enjoyed cooking meals for them, and looked forward to spending evenings and mornings together.

"Don't you miss the companionship?" Dev said, looking over his shoulder for the kids before lowering his voice. "Or at least the *sex*?"

Jaya smiled and lobbed a green bean at him in jest. He caught it and popped it into his mouth. She did miss the companionship. And the sex. For years, she hadn't. She had been so shrouded in her own grief that she felt disconnected from her physical body. Then, when she had discovered the Guru, she convinced herself that the feminine, sexual part of her had served its purpose—mating, reproduction—and now she'd moved on to another phase of life, intended for higher order concerns.

". . . just want you to be happy," Dev was saying now.

"I'm fifty, Dev," Jaya said.

"Exactly. You can find a nice, mature gentleman who already has an established career, who's comfortable with himself. You don't have to go through any of that tedious child-raising, career-building stuff. You two can just have fun together, travel, enjoy life."

"I told you guys, leave the profile description to me. You old farts are hopeless at romance," Smita interjected as she returned to the room, carrying two dresses with plunging necklines. Jaya recognized the black one from her last romantic getaway to San Francisco with Keith, Before. She hadn't even realized it was still in the back of her closet; the woman who'd worn it seemed so far away, but perhaps not entirely forgotten.

Smita grinned, proudly holding the two hangers in front of her. "Okay, Jaya Auntie. It's showtime."

45 | serotina

MAY 17, 2015

Serotina, Jasmine and Rufus were in the basement, working on a large Greenfields order for Alaska. Sero was snipping dying leaves off the cannabis plants with miniature clippers. The memory of working on bonsai in Mrs. Galbraith's science lab came to her, so long ago and far away, when Micah descended the stairs toward them. "How we doing, team?"

"Dude, this is the biggest order we've ever had," Rufus said, gleefully. "Four pounds. *Seven grand* in a single transaction. Hopefully, this guy is a repeat customer."

Micah slapped him on the back and peered at the tray Jasmine was working on. "Great work, guys. I'm really proud of what you've created here." He turned back to the group. "I think it's time to share this with everyone."

"Oh, thank god," Jasmine said. "I'm getting tired of not being able to talk about it outside this room." She shared a glance with Rufus, then looked over at Sero. "I mean, no offense, but it'll be nice to be more open about it, you know?"

"Yeah, we should share the love." Rufus grinned. "Everyone should be able to partake in the premium Greenfields weed."

"I'm planning something very special for tomorrow," Micah said. "I'm going to share it with the group tonight, but you guys should start getting ready. Finish up your big order and get this space cleaned up." He gestured to the side wall, where bags of supplies and unused equipment were stacked. "Good?"

"Yup, I'll do it right now," Rufus said, rising from his seat behind the computer.

Micah wandered over to Sero's table. She anticipated his hand on her shoulder, some touch from him that she still craved, but he just leaned up against the wall next to her. "You're very quiet."

Sero shrugged. What could she say? There was so much bottled up inside of her, but she was afraid to let it out, lest she rouse Micah's temper. She longed for things to go back to the way they had been a few weeks ago, before Cerise and Daphne moved in, before Justin left, before she discovered those papers in Micah's office, which she could no longer explain away or ignore.

"Hey," Rufus called from across the cavernous space. He'd ducked into the area under the staircase and pulled out a large plastic jug with red lettering. "What should I do with this?"

Micah took a few steps toward him and read the words printed on the jug. "Rodenticide?"

"Rat poison," Sero explained.

"Yeah, do we need it, or what?" Rufus said.

"Not unless we want to kill off plants," Sero said.

Micah took a few steps closer and took the jug from Rufus, turning it around to read the back.

"What are you thinking, man?" Rufus said.

"Micah?" Sero asked.

Rufus grinned. "Maybe those prize rosebushes next door?"

"Micah?" Sero stopped snipping leaves. "You can't really—"

Micah wheeled around to face her so quickly, she instinctively drew back. "Don't you get it, Sero? That asshole is making life very difficult for us. He's submitted all kinds of complaints to the community board, which get forwarded to the landlord and then to us." He was speaking rapidly, gesturing wildly with the jug in hand. "He's just going to start up again when our dairy cows get here next week."

"We'll just send him a little warning." Rufus took the jug from Micah, unscrewed the lid and pulled back from the sharp odor. "Show him it's in his interest to let us be."

Micah nodded. "And if he keeps messing with us, the karma's going to come around to him. Use it *liberally* on the fruit." He wiped his hands on his jeans. "Live and let live. That's all I'm saying. Not like it's strong enough to kill people."

"I'm not sure about that." Sero rose slowly from her chair.

"Ah." Micah waved his hand in her direction. "Don't worry so much, Sero. It's fine."

"Hey, Jas," Rufus said. "You want to give me a hand with these?" He hoisted the two large black trash bags he'd filled.

"Sure." Jasmine jumped up to help, and as Sero watched them ascend the stairs, she wondered if there was something going on between the two of them.

Once they were alone in the basement, Micah stepped toward her. "Hey, don't be angry with me. I can't handle that right now." He reached out a hand, and Sero, softening, took it. He caressed her face with both hands, then closed his startling blue eyes and leaned forward to kiss her, long and slow. Despite herself, she melted under his prolonged touch. "Thank god for you, Sero. You, and *this* . . ." He gestured around the basement. "If it wasn't for Greenfields, none of this would be possible. I don't know what I'd do without you."

"What *are* we doing here, Micah?" She couldn't hold it in any longer; she needed answers.

His mouth formed a lopsided half-smile and his eyes narrowed. "What do you mean?"

"I mean, what are we *really* doing?" She let go of his hands. "I'm not sure anymore. First you said Justin decided to leave, then you said you kicked him out. All decisions are supposed to be unanimous, but you just decided yourself on Cerise and Daphne. You didn't even ask *me*, and they're sharing my room."

Micah's smile twisted into a sneer. "Oh, so now you want to *question* me? Because you're *jealous*? Don't do that, Sero. That is so predictable, so *beneath* you, common jealousy." He shook his head and she noticed the pulsing of his jaw muscle.

Sero felt perspiration moisten her armpits. She forced a smile onto her face, stepped forward and took his hand again, hearing the thud of her heartbeat loud in her throat. She stood on her tiptoes and kissed him, lightly on the lips. "You're right. I'm so sorry. I just . . . miss you."

Micah gave her a small smile, but she saw a distinct coldness in his eyes.

———

After Micah left the basement, Serotina walked out the exterior door to the stairwell at the side of the house. She sat on the top step, staring out over the grounds of the Sanctuary, where the sun would soon be setting. She loved this place, how it shaped her view of what was possible. She loved the people here, who had been so welcoming and supportive, seeing only the best in her. Ericka had offered her friendship and vulnerability. Zoe had taught her through yoga how to integrate parts of herself that hadn't made sense together before. Jeremy and August had helped her move out of her lonely apartment. Micah was the first person to truly see her for who she was. He had held her hand when she entered the ocean, helped her face her fears with gentle confidence.

The money, the papers in his office, Justin's accusations—it didn't add up. Sero suddenly felt as if she couldn't breathe freely. She knew there were problems brewing here, but she didn't know if she could bring herself to leave this place. What about her friends? How could she just leave them behind if she cared about them? She could be more effective by staying. She'd been able to influence Micah before; she could help him get back on track now. And if not, perhaps she could convince some of the others, at least Ericka, to leave with her.

Serotina stood and walked toward the swimming pool. She pushed off her sandals and wrapped her toes over the edge. The scent of chlorine drifted up and began to itch at her nose, but she stood in place and inhaled deeply. Her mind drifted back in time, running over the years like a stone skipping water, alighting on certain memories. She thought of Prem's bright smile, her mother with her roses, her father teaching her to play golf. She thought of Izzy and her dog and Mr. Chuckles, Mrs. Galbraith and her bonsai. She remembered the glory of winning a trophy at the Science Olympiad, and the pride she felt when she was awarded her scholarship. She thought of James, and she allowed herself to linger on those memories—the good ones—for a while.

She sat down at the pool's edge, observing how the water distorted the size and color of her feet. Last year, she hadn't been able to get this close to a pool without panicking. Her mind returned to Micah and the things he'd taught her, the things he'd said. *If it wasn't for Greenfields, none of this would be possible.* She heard something deep inside her, barely discernible: a voice telling her what to do. But fear shrouded her, paralyzing her.

"Hey, Sero!" A voice from behind startled her. Ericka was leaning out of the back patio door. "Dinner!"

Sero waved at her, then stood, shook off her feet and returned to the basement. Inside, she locked the door and worked quickly, some force propelling her through the next motions. She carefully poured the large jug of rat poison into the newest batch of seedlings, young and vulnerable. She rinsed out the empty jug in the utility sink. After filling it with water, she placed it in the same spot on the basement floor, this one small act of courage all she could muster right now.

By the time Sero joined the group in the dining room, Micah was speaking, holding a wineglass in the air.

"There are those who are threatened by what we represent," he said as she entered. "We must fortify ourselves. Tomorrow night, there will be a new moon—it won't be visible in the night sky, but it is a new beginning, and I propose a celebration at the Sanctuary. A bacchanalia. A ceremony of rebirth and recommitment. We will pledge ourselves to one another, and to our vision of the Sanctuary. Let us all wear white, the color of purity. We'll enjoy a tremendous feast, music and swimming under the stars. I will share an exciting new initiative that will change everything we do at the Sanctuary." He smiled over at Sero. "And each of the rest of us will present an offering to our family here at the Sanctuary—words of what this place means to you, food you have prepared, music from your heart. It will be . . ." He cast his glance skyward for the right word. "A *Renaissance*." A broad smile spread across his face. "We will recommit to one another and look to the future."

How badly Sero wanted to believe him, to fall into the vision of comfort and love he presented.

"Are you with me?" Micah asked softly, and someone in the group murmured. "Are you *with* me?" he said, louder, and several voices assented. "Are you with me?" Micah's voice rose, had risen, turning his question into more of an exclamation, and as the group shouted, "Yes!" Sero found herself joining in.

Later that night, upstairs in the theater room, Cerise and Daphne were preoccupied, planning their contribution to the Renaissance. Serotina pulled her journal from the top drawer of the dresser, flipped to the back and pulled out the page torn from the calendar in her room years ago.

The grainy image of Prem, with his missing front teeth and ice-pop blue tongue, made her smile. He would look nothing like that now, of course. She tried to see him as he would be today at fourteen: as tall as her, with oversized man feet, and a thick swath of hair falling into those thickly-lashed eyes that the girls would love. Touching his nose, she refolded the picture and slid it under her pillow.

46 | serotina

The next day, everyone was in heightened spirits as they prepared for the evening's festivities. Ericka and Zoe offered to do a load of laundry with bleach to ensure that everyone would have enough white clothes. The spirit of celebration reminded Serotina of her Thanksgiving visit, when she had felt swept up by the collective energy. She collected eggs from the coop and harvested some vegetables, then helped Ericka roll out pastry for an apple pie. Along with everyone else in the house, who had showered at staggered intervals so they could all have hot water, she dressed in white clothes—a pair of skinny jeans and a long-sleeve T-shirt. She took the folded calendar page from under her pillow and tucked it into her back pocket, wanting Prem close by.

As the sun began to set, Micah called them all out onto the patio, where he opened two bottles of champagne and passed them around to kick off the festivities. Sero stood at the back of the group, leaning against the house. Micah stood in front of them, fingertips touching, as he waited for everyone to have a glass in hand. "Tonight, our Renaissance will serve as our recommitment to one another and the community we are building here at the Sanctuary. And to initiate the newest members of our family." He smiled generously at Cerise, who was sitting practically at his feet, and Sero felt her expression curdle before she caught herself. "But first," Micah continued, pacing the width of the patio. "I want to share an exciting announcement. Serotina, Jasmine and Rufus have been working for months to build an important new initiative here at the Sanctuary, down in the basement. It's called Greenfields, and it produces the best medical marijuana on the market today."

Sero saw the others share looks of surprise and approval. David smiled widely and pumped a fist in the air. "Just medical?"

"Well," Micah said, smiling, "it meets the rigorous testing requirements for medical marijuana." He paused. "But we're all adults here, and you'll all get a sample tonight."

Cheers and hollers went up in the crowd. Sero noticed Zoe put a hand on August's arm.

"Let's thank Serotina, Jasmine and Rufus for their efforts," Micah continued. "Their work enables us to do so much good for so many people, and we can feel good about that, as a family."

Sero heard a low snort. As she looked around to see who might have made the noise, Micah began to walk the perimeter of the patio. "And this, in turn, gives us greater freedom. We can now afford to focus all our energies, collectively, here at the Sanctuary. Those with outside jobs can leave them." Jeremy cheered and whistled at this news. "No more dividing your time and energy. No more working for someone else." He held his champagne glass high in the air. "You can work for *your* family and *your* community and *your* future!" The group erupted into cheers, and as Micah waited for them to die down, he walked around the circle, touching shoulders and arms as he passed. "The earnings from Greenfields will finally allow us to make the investments we've been wanting to and get us one step closer to making our dream a reality." He stopped behind Jasmine, resting both of his hands on her shoulders as he looked around the circle. "Solar panels. Dairy cows. More fruit trees."

The snorting sound came again, louder, and this time Sero knew its source was unquestionably August.

"How about some hot water?" August spoke up. "It would be nice to take more than a three-minute shower." There were a few chuckles from the group, but not Micah, whose expression remained serious. Sero watched him nervously.

"Well, if small, individual comforts are more important than investments that benefit the earth, then yes, I suppose we can consider *plumbing*," Micah said with distinct sarcasm. "But we did this so we can—"

"We?" August interrupted. "*We* did this? C'mon, man." He looked to Zoe and Ericka on either side of him. "*We* didn't take a vote and *all* decide to build a pot farm in the basement." Zoe put a hand on his elbow and gave him a pleading look.

There was silence while Micah and August locked eyes. Sero suddenly felt cold and wrapped her arms around herself. Micah turned away, and when he spoke again, his voice was calm and slow. "After dinner, we will begin our offerings to the Sanctuary, including our beautiful Music Salon. You guys are in for a real treat tonight. Daphne is a wicked guitar player." He placed a hand on her shoulder and she beamed at him.

August pushed back his chair, the legs scraping loudly against the patio stones, and he walked toward the swimming pool. Zoe stood to follow him, but Micah held up one palm. "Let him go, Zo. Give him his space."

Slowly, Zoe sank back down in her chair.

"Cheers!" Micah held up his champagne glass and took a long sip, and everyone followed suit. After the toast, Micah asked Serotina to lead the group into the basement, where she explained the Greenfields operation, and Micah and Rufus rolled a few joints to take back upstairs. The group sat on the patio together, passing the joints and drinking champagne, watching the sun set on the horizon. Sero faked her turns at the joint, the way she'd learned to do at parties in high school. Down on the pool deck, August sat in a lounge chair, his back to them, the glow of a lit cigarette dangling from his fingers.

Cerise leaned over to her. "Sero, it's so amazing what you're doing down there. I'm totally blown away." Her words were slightly slurred.

"I'm going to ask Micah if I can work with you guys. I bet he'll let me."
She smiled and tried to raise an eyebrow but was too impaired and bent
over laughing instead. Daphne was dancing by herself on the lawn;
Jasmine and Rufus were slow dancing seductively together.

After the sun dipped below the horizon, everyone went inside to
help Chef Guy prepare their five-course feast. The air was suffused with
the scent of marijuana. Sero watched Micah enter the kitchen, his arm
around Zoe's shoulders. Sero stood up, walked down to the pool deck
and sat on the lounge chair next to August. He took a long draw on
his cigarette and blew the smoke out the other side of his mouth. From
behind them came the sound of the amplifiers starting up in the house,
followed by a few twangy notes on electric guitar. August winced at the
screech. "Jesus," he muttered.

"Hey, you want to talk?" Sero said gently.

August shook his head. "Why, Micah send you to check on me?"

Sero flinched. "No, I . . . ," she stammered. "I was actually just going
down to check on Buddy." She put her hands on her knees as if she was
ready to go. She had left her shoes inside but didn't want to retrieve
them now. "See you at dinner?"

August dropped the stump of his cigarette onto the patio and took a
new one out of the package.

Serotina followed the path toward the stables and slowed her breath as
she tried to compose herself. She checked the feed trough and noticed
that Buddy was still not eating much. It had been a couple of weeks
since she had noticed the lump near his mouth, which was still there.
She began to brush out his coat and Buddy nickered quietly. She felt
unsettled by August's reaction, and hurt that he had dismissed her so
brusquely. Suddenly, the music from the house stopped with a loud
crashing noise, and moments later, a door slammed. She peered out the
window to see August storm out of the house. He was heading down
the path toward the stables, and she was about to go to him when she

saw Micah chase after him. Sero drew back into the stable, where she could watch through the open window, out of view.

"August!" Micah shouted, catching up to August outside the stable. "Hold up, Auggie! C'mon, man. You can't be mad at me."

"I can't?" August yelled. "I'm a fucking addict, Micah. You *know* that. You brought me here because it was a safe place. I've been clean over a year—"

"Dude, this isn't coke or heroin we're talking about—it's *weed*."

"Doesn't matter, Micah. It's still a *drug!*"

"We have liquor in the house, and that's a drug. Did you have champagne tonight, August, or am I mistaken about that?"

"*Fuck* you, man!" August spat, pulling the box of cigarettes from his shirt pocket. "You're a fucking hypocrite."

"And nicotine? You think that's not a drug? Don't fool yourself. I'm not the hypocrite here."

August pointed an unlit cigarette at Micah. "I see through you. She may not, but I see right fucking through you."

Micah turned his head slightly and considered August. "Ah, so that's what this is about?"

"You know damn well what it's about." August's voice was tight and angry. He stood with his back to the stable, facing Micah.

"Listen, man," Micah said. "We are all free to exercise our will, to be our own people. Zoe is free to make her own choices. The two of us go *way* back, man, before you were even here. There's a deep connection between us. It's undeniable."

Sero sank down to her knees as she unfolded Micah's words, the same ones he'd used to describe the two of them. A hot flush of shame rose to her face, and she dropped her head into her hands.

"I'm sorry you're hurt," Micah said, "but you know everyone here loves you. Zoe loves you. I love you."

"Why her, Micah? You can have anyone. Why *her*? I just can't—" His voice broke off and he began to sob. "I thought this was my home. I thought you were my *friend*, man."

"We are all free, Auggie. All of us. You are too."

"Yeah, well," August said, his voice turning harsh again. "Then I'm getting the *fuck* out of here." He spat the words in Micah's direction. "And Zoe's coming with me."

"No, she's not." Micah's voice was icy calm. "You can make a choice for yourself, not for someone else, not for her."

August threw the cigarette carton onto the ground, ran his hand through his hair and laughed. "God, I could really use a fucking joint right now."

"Auggie," said Micah, shaking his head slightly, "you know it's only you who can control those urges."

"You bring drugs in the house and tell me to resist, Micah? You're full of shit and I finally see it."

Micah hooked his thumbs into his front pockets and smirked. "Well, I could say the same about Zoe. After all this time, how can you expect me to resist?"

In a sudden burst, August took a swing at Micah, whose head twisted to the side as the punch landed. Sero covered her mouth with her palm to contain her gasp. Micah stumbled and, after he regained his footing, touched his mouth and saw blood. The expression around his eyes hardened. As if in slow motion, Micah reeled back his arm and his fist made contact with August's jaw with an unmistakable crack. August flew backwards, his head slamming against the hard concrete wall of the stable. Buddy whinnied and shook his head. Sero wrapped her arms around Buddy's neck and buried her face there, unsure if she was comforting him or herself.

"August!" Micah shouted. "Come on, Auggie." Sero turned to peek through the window and saw Micah crouched on the ground, slapping August's face. "Oh god. Oh no. Auggie! Oh *shit*." She watched as he checked for August's pulse at his wrist. Serotina felt her mind separate from her body, float up and high above it, watching the futility of the scene below. Micah put his ear to August's mouth, shook his shoulders, then fell onto August's chest. "Goddamn, Auggie. Goddamn you!"

Sero sank down to the hay-covered floor and rocked back and forth. Something sharp and metallic glinted at her from beneath the shavings and she unearthed an old horseshoe nail. She clenched her fingers around it, then pulled its sharp metal tip across her forearm, slowly at first, then faster and harder until there was a series of crisscrossing red lines across the length of her inner arm: four, then sixteen, then sixty-four, and she lost count. A mixture of pain and relief flooded her body, her mind swirling with shame and guilt.

When she came back to herself, she realized it was silent outside. On hands and knees, she peered through the doorway. August's unmoving body lay on the ground, but Micah was gone. Sero crawled out of the stable, over to her friend. Memories flashed through her mind: the floating spaceship, his arm underneath. This time would be different. She would stay calm. She placed two fingers on August's wrist and closed her eyes, willing herself to feel a pulse. Was it there? She couldn't tell. She switched to the other wrist and tried again. Her breath quickened. She placed her ear to August's mouth to feel his breath, to his chest to listen. She felt a drumming in her ears. Sirens? She looked around; the night sky was dark. The only sound was music coming from the house, a furious drum riff. She reached to her back pocket, but of course her phone wasn't there. She had to call for help—how could she call? The house was so far away, and she couldn't leave August here all alone.

Just then, she heard a rustle. When she looked up, Micah was standing a few feet away, a shovel in his hand. "You shouldn't be here," he said.

"We have to call for help," she stammered. Buddy whinnied from the stable.

"It's too late. He's gone."

She choked back tears, laying her palm on August's chest. "No."

"You shouldn't be here," Micah repeated, his voice cold. "Go back to the party. Tell them everything's fine. I'll be up in a minute."

"What? We have to at least get Zoe. She deserves to know."

"I'll tell Zoe later."

"What . . . what are you going to tell her?"

"The truth," Micah said. "August wasn't committed to our cause anymore. He stopped believing in what we're trying to do here. Did this to himself. Relapse."

She stood up slowly, shaking her head. "No."

"You know she'll believe me," Micah said. "It's better for everyone this way, trust me. Now, go back to the party."

Something inside her boiled irrepressibly and the words erupted before she could stop herself. "You can't do this, Micah. It's . . . wrong."

"Wrong?" A dark shadow passed over Micah's face and he smirked. "Like growing marijuana without a license? I can't take credit for that. That was all you, wasn't it? You purchased that equipment, using your credit card. You nurtured those plants and harvested them. There are a dozen witnesses in the house right now who will attest to that." Micah held his arms wide, the shovel dangling from one of his hands. "Hell, it was even *you* who shipped those first packages across state lines. Don't forget that, *Karina*." That name punctuated his statement, his warning clear. "Now. Go back to the *fucking* party before people start wondering where we are." He stabbed the tip of the shovel into the dirt. "Tell them August and I went for a nice long walk."

Sero looked down at August's lifeless body one more time before making a wide circle around Micah and taking the trail back to the house. In darkness lit only by the moon, she picked her way carefully across the fields, not daring to look back toward the stables, where Buddy's whinnying continued. Her mind ran through all the incidents he'd mentioned, forming a pattern. Micah had purchased the plants, but with a thick envelope of cash that left no trace. Her left arm ached with the angry gashes she'd made. She closed her eyes and felt them burning behind their lids, images of Micah's hard expression and August's lifeless body flashing across her mental screen. What had really happened to Justin, when he'd left all his belongings behind?

Loud music emanated from the house, and she could hear the voices and laughter of her friends inside. Quietly and deliberately, she moved along the side of the house to the front, carefully making her way around the broken driveway stones in her bare feet. Her heart beat out a syncopated rhythm in her chest as she reached the bottom of the driveway and turned onto the road, then made her way down to the end of the cul-de-sac. Not until the festive sounds of the Sanctuary could no longer be heard behind her, did she finally feel safe.

And then, she began to walk toward the Pacific Ocean, drawn to the largest body of water she could find.

47 | prem

Before that day—the day Kiki found me in the swimming pool—she loved the water. She liked to do somersaults underwater and practice her swan dives off the board, and she really loved being in the ocean, especially in Hawaii, where the water was warm. Neither of us could believe that was the same frigid body of water we saw when we drove up to San Francisco for Easter brunch. Kiki tried to walk into those cool, gray waves, but she couldn't get in all the way; she couldn't be the super-mermaid I drew into my award-winning graphic novel, *WaterMan*, who saves the world from drought.

But she just stopped, after that day. She stopped going in the water, or even near the water, which made me sad, because in addition to me and Gilly, that was just one more thing she loved that she didn't have in her life anymore. I was really proud of her when she was brave enough to do it again, to visit the ocean, then try surfing. I was proud of her when she dipped her toes into a swimming pool just like the one where she found me; I know she had to be really strong to do that. One day, I hope she'll make it in all the way into a pool again.

Kiki didn't want to swim with me that day after school, and she didn't want me to swim alone, but that's no reason to be afraid of the water forever. There are good reasons to fear the water. It's big, it's powerful, it's controlled by forces we can't see, and it can make us feel really small when we stand next to it.

But the water is also full of magic. When we go underwater, our bodies feel like we're floating in outer space. Our ears feel like we're in a tunnel. We can make bubbles and do somersaults and try all kinds of things we can't do on land. All those amazing creatures live under the water: the colorful fish we saw in Hawaii, and some that don't even look like fish, just like rocks or leaves. There's a whole different world down there.

I just wanted to look at the water that day. That's why I climbed up onto the chair. Once I saw it, the clear blue pool with light dancing on its surface, I thought I would just dip my legs in. It was so refreshing and so playful, lapping at my legs, begging me to slip in. It couldn't hurt, I thought, to play in a different world, where the rules of gravity and movement were different, just for a little while. And I had so much fun in the pool, steering my spaceship into another galaxy, hiding underneath it from the invading forces, shooting the spray gun I got at Tommy's birthday party. It was so much fun. I can't think of a better way to spend my last moments on earth.

I wish my family could understand that. They always think about my death and me missing from their lives. But I had a pretty wonderful eight years with a family I loved, who usually laughed at my jokes, friends to see every day at school, pizza nights and vacations and birthdays filled with love. And I had the best sister in the world. My death was just a moment, and not even a bad one. I was joyful up until the end, then peaceful when Kiki was with me, then nothing.

I've been with my family ever since that day, and if they could really let go of all those feelings of guilt and sadness, they would feel me there.

That's what I tried to tell Kiki that day she reached the Pacific Ocean. I think she finally heard me.

FOUND

48 | the olanders

Keith's hands grip the steering wheel as he drives faster than the speed limit, faster than is safe, the way people expect a middle-aged guy to drive an expensive sports car. He feels a twinge about how his life has turned into a cliché: a high-flying career, financial success (for now), failed marriage . . . wayward child?

"Tell me again what the police said?" Jaya asks.

Keith glances in his rearview mirror and down at the radar detector. "They picked her up this morning on the beach, alone, about twenty-five miles from campus. She was disoriented and gave them the wrong name at first, which is why it took a few hours for them to track us down. She called herself Sarah. Does that sound familiar to you, one of her friends?"

Jaya shakes her head, stares out the window. Tension fills her chest cavity and her fists clench an imaginary steering wheel as they did that day after the phone call on her way home. She feels the terror of seeing emergency vehicles parked out front, and hears the screech of her tires as she drove up onto the flower bed. Once again, she is suspended in time and space, waiting for something terrible to arrive. She forces herself to breathe deeply, even as the image of Prem's lifeless body on the pool deck intrudes.

"Jaya." Keith takes one hand off the wheel and places it atop hers. "I don't know what's going on, but it'll be okay. If she's in trouble, we can sort it out." He doesn't share what he learned on the drive over to the house, when he called the university and was told that their daughter was no longer enrolled, that she had not, in fact, been on campus in five months, ever since they saw her over winter break. Keith is wary of telling Jaya everything at once, uncertain of how much she can handle.

Jaya closes her eyes and leans her head against the cool window, repeating a mantra softly under her breath, masked by the hum of the car's engine. In her mind, she sees young Dev spinning away from her on the merry-go-round, then Prem sailing off into the universe. Now her daughter. The distance between Karina's life and hers is increasing with the passage of time—a runaway bunny she cannot catch.

———

At the precinct station outside Santa Barbara, a young female officer meets Keith and Jaya at the front desk to escort them to the room upstairs where Karina is waiting. "Has your daughter ever been diagnosed with mental illness?" she asks as they climb the stairwell.

"What?" Keith exclaims. "Of course not. She's a scholarship student."

"It's not unusual for bipolar disorder or schizophrenia to manifest for the first time in a person's early twenties," the officer says. "You should have her assessed when you get her home. In addition to the disorientation and name confusion, she appears to be food-deprived and have some self-inflicted wounds on her inner arm."

Keith stops on the landing. "She . . . you mean, she tried to kill herself?"

The officer looks slowly from one of them to the other. "They don't appear to be those kinds of wounds, not a serious attempt at suicide anyway. But there are signs of self-harm."

"What was she doing at the ocean?" Jaya asks.

"According to the 911 caller, she stood in the water for a while before walking farther in. She was dressed in street clothes, so I don't know what her intentions were, if she was in possible danger of . . . well, drowning can happen quickly in those currents. Even for a strong swimmer."

A small cry escapes from Jaya as she stumbles on the step, grabbing the banister just in time. Keith moves to hold her up and keeps his arm wrapped around her shoulders as they take the last few stairs together.

"Mr. and Mrs. Olander," the officer says as they reach the top landing, her hand on the door handle. "I'm not sure what's happening with your daughter. All I know is she needs all your love and support right now."

Keith and Jaya nod solemnly, at the mercy of this stranger who seems to know more about their daughter than they do.

————

The cardboard container of fried eggs and hash browns is nearly clean, after Karina wipes up the last morsels of cheesy yolk with the toast, then her finger. It tastes so good, and she hadn't eaten anything since early the day before. A scratchy gray blanket is draped over her shoulders, sealing in the chill of clammy clothes against her skin.

The door to the room swings open, and the female officer who brought her the food enters. "How was your meal?" she asks.

The kindness this officer has shown Karina makes her want to cry— this person who doesn't even know her. Karina nods in thanks and offers up all she has to give. "Do you know, when an egg comes out of a hen's body, it has a natural coating that seals the pores of the shell against bacteria in the air? It's a natural insulation system. As long as you don't wash fresh eggs from a hen, they don't have to be refrigerated. They can stay out on the counter for two weeks."

The officer gives her a small smile. Her eyes look puzzled.

"At commercial farms," Karina continues, "the eggs are all washed and disinfected with bleach to kill any traces of salmonella, and the protective layer is also washed away. That's why store-bought eggs have to be refrigerated right away."

"There's someone here for you, Karina," the officer says gently, and now Karina notices two other figures emerge from behind her. Her mother and father. "We gave her some food," the officer says to them. "And we offered her a change of clothes since, you can see, hers are soaked. But she refused."

"Thank you," her mother says to the officer, putting her palms together in a gesture of gratitude.

The officer smiles. "I'll give you some privacy. Take as much time as you need." She pulls the door closed, leaving Karina and her parents alone.

They approach her tentatively, as they would a wild animal. The distance feels enormous. Karina stands and takes a step toward them, her mask crumbling as she falls into her mother's arms. "Shh," Mom says, stroking her head, rocking her gently side to side. The rhythm of her mother's movements soothes Karina; from behind, her dad's strong arms wrap her in an embrace. She stays there, comfortable in the safety of their cocoon, until Dad pulls away.

"We're so glad you're okay, honey. Can you tell us what happened?" His face is worn, his eyes tired, and suddenly Karina feels the weight of her own exhaustion. She cannot hold herself up any longer. She slumps back into the chair, rests her head on the table. Her parents sit down on either side of her, Mom's hand never leaving her back.

Where should she start? The Sanctuary, Greenfields, Micah, August? Further back: Natural Foods Market, Henry, James? How far back does she have to go to unwind the bad decisions, the poor judgments and all the pain? *Prem.* Karina sits up and pulls from her back pocket the wet piece of paper. She unfolds it on the table, smooths the creases with her palms and looks at the smiling face of her little brother. She hears

Mom's breath catch. "He spoke to me," Karina says, softly at first, then again louder so they will believe her. "Prem spoke to me at the ocean." She looks at Dad, his eyes full of sorrow and confusion, as if he pities her or thinks her delusional.

But Mom squeezes Karina's hand resting on the table, and her eyes glisten as she smiles. "And what did he say?"

"It wasn't my fault."

"What wasn't, darling?" Mom asks.

"It wasn't my fault he died." With the voicing of these words, a torrent gushes from her, a sobbing she can't choke back.

"Of course, it wasn't, honey," Dad says, his brow furrowed.

Karina places her palms on the edges of the photo, its color faded along its creases. Prem's boyish face and missing teeth. His expression of sheer joy. She smiles at her brother, touches the tip of her nose, then his. "He was happy," she says in a whisper. "He had a good life."

"Yes, he did." Mom smiles as she takes Karina's hand in both of hers and grips it tightly. "And he is always with us."

Karina meets Mom's eyes and nods, sharing their first moment of true understanding in a long time. Dad looks uncertain, but his eyes are brimming with tears and he picks up her other hand and grasps it. For a few silent moments, the three of them, enjoined, look back at Prem's smiling face.

———

Keith excuses himself from the room, and Jaya takes in the image of her daughter. It has been only five months since she last saw Karina, but in that time, her body has grown leaner, her face colored by the sun, and there is something new behind her eyes that Jaya can't quite place.

"It's okay now, honey. We're going home." She squeezes Karina's forearm and sees her flinch. Jaya thinks this is a response to her words, but when Karina pulls her arm away, she realizes it is her touch. Recalling the officer's words, Jaya gently pushes up the sleeve of Karina's white shirt and sees her inner forearm covered with fresh cuts and scratches. It first seems like a disorderly mess, but when she looks closer, there is a grid of parallel lines underneath that can only be intentional. She looks up at Karina's face, but her daughter won't meet her eyes. Jaya moves the sleeve back down and Karina pulls her arm close to her chest, protectively.

Jaya recognizes her daughter has chosen the physical pain of hurting herself to mask the internal pain she suffers. Physical pain can often be easier to tolerate, Jaya has learned through the discomfort of traveling with the Guru and working at the ashram—sleeping on floors, traveling on buses, fasting for periods of time. Inner suffering is harder to endure, but only when you face those emotional and psychological demons can you truly find peace. After suffering the worst loss imaginable, she has spent years struggling with her interior terrain of guilt, pain and sorrow to find meaning in the world and her life again. She can even find beauty now. Karina will find those things too, she knows.

What Jaya sees when she looks at her daughter now is the fierce young girl at her core, the girl who fought for the runt of the litter, who loved her brother intensely, who has always forged ahead for what she wants, never seeming to need anyone else. But Karina needs her now. Her daughter is reaching a hand above the surface of the water, flailing for something to hang on to. And this time, Jaya will not let her fall.

"Do you remember," Jaya says, gently taking her hand, "when Prem was seven years old and woke up early to make us breakfast on his birthday?"

Karina smiles, her brow wrinkling. "Didn't something catch on fire?"

Jaya nods. "The toaster oven. He put the butter on the bread first—you know how much he liked butter—so it dripped down and the whole thing went up in flames. Poor thing, he tried to reach in to save the toast and burned his hand."

"Dad was so angry." Karina laughs. "He had to spray the extinguisher and that foam got all over the kitchen, the coffee maker."

"Yes, two appliances destroyed along with our breakfast." Jaya smiles. Karina smiles. "I forgot about that."

A moment of silence passes between them. "I remember it every single day," Jaya whispers. "At the time, it was a disaster. But now all I think of is the joy of a boy who loved life so much he couldn't wait to celebrate his birthday."

Karina closes her eyes, remembering. "He said he wanted to do something to thank us for bringing him into the family." A tear runs down her face, past her smile.

"Pain is always there to serve a purpose," Jaya says, "to teach us something, whether it's to not reach into a hot oven or to not fall in love with the wrong person." Karina looks up at her with startled eyes, but of course there's love involved here. What else could cause such pain? "And once we've learned what we're meant to learn," Jaya continues, "we are better than before. The wounds will heal." She lightly touches Karina's arm. "And that pain inside will help you grow."

———

Keith re-enters the room, confident about what to do next. "It's too late to drive back, so I've booked us two hotel rooms for the night. We can get some sleep and a fresh start in the morning." Jaya nods in agreement and looks at Karina, who simply stands up, shedding the gray blanket onto the chair.

They stop at the first restaurant they come upon, a family-style spaghetti house where the music and merriment create an ironic backdrop to their mood. It is neither lunch nor dinner hour, and none of them are particularly hungry, but it seems like the right thing to do right now, to nourish their daughter. Keith and Jaya sit on either side of

Karina in the half-moon booth and watch her pick unenthusiastically at oversized platters of fettuccine alfredo and Caesar salad.

Keith chooses a blue crayon from a glass on the table and draws a large oval in the center of the paper lining the table. He nudges Karina with his elbow. She takes a green crayon and draws a squiggly line touching the oval with such disinterest, he feels worse than if she'd declined to play along. He tries again, delicately, to start a conversation about whatever has transpired over the past few months. "Honey, you know you can tell us anything."

But Karina doesn't respond; she is a worn, watered-down version of herself. Jaya shoots him a warning look, and Keith is so spent himself, it's easier to numb himself with another glass of bad Chianti. With the red crayon, he draws a flag protruding from the other end of the oval, hoping Karina will recognize the beginnings of a horse and add some legs. He pushes the crayons toward her, hopefully. Karina stares at the image for a few long moments, then covers her face with her hands, and her shoulders shake as she begins to cry. Jaya looks at him in alarm. Neither of them understands what has just happened.

"I couldn't save him," Karina says, crying. "I couldn't . . . I couldn't *save* him." Her words turn to sobs, then great big gulps of air as she gasps and chokes.

Jaya wraps her arm around Karina's shoulders. "Honey . . . we talked about this. You know Prem's death wasn't your fault. No one blames you."

Karina shakes her head violently, as if trying to rid her mind of something. Keith is frightened, watching her battle with herself. "August . . . ," she whimpers. "I couldn't save him."

Jaya flashes Keith a worried glance. "Who's . . . August?"

Keith feels the ground slipping out from under him as Karina begins to explain. A scuffle between friends, a fistfight, an accidental death. Then it all comes rushing out of her, an unstoppable stream of words. She admits to taking a leave from college to move into a house in Rancho Paraiso with a bunch of hippies. Keith has been to Rancho Paraiso a few times, with clients for golf outings or business dinners at the tucked-away French restaurant. It's the kind of sleepy hamlet he could imagine retiring to, back when he thought about such conventional life stages. Apparently, his daughter has been living there all this time with a dozen other people, some sort of crazy commune.

Karina tells them about the marijuana farm, and when Keith hears about the absence of a license, the intra-state shipping and the equipment purchases on his credit card, paid automatically by his assistant, his heart plummets. It is clear that Karina has been complicit in several criminal activities, and the argument can probably be made that she was, in fact, the leader of the operation. He has learned over the past year how lawyers can twist things to make people look guilty.

The revelations accumulate until Keith realizes he doesn't know his daughter at all. What he took to be a natural part of her growing into an adult was in fact a series of well-crafted lies and deliberate omissions, designed to keep him in the dark. How did his smart, responsible daughter fall into this kind of racket? This guy—Michael or Micah, whatever the hell his name is—Keith is going to make him pay. The thought of Karina associated with such an obvious charlatan, caught up in drug smuggling, IRS violations, property disputes, *manslaughter*—his entire body pulses with the desire for vengeance.

They leave the restaurant and drive to the hotel in silence, Keith quietly fuming. Jaya goes upstairs to get Karina settled in bed while Keith says he'll wait for her at the hotel bar. He paces the lobby as he dials his attorney's number and waits for him to pick up. "Carl, thank god—"

"I swear, Keith, you have a sixth sense," Carl says.

Keith is puzzled. "About what?"

"The SEC. I assume that's why you called?"

"What? No. I . . . What? You heard?" Keith turns toward the wall and closes his eyes to brace himself. "Tell me."

"We're lucky, Keith. They're going to deal. You'll have to pay a fine, a hefty one. Three times your gain is $2.5 million, but in exchange, they're willing to forgo pursuing a conviction through the U.S. attorney."

"That's . . . ah . . . that's a big number. But I guess I can earn it back in a few years, right?" Keith turns away from the wall and runs his hand through his hair, filled with a strange relief. "Thank you, Carl. Thanks so much."

"It's not all good news, Keith," Carl says. There's a long pause on the line. "You don't have to admit fault, but you will be barred from the securities industry for five years."

"What?" Keith speaks in a near-whisper. "I . . . I can't do that. There must be some other way."

"There isn't." Carl's voice is firm. "I already talked them down from ten, which is standard for your case. This is a deal-breaker, Keith: it's either the fine and five-year bar or a trial. And we've discussed why you can't go to trial."

"Banking is all I know," Keith protests weakly. "How . . ." His voice cracks a bit. "How am I going to provide for my family?"

"You'll figure it out. You're a smart guy, Keith. This is a road bump, a big one, but you'll get past it."

Keith closes his eyes. He can't think about this now. He lets out a long breath and lowers his voice. "Carl, listen, the reason I called . . . I'm in Santa Barbara with my daughter, and she's in some trouble. I need the best criminal attorney you know down here."

———

When Jaya enters the bar, she sees Keith sitting at a quiet corner table with two glasses in front of him. She recalls their family vacations when the kids were young: she and Keith would sneak out of the room for a nightcap after the kids went to bed, going as far as the baby monitor would allow, sometimes just a few feet down the hallway from their room.

"How is she?" Keith asks, as she joins him.

"Asleep. She's exhausted." Jaya picks up her glass for a sip. His is already half gone.

"I can't believe . . ." He shakes his head. "She seemed so happy in December. We were talking about *graduate* school, for god's sake." Keith is quiet for a moment. "When I think of what she's been through." He runs a hand through his hair. "How did I miss it—the signs, the lies?"

Jaya surprises herself by reaching out and clasping his hand. "I missed it too. The important thing is where we go from here, what we do now."

"I spoke to an attorney," Keith says. "He's coming by here in the morning to discuss options, but I think we probably need to go back to the police."

Jaya nods, her shoulders beginning to relax. She rarely drinks these days, and two deep sips in, she is already feeling the effects of the smooth, expensive Scotch.

"And," he continues, cautiously, "that officer said she should see someone."

Jaya remembers the patchwork of angry red marks covering Karina's forearm. "Yes," she says. "A therapist. I think we should all go. I'll make some calls tomorrow."

Keith exhales and a look of relief passes over his face. "Good. Thank you."

"She's stronger than you know," Jaya says. "She needs time to heal, but she's a fighter and she'll be fine."

"How do you have such faith?" Keith's eyes glisten. "It usually drives me crazy when you do, but I have to admit . . ." His voice cracks. "Right now, I'm really desperate to believe everything will work out."

"It will," Jaya says, squeezing his hand tighter. "We've already survived the worst possible thing."

———

With no gong to rouse her the next morning, Karina sleeps late. When she wakes, she is alone in the room, and she goes down to the hotel restaurant to find her parents waiting for her, cups of coffee before them. They place their orders, including the full American breakfast of pancakes, eggs, bacon, toast and fruit for Karina, who is famished again after barely eating the night before, as if her body is vacillating between whether to nourish itself or not.

"Karina." Dad reaches across the table toward her. "You were right to tell us everything yesterday. You may not fully understand it, but you were mixed up with some pretty serious criminal activity at that place."

"The Sanctuary," Karina reminds him. The way he refers to it makes it sound like nothing special, failing to grasp what drew her there in the first place, the vision she still believes in.

"Yes, the Sanctuary," he says, glancing over at her mother and nodding. "So, given your involvement in some of those activities, we spoke to an attorney this morning and got some advice."

We? Karina looks at Mom, who is nodding solemnly.

"He advises going to the police and telling them everything you know—the cannabis operation, the fraudulent behavior with the landlord, the . . . death . . . of your friend."

"August," Mom supplies.

"Yes," Dad says. "The attorney will go with us and try to secure some protections for you in exchange for your testimony."

Karina feels anxiety begin to rise. What will happen to her friends—Ericka, Zoe, Jasmine—if everything comes out? What will Micah do to them, to her?

Mom reaches over and grabs her hand. "It's going to be okay, darling." The waitress interrupts to deliver their orders. The plate of food she places in front of Karina is grotesque in size and brings with it a fresh wave of nausea. Karina pushes the plate away as she tries to process what her parents are saying.

"I know you're scared, honey," Dad says. "But you have to tell the police everything you know. You'll probably have to come back and testify if there's a trial."

Karina feels her body trembling. "What's going to happen to my friends?" She sees her parents exchange a glance, silently deciding who will respond to her, a form of communication and alignment in them that she hasn't seen since Before.

"Darling," Mom says, leaning forward and grasping Karina's hand in both of her own. "You love your friends, yes?"

Karina nods back. She digs the fingernails of her free hand into her thigh, but the sharp pain cannot distract her.

"And aren't you worried about what might happen to them there?"

Karina hears the crack of August's head against the stable wall and sees his lifeless body. Tears begin to drip down her face, and she wipes at them with her sleeve.

Mom leans closer, steel in her eyes. "I know you couldn't save August," she says, "but you can save your friends now."

Karina feels Mom's strength electrifying the air between them. Dad's eyes are glistening as he nods silently across the table. She thinks of what can't be undone and tries to summon the courage to do what she knows she must. When she finally finds the voice to speak, it is barely above a whisper. "I can save them now."

49 | the olanders

Jaya brushes the hair out of her eyes with the back of her gloved hand. She and Karina are planting the two new raised beds Keith installed in the backyard. They had to tear out some grass to make space for these—some of the new turf they installed years ago, in fact, where the swimming pool used to be. Karina came up with the idea of intermingling flowers, herbs, vegetables and berry bushes all together in these beds, a more naturalistic design that should increase yields. Jaya has not gardened in years, having relinquished the planting to the weekly landscaper. When she did garden, she arranged all her plants in separate, tidy rows. She's never seen the type of garden Karina has designed, but she is excited about its potential. The lady at the nursery agreed the diversity of pollen would attract lots of honeybees and butterflies.

A hummingbird vibrates close to Jaya and she watches it for a moment: its head improbably larger than its body, its wings buzzing so rapidly they are a blur. The bird migrates over to where Karina is tilling the new soil and mixing it with nutrients. Jaya watches her daughter stop and observe the miraculous creature for a long moment before she returns to her task. Every morning, Karina comes out here on her own. Jaya often finds her meditating on the wooden bench they installed. She sometimes joins Karina, silently reciting her prayers or simply recounting her gratitude for having her daughter home safe.

Then they get to work, sometimes on the same tasks, other times near each other but separate.

Jaya has been relearning what it is to be a parent this past year. When her children were younger, it was about the basic tasks: feeding them, clothing them, ensuring they had a good education and dental check-ups. Keeping them safe from harm. When she couldn't ensure that most elemental duty with Prem, the rest of it tumbled down like a sandcastle. Jaya's subsequent search for inner peace felt essential to her survival at the time, but she now realizes it came at a price. She did not teach her daughter how to develop confidence, rather than insecurity, in what makes her unique. Show her how to fortify her heart against life's inevitable disappointments and betrayals. Help her cultivate an instinct for people. Jaya could blame herself indefinitely for these failings, but it wouldn't remedy anything now.

One important thing she and Keith did manage to instill in their daughter was a core of strength. Only a strong person would be able to endure everything they've learned Karina has endured—the terrible things that happened to her, those she did to herself, and the ones she's been carrying in her mind. Now, when Karina feels the desire to inflict pain on herself, she talks about it with one of them: Jaya, Keith, her friends or the therapist. And now, Jaya is equipped to support her daughter. She has been given another chance to be the mother Karina needs at this crossroads.

Life is wondrous that way. It has been a test of Jaya's spiritual beliefs to integrate them with the world she and Keith must help their daughter navigate. It is possible, though not easy, to balance the challenges of a worldly life with divine truth. Sometimes her mind alights on how things might have been different, for Karina, or in Jaya's relationship with Keith, had she attained this equilibrium earlier in life. But she cannot serve her daughter now by dwelling in the past. It is enough to know that, together, they have now closed the chapter of their family crisis that began with the loss of one child and ends with the healing of another.

"Hey, Ginger." Jaya bends down to pet their newest family member, a golden-brown beagle mix, who bounds off to dig for some unknown treasure in the corner of the yard. Jaya smiles as she sees the hummingbird return to Karina, perching on the flowering branch near her. Karina holds out a finger, encouraging the small creature to land on it. Jaya sees Prem everywhere these days, especially in his sister.

———

Through the kitchen window, Keith watches Karina and Jaya as they work in the backyard. He feels an unfamiliar pride every time he looks at those raised beds, constructed from six-foot-long solid cedar beams, completely parallel and level, with netting in the bottom to keep out the pests. They are the first things he's ever built completely with his own hands, and they give him a strange sense of accomplishment. He has already begun his next project: a dog house for Ginger—more of a canine cabana—which his father, who insisted on housing their dogs in the garage, would think ridiculous.

The past year has not been easy. Learning about all that Karina suffered has been nearly unbearable. But Jaya surprised him. She has been stronger than he would have thought—stronger than him, for certain. After Prem died, Keith tried so hard to carry their family and failed. Now he feels, above all, like he is not alone in this crisis. He follows Jaya's lead these days, because she seems to know how to respond to Karina when he is not sure.

He has taken on the responsibility of staying on top of the situation in Santa Barbara, communicating with the police and the district attorney's office about the case. There won't be a trial after all, since the defendant (Micah, as Karina still refers to him), tied a trash bag around his neck to hang himself in his cell after being arrested. At first, Keith felt cheated by that: losing the opportunity to see the bastard suffer and pay for his crimes. But Jaya has been helping him let go of his anger, and now he can see it's all best for Karina, enabling her to move forward without the repeated trauma of testifying.

It took over three months for the police to fully process the Sanctuary as a crime scene, during which they confiscated forty pounds of unlicensed cannabis and discovered one body buried in a shallow grave behind the stables. There was not enough evidence to charge any of the other residents with the crimes that transpired. Karina has tried to track some of them down, insisting they are still her friends, but most seem to have disappeared. There are rumors they have regrouped in a new house under a new leader, somewhere outside Calabasas.

Once the property was finally vacated, the landlord, Joe Petrosyan, sold it at a bargain price to an overseas buyer who had been looking for just such a piece of land in Rancho Paraiso to build a world-class equestrian facility for her dressage competitors. To protect property values and privacy, the community board quickly voted to change the name of the road on which the Sanctuary was located, so that the group was not only disbanded but written out of history.

Although Keith had a hard time adjusting to his newly unemployed status, the past year has been a gift in many ways. Primarily, it has been a chance to focus on Karina. He comes over to the house every day, and they feel like a family again in the best possible way. He and Karina took some cooking classes, and they have learned to make more vegetarian meals: lentil stews, tofu curries and cauliflower steaks, which Jaya appreciates with a hearty appetite. But some things haven't changed: when they order pizza on Friday nights, he and Karina still polish off a whole pepperoni pie between them. It all reminds him—though in a different way—of those early days in London when he and Jaya discovered food together as they learned how to be a couple. Now, it is the three of them, a re-formed unit, learning how to shape themselves around a missing piece without losing themselves to it.

Keith sold his condo, which had appreciated considerably with Silicon Valley's growth, and moved into a simpler duplex close to Jaya's house in Los Altos. These days, he only returns to his place to sleep anyway, and the move has given him greater financial security after paying the SEC penalties he incurred. In the end, neither of his remaining family members derived much benefit from the money he'd worked so hard to amass. Jaya has always believed too much money is corrupting, and Karina was eager for her financial independence. That single illegal trade was driven more by his ego, truthfully, than anything else. And it was that ego that drove a wedge between him and Jaya, even him and Karina—his limited ability to value them for who they were, rather than who they could be. He has come to these realizations painfully, working with the therapist they each see individually and also together as a family. They have all been speaking more honestly than ever before, and sometimes that is shockingly painful—more painful even than the therapy after Prem died. But their honesty is buying them something more valuable than the pain it causes: a way to move forward, a way to forgive each other and themselves, a future as a family rather than just three individuals.

———

Karina notices the mingling of iridescent colors in the rapid movement of the bird's wings, not unlike the spill of oil in a rain puddle. The garden she has designed, though it is not yet finished, is already attracting all kinds of curious visitors. She imagines a communion of them, coming to harvest pollen through the upcoming season. It is difficult to believe it will soon be a year since she came back home. Time is passing more fluidly now, but it was painfully slow at the beginning. It took all her strength to relive her experiences at the Sanctuary, baring to the authorities not only how she'd suffered, but the wrongs she'd committed out of faith and loyalty.

Most of the things she'd told the police about Micah turned out to be lies. His real name was Myron Williams, and there were charges pending against him for operating an E. coli–stricken mushroom farm in Oregon and embezzling from a crystal shop in Vegas. He had never attended Juilliard or even registered for a marathon. He could not have traveled around the world because he had never held a passport. For the past several years throughout Southern California, he had perpetrated a con known as "luxury squatting" by intentionally damaging multi-million-dollar properties to live in them rent-free. It had caused Karina fresh pain to know that nearly everything she had believed about him was untrue, that her judgments and instincts had been so grievously wrong. In contrast to Micah's claims, the police were, in fact, more intent on halting widespread illegal growers since the legalization of marijuana. Karina felt some consolation in taking responsibility for her actions and working with the police to liberate the friends she left behind. The authorities, in exchange for testimony that enabled them to finally arrest a career criminal, granted her a community service requirement.

When she first returned from Santa Barbara, Karina had little reason to get out of bed, until the day Mom brought home a rescue dog from the shelter, a four-year-old beagle-retriever mix. They had a few days to decide, Mom said, but as soon as the dog bounded up to Karina, with her gentle eyes and coat the color of gingerbread, she belonged to them. Karina began waking up every morning to walk Ginger, then running with her through the neighborhood, which she now does twice a day. She hasn't run since the cross-country team in high school, and that familiar burn in her lungs is a welcome discomfort.

A few weeks after Karina's parents brought her home, Izzy returned from college. When she learned what had happened, she cancelled her trip to Spain and spent the entire summer at home. She and Karina went to her old barn together every day and helped care for the horses, brushing coats, refilling feed, raking out stalls, going on leisurely rides. Karina plans to move Buddy up to these stables, once the rescue farm where he's been recovering in Santa Barbara deems him strong enough for transport.

Karina leaned heavily on Izzy in those early days, confiding all the shameful and embarrassing things she'd carried alone for so long, and her friend did not falter. Izzy's unconditional support enabled her to then share those truths with her parents: what had happened the day Prem died, the cutting that started soon after, the mistakes she continued to make with Henry, with Micah. Karina called Claire and finally explained to her what had happened that night with Henry. "It may have been my fault too. I don't know. I shouldn't have drunk so much. I shouldn't have made myself vulnerable like that."

"Karina, don't," Claire said. "Stop blaming yourself. I didn't know, I just assumed you knew what you were doing . . . And maybe Henry just assumed too, because I really don't think he's that kind of a guy." Her voice dropped. "He's a good guy."

The words cut into Karina with their implication, but the pain was not unfamiliar. She and Claire wept together on the phone, both apologizing for the mistakes they'd made and for the withering of their friendship that had followed.

James came up to visit too, once he heard the news. After the many times Karina had imagined such a scene while they were dating, James finally met her parents over a very normal dinner at their kitchen table. Dad cooked polenta pizza on the grill and Mom made a kale Caesar salad. Afterwards, Karina and James went for a long walk through the neighborhood, where Karina pointed out some of the childhood spots she'd told him about. She didn't talk much about what had happened at the Sanctuary, but she did divulge how she'd felt after their breakup. "I really trusted you, and you hurt me. Everything just spiraled from there."

James stopped, turned to her on the sidewalk, took her hands. "I really am sorry, Karina, for being such a jerk." Yoga Girl hadn't lasted long, he told her, only a few months. "But what you and I had was real. You were my first love, Karina, and it's true, I won't ever forget that."

Karina remembered all that had been good about James and the time they'd been together. He had made her feel special, beautiful. He had encouraged her to go to Ecuador even when it scared her. Though their relationship ended, James showed her what real love felt like, and she is hopeful she can find it again. Her love with Prem will also have a lasting impact—the way he trusted her unconditionally and believed her to be stronger than she felt. Each love she encounters will change her, she has come to see, shaping the person she will become.

Karina has spent many hours in the past year in therapy, trying to understand what truly happened at the Sanctuary, how she was manipulated into following Micah and his destructive authority. The therapist helped her recognize that the techniques he used on her—love bombing, sensory deprivation, social isolation, breaking her down and building her back up—were all well-known tactics in such groups. She has been working to understand how she was susceptible to Micah and his message, why her life was such a mess even before him. She drew the wrong conclusions from some events in her life, blaming herself for Prem's death and James's betrayal. Others, she never spoke about at all, like the night with Henry. But when she looks back now, she sees her strength has always been there, if not always constructive. Sometimes, she has directed that power against herself and it has turned to self-hatred, making her vulnerable to someone like Micah.

One of the first things Karina did after starting therapy was track down Justin, in an online community for cult survivors. She was relieved to learn he was alive, that Micah hadn't lied about his departure too. She and Justin speak frequently now, to make sense of what happened to them at the Sanctuary. Sometimes, Justin says he should have stayed longer once he understood what was really happening; perhaps he could have prevented August's death or the damage inflicted on others. When Karina tells him he can't blame himself, she is also reassuring herself. Everyone at the Sanctuary was seeking, just as she was. Everyone was looking for a place to belong. Even Micah, if she's truthful, wasn't wholly bad. He did some good things for her, taught her some valuable insights about herself. There was some truth in his beliefs and his vision; that was why he spoke to all of them.

Karina has finally come to realize that the kind of belonging she seeks is already here. She has told her parents every awful thing she'd kept from them for years and, after hearing it all, they have stood by her. They are flawed, all three of them, but they belong to each other.

For Thanksgiving last year, Karina and her parents joined Stephanie Cortez at her family's home in Redwood City. It was a celebration like none she'd ever seen. The crowd of fifty or more brought dishes of tamales, posole, stuffing, turkey legs—a fusion of two cultures that harmonized perfectly and tasted delicious.

"Mashed potatoes with mole should be a thing," Karina said, sampling the combination for the first time. "Much better than gravy. I'm definitely doing this next year."

"What? You're coming here next year." Stephanie smiled. "Once you're on the Cortez guest list, you can't get off. Besides, I've tasted your cooking, remember?"

"I'm much better now," Karina protested. "I took a class with my dad." Stephanie raised a skeptical eyebrow, and Karina grinned. She was looking forward to seeing more of Stephanie over the summer, when she was doing a teaching internship across the bay in Oakland. Stephanie didn't treat her as if she was fragile or damaged; she treated Karina, as she always had, with the assumption that she was strong and smart and would find her way back.

"I fell for him too. I thought he was cool and *cute*, and charming," Stephanie told her after learning what had happened. "I was a little jealous, truth. It could easily have been me."

Karina is not sure this is true, though her therapist has explained that all kinds of people fall prey to the Micahs of the world. "There are more Sanctuaries out there than you can imagine," she said.

Karina is taking some courses online to make up for the time she's missed. If all goes well, she will return to the Santa Barbara campus in the fall and graduate one year after she was supposed to. But she has learned not to plan too far out. Mostly Karina has been working with her therapist toward the goal of entering a swimming pool again one day. She imagines what it will feel like to dip her toes in the water and close her eyes. She practices clearing her mind of the old images and summoning new ones into existence.

The gray spaceship floats atop the water, Prem's lean frame balanced on top, his hair tousled and a big smile on his face. He dives under the spaceship and around the back, darting through the water with speed and agility. A long stream of water from the neon green sprayer arcs through the air and nearly reaches her, but not quite. He laughs. "Kiki," he calls out, waving to her. "Kiki, come in!" As she steps in further, she feels the water level rise to her calves, her waist, her chest. Slowly, she descends the last few inches and glides through the water.

She is not yet ready to do this, but one day, she will be. Prem will be with her, not haunting, but encouraging her, just as he did at the shores of the ocean. Karina breathes deeply, reclaiming the memory of a boy who loved life, who loved the water, who lived with joy.

50 | prem

There are so many ways to die without actually leaving the world: You can cut off a piece of yourself, or your feelings. You can stop doing the things you love, or lose sight of your dreams and goals. You can separate yourself from those who love you, or you can never be willing to find love at all. You can withdraw from the world, or you can go through life without seeking anything bigger than yourself. These may all look like ways of living, but they're not. They're ways of dying.

We are fortunate to get a turn on this rotating planet, however long it is. I had only eight years on the merry-go-round, which means I got to eat the frosting off the cupcake, but next time, I'd like to stay longer. I've watched the people I love most in the world endure grief, loneliness and pain. The hardest part is knowing that I changed the shape of my family. We weren't perfect Before, but we were something strong and beautiful together. They are finding their way now—Mom, Dad and Kiki—finding a new way to take formation without me. I know their peace and happiness comes at a cost: they have to think of me a little less. They have to learn to keep the best parts of me, the parts they can remember with a smile.

I have been with them ever since that day. They can see me in the sun peeking out from the clouds, in the cool breeze on a hot day, in the feeling they have when they remember me and smile. I am always there. Just like the air, just like the water.

acknowledgments

I was fortunate to have not one but two thoughtful, astute editors who helped guide this novel to its final form. Thank you to Kate Nintzel of William Morrow/HarperCollins and Iris Tupholme of HarperCollins Canada for their personal attention, insights and patience.

I am grateful to the many people at William Morrow/HarperCollins who helped usher this book into the world and who have championed my work over the past decade, including Liate Stehlik, Jen Hart, Amelia Wood, Kelly Rudolph, Bianca Flores, Vedika Khanna and many others in the publicity, marketing, production, art and sales departments. Thanks to Tessa Woodward for picking my first novel out of the slush pile, and to Carrie Feron for making it a success. I feel fortunate that Mumtaz Mustafa has designed beautiful and artistic covers for each and every one.

It is a joy to continue working with the dream team at HarperCollins Canada: Leo MacDonald, Sandra Leef, Michael Guy-Haddock, Cory Beatty, Alan Jones, Noelle Zitzer, Lisa Bettencourt, Natalie Meditsky, Irina Pintea, Karmen Wells and many others, as well as freelance copy-editor Stacey Cameron. Thank you all for your tremendous work and enthusiasm.

My agent, Ayesha Pande, has been with me from the beginning as a strong champion and trusted adviser, and I am perennially grateful for her wisdom and support. Thanks to the entire Pande Literary team for making everything run smoothly, including Serene Hakim and Theresa Soon-Young Park. I am also indebted to all the foreign agents and publishers who've brought my stories to over thirty countries around the world.

Thank you to the many independent booksellers around the country who embraced and shared my first two novels; a special shout-out to the fabulous staff at Warwick's of La Jolla and Teresa Lee Rushworth of Vero Beach Book Center. Thank you to all those readers who wrote to me with your thoughts and questions, invited me to your book clubs and shared reviews on your blogs. Without your support, this story would have remained in my imagination.

My deepest gratitude to Katherine Kirby Dunleavy, who read an early draft of this story and provided much-needed encouragement when I was about to hang it up. She was a careful and astute reader, and always generous with her time and opinions, not to mention her unyielding friendship.

My writers' posse—Lori Reisenbichler, Cindy Corpier and Erin Burdette—came out of retirement at exactly the right time to convene for a magical retreat that helped me unlock the ending for which I'd been searching.

To delve into the world of cults, I read and watched everything I could find, and two experts I consulted were of tremendous value. Paul Morantz is an investigator/attorney, whose memoir, *Escape: My Lifelong War Against Cults*, details his harrowing experiences as a cult prosecutor. Rick Ross founded the Cult Education Institute and wrote the book *Cults Inside Out*. Rick was very generous in speaking with me on several occasions, helping me comprehend the mindset of both nascent cult leaders and those who fall prey to their manipulations.

Dr. Elena Mikalsen, a clinical psychologist specializing in trauma, helped me understand the development of post-traumatic stress disorder in young Karina, and how this would manifest, multiply and ultimately be healed through her life. Gene Glazier graciously shared her expertise about the psychology behind cutting, and how it occupies the minds and bodies of adolescent girls.

Thanks to the many folks who helped me learn about things of which I knew nothing. Tim Fox introduced me to Ernie Hahn and Matt Yamashita of Grizzly Peak Farms, where I observed the detailed process of marijuana cultivation. Sean Prosser advised me on the finer points of insider trading violations and settlements. Anjou Parekh and Pratiksha Lakhani educated me on the practice of Bharatnatyam dance. Charlene Stein showed me how to raise chickens, and Stephanie Walker patiently explained the care and feeding of equines.

Thank you to my virtual tribe, Fiction Writers Co-op, for making the solitary life of a writer a little less so.

Finally, thanks to my family and friends: Mom and Dad, for their unwavering support and love; Preety and Vikas, and Nikhil and Brahm, who helped reacquaint me with the heart and soul of an adventurous adolescent; Ram and Connie, for always being there through good and bad.

My deepest thanks to Anand, who read and believed in this story first, and who remains an unflappable champion and solid rock of support when it matters most. To Mira and Bela, who, amid the complexities of adolescence, always inspire me to see the immense possibility and utter wonder in the world.

And to my dear friends, for forgiving me when I disappear for long periods into my writing mind, and for always being there when I emerge, to share joys and divide heartaches.

The shape of my family includes all of you, and for that, I am ever grateful.